I0702514

THE WOLF QUEEN

THE WOLF QUEEN

MARIE MCCURDY

Marie McCurdy Books

CONTENTS

To my mom, my first reader and biggest fan. I could never have done this without you.

Copyright © 2023 by Marie McCurdy

All rights reserved. No part of this book may be reproduced in any manner whatsoever without written permission except in the case of brief quotations embodied in critical articles and reviews.

First Printing, 2023

To request permissions, contact the publisher at contact@mariemccurdy.com
eBook ISBN: 979-8-9877208-1-3
Print ISBN: 979-8-9877208-0-6
Cover by: Nicole Lecht
Copy edited by: Mollie Madden
Prologue art by: Joe Strela

Acknowledgements

First and foremost, thank you to Mollie Madden and Ann Leslie Tuttle. Your editorial feedback was invaluable. Thank you to Nicole Lecht, Joe Strela, and Alex MacDonald, who created all the artwork for this novel.

In my journey to publishing, countless people and groups offered support and feedback. Thank you to Shut Up and Write NOLA, Third Lantern Lit, and "the rowboat," who know who they are and inspired me so much as I began my writing journey. Most especially, thank you to Caitlan McCollum, who has been my "rowboat" writing buddy, feedback partner, and inspiration for years, for the entire journey of this novel from a short story to the final product.

Glossary

Roman Terms

Ala/alae (plural): Cavalry squadron(s)

Centurion: Commanding officer of a century, a unit of one hundred legionary soldiers

Equestrian: Though literally translated as "horseman," the title is the equivalent of a knight, generally awarded to men of the property-owning class, a step below the Senatorial class

Lanciarius/lanciarii (plural): Light infantry skirmishers, best used for reconnaissance and loose formation fighting, considered the "special operators" of a Roman legion. Lanciarii were not a permanent fixture of a Roman legion until the 3rd century CE and are used here by the grace of artistic license.

Legatus: Equivalent to a modern general, the officer in command of a legion

Optio: Officer second to a Centurion, responsible for enforcing the Centurion's orders, keeping the troops in order, and other administrative duties

Panem et circenses: Bread and circuses

Testudo: A type of shield wall formation named for its appearance to a tortoise

Tribune: Officer second to the Legate, above the Centurion, usually a young man of Equestrian rank

Usus: The Roman equivalent of a common law marriage, an informal agreement between two consenting adults who lived together

Baduhenna: Goddess of war and revenge,

Donar: God of thunder

Haustblot: Fall festival celebrating the autumnal equinox

Landvættir: Guardian spirit of an area; nature spirit

Männerbund: Brotherhoods of male warriors who completed their warrior training together

Offnüng: Vent in the ceiling/roof

Ôstara: Goddess of Spring, celebrated at the spring equinox

Wald: Forest

Scalc: Slave or indentured servant

Tyr: God of war

Vetrnaetr: "Winter nights," winter solstice festival

Wîblîhbund: a theoretical sisterhood of warriors

Wodan: Chief of the gods, the one who determines the outcome of battles

Germania Magna,
circa 7 CE

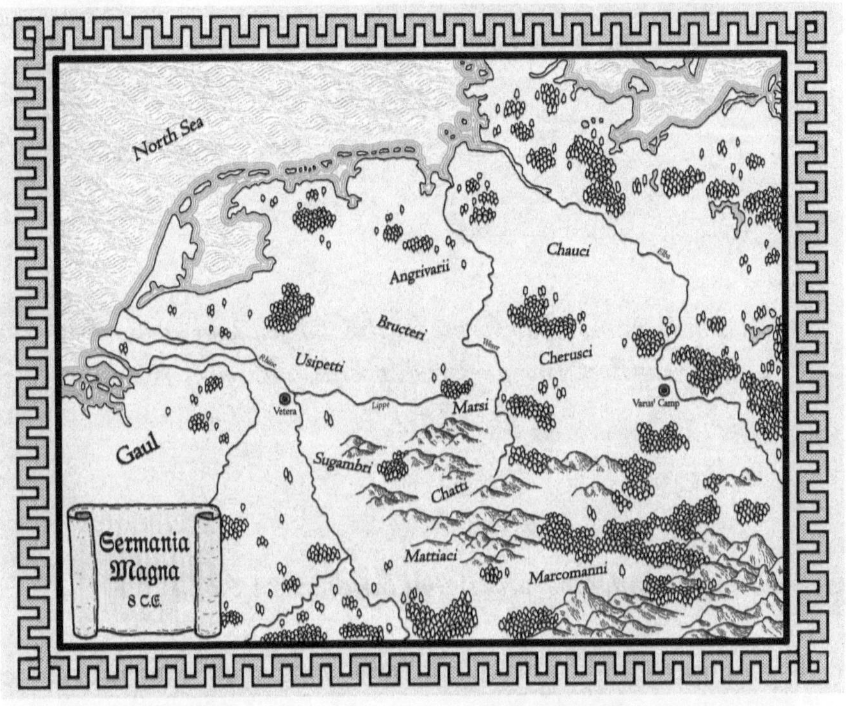

Map by Alex Macdonald

Prologue

You Romans are to blame for this; for you send as guardians of your flocks, not dogs or shepherds, but wolves. (Cassius Dio)

Germania Magna, Cherusci tribal lands, circa 6 BCE

My damned brothers wouldn't leave me to milk the goats alone again. Cursing with each step, I ran out of the roundhouse and down the path to my family's animal corral, bare feet slapping in the dust.

So help me, I would drag them back by their ears and tie them to farm tools. Though the twins were only six years to my nine, every day they grew in strength and height, and speed, damn them. If I could just wrangle Levin to a shovel, he'd be forced to help me. I could worry about catching Lennart later.

Milking the goats and corralling my younger brothers was my job, and I took it with utmost seriousness. The day was early yet, but a cloudless sky promised a sweaty afternoon. The sooner we finished our morning chores, the sooner I could sneak off to the meadow where Mama and her warriors trained. If I was lucky, one of the younger women would take pity on me and let me train with her. I was supposed to train with the other village children, but by my logic, the best training happened with the best warriors. Mama's troop of women and men were the best in our whole tribe.

Fortunately for me, I found the twins arguing in their half-spoken, half-unspoken secret language in the aging lean-to where we stored our tools.

"Did you see it?" Lennart whispered to Levin.

"Of course I saw it." Levin gave his brother a playful shove. "He's been showing it to everyone."

In my very best imitation of Mama when she tired of our antics, I sighed gustily. "Levin, go get a goat and start milking. We'll never get done if you two don't stop gossiping about that treasure."

Levin stuck his tongue out at me but did as I instructed.

"But Thusnelda," Lennart whined, "it's *Roman* treasure. Our warriors pummeled a whole band of them!"

"And I'll pummel you if you don't make yourself useful. Go collect the eggs."

I took up my stool and bucket and collected the goat I called "Brown Goat," for obvious reasons. The matter with the Romans was settled in my mind. They had attacked a farmstead belonging to a family of our tribe, the Cherusci, after the farmer had refused to sell his crops for coin, coin we didn't use. They had taken the women as slaves, put the men to the sword, and taken the boys for their army. We struck back to teach those whoresons a lesson, and the band, mostly comprised of Mama's troop, returned to much merriment and celebration for their victory. Our fighters laid waste to nearly fifty of theirs and returned with trophies of armor, short swords, horses, tents, anything we might use. This was Cherusci justice.

Lennart's egg collecting resulted in outraged squawking from the birds and an impressive litany of swearing for a six-year-old. I laughed at his antics and Levin shouted, "There wasn't enough smart in Mama's belly for both of us!"

"What's going on over there?" Mama called. Papa and Wout, my older brother by a few years, stood behind her. Wout held two fishing poles, a bucket, and a fish knife on his belt, and Papa had slung not one but two water skins across his shoulders and wore a large floppy hat to shield his eyes. Today was his day to mind the village cattle, an unspeakably boring and smelly chore I didn't envy.

"Lennart still can't collect eggs right, Mama." She grinned at me. I lived for those conspiratorial grins, as though I shared secret knowledge with her and only her. I didn't yet, but that grin told me one day I would. One day I would understand all her private amusements.

"I can see that." She chuckled from across the corral fence. "I'll be fishing with Wout for a few hours down by the river in case you need me for anything."

Her hand smoothed over her massive belly in the unspoken reminder that at this stage in her pregnancy, sitting in the shade by a calm river was second only to remaining in bed all day. Three different midwives agreed it was another set of twins, what with how large her belly had grown so early in her pregnancy.

Papa frowned behind her. We all knew he'd prefer it if she remained abed all day until the time came, not walking down to the river shore and certainly not overseeing the day's training. She'd barely survived the twins' births, and her last two babes had died in the womb. It wasn't uncommon, but Mama was a hearty and muscular woman with the soul of a warrior, and she wouldn't be taken from us so easily. My Mama wouldn't die without a sword in her hand.

I tried not to take umbrage at Mama's suggestion that I might need her help managing the twins through our daily chores. The fact that I was only nine years old seldom stopped me from demanding adult treatment.

Instead of snapping about the silliness of her reminder, or pouting, or rolling my eyes, I pushed back from Brown Goat and offered her what I thought was my most reassuring smile. "I know, Mama. We'll be fine here."

Though Papa and Wout marched off with absent waves, Mama hesitated, her eyes flicking from Levin and me with the goats, to the chicken coop still loud with offended birds. After a moment, she shook her head, bade us farewell, and followed down the path.

It took another hour for the three of us to work through the goats. After that we raked the corral free of goat droppings and other mess, then checked each length of fence for weak spots. Squinting against the bright afternoon sunlight, I spotted a figure in dark clothes sprinting toward us down the dirt lane. Once he got closer, I recognized Ermin, and my heart raced. We'd been betrothed since my birth, but only that spring had I grown to appreciate his handsome features and the impressive height promised by his gangly, fifteen-year-old body. As chief Segimer's eldest son, he would one day be chief himself and I would be his wife, queen of the Cherusci. I sat up straight and tried to smooth my fair hair into something respectable with grubby, dirt-stained hands.

Levin noticed Ermin's alarm before I did and abandoned his fence-kicking. "What's wrong?"

"Romans," he wheezed, "hundreds of them. Spotted near here, heading this way."

I called Lennart, who'd returned to cursing and banging around the chicken coop.

"Come." Ermin snatched my and Levin's hands. I took up Lennart's when he wandered over to us, shaking his head and frowning in confusion. "Get to the woods."

"But Mama—" I tugged to get free and rush toward the river. Mama and Wout were at the river. I could warn them.

"No time." Ermin tightened his grip. Poor Lennart hadn't the first idea what was happening and burst into tears. Ermin scooped him onto his hip, skinny yet strong from his training and toiling in the fields, and I took Levin by the arm.

Ermin yanked me along despite my protests. I was too little to put up much of a fight, and his urgency inflamed my rising panic.

Levin and I barely kept up with his fast pace; Ermin was outrunning us even with Lennart in his arms and slowing himself for our sakes. Levin stumbled and cried behind me, but I wasn't big enough to carry him. The twins were big like Wout and though I was three years older, I was only a few inches taller.

We darted up and over the tall palisades encircling our village. When Levin slipped, I jerked him back to his feet and kept us going. Ermin turned south, through the spelt and oat fields. The tall grasses whipped at our faces, and it was only Ermin's height that kept us on a straight track. At last we burst into the trees and still Ermin ran on, deftly avoiding the myriad natural obstacles at his feet and protecting Lennart from the swipes of brambles and low branches. When he stopped by a copse of alder trees, we were all panting and sweating. I swiped at a biting fly swarming around my face and earned myself a stinging bite to the arm.

"Up." Ermin lifted Lennart to the nearest thick branch. "Everyone up there, as high as you can."

With my knee, I gave Levin a boost to follow his brother and turned to Ermin. "What about you?"

Instead of answering, he pulled a dagger from his belt and handed it to me.

"Take this." He held my hand in both of his and looked at me with a gravity I'd never seen from him. Good humor, often. Annoyance, most definitely. A feigned sobriety, the kind boys put on when they wanted to act more adult than they were, regularly. This look, however, chilled me. "Don't let them take you alive. The twins will be all right. They've been taking our boys into their army. But not you. Do you understand what I'm saying?"

What they would do to me that was so awful I should choose death, I didn't understand. Many years later, I'd at last sympathize with why Mama had sought to shield me from the horrors men wrought on women and girls. At nine summers old, I didn't know anything.

"I can fight them," I said, brandishing the blade for good measure.

"No, Thusnelda," he shook his head. "You can't. There're too many of them."

"But—"

"Promise me!" He gave me a shake. "Promise me you won't let them take you alive."

He was red in the face, wild-eyed and frantic. I had no choice but to go along with him, though I had every intention of fighting my way free.

"Yes, Ermin."

"Good," he said. "Whatever happens, whatever you hear, don't come down from this tree. Don't reveal yourselves. I'll come back for you, I promise."

Without warning and to my shame, hot, wet tears burst from my eyes. I didn't wail or sob despite the tremors wracking my body. *He's not coming back*, I thought. He was going to run back to our village, fight, die, and I'd never get to marry him. I had eagerly anticipated the day when I got to marry such a fine man, the kind of man who rushed to my side to protect me and my little brothers. I was only a child, but I knew enough to understand that was special.

He wrapped me in a tight hug against his sweaty chest and patted my head. "Don't worry, Wildberry," he said, using the nickname he'd invented for me. "I swear I'll be back for you. But I need you to get in the tree and be strong for your brothers. Can you do that?"

I sniffed and brushed my tears away with the back of my hand. "Yes."

"Good. Go on, get up there."

Only once I was up the tree did he leave. As he disappeared from view, the steady, rhythmic clomping of heavy feet, the clatter of armor, shouts in a lyrical foreign tongue overtook the natural sounds of the forest.

Through the leaves, I caught glimpses of their army in the distance. There were so many of them. They marched in strict order and straight lines, each step matching a steady beat. In that moment, I learned the horror of discipline. This was no mob of warriors competing for glory, but a machine of death.

They blew horns, a menacing noise so deep and loud our tree shook with it. The Romans shouted and their voices rose into a chant so clear I made out the word.

"NECO! NECO! NECO!" When I at last learned Latin, I thought back to this day and recalled their chant.

"KILL! KILL! KILL!"

Then came the screams, so much screaming. My people responded with their own battle cries, but they were half-hearted, surprised. The pleasant smell of burning wood drifted to us and it forever altered any comfort I once took in the scent. Though the words were lost over distance, I recognized the sound of begging. Animals howled and yelped and squealed. Metal weapons clashed and rang out. A few branches above me, the twins wept and moaned as quietly as possible. I feared that by the time the Romans finished and we climbed down, the village would be destroyed. No family, no tribe, and I would be responsible for raising the boys, keeping us safe and fed. Silent tears streamed down my face. That task was impossible for a child. We'd be lucky to survive the winter all alone. We'd be lucky to be taken as scalcs by another tribe.

Finally, blessedly, the noise dwindled. Smoke rose, gray and thick. When the Romans marched back the way they came, flashes of brightly colored tunics and trousers in the Cherusci fashion joined their ranks, shuffling along in a mass of bodies and clanking iron chains. With an eye on the sun moving across the sky, I made the twins wait several hours more, certain this was a trick or, if the Romans fought anything like us, they'd be back after this initial assault.

When they didn't come back and Ermin remained absent, I eased to the forest floor and coaxed the boys with me. Someone had to take charge. We held hands on the walk back. The dagger weighed heavily on my belt, and I hoped I wouldn't have to use it. Our world smelled of smoke and death, but I heard low voices speaking in our tongue and I swelled with relief. We weren't left alone to fend for ourselves! Perhaps our family had survived. Perhaps Ermin was wounded or busy, and that's why he hadn't returned for us.

The fields to the north burned, and the smoke stung my eyes. A few roundhouses also burned, but not nearly as many as I expected. Smoke billowed from grain and food stores dotted throughout the village. Men dragged bodies into our square. I fought the urge to shield the boys and myself from the sight. We all needed to witness what Rome was. We needed to know our enemy.

But for the murmur of voices, our village was strangely silent. Blood coated our central road, and I breathed in its coppery tang. This was battle, and I had to inure myself to it if I was ever going to be a warrior. Shocked, grief-stricken survivors cried in near total silence over the bodies of their loved ones. It was as if any loud noise might call those demons back to finish what they had started.

"Children!" Papa cried, almost shrill. He staggered to us, tears streaking through dirt and ash on his face. I had never seen him weep before, and the sight stunned me into stillness. He hugged and inspected each of us with rough pats. "Thank the gods you're all right. Where were you?"

"Ermin took us to the woods. Where is he?" I coughed over the smoke scratching at my throat.

His face darkened and behind him, Wout sat in the dirt, sobbing. His lip sported a gash, and blood dribbled down his chin.

Papa grabbed all three of us and pressed our faces into his soiled tunic.

"Don't look at her," he said. "Don't look."

I twisted until my face poked out beneath his arm and immediately wished I hadn't. Among the bodies littering the road, I recognized Mama's tunic. Dark red blood stained it and she wasn't moving. Her sword was still in her hand.

Move, I willed her with my mind. *Get up. You have to get up.*

She didn't; my mind refused to make sense of it. I'd seen death before—animals, babies, people who suffered accidents—but not my mother. Not a woman so hearty. Not a woman I loved so much, a woman I needed.

Beyond her, Chief Segimer lay dead, slashed from shoulder to groin, and his wife knelt over his body with a face of stone. Nearby, Segimer's brother, Ingomar, sat in the dirt holding the body of his young daughter, rocking her back and forth as though she were sleeping and her skull wasn't cracked open. His own wife's body lay next to him. Our chief was dead and his family decimated.

I didn't cry. The twins wailed and ran to Wout, who took them in his arms and together they let their grief take the form of a flood. Not me. I pushed away from Papa and stood in the middle of the road, swaying beneath the weight of it all. Mama was gone. I screwed my face up tight lest I crumple, like the men. Mama was gone, our chief was dead, and before the day was out, I'd discover all the friends and cousins we lost, too. I couldn't breathe.

"Do you see?" Papa's voice broke in a shout. "Do you see what happens when you fight them? I told you to make peace!"

A few faces turned his way, but most remained lost in their own pain.

"No one had to die!" He railed on, tugging at his hair until his side knot loosened and hung down his cheek. "Never again. I will never let this happen again."

He wandered away, muttering about all the things he'd do to save us from Rome. If I had listened more carefully, I would have known then what he intended for us and it wasn't salvation from the invaders.

Ermin wasn't there to stop him and claim the chieftainship that was rightfully his, nor was his little brother. It would be many years before Ermin returned to me, but over one devastating afternoon, I lost my mother and became the female head of our household, responsible for everything Mama had seen to. With Ermin's dagger always at my side, I spent the next fourteen years shaping myself into a warrior and fervently praying to the gods I would be ready the next time the Romans came for us.

Chapter 1

For lo! Were they not happy in the Latin embrace? (F. Matania)

Germania Magna, Cherusci tribal lands, 8 CE

I both loved and hated our holy festivals. At the festival of Ôstara we welcomed the goddess of dawn and cast aside another gloomy, cold winter each year. In generations past, Cherusci volunteered themselves for the honor of being sacrificed. Their gifts pleased Ôstara, who, in her pleasure, granted us plentiful crops, healthy children, and strength in battle.

Friends and distant relations spread across our various settlements reconnected and enjoyed plentiful ale. I enjoyed that part. What I didn't enjoy were the weeks leading up to the festival, when I spent every day from before dawn until after midnight hustling between the kitchen house, the smith, the granaries, the butchers, the priestesses, and so much more, ensuring everything ran according to plan. At the festival, I had to listen to my father drone on about all the glories and gifts granted to us by the gods and our Roman benefactors.

Tonight, our priestesses would sacrifice the largest aurochs in the tribe and others would offer their personal sacrifices in the way of small animals, grains, corn, and personal property. Whenever I had a moment of time, I had spent the winter shaping and honing a beautiful spear for just this purpose. The oak shaft gleamed as though it emitted its own light, and the meticulous patterns carved into the spearhead marked it as a work of devotion.

The sun sank low on the horizon before I stole away long enough to dress myself. Though the evening promised frigid air, in honor of the equinox we all wore the sleeveless tunics and gowns that only further marked us a *gens* wholly apart from Romans. They found our bare arms and trousers trademarks of our barbarism, things to be corrected in their superior image.

As the chief's family, we occupied the largest house in the village. Other clans had their own smaller villages dotted throughout our territory, wherever the earth was good for planting and animals. Most of them lived in roundhouses with wattle walls and thatched roofs. A longhouse was different and reserved for chiefs and clan leaders. Our longhouse featured straight walls that stretched nearly sixty feet long, room enough for a large dining hall offset by stalls to keep the animals warm during our long winters—though this quickly turned to unbearable stench—private bedrooms, a cavernous attic for storing hay, grains, and sundry dry goods. We boasted a small roundhouse for our personal scalcs, the indentured servants who saw to the daily needs of our household. I enjoyed the familiar smells that said *home*: hay in the loft; freshly baked bread; and coals in the central fire pit.

With its cozy stuffed mattress and fragrant rushes squashed beneath the rugs on the floor, I always reveled in the restfulness of my room. In winter, when the scent of manure and pigs permeated the whole house, gentle lavender and rosemary and dried herbs by my windows blocked it out. I slipped my mother's golden arm bands over my biceps and let my fingers linger, tracing the intricate whorls and patterns. I remembered cooing over them whenever Mama wore her bride jewels, and biting back sobs the first time I was expected to wear them and the bands didn't fit my skinny arms. The memory made me shudder, so I pushed it away and called for a scalc to fix my hair. My personal scalc was the closest thing I had to a friend. A sorry state. For both of us.

Jotapa entered and immediately launched into a rant about her own busy day while crafting a riot of golden braids and curls atop my head.

"Will Reimar be at the festival?" Jotapa eventually asked.

Her fingers stilled when my body stiffened. I forced a low chuckle. "No, he will celebrate with his own people. I don't believe I will see him again until the wedding."

She continued merrily fixing my hair, sliding pins and jewels this way and that. I seldom troubled myself with mirrored bronze, instead trusting in Jotapa's deft hands and innate sense of style. Truly, for a young woman confined to simple undyed woolen tunics and short trousers, she had a singular beauty about her. Though such beauty could be a plague with Cherusci men, Jotapa wore her black hair in neat yet elaborate braids. Her tunics were always clean and belted just so. She carried herself with that nameless, effortless *something*. I carried myself like a warrior, even in a fine white gown and gold jewels. Some found this appealing, but without needing to ask, I understood I lacked that special spark that burned so brightly in Jotapa.

Jotapa would thrill over a match like mine with Reimar, son of the Chatti chief, thus heir to their chieftainship. Such a marriage meant becoming queen of the Chatti, even for a scalc. Jotapa sold her services throughout our village as a hairdresser and steadily amassed wealth worthy to buy her freedom. We were of an age, and she could marry Reimar in my stead. I doubted I'd feel anything about it other than relief. Yes, it meant surrendering my title as a future queen, but I had no reason to want it while I remained the chief woman of the Cherusci. Until my eldest brother, Wout, married and took my father's seat, I remained the de facto queen here. A queen without a husband. It delighted me. After Wout took his rightful place, I'd remain something of a dowager queen. None would dismiss my fourteen or more years as a leader. My voice and leadership would still be crucial to our tribe.

Reimar and I had met only twice. Closer to my father's age than my own, he was a large man, even for us, and fiery headed. We'd hardly exchanged more than a brief greeting, yet I was to marry him during our fall festivals. The thought chilled me to the bone.

"May I ask," Jotapa's nimble fingers worked their magic through my unruly hair, "do you find Reimar himself distasteful, or do you wish to remain unmarried altogether?"

That was the question, wasn't it? I'd met men I found attractive. I had my share of infatuations, even as a young girl with my lost Ermin. Strong in the jaw, brilliant blue eyes that put the sky to shame, and a warrior initiated into his *männerbund* at just twelve. Yes, there was a man I'd wanted to marry.

The earliest most boys endured their initiation was thirteen or fourteen. As a woman, the details of the initiation remained a mystery to me. I didn't understand the purpose of a *männerbund*, the brotherhoods of warriors parceled out by age groups, exclusive to men. I, and many Cherusci women, had fought in more battles than my younger brothers. I still bested them each in training, despite their ungainly height and strength.

Like all women, my initiation came with blood, my strength, and no fanfare. There was no *wiblihbund* for us.

As a *wiblihbund* would never properly initiate me into our warrior class, I also had no hope of ever choosing my husband. Since Ermin was taken as a hostage to Rome that horrible day my Mama left us, I found little purpose in setting my heart on any man. My father harbored grand designs on making a profitable match for me, my feelings and welfare be damned. If he could marry me off to a high ranking Roman officer, a citizen and noble, he would. I'd end my own life first.

"I give it little thought." My tongue scraped, dry as wool in my mouth. "I have no choice."

Jotapa hummed. Did she understand my meaning, or did she passively agree with my assessment? I didn't realize she'd walked away until she slid my mother's golden torque around my neck.

"There." She smoothed her hands across my bare shoulders and knelt at my feet, granting me her shining eyes and brilliant smile. "You are a vision, Princess. If I may say, there is no woman in the tribe better suited to cutting off the cock of any man who dared not appreciate her as such."

I sputtered, and together we dissolved into giggles. "Are you sure I can't convince you to accompany me tonight?"

"No." Jotapa rose and I followed. "You know how the men are with scalcs at these things."

"I would make sacrifices of them all and take us back to the old ways." I smiled at the thought.

Jotapa handed me a simple white shawl. It would hardly keep out the chilly air, but spring clothes were one of many ways we honored Ôstara. It would insult her glory to treat her arrival as though she were winter.

"Yes, you would; that's why I must decline." She grinned and made a few more adjustments to my hair and gown. "I will make my own sacrifices in my quarters."

A sensible reason and a sensible alternative to violence. Damn it. When she purchased her freedom from Segestes, I would see to it we accompanied each other everywhere. For this evening, I left alone, spear in hand, for the sacred woods over the priestesses' chosen bog. I didn't quite understand what they found so sacred in a bog, except death. Nothing that sank into one ever came out. Perhaps if we sacrificed enough, murky wet arms would reach from the depths and take the Romans.

Drums pounded. Their steady *whump whump whump* echoed a tattoo on my bones. My heart followed the beat, and I felt myself slipping into the oblivious ecstasy of our ceremonies. Horns joined the rhythm, deep and bellowing—not music, but a primal energy reaching to the gods themselves. I didn't make note of my path, stepping over branches and bushes by memory alone in the darkness, a slave to the call of the Cherusci.

Firelight glowed in the darkness, and voices from thousands of villagers overtook the horns and drums. I passed outliers, men and women already drunk beyond reason, laughing and tripping their way around the celebration, coupling in the near darkness. I continued on until I had to push my way through the crowds to the central fires, past torches, past smaller sacrificial gatherings. My place was at the heart, where Segestes promised to offer the massive aurochs our tribesmen had

snared and much more. He intended to call for blessings from our conquerors, that they might continue to grace us with their civilized gifts,
as they had since he struck the treaty that secured his place as chief and
our place as Roman clients. As though hunger so sharp it drove families
to sell their children in exchange for dogs to eat was a blessing. As
though being forced into a collar to pave their roads was civilization.

My spear would go to Ôstara with a different purpose—that I might
shed Roman blood in her name.

I found my father and trio of brothers at the largest fire. Segestes'
dark hair bore more gray than black, though he and I shared the same
dark eyes. It was the only thing we shared anymore.

On seeing me, his face lit with happiness. *He must be well into
his ale*, I thought. He wore his wolf pelt headdress, the mark of his
station. Other clan chiefs wore the same, though his was particularly
elaborate. All four limbs and tail remained from the large snowy white
wolf that had fallen to my father's spear. A necklace of bones—fingers
taken from men Segestes had slain in battle—graced his neck beneath
his own torque.

"My daughter!" He raised his alehorn, and Wout grabbed me about
the waist and spun me in a circle. Oh yes, they swam deep in drink.

The priestesses in their spindling antler headdresses and white, veiled
robes sang incantations with each proffered sacrifice. Words repeated in
passion, on important nights such as this, granted the speaker a special
magic. Only our priestesses spoke certain spells and prayers, but these
sacrificial rites were not among them. We liked to have them present
as we believed their deep connections to the gods and fates and earth
itself endowed their words with a magic that eluded the common folk,
mingling in the air with their incense and oils into a mystical otherness
our daily lives lacked.

At Segestes' whistle, the crowds parted, and a scalc ushered the inky
black aurochs forward. His horns jutted high and thick. A magnificent
animal would die, and we would put no part of it to use. Behind it
was a cart overflowing with rich grains that might have seen us through

another winter, wool to clothe the tribe, and an armory of new, finely honed weapons.

The crowds fell silent. Only the drums and horns kept up their call until, as one, the five priestesses raised their arms.

They circled the aurochs in choreographed movements, practiced throughout their lives and passed down each generation. He stamped a hoof and air burst from his nostrils in steaming puffs. Each priestess held a long, curved blade. Without cue, they resumed chanting. On and on their words circled each other until they blended in my ears as nothing but noise and ululations. As one, they stopped.

Segestes stepped forward and faced the bulk of the crowd. "Honored guests, friends, family," he tipped his alehorn at us, "I dedicate this sacrifice for all of us."

A cheer rose up.

"May we all see bountiful harvests, fattened animals, healthy babes—" uproarious shouting and laughter answered that "and the continued strengthening of our friendship with Rome."

Silence sucked the air from the gathering. Segestes cleared his throat and continued. "My sacrifice also honors my daughter's betrothal to Reimar of the Chatti. As a united front, with Rome at our backs, never again will our people face raids! Our trade in Gaul will blossom! We stand at the precipice of peace and prosperity such as we've never known!"

The crowd roared. I grimaced. Two blades arced through the firelight and sank into the animal's fleshy neck. Blood gushed to the forest floor and pained bellows joined our battle horns and drums.

It would fall to Ôstara to determine whose sacrifice she honored this night.

———————————➤

"Again!" I shouted.

My young charge, Konrada, rolled to her feet from the bed of short grass, shook her shoulders out, and assumed her fighting stance. Her youthful face, no more than fifteen summers, split into a wide grin. Like me, she lived for this. Unlike me, she'd only just started her training to join our warrior class. Unlike me, she didn't require days to recover from a celebration. She'd been pestering me to train since the morning after Ôstara. Putting her off for three days was a challenge, though my years training new warriors had prepared me well for her enthusiasm.

I stood at least a head taller than Konrada, though the nearly eleven-year gap in our ages meant she might still grow. I hadn't achieve this height until my eighteenth summer, when I was nothing but rangy limbs, eyes the color of wet soil, and a viper's tongue, or so my brothers liked to tell me.

"I'm bored." Lennart tossed a clump of grass my direction from his seat in the grass. "I told you I don't need to practice with the spear."

He did, but Wodan himself couldn't convince the surly twin he wasn't already a master of warfare. Lucky for him, my head still suffered the lingering effects of too much drink at the festival, draining what little patience I still had for his antics.

"Then go help Levin finish grooming the horses." I avoided Konrada's curious gaze, unwilling to reveal exactly how exhausted Lennart made me.

He stood and narrowed his eyes. "Wout wants to go hunting. I think I'll do that."

One deep breath in, one out. "There are more than twenty horses with mats and overgrown hooves—"

He scoffed. "If Levin wants to keep acting like you're our mama, that's his problem. I'm a grown man, so how about you fuck off?"

Years of practice meant the stab of his words didn't show on my face. Since his last growth spurt, he'd sniped and bit at me at every turn, mostly to tell me I was not our mother. As if anyone needed to remind me. He made a point of shouldering past me in the open meadow and stomping off. To Konrada's credit, she'd turned away during the conversation and started practicing her overhand thrusts. Her parents argued often, especially about her own troublesome brothers, so I imagined pretending to ignore arguments was a skill she'd finely honed.

I took another deep breath, pushed Lennart from my thoughts, and said, "All right, let's try something new. Take your stance."

Our long, heavy spears forced us to position far from each other, much farther than sword fighting. I preferred our single-edged swords, but a good spear offered its own benefits. The length kept enemies at a distance. I could land cut after cut without my opponent getting anywhere near me. I felled enemies with a single thrust, never close enough to see the whites of their eyes. A well-thrown spear could kill from fifty yards or more. On horseback, our circular formations ensnared and demolished even the sturdiest Roman formation. Spears weren't my favorite, but they were damned effective.

I whirled my spear over my head, round and round, letting it gain momentum with each sweeping arc. Konrada stepped in a slow circle around me, tracking each turn of my weapon, waiting for her moment to strike. All around us, the forest loomed, pulsing and breathing into the open meadow where we practiced, close to the village proper.

Each time I turned the spear, the shaft slipped a little further down my grasp until I gripped only a few inches from the end. The turns lengthened like a spiral. An unwary opponent would find themselves within my reach before they realized it happened. I hadn't yet taught Konrada this maneuver, so I didn't fault her missing it. She was about to learn one of the trickiest spear skills, difficult for the wielder and too fast for any but a trained eye to catch.

She waited, timing her lunge just right...if I hadn't closed the distance between us. As I'd predicted, she didn't account for the increased length of my spear. The flat of my spearhead caught her hip and sent her tumbling into the wet grass again with a heavy *oof.*

I guffawed into the milky blue, cloudless sky above. A light breeze deflected the sun's heat, whispering through the trees, grasses, and wildflowers newly in bloom. Spring arrived in earnest. Our nights warmed and the days would soon turn blisteringly hot. Each village worked as one body to plant and tend the fields—spelt, wheat, corn, cabbage, anything that took to our soil. These few weeks before summer, we took advantage of the cooler weather and soft rains to complete our work.

Instead of tilling a field, I lingered here, an escape from listening to my brothers squabble and my father prattle on about my impending marriage. If I had to sit through one more fervent lecture on how the future of our tribe rested in my ability to procreate, I'd take to the woods and never return. Konrada could avoid tilling a field with her family, and I could enjoy a few hours managing just one thing: training an eager young warrior.

"How did you do that?" Konrada dusted herself off and retrieved her weapon.

"It's actually quite simple." I took my time demonstrating the maneuver for her eager eyes. Then demonstrating a few more times, allowing her to finally comprehend the subtle flexing and loosening of my grip that enabled the technique.

"Again?" She pushed the loose curls of her dark hair off her sweat-dampened face.

We resumed our positions and this time, I let her try the spiral trick. It wasn't as smooth as mine and she required a few false starts before executing an even, if a little slow, mimic of the move. I shot my spear up, effectively knocking hers out of her hand.

She lunged to retrieve it. "That was pretty good, wasn't it?"

I hummed a noncommittal noise. It was good, but it needed more practice.

"Next, we have to work on—"

Clapping echoed through the meadow. A legionary materialized from the wood, clapping and grinning like a child with a new toy. Konrada jumped like a startled cat, then fell in at my side. The smug little man appeared far too pleased with himself. I would wipe that smile from his face. More soldiers appeared, six in total. A patrol. Each passing year brought more of them into our territory. More to collect our goods and people in tax, more to stir up trouble I inevitably settled before our people ended up on their wooden crosses.

I should have brought my dogs with us.

"See?" The first man spoke in Latin. "I told you these Germani bitches are big. They can fight, too."

I didn't react to his insult. No sense in revealing I spoke Latin as well as I spoke our native tongue. Segestes had forced me to learn it not long after he was elected chief.

"That's a fine piece of meat, though," another said as he flanked us, appraising our figures in high boots, wool trousers, and short tunics. "I'd let her ride me."

Their stench wafted through the clean, airy meadow, ripe and sour. All except the leader bore gaunt faces marked by darkened eyes. They must have just marched in from the west, across the Rhine where the Roman empire ended and the free land began, fresh troops for the encampment.

The soldier circling nearest to me reached out to touch my hair. I ducked out of his reach, hissing like a cat and brandishing my spear at him.

His face reddened, but his peers burst into uproarious laughter.

"I think this one bites." The leader clapped his friend on the shoulder. "I'd watch myself. These bitches learn to fight like men. I wouldn't be surprised if this big bitch had a cock."

And I wouldn't be surprised to find you entirely without beneath that tunic. Of course they'd think me tall and muscular. I was, compared to their stunted people and soft women. The Cherusci never bred weaklings.

"You remember what I taught you?" I kept my words low, for Konrada's ears only, lest one of these animals understood our tongue.

She nodded once, her knuckles white around the wood of her spear. She positioned herself at my back, each of us canted to face the semicircle the soldiers formed around us.

Six against two were not good odds, but knowing I would make them suffer dearly for their assault, win or lose, brought a cruel twist to my lips.

One idiot removed his armor, as if victory was so readily assured. Romans would believe that. *Let them underestimate me. Let them believe I'll make this easy.*

The leader twirled his sword in his palm, eyes alight with predatory satisfaction on me. "Look at her, men. I think she wants this."

He gripped his cock beneath his belt and tunic and opened his mouth, waggling his tongue. His intent was clear enough. The damned idiot turned his back on us to share a congratulatory laugh with his men. I lunged forward with a powerful thrust of my spear. The other men shouted a warning, and he jerked out of the path of my weapon. I didn't stop the assault.

Keep him off balance.

Tangle his feet.

Finish it quickly.

Bring him down.

The march had exhausted the others. They were too new, too tired. Easier to defeat. I heard the crack of Konrada's spear against blades and armor, and the air moved with her behind me. In my periphery, her vicious swings and thrusts kept her opponents at bay. *Good girl.*

Fury pushed me beyond reason, and I chose a different approach. I would see the whites of their eyes before I killed them.

The leader of this patrol fought me with skill and experience. Our weapons clashed and rang off each other. Each impact jarred my bones. The earth churned to mud beneath our feet. Two others circled, but he barked them away.

He grew tired. His steps faltered and his blows came slower, weaker. I felt another man coming before I noticed his absence from the group.

I choked up my grip on my spear and sent it in a clean sweep across the chest and belly of the soldier who'd been foolish enough to not only remove his armor but also attempt to sneak up on me. I didn't slow to assess the extent of the damage and whirled back to face the leader. He stood transfixed between shock and rage. His rage won out.

With a roar, he lunged forward again, but his roar turned to a sharp cry and his body jerked. His sword flew from his grasp and he stumbled to his knees.

A spear grazed his right shoulder and sank into the earth behind him.

Soldiers of the most professional army in the world, the army that so easily conquered my people, fell to chaos. Leaderless, they scrambled, some to their wounded friends, one leveled an enraged snarl at me, and the others converged on Konrada.

Foolish girl. She was unarmed, and there were too many of them for me to defend us both.

Distracted by the imminent peril of my young charge, I lost focus. A blow cracked against the back of my skull. The noise of it was deafening, or perhaps my senses lost track of the pain and expressed themselves through a grating, shocking sound. I stumbled and fought to stay upright even as the earth wobbled beneath my feet.

Two came at me at once. My head rang and spun. They moved in a blur. Sharp stings burned my arm and leg.

A blow to my stomach.

A blow to my back.

My spear met flesh and a fist met my jaw, and I dropped to the mud.

The leader stood before me, panting, a little gray around the edges, with his sword under Konrada's chin. Another hand gripped my hair and jerked me back to my knees.

"I'll kill her!" the leader shouted.

My body seized with the desire to rip him apart for his rough handling of her. She was so small, even compared to Romans.

"Secure them." The leader shook so badly the tip of his blade dug into her skin, drawing a trickle of blood. My breath stuttered for her. Warm blood trickled down my arms and legs and face, coppery against my tongue.

It took a bit of fumbling and arguing as they hadn't brought rope, but they managed. Strips of cloth dug into my wrists, and my shoulders protested at the binding.

Two of their own lay dead in the meadow, a macabre scene fit for the days when people sacrificed other people. Blood and weapons and feet churning in fight turned the once beautiful meadow into a gruesome battle site. If only a priestess was here to perform the rites, then it could have been my sacrifice to the gods, beseeching an end to Rome. Perhaps the gods longed for such a worthy sacrifice.

"Let's go," the leader said.

The one with a meaty, unwashed hand digging into my shoulder shifted from foot to foot. "But Patrin, the men…"

Patrin, their leader, snarled back, "Unless you think you can carry two dead men and keep control of these barbarian whores, we'll have to come back for them, won't we?"

Yes, I definitely should have brought my dogs.

Chapter 2

And, beside the perils of rough and unknown seas, who would leave Asia, or Africa, or Italy for Germany, with its wild country, its inclement skies, its sullen manners and aspect, unless indeed it were his home? (Tacitus)

After they disarmed and marched us to the garrison, taking any opportunity to spit at and curse us, I took comfort in the fact that they didn't rape us. I failed to protect Konrada from their mistreatment, but at least they hadn't subjected her to *that*. Patrin needed help remaining upright and moving forward with his wound, which was deeper than it had first appeared. Blood flowed steadily, dripping from his fingertips. He didn't speak, content to glare. Spittle dotted his curling lips. This man frothed at the mouth to tear us limb from limb.

Konrada and I kept silent, though tension rolled off her in waves. Darkness fell and mist oozed in a fragile dance on our path. I hoped these idiots knew their way, because a false step could land one or all of us in a bog. It wouldn't be so bad if I cast a few more to the underworld by way of our inescapable swamps. To my disappointment, they followed where our wooden roads created safer travel.

After nearly an hour, the sprawling camp loomed ahead. No matter how many times I saw it, it remained a marvel. Orderly rows of identical tents stretched far beyond the high wooden walls and intricately spiked ramparts. Evenly placed torches lit meticulously aligned paths. Three golden eagles marked the divisions between legions. Torch light made the them dance, giving the raptors the illusion of life.

This is what civilization meant to them: lines, rules, order. Our disorganized villages and few leaders represented chaos to them. If Rome was civilization, we were its antithesis.

Soldiers stared, stopping whatever they were doing to watch our bloodied procession. Someone called for a centurion and a medicus.

We halted in front of one of the larger tents as a harried and tunic-clad soldier emerged. He assessed our bedraggled troop and set his jaw.

"Stand by," he spoke in a low growl.

"Centurion—" Patrin started.

The centurion whirled, the veins on his neck bulged, and in the torchlight he turned a lovely shade of red. "Where the fuck have you been? No, nevermind. I don't give a fuck. The medicus can see you while you await my escort to the general. This was your last chance, Patrin."

Droplets of moisture flew with each word.

When the centurion next appeared, he wore his full regalia, from his segmented armor to the horsehair crested helmet. He sent an optio ahead to alert whomever—I didn't care—of our impending arrival.

More waiting followed our arrival at the largest tent. We interrupted their evening meal. I listened to the masculine voices, laughing, shouting, almost boyish in their unguarded state. Layers of fabric and furs muffled their voices too much to hear clearly. After a parade of slaves— my people and others, collared like dogs—cleared away the dishes, a voice beckoned us.

I knew that voice. I'd seen him enough on his tours of our villages. General Publius Quinctilius Varus' tent was appointed befitting his rank and position as the governor of our land, as far as Rome was concerned. Sumptuous carpets and furs lined every surface. Silver and gold glittered in the lamplight and the smoldering brazier. He sat at a heavy, polished wooden table in an equally ornate chair. More solid furniture and thick couches filled the space. I pitied the men who had moved this furniture all the way from Rome just to make a little man feel important. His quarters smelled of seasoned meat, wine, and scented oils. Each man present glistened with it.

I almost missed one man. He stood behind Varus, leaning indolently against one of the tent poles and shadowed behind the overly warm brazier. Once I saw him, he filled my vision. He stood tall, taller than any Roman and most of the conscripts from across the empire. Bronzed, thick arms crossed his chest, making him look even bigger.

His light hair, a burnished gold so dark it might have been brown, shorn in the Roman style, marked him. One of our own stood at Varus' shoulder. His presence incensed me more than the whole of Patrin's attack. Many of our boys had been taken as hostages to Rome after their assault some fifteen years ago, Ermin and his little brother among them, but it was widely believed Rome had enslaved those sons. Cherusci spoke rumors of our lost princes becoming great Roman warriors, but until this moment, I'd refused to believe it possible. None of our people survived capture, let alone gained position as Romans. At best, they toiled in the auxiliary.

This man was no slave, no nameless soldier. They had made him a Roman in a truly inventive insult, sending one of our own to enslave and oppress his people. It was all true. In my mind's eye, fury gave me the preternatural strength to burst free of my bindings, steal the centurion's sword, and leap across the table to fell this bastard with a mighty war cry. Instead, my wrists chafed and my body quaked with unspent delirious madness.

He saw it, too, while the others ignored me, instead focusing on the centurion and Patrin. Icy blue eyes bored into me so intently my chest constricted at their impact. Konrada cleared her throat and brought me back from the brink. More than my life hung in the balance, so I forced a kind of calm I seldom required.

In an eruption of noise, they volleyed questions from all sides. Patrin insisted Konrada and I fell on them without provocation. The centurion declared we were to be held accountable for wounding and killing his soldiers. One man pushed to his feet and shouted at the centurion about having no control over his men, who had left the camp without permission. Not a patrol, after all.

Varus sighed and leaned back in his chair. "Arminius, ask the women for their story."

The man, the Germani, stepped around the table, and I finally got a good look at him. He was handsome enough, for a vile traitor.

"What is your name?" Arminius asked me in our tongue; his accent was atrocious.

I wanted to spit on him so badly my teeth ground together. Instead, I responded in clear Latin to Varus, "I am Princess Thusnelda, daughter of Segestes, Chief of the Cherusci, and I demand you release us."

The air sucked out of the room. Konrada flinched at my back. Patrin lost himself and lunged for me, hurling expletives and insults, accusing me of lying. Rage boiled over until my wrists tugged at my bonds. How dare he? My lips curled back in a snarl just as Patrin's good arm came within a breath of my throat. Quick as a wildcat, a brawny arm shot out and caught the smaller soldier by the throat. With a growl, Arminius shoved Patrin into the centurion.

"Eggius, control your man." Arminius took a breath and settled himself, but for a moment I envisioned him bearded, wearing our armor, leading our armies. More the pity.

In a sea of simmering tempers, Varus let out a delighted laugh. "Wonderful! She speaks! Your father has mentioned you. Tell us, Princess Thusnelda, how it was you came to kill two of the Empire's fine soldiers."

I hesitated to answer. It was highly unlikely they would believe my account over the men who attacked us. Arminius nodded at me, encouraging me to speak.

As if I needed his help.

"I took this girl for training," I said. "We were practicing with spears."

The centurion, Eggius, scoffed. "I am well aware it's commonplace among these people for women to hunt and join men on the battlefield, as these women have already demonstrated, however—"

"Centurion," Arminius fixed his attention on the man, "how long have you been stationed here?"

"A little over a year."

"Then you should already know Germani warriors are smart enough to pick their battles. They wouldn't have attacked a patrol without reason."

Varus watched the exchange, vibrating in his amusement. With a magnanimous nod, he said, "Continue."

"As we were preparing to spar again, these men came upon us. They stated their intention to violate us. We fought back."

Varus erupted in laughter. No one joined his eerie humor, though he had to wipe tears from his eyes. "Are you telling me," he gasped between body-shaking spasms of laughter, "that one woman and one child successfully repelled six of Rome's finest soldiers, killed two, and wounded three before being subdued?"

He continued laughing. The centurion shifted his weight and cleared his throat. "General, I—"

"Enough!" Varus slammed his fist on the table, all traces of humor gone in an instant. "Your incompetence as a leader has cost me two trained men and imperiled my control of the strongest tribe in this region. Now I have to deal with Segestes and assure him his own daughter is safe under our rule because your men respect you so little they apparently come and go as they please, not to mention the obvious deficiencies in their training."

The centurion colored. "General, I will handle it."

Varus shifted in his seat and adjusted his fine tunic with more force than necessary. "Segestes will see this as a great insult and it's your fault."

One of the other men stood from his seat. Like Varus, he wore a snowy white tunic trimmed in purple. The others wore the simple red garb issued to soldiers. "I will handle the men, General."

"See that you do, Legatus. Do something about our guards and patrols, as well. Every man who was on watch and missed their departure from the gates must serve as an example to the others. Princess, this man," he gestured to Arminius, "is one of yours. He's here as my aide and something of an envoy between our two nations. Arminius, ensure the princess and her companion return to their homes without further harassment. If you can do anything to ease my way with Segestes, then…" He gestured vaguely.

"Yes, General." Arminius saluted crisply. He turned to another soldier, "Escort them to my quarters and wait with them while I get my armor."

Once placed in front of yet another tent, the optio released our bindings. Ever the child of a combative family, Konrada lurked at my back, close enough that I couldn't forget her but far enough to give me space. Arminius emerged after just a moment, now encased in the well polished molded armor Romans used for ceremonies. He cut an impressive figure, particularly once he donned his crested helmet.

He was a Cherusci remade in their image, and I hated him.

With the snap of his fingers, a legionary returned our spears, but not my precious dagger.

"Where's my knife?" The legionary didn't answer me. Arminius reached to take me by the elbow, but I jerked out of his reach. "Where is it?"

He pressed his lips together and waited until the legionary was out of earshot. "I'll explain when we're outside the fort."

Without waiting for me to argue, he strutted off, leaving us no choice but to follow. To stay in this encampment alone was foolishness. We walked on in silence, Konrada trailing behind us, until we were well past the camp, enveloped in the night.

"Thusnelda, do you remember me?" Arminius asked.

I studied him out of the corner of my eye. He was handsome. Not handsome enough to diminish his betrayal but objectively well formed.

"Should I?"

He didn't reply for a few steps before he cocked his head. "Do you think Segestes will still honor our betrothal?"

I stopped and whipped around to stare at him, aghast. "What?"

Konrada squeaked and, after an initial rush to get closer, fell back even further.

"You grew up well. Killed two legionaries. I'm not supposed to be impressed, but... You still have your fire. I like that."

Arminius chuckled and kept walking, leaving me scrambling and sputtering to keep up. My pulse turned erratic. A quick glance behind us revealed Konrada staring with eyes so huge they looked like twin stars following our path. There was only one among my many made and broken betrothals who had wound up in Roman hands. But no, it was impossible. Ermin and his brother were hostages, glorified slaves, not Roman officers.

My hand tightened on the spear. With a few quick steps, I blocked his path and put the tip in his face.

"Who are you?" It wasn't him. I refused to allow this. Not my Ermin, the young man I'd worshiped, the man who was supposed to be our chief and my husband. The man who promised to come back then never did.

"I'm glad you didn't have to use this on yourself." He proffered the bone-handled knife and suddenly I was nine years old again, terrified and confused.

Bless her, Konrada took a fighting position next to me.

"Princess?" she whispered.

"No." I shook my head. "No."

Arminius held his hands up and stood his ground. "Wildberry, I told you I'd come back for you."

I shifted the spearhead to his throat. "No."

Perhaps if I denied it enough, it wouldn't be true. I'd wake in my bed and discover this was a perverse dream. My Ermin would never wear that uniform. He'd never fight for our enemy, our oppressors. Gods above, he'd never twist his name into something the Roman tongue liked.

"I'm sorry you're finding out like this. I see I shouldn't have started with a joke. I meant to come to the village and—"

"And what?" I pressed the spear hard enough to draw a thin trickle of blood. He didn't flinch. "Pretend you're still one of us? We mourned you, and you...you..."

You betrayed us. You betrayed everything. You abandoned me for them. You didn't come back.

"Elda" With meticulous care he pushed the spear aside, "I'm sorry. I can explain everything, if you just—"

On a growl, I stepped back and kept the weapon raised. "No. I don't want to see you again. Konrada, let's go."

"Please," he said, face pulled in pain. It looked so genuine, I almost stopped my retreat. Almost.

I hardened my heart. Ermin was dead, and this *thing* wearing his face was an abomination.

"You disgust me." I grabbed Konrada by one of her short sleeves and turned my back on him.

→

A week later, dinner was a tense affair, though one would never have known it from the way Arminius wolfed down his plates. Every few minutes he paused long enough to explain a dish or custom or turn of phrase to Varus, who had the good graces to feign an interest in learning more about the people he governed.

I longed to be anywhere except the family table at the head of the hall. I loved the rows of beaded necklaces and bronze bracelets I wore, but they threatened to strangle me this evening. My gown, a lightweight wool in cornflower blue with blood red details, felt too cumbersome, especially with its long sleeves, a concession I'd made to Roman propriety. The fire burned too hot. Sweat dotted the back of my neck. Between bites of food, I tugged at my sleeves, my bracelets, the neckline of my modest gown.

Segestes had surrendered his usual position of honor at the head of the table to Varus, and my brothers and I had arranged ourselves alongside Segestes by age. Wout took the seat next to father. I took the next, and Lennart and Levin filled the rest of the bench. I wished Levin was next to me. The legatus and a tribune—Lucius or Marcus or something else painfully Roman—who'd been in the tent when I was first taken before Varus took the seats flanking their general, which placed Arminius squarely across from me.

If I was peevish over the seating arrangements, Reimar was furious. He'd ridden hard from his Chatti lands to check on my welfare as soon as word of what had happened had reached him. Of course, by "my welfare" he meant assurances from Segestes that I had not been so badly violated by a troop of Romans that I was no longer a worthwhile investment.

He bristled like an angry boar to be seated at the end of the table and grumbled in our tongue that as a prince and soon-to-be son-in-law of Segestes, he belonged in Wout's seat. He took particular offense every time Arminius winked at me and snickered at one of Reimar's comments, which was often.

I itched to give Arminius a swift kick to the shins, but I'd only hurt myself against one of his greaves. The bastard.

If Segestes noticed Arminius' behavior, he didn't care. My father would chop off his own hand at Rome's request, lest he offend his great benefactors. Sometimes his eyes shone with unmistakable love for these men, more so than he'd ever shown me.

"You're a lucky man, Reimar." Arminius kept his voice low enough to avoid drawing away attention from the conversation at the head of the table.

A hot flush crawled up Reimar's neck before disappearing beneath his thick red beard. Though not as tall as Arminius, Reimar possessed a sturdy frame and a reputation on the battlefield envied by warriors across Germania. If there was to be a fight between the pair, I would be hard pressed to determine the victor.

Arminius slowed his chewing and cast an innocent look between us. "She can cook." He gestured at me with his spoon. "A wife who can cook this well is a rare gift indeed." He tucked back into his meal with gusto.

I wanted to hit him with a plate. One quick thrust with a carving knife and we'd all be rid of his poison. Instead I plastered a sickly sweet smile on my face. "You are too kind, Arminius, but I merely gave the kitchen scalcs instructions."

Arminius gripped his alehorn and set his attention squarely on me. My skin prickled with gooseflesh under the intensity of his stare. All other noise and activity dimmed, leaving me alone in the longhouse with Arminius, who traced his long, blunt fingers up and down the sides of the horn. I suppressed a shiver under all that unrelenting focus. Beneath his boyish facade hid a dangerous animal indeed.

"A wife so comfortable in command is an even rarer gift." He took a long pull of ale and clapped a hand across Reimar's shoulders, shattering the strange sense of solitude we'd shared. "Besides, a man could do worse than taking to a wife a woman who stood against six legionaries and lived to tell the tale with hardly a scratch on her."

"Yes." Reimar's voice boomed. He hadn't taken to Latin as naturally as I had, and oldiers still mocked his guttural mispronunciations. "I would like to know why this insult to our honor we have not discussed."

All eyes turned to Reimar. My father looked ready to boil over, but before he spoke, Varus waved a hand.

"No, the boy is right."

Reimar was hardly a boy, graying at the edges as he was.

Varus swirled the wine in his cup. Father ensured he always had an amphora available for notable Roman guests in our home, although this marked the first occasion he had to serve it.

"My soldiers insulted both your fine houses. I am here to build bridges, not burn them. Please, accept my apologies and assurances that the four survivors have been made an example of."

Segestes' face pinched. "And when they attack again? I'm sorry, General, but this matter calls into question our entire arrangement."

It took several heartbeats before I understood him. Many years had passed since Segestes last expressed concern for my personal welfare. I didn't know how to respond to a concern so significant he took a stand against any Roman, let alone our governor.

"Is that so?" Varus was a small man with no discernible physical strength. I couldn't picture him in battle. Yet the entire table stilled when he spoke. The Roman emperor, a chief of chiefs, chose him to bring us to heel. I did not imagine slow-witted men became emperors of such cunning people.

"Yes," Varus's voice remained deceptively calm, "our men violated one of our most basic disciplinary principles and nearly lost a fight to two girls, no less. I can understand why you might feel that way. However, I swear on my gods and my legions that Rome will honor her promises to you."

"How?" Reimar spat. "How you will do this? Cherusci and Chatti have been most loyal, but our women still not safe."

For the first time since our betrothal, my interest in Reimar was piqued. I was to marry a man who stood up to Roman bullying. Fourteen years watching Segestes lick boots weighed heavily on my pride.

Varus studied Reimar, much the way a cat studies a mouse, indifferently vacillating between killing the small creature and sharing his crumbs.

"Legatus Vala and Tribune Belenus are working closely together to address the training concerns raised by this incident. Our mutual friend Arminius—" Segestes barely hid his snarl "—is here not only to help your people adjust to Rome's way of life, but also to help me guide my legions in understanding Germania. Together, I believe we can prevent such misunderstandings in the future."

I indulged in a silent scoff. A misunderstanding. Six armed men attempted to rape a young girl and me because we'd had the misfortune to cross their paths. This was of little matter to the fine men at our table. The insult to Konrada was nothing to them, and the insult to me was an insult due to my value as a potential wife. Any goodwill I inferred from Segestes' defense of me evaporated. I lost my appetite, instead choosing to drink my ale as quickly as possible. My hand trembled, and the drink turned to dust in my mouth. Pushing my plate away would be rude, so I settled for moving the food around aimlessly with my wooden spoon.

Reimar opened his mouth to argue, but Segestes silenced him with a single look. "I understand and appreciate your efforts, General, but as you can see, it is not common for Germani to accept redress in this manner. We are a barbaric people, and the Chatti may view Reimar's acceptance of these terms as weakness. I'm sure you can understand."

"He's correct, General," Arminius said. "Such an assault, particularly of the daughter of a chief, would normally call for war between the tribes, or at least an opportunity for the offended party to face the aggressors in single combat."

With a snap of Varus's fingers, a slave materialized from a darkened corner of the longhouse. He placed a small but heavy sack before Segestes, then another before Reimar.

"Perhaps this will help ease relations between us."

Reimar tugged the sack open and grunted. "We do not use coins here. These are without meaning."

Varus shot a hard look at Arminius, who cleared his throat and said, "More and more Germani are using our coin for trading, especially outside of Germania. You will find—"

"What business do Chatti have trading beyond Germania? We have good trade here. Merchants come to us. You should know this."

Our coin. *Our.* My skin crawled. It was not ours; it was Rome's and Arminius was a Roman. I wanted to rail at him, but if I were to speak now, Segestes would beat me later, or at least try. It may not have been the bravery our people sang in songs, but I believed a smart warrior waited until the most opportune moment to strike, when her blade landed a killing blow.

"Tell them," Varus said. "It will soon be your duty to liaise with the tribes, so you might as well get used to it."

Vala drummed his fingers on the table, a small smile playing at the corners of his thin lips.

Arminius shifted in his seat and cleared his throat. "The General plans on eliminating trade-based taxation. Within the year, Germani in the region will be expected to pay their taxes in Roman coin."

Even Segestes balked. "Forgive me, but what you ask is impossible. In a few years, perhaps, but just one? We Cherusci number in the tens of thousands. Distribution of the coins will take years, let alone convincing my people to use them."

"I'm not asking," said Varus. "I am telling you this will happen. The border tribes have adapted well enough. Rome did not become what she is by hiding behind caution."

No, she grows like a plague, relentlessly sweeping across the land, killing indiscriminately, leaving the survivors marked by her disease.

The survivors became Roman, like Arminius, and all traces of their old identities vanished.

My father accepted the rebuke while Reimar chose silence, staring at Arminius with hard eyes. Defiance rolled off him in waves. Living under Segestes' rule left me with few options for expressing defiance of my own, so I was left instead to stew alone in impotent frustration. I wondered if Reimar might be the answer to my inability to protect my community, my people.

"We are not on the border," I said. All eyes fell on me. My spine straightened under their scrutiny. "They use your coins to trade with your people. We don't."

A bright crimson flush colored the men of my family. Wout hardened beside me. Levin choked on his drink, and Lennart's hand shot under the table to my wrist in a punishing grip. Reimar studied me impassively, his expression betraying nothing, though it marked the first time he spared more than a glance in my direction.

Segestes contorted his features into an obsequious smile for Varus. "Please forgive my daughter. I'm afraid I've been indulgent with this one. Wout—"

"Yes, Father." Wout stood and snatched my arm hard enough to bruise. The table bumped and rocked as Wout and someone else rushed to their feet.

"Bah." Varus waved a dismissive hand. "She speaks the truth. Don't send her away on my account."

His fixed, predatory stare belied his light tone. I resisted the urge to wilt under that stare.

The gathering turned its attention to Arminius, who looked bewildered as he settled himself back into his seat. He chuckled, two or three forced laughs. "Apologies, gentlemen. The last time someone put hands on this woman, two men died and another got speared."

Once Varus erupted in laughter, the rest of the party followed. Everyone but Legatus Vala, who flicked his attention between Arminius and me. Something in his deep set eyes, thin cheeks, hard chin said he knew something we didn't. Something none of us knew but would pay for later.

This was to be a long damn night.

Chapter 3

... for the greatness of the Roman people has carried a reverence for the empire beyond the Rhine... (Tacitus)

As evening wore on, more villagers piled into our home at Varus' request. His slaves left and returned with amphoras of wine, baskets of bread, olives, cheese, a horrifying fish sauce, and their beloved olive oil. I hastened about the village to assemble more food and drink for our guests. To their credit, our scalcs responded admirably, especially under Jotapa's skilled supervision. Hospitality was serious business across Germania. In a land as unforgiving and hostile as ours, welcoming people was no idle matter. All visitors were to be fed, offered drink and warm blankets, and places to sleep comfortably. The fires must be carefully controlled, never too cold nor too hot. A chief's home, in particular, needed to excel in comfort.

The salty-sour stench of hardworking bodies mingled with that of wine and food. I was glad to have dined so lightly; far less to lose later.

Cherusci imbibed in the unwatered wine with gleeful abandon. Segestes reveled in the opportunity to show the Germani how wonderful civilization was, even while their backs ached from the extra labor required to pay Roman taxes, while their sons and daughters disappeared into slavery, while their most prized son dressed, spoke, and ate as a Roman.

The man in question sidled his way to where I stood, observing the crowd, checking for any deficiencies to meet before anyone accused the chief of the Cherusci of lackluster hospitality.

Naturally, Arminius didn't smell like a filthy man fresh from the fields. He smelled of leather and forest, like he belonged here. I only barely made out the scented oil Romans used after a bath. I found it uncomfortably pleasant. My skin crawled.

He took a sip of ale, one of few in the expansive room who didn't choose the wine.

"*Panem et circenses.*"

I hardly heard him over the general din of voices, laughter, and clattering dishes. A piper whistled a merry tune and those nearest clapped along.

"What?" I understood the words—bread and circuses—but not why he would seek me out to say random things. Why seek me out for anything? His focus on me turned quickly from odd and welcome to vexing and infuriating.

"All this," Arminius nodded at the room, "it's what Romans do to smooth things over. You give people good wine, food, some entertainment, suddenly they're not so worried about their taxes, crime, and poverty."

Despite my deepest desire to ignore him until he ceased to exist, I responded to his little verbal thrust. "And what is the entertainment here?"

My father laughed too loudly at something Varus said. A chorus of Germani joined him.

"They get to spend an evening pretending Varus is their peer, that he is a man of the people who cares about each of them personally. When legionaries and that ghoul Vala come for their taxes, these men will remember this night and think more kindly of their Roman benefactors."

I crossed my arms and squared myself to him. "Is that how you see yourselves? As our benefactors?"

Something dark flashed behind his cool gaze. "I am Cherusci."

"So you say."

A muscle in his jaw twitched. "Believe whatever you want."

His back retreated into the crush and to my great consternation, I found myself catching him in the corner of my eye as I went about my duties. Tall even for one of us, but bedecked in a Roman tunic, he didn't belong to either group. He dwarfed the pitifully small and wiry Varus and the relatively larger tribune and legatus. Cherusci and Chatti folk watched him openly, uncaring if he caught their curious stares.

Determined to get him out of my sight and, hopefully, remove him from my thoughts, I turned on my heel and left by the main doors. The cool night air cleansed my tired nostrils. I breathed in the trees and moisture. Even the hay and animal scents from the barn, where we kept our stock through spring and summer, soothed my frayed nerves. My dogs loped to my side, a pair of wolf half-breeds I had found starving in the woods. I slipped them each a crust of bread, and they stuck by my heels on my slow meandering toward the wooden corral where our stout, thickly furred horses munched lazily at patches of wild grass. Segestes hated how I treated the dogs. He wanted them at least half feral, ready to rip apart any who dared to trespass on our territory. I preferred them like this—loyal and infinitely biddable. When they joined me on hunts, they followed my commands with a discipline to rival any Roman legion. Donar, my biggest dog, leaned his body against my leg, so I lazily scratched his head and rubbed his ears. My quiet friends soothed me out of my worst moods. When they howled, they spoke to the gods.

Donar's ears perked, and he turned to look behind me. Sunna's low growl rumbled through the night. I followed the direction of their attention and saw the shape of a large man striding our direction. When I recognized him as Reimar, I ordered the dogs, "*Plotz.*" They both dropped instantly to their bellies.

Reimar smiled down at me with glassy eyes and wine on his breath.

His meaty hand gripped my arm. "'Elda, there you are." He gave my thick braid a light tug, rubbing the loose ends between his thumb and forefinger. "Are you sure you are well?"

"I'm fine." I took a casual step back and returned my attention to the horses. "I needed fresh air, is all. Thank you for your concern."

Reimar joined me, leaning on the fence a respectful distance away. Drink loosened his tongue and his posture. "I know you don't want this marriage. That's fine. I don't want it, either."

Too stunned to speak, I watched him in the moonlight. Our people weren't prone to dissembling, not the way Romans were, but matters of courtship and marriage generally required at least a feigned attempt at liking each other.

"I already had a wife," he continued. "I swore she was the only wife I'd ever take, but the Chatti will need a queen. Does this upset you?"

His age indicated that he'd already been married at least once, so I wasn't surprised and certainly not angry about that. Part of me wanted to be upset that he wanted to marry me about as much as I wanted to marry him, but I didn't like to consider myself a hypocrite.

"No," I said. "Does it upset you that I'd rather not marry at all?"

He shook his head. "I know you'll do your duty, as I will do mine. I need a queen, and a son. I've no need or want for a wife, you understand?"

I caught myself smiling. Reimar offered everything I wanted: a tribe of my own to manage, a little queendom Wout's chosen bride could never usurp, children, and no expectations of love. Love was out of the question for me, a gift I wasn't sure I could even give, not when I gave so much of myself back to my people every day, and would do so with the Chatti.

"Yes," I said. "I understand, and I agree. I don't want to be your wife."

———————➤

The next morning, I sat near the main fire in our dining hall, stitching a tear in one of Wout's tunics. I listened to the quiet chatter of the scalcs as they cleaned up from the evening's festivities. Two younger girls blushed and giggled over the attentions of the Chatti men. It brought a small smile to my lips and a twinge of grossly misplaced jealousy. They were slaves by another name and I was to be a queen, yet they had certain freedoms I lacked. I couldn't afford dalliances with handsome strangers, nor even the friendships they shared. The sole exception happened years earlier, with my own little rebellion. One night with a Marsi warrior was all I thought it would take to deter my father's marriage ambitions. I thought I'd wed the handsome nobody and go on about my life miles and miles from Segestes. It was not to be. Unless I got with child, it didn't matter who I fucked. Cherusci, and most Germani, didn't concern themselves overly much with chastity, so long as a child's father could be identified. Not like the Romans who apparently guarded their women like sentries of cunt.

Footsteps pounded from the rear of the house. I didn't look up from my work, but Segestes hovered over me with palpable intent.

"Arminius isn't welcome in our home. See to it."

For that, I paused and set my needlework aside. "I don't see how that will be possible, given his position. Besides, I'm not sure why you hate him so much. He is exactly what you hope for all of us."

He wanted to strike me. The desire quivered from his hair to his toes. I held his challenging stare. Let him try. He had struck all of us throughout our childhoods until we grew strong enough to fight back. It had taken longer for me to catch up with even the twins, but in my twentieth summer, when muscles thickened with hard work to fill my long limbs, when they grew fast and lethal with hunting and training, I hit him back. He had been simultaneously proud and furious, and his blows came less and less often.

Instead of slapping me, he pointed a dirty, calloused finger in my face. "You know damn well why."

"I really don't."

The veins bulged in his neck, and he swept his hand out to knock everything he could reach off the table. "This is his fucking house, Thusnelda! Don't you understand how precarious our situation is? Everything I've worked for, all the sacrifices, the safety I built for us, all gone with a few words from his lips."

I wanted to roll my eyes and finish my work, but that would provoke him further. "Is he not one of their horse lords? What would he want with being chief of the Cherusci?"

The concept of strict ranks beyond chiefs eluded Germani, myself included. I understood they had awarded him citizenship and they called him an *equestrian*, but what that meant was beyond me.

The anger drained from his body. He ran his hand through his scraggly hair. "I've shielded you from too much. I can't expect you to understand this, but hear me now, daughter: You don't know what he really wants. We may not be able to keep him out of this house, but if I hear of you conversing with him again, I will put you out. You will no longer be my daughter. Reimar will not have you. No man worth having will take you."

He left me alone in the hall to stew on his proclamation. He'd taken a hard line, even for him.

What did he think I had to do with Arminius reclaiming his seat?

* * *

I took to the woods again, though I should have been making my rounds in the village. At least two women were due to give birth soon, one family was refusing to take their share of the planting duties, and a few of our elders hadn't made it out of the winter without ailments. These were problems I could, if not fix, soothe. That was my role in life, and I was damn good at it. But in the days since that dinner, I had lost focus. Tasks that had once seemed clear—did Ulfhir and her husband have sufficient swaddling clothes? Which children were responsible and quiet enough to look in on the grouchy Adelfried every day?—turned hazy, things just out of reach.

My impulse to fetch Konrada and bring her along died as quickly as it rose. The last time I was supposed to protect and guide her, my foolishness nearly got both of us raped. I'd been mentoring would-be warrior girls since I turned sixteen and never, not once, had I put one of my charges in such danger. Thoughts of what might have happened haunted my dreams and waking nightmares. I had failed, and I sensed my role as head woman of the Cherusci slipping through my fingers.

Something nebulous had shifted the day Ermin—no, Arminius— returned. Instinct said my life would now take a different course, and I was powerless to stop it.

My mother often said I was more *landvættir* than girl, an earthen spirit tragically confined to a house when my true home lay in the wilds. While my brothers played in the village, I wandered among the trees. The darkness, the mist, the crush of towering alders, beeches, and oaks never frightened me the way they did most children. My fingers traced the vines climbing the trunks and my skin cooled with dew brushed from buckthorn leaves. Where others saw evil spirits, I saw a multitude of life and opportunity. All manner of plants and animals thrived here. At every glance, well hidden clutches of flowers reached for the sun. After all my years, I still sighted new birds almost every time I entered these woods. A babbling brook was my music, its watery scent blending with soil, leaves, grasses, tree bark. Petrichor was my perfume of choice.

Sunna and Donar trotted along, the three of us nimble over the tangle of branches, mud, and dense understory. Moss and bark and moisture mingled in the air, their smell heightened in the rolling wet mist. One mistake I would not make again was wandering from the village without my dogs.

I snaked my hand out to a clutch of plump blackberries on my path. Each dog got one, though they never actually ate the berries. I chewed them slowly, one at a time, savoring their sweetness.

When I married Reimar, would he permit me this kind of freedom? I liked to think so, but I didn't know him well enough to be confident. In truth, I took my situation for granted. For all Segestes' faults, he allowed me this whenever I needed it. I never quite gathered why, though I liked to imagine that somewhere inside him was a father who loved his daughter. He let me dictate the course of my own days, as long as most of my days were spent in service to the Cherusci, which suited me fine. Many men kept their women on much tighter leads. Would Reimar be among them? He hadn't scolded me, nor looked affronted by my interruption at dinner. He'd followed me outside and respected my need for space. Yes, I believed he wouldn't keep me as though I were his personal dog.

A gap in the trees filtered sunlight to the forest floor. At least two hours had passed since I first set off, making me a healthy distance from our village. I should be close to another Cherusci village, but sticking to the wald meant I was unlikely to encounter anyone else.

Faint voices drifted through the trees and I cursed myself twice a fool. I must have wandered closer to the roads between our villages than I thought.

"It's never going to happen," a male voice said. He spoke our language, but his accent was unfamiliar. *A Germani auxiliary?*

"You are absolutely correct, Ermin," a familiar voice answered. I'd recognize Arminius's strange blending of our language and accent with the lilting notes of Latin anywhere. How strange to hear him calling another man by his own name. But then, Ermin wasn't his name anymore.

With a hiss and a sharp hand gesture, both dogs dropped to their bellies. I followed the voices on light feet, careful to minimize the noise of my body traveling through brush. Sunna and Donar would remain just as I left them until I called, or if they heard me in distress.

"Watch how Varus works," Arminius continued. The understory blocked my view, but I was close enough to hear the steady clopping of several horses. "He sets an impossible standard he knows damn well the people can't meet. They'll be harried and desperate by the time we come to collect. Then, in his magnanimity, we will graciously accept alternative payments; grain, livestock, men for the auxiliary, slaves."

"But that's what they're already paying," another voice answered.

Mail armor and saddles creaked with the rocking gait of their horses.

Arminius said, "Precisely, but the people will view it as a gift from a forgiving governor. He will soften them, convince them that Rome's taxation is fair and just. Overnight, they won't mind so much anymore."

A chill shivered up my spine. He was right. It was Roman dissembling, manipulation. As our people softened toward the Empire's demands, so, too, would they soften toward Rome.

The trees thinned, so I ducked behind a clump of thick, thorny holly bushes. Arminius rode ahead of six auxiliary soldiers in their chainmail shirts and mismatched tunics. His size made the massive Roman war horse he rode looked like one of our stout nags.

"You all need to pay attention, study their methods, how they think. What we are about to undertake requires all of you to be observant." Arminius pulled his horse to a halt. "Everyone go on. I'll catch up. I think that Greek cook is trying to kill me."

Ermin laughed and took the lead. "C'mon lads, let's give the man some privacy to shit his brains out."

The others followed, laughing and tossing ribald comments to Arminius as they rode away. Once out of sight, he dismounted. First, he removed his helmet and then his scarlet cloak with the methodical precision of a man not remotely ill. He strode into the tree line a few yards ahead of me, and I tracked him until he disappeared.

He'd seen me; I knew it. I gauged his distance and direction, then pushed forward on silent, well-trained feet where he entered the woods. He wouldn't expect this. He'd make a wide berth to circle where he thought I was and sneak up from behind. I could do the same.

The wald, what Romans called *forests*, fell silent. No birds called, no small animals scampered, and the distinct sounds of a food-sick man never materialized. I predicted his intent correctly. More silent steps brought me closer. He did a good enough job concealing his path, but his size and armor glinting in the dappled sunlight betrayed him. I drew my sword at the precise moment he spun and drew his own. Mine remained aloft, but he immediately dropped his weapon and his shoulders sagged.

He held his hands up in supplication. "I'm sorry. I wasn't sure it was you at first, then I didn't want you screaming and calling the men back."

"What do you want?" I kept my body angled to his, ready to flee or fight.

"What do *I* want?" His eyes widened in surprise. "I'm not the one lurking about in the woods, listening in on people's conversations."

"I was not lurking, you—" I bit back a useless insult. "I was out for a walk. I didn't think it wise to announce my presence to seven soldiers, particularly after how the last lot treated me."

"Fair enough." His blue eyes softened. "You still wander the woods?"

I didn't answer him. I stayed on my feet while he found a seat on a felled log, as casually as if we were two friends sharing a pleasant afternoon. He reached into a pouch on his belt and produced two shiny red apples, tossing me one and keeping the other for himself. I caught it reflexively, then sneered and dropped it. He frowned and hummed in disappointment.

"Do you have any idea," he crunched into his fruit, "how many times over the years I followed you through these woods? It drove me mad. I'd beg my father to tell Segestes to make you stop and he just laughed at me."

I turned away, unwilling to associate this man with the boy of my childhood. "Why?"

If my vague question confused him, he didn't show it. "A man has a responsibility to his future bride, even if she is a reckless and annoying child. No matter how badly I wanted to take you by your little arm and march you back to your father for the punishment I was certain you needed, I couldn't bring myself to do it. You looked happy out here."

A fresh shiver danced across my skin. I never knew I'd had a silent guardian on my childhood adventures. When I glanced over my shoulder, Arminius the Roman officer stared back.

"Don't tell anyone about this," I snapped.

The pleasant haze of childhood memories dropped from his expression, replaced by the granite countenance of a hard man.

Arminius stood. He adjusted the leather bracers on his forearms and straightened his armor. "That you shared two minutes of friendly chatting with the most hated man in Germania Magna will remain a secret. I'll go."

Friendly chatting was hardly how I'd describe it. I knew his game. He wanted to soften me, the way he described Varus softening my people. He wanted me to see him as Ermin the Cherusci prince, though I didn't know why.

"Wait." I reached for one of those bracers to stop him. As soon as my fingers made contact, I jerked back as if scalded. "I mean it. Segestes has forbidden me from speaking to you. He says he will disown me if he finds out we've... socialized."

I don't know why I felt the need to justify myself to him. It's not as though a traitor deserves an explanation.

"Why?" he asked with a smirk. "Afraid you won't be able to resist tumbling into my arms after all these years?"

The gall of him. We stood too close to each other, but neither of us backed away. Ensconced in the tall trees, it was easy to believe we were the only two in the world.

I had to tilt my head to look him in the eye. "Hardly. He knows I don't lie with animals. He thinks you will challenge him for the chieftainship. He thinks you've come back to reclaim your seat, and I'm not sure he's wrong."

He huffed a dry laugh. "I don't want to be chief of the Cherusci."

"Then what do you want?"

My stomach flipped within my belly when he only gazed at me. Heat radiated from him like a warm embrace. His eyes flickered to my lips, and he leaned as if to close the distance between us. Baduhenna help me, I couldn't bring myself to back away. I didn't want to back away. I wanted to taste the fire he offered, the only clear sensation I'd experienced since his return.

He abruptly stepped back and cleared his throat. I froze, mentally scrambling for all the reasons I should be outraged instead of bereft. Outrage was easier than reconciling the confused tumult of my racing heart and pulsing lips.

"We should go." He spoke gruffly.

Again at a loss for words, I whistled for my dogs. They bounded through the brush with all the subtlety of a pack of wrestling bears.

Arminius turned to leave, but then stopped. "Thusnelda?"

"Yes?" There was no reason to whisper, yet I did.

A muscle in his jaw flexed, and the corners of his eyes wrinkled.

"I know what you think of me, what everyone thinks. I want you to know it's not true. I was a hostage. This." He gestured to his uniform. "It's not what you think."

He didn't wait for me to reply. He left to rejoin his men and I returned to the village, telling myself over and over that our paths were unlikely to cross again.

Chapter 4

Thereupon appeared a young man of noble birth, brave in action and alert in mind, possessing an intelligence quite beyond the ordinary barbarian; he was, namely, Arminius, the son of Segimer, a prince of that nation, and he showed in his countenance and in his eyes the fire of the mind within. (Velleius Paterculus)

Wailing drew me from slumber. Voices blended into a cacophony of fear and outrage.

Instantly alert, I jerked from the comfort of my bed and lunged for a clean tunic and trousers. A flurry of scalcs' feet thumped across the wooden floors. Usually quiet, especially at this hour, their voices echoed through our halls. From what I could hear, they were arming Segestes and my brothers and chattering about legionaries arresting young men in the village. The word "crucifixion" echoed through the hall.

I finished tying on my boots and belt. My sword hung heavy on my hip. My pulse thundered. At last, the Romans had crossed a line even Segestes couldn't abide. In our land, the entire community meted out justice. No one man, not even a chief, had the right to unilaterally punish a criminal. The most egregious and untamable criminal possessed a fundamental right to live and still served a purpose within a tribe, even as a scalc, where he might earn his freedom back should he prove himself worthy. Death was the realm of the gods. It was not for men to decide who lived or died in judgment. Even in the old times, generations long past when our priestesses called for human sacrifice, the most noble of our people volunteered their own lives in tribute, they were never unwilling.

We found the Roman practice of crucifixion profoundly barbaric, though few among us spoke of it. That one man—a governor, a general, a magistrate—could order a slow, painful death upon a wooden cross for crimes as minor as theft was an affront to our way of life. Our gods would not abide an offense like this, and it was for us to prevent a Roman-led atrocity.

I found Segestes and my brothers in all their battle finery. Unlike Romans, with their chainmail and brilliant silver armor and scarlet tunics, Cherusci favored camouflage and the freedom of movement metal armor inhibited. Simple leather overshirts covered tunics and trousers. As chief, Segestes wore a wolf skin headdress to mark his station, while my brothers donned dull helmets, dented and worn. They each held their spears, but to my confusion, their shields remained mounted above our head table.

"Father," I said, "What is—"

His face clouded. "Thusnelda, stay in the house."

"I have seen more battle than Levin and Lennart combined. I can help."

The twins argued over each other and Wout scoffed. "We are not going to war with the legions, you little idiot."

I crowded into his space, toe to toe. He looked so much like our father with his dark features. His braids and beard hung longer, without Segestes' mottling of gray. Same nose, same thick brows, same woody eyes. Is that why he followed Segestes' temperament, he was predestined to age into our father? As children, we'd been thick as thieves. Now we faced each other as two tribes, war looming beyond the horizon.

Segestes stepped between our standoff and smoothed a hand over my shoulder. I tracked the gesture with wary eyes. He pulled his hand back and clenched it at his side.

"We go to negotiate with Varus. Some Cherusci men were caught stealing from Roman supply stores. I will do everything I can to smooth things over, at least convince him to let us handle their punishment."

I pulled away from him. "You believe you can negotiate with them?"

Again Wout prepared to censure me, derision already curling from his tongue, but my father stayed Wout's words.

"I know who I am dealing with. I am not the fool you think I am. What I do, I do for all of us," Segestes said.

He repeated those words almost every time we argued about how to handle the Romans. I grew weary of his excuses to bow and scrape. He didn't go to negotiate, he went to beg.

Each brother made a point of jostling me on their way out, while I remained rooted in place, silent and scrambling for better answers. Anything was better than begging mercy from well-dressed barbarians.

Jotapa materialized from a darkened hallway. She set a basket of linens on the nearest table and took my chilled hands in her warm ones.

"You're upset, we all are, but if you rush out there and stir things up, you will make it worse for everyone."

Angry tears burned my eyes, but I refused to let them fall. She was right and read my intentions correctly.

I nodded once. "I'll go out the back door. I want to see what's happening."

Her face drew tight, but she stepped aside to let me pass. Before I got to the door, she called out, "Perhaps you should leave your sword. I'll put it away for you."

That gave me pause, just enough to consider it. It would be safer for everyone if I were unarmed, but the weapon at my hip was an extension of me. I shook my head and left through the back door.

I made it three steps outside, preparing to loop behind a few small buildings and stay out of sight, when a throat cleared behind me. I froze and steeled myself to face one of my brothers, who had no doubt anticipated my plan.

Instead, Arminius stood on the other side of the door, arms crossed and lips pulled into a frown.

"Whatever you think you're doing," he said, "don't."

My fury, the fire only he lit within me, flared white hot. Thought never entered my mind before I lunged at him. Had I a modicum of self-control, it might have been a fair fight. Arminius's eyes widened, but he sidestepped me easily, caught my outstretched arm and pivoted until he was behind me. He caught my other arm just as quickly.

I kicked my legs and feet, but they only hit his greaves and flailing earned me a sharp pain in my shoulders. He urged me to settle down, but the roaring in my ears drowned him out. In a last ditch effort, I pushed off my feet high and hard, then slammed the back of my head into what I hoped was Arminius's face.

It was.

Unfortunately, it felt like willfully ramming my head into a boulder. He dropped me, and I stumbled to my knees, scrambling for purchase as the world tilted this way and that and black dots filled my vision. Arminius groaned and cursed, then recovered too damned fast.

While I fought for equilibrium, his big, heavily armored body crashed into mine. Before I made sense of the attack, I was on my back, legs pinned beneath his, arms pinned beneath me, locked in place by a single hand with his other forearm across the breadth of my chest. A warm drop of blood from his nose fell onto my cheek. I tried once, twice, and a final third time to unseat him before admitting my fight was a lost cause.

"Are you finished?" He was so close his breath mingled with mine.

Dirt and small rocks dug into my shoulders and arms, and struggling only made it worse. I let my head fall back into the dust and regretted it immediately. More dots spun and blinked before my eyes, following a fresh wash of pain.

The bastard on top of me had the gall to smirk. "I ask you again, are you done?"

I had no choice but to nod and let my body relax. He loosened his hold but didn't release me. At least some of the pain in my shoulders relented.

"Why are you here? Shouldn't you be executing our people?" I gritted my teeth and hissed the words, anything to mask the devastation I felt.

The depth of his sigh echoed through the length of my body. He closed his eyes, and that muscle twitched in his jaw. The thick bristle along his chin and cheeks told me he hadn't shaved this morning.

"I am trying," he said, eyes still closed. "I will push Varus to release them back to Segestes, I swear it, but they were caught in the act and Varus sees it as a rebellion. I cannot do any good here if you and I run into the square swinging swords."

"How many?" The village center was too far to see. I saw him, though, eyes dark enough to match the northern seas and wrought with pain. Perhaps the blood drying beneath his nose and around his mouth made them stand out more.

"Four, all grown."

He sat back on his haunches and though I was glad to free my arms, his familiar scent left with him.

I pushed away from him and drew my knees to my chest. Puffy clouds looked friendly enough for now, but by afternoon they would amass into a gray storm. The scent of soft watery air promised rain and the wind kicked hard.

"What do you want, Thusnelda?"

The question was a trap, just like his "you and I" comment was a trap. It was one thing for me to kill Romans in self defense, quite another to rebel against their version of justice. He'd no intention of having my back while I fought his compatriots, he just wanted me to admit my seditious impulses. So I held my tongue.

He grunted. I couldn't tell if it was a laugh or not and kept my attention on the dirt between my boots.

"If you do that, you'll be dead and the Cherusci will pay for it. First, they'll be punished. There'll be crucifixions, more will be sold into slavery, and Varus will demand even more in taxes. To make it worse, you won't be here anymore. The Cherusci need you."

He stood and dusted himself off, then produced a water flask and cloth strip to clean the blood from his face.

"I know you don't trust me," he said. "But I need your help. The Cherusci need your help. I need...can I show you something?"

Bathed in the glow of morning sun, he might have been a Roman statue before me, tall and strong and untethered to our mortal world.

Despite my better self, my more suspicious, guarded self, he intrigued me. It was a trick; I knew it. Yet it seemed strange to single me out like this. Though I had power in my tribe, the Romans didn't acknowledge women as leaders. It wasn't as though I'd be some grand prize for Varus to capture, and it wasn't as though I hadn't already offered myself up on a platter by killing two legionaries, no matter how justified. Arminius was going to bizarre lengths to trick me into something, and I intended to find out what.

"Fine."

"Do you remember where we met yesterday?" he asked.

"Yes."

Arminius held a hand out to me. "Be there in five days, at dawn. Stay hidden and follow us. Do not speak. Do not reveal yourself. If you do, I slap you in chains and take you Varus myself."

I stared at his hand, then his face, searching for treachery, the knife he planned to slide between my ribs. He said, so softly I almost believed he didn't say it, "Please."

I took his hand.

———————➤

Jotapa said nothing when I re-entered the house, though it seemed she'd been standing on the other side of the door throughout my altercation with Arminius.

"Everything is fine," I said. Jotapa's eyes trailed up and down my disheveled and dirty form. She clucked her tongue and sauntered back to her duties. I'd explain later. Or not. At the moment, I wanted a nap. The succession of startling, stressful events throughout the morning had taken their toll.

In the safety of my room, I disarmed. I longed for a warm bath, but the house only echoed in silence. Most of our scalcs had gone to the center of the village, it seemed.

Levin burst into the room. I knew it was him without having to ask. Though he and Lennart were identical in all ways—looks, height, voice, even the way they hit—I always differentiated them immediately. Jotapa couldn't. Even Wout and Segestes could be confused, but not me. They were as different as night and day, though I wasn't able to articulate the differences. Perhaps it was Levin's more gentle spirit.

A spirit he overcame long enough to shove me. My feet tangled over my stool, and my rear hit the floor with a thump. I opened my mouth to shout my outrage, but Levin thrust out his index finger, quivering with fury.

"You shit!" I snarled, pushing to my feet. He dropped his hand and his face fell. A twinge of sisterly guilt tugged at my heart, but not enough to ignore this offense.

Levin closed his eyes, and the wild anger that drove him faded. "I saw you. With him."

"You saw us fighting and did nothing?"

"I came to check on you. I was coming to your aid," he said, "then I saw you talking to him."

I sneered and turned away from him. "That's all it took? You saw us fighting. We exchanged words, and he left. So you barged in here and shoved me?"

I wanted to scream and tear my hair out. Our lives were hard; this was apparent long before I learned how the Romans lived. But these past two weeks left me raw, bruised, and bleeding. Literally and figuratively.

"Father forbade you from cavorting with him." Levin shifted his weight from foot to foot. "He is a villain."

"As far as I can tell, he is exactly what Segestes wants for all of us."

A steady throbbing pounded in my temples and rubbing at them did no good. Intrigues and secrets were Roman ways, not Cherusci. Moreover, I wanted few things less than to defend Arminius from my increasingly erratic family. Segestes spent every waking moment, and likely his dreams, yearning for the day when all the Cherusci turned as

Roman as Arminius. Segestes' suggestion that Arminius might want to take over as chief was ludicrous.

"He's not what he seems." Levin spoke with such gravity, I didn't deny the depth of his feelings, his certainty. "Father told me... never mind. Please trust me. Stay away from him. He's only going to cause problems."

Now that was something with which I agreed.

Levin stood by the door as somber as I'd ever seen him, imploring me to hear his words.

"I would better trust you if you told me the truth." I tipped my chin at the door and Levin got the message: He'd been dismissed.

He paused in the doorframe. "Please, be careful."

I'd be careful, but who was my enemy here?

Chapter 5

They had not, however, forgotten their ancestral habits, their native manners, their old life of independence, or the power derived from arms. (Cassius Dio)

Baduhenna bless her, Konrada didn't shed a tear as she told me how her oldest brother had been pressed into service in the Germani ala, the auxiliary cavalry squadron. The tears glassed her big dark eyes, but she refused to shed the first one. Anger and fear mottled her skin a ruddy red, and she sniffed through her tale. Only a day had passed since the arrest, and already her life was irreparably altered.

"They just took him from the stocks. They didn't even let us say goodbye." She stuffed her brother's bedding into a basket for washing under the dim light of their closed roundhouse. Her mother lay abed in the darkness, where she'd been since her son was first arrested. Konrada's father and other siblings kept to the fields during the day, choosing to focus on daily mundanities.

Where Konrada got her spark was a mystery to me.

It seemed Arminius was true to his word and had secured auxiliary positions for the thieves, an outcome far better than execution or Roman enslavement. Perhaps even better than being bartered as a scalc to another tribe. Twenty years in service to Rome over a few stolen amphoras of olive oil and preserved fruits was excessive, however, and twenty years gone was twenty years gone regardless.

I toed the edge of her brother's cot. "Do you think you'll need this? Luter and Fred offered to take Adelfried in until he passes, but Adelfried's bed is too large."

My question distracted Konrada long enough to clear some of the red mottling from her cheeks, as I hoped it would. She pursed her lips and looked to her silent, unmoving mother.

Useless bitch. You have five other children and working limbs. Get up and be a mother to your family. Don't make this child do your job.

"That's fine," Konrada said. "Wandis hasn't shut up since last spring about building a new pantry and cooking table. Now she'll have room."

From there, Konrada made swift work of piling her erstwhile brother's belongings into three separate piles: keep for the other men in her family; give away in the village, and items too soiled, old, or damaged to salvage. When it was all done, we stood over the piles, looking down at the remnants of a young man's old life.

After a long silence, she asked, "Am I ever going to see him again?"

How easy it would be to lie to her. "I don't know. As long as he stays with this ala, he'll be close enough to visit."

"And when they get called somewhere else?"

For lack of better answers, I pulled her into my arms for a hug. She stiffened in shock at first, then melted.

"Thank you for your help." Her words were muffled in my chest.

"Whatever you need." I stroked her hair. "You don't have to shoulder all this on your own."

———————▶

Three nights later, I didn't sleep, then took off to our meeting place hours earlier than necessary with my sword, cloak, a water flask, and a small sack of food. For the hundredth time, my mind insisted this was a trap. A lifetime of hating anyone and anything that marched under a Roman eagle insisted Arminius must be treacherous. A lifetime learning that miracles were children's stories insisted Ermin died, the way Mama died, and boons were temporary at best, and crippling snares the rest of the time. I'd spent so many years praying for my Ermin to fulfill his promise and return for me, only for Arminius to arrive in his stead.

It was slower going to this spot than I expected. The predawn darkness brought the native dangers lurking in the wald to life. The animals turned bold, and each step I took on the mist-wet earth filled me with dread. Wolves lurked in these woods.

I reached the spot with the doggedness of an experienced hunter. Tree bark dug into my back, and my trousers were soaked through within minutes of sitting on the ground. The mist thickened as the sun began its slow journey over the horizon. I tugged my cloak tighter around my shoulders. It was always colder as the sun rose.

I needed to eat, but tension tied my stomach in knots. My nose scrunched in protest at the sight of the hard roll I'd packed. Too restless to sleep, too anxious to eat, and far too committed to listening for the first sound that announced their arrival. I jerked at every whispered breeze through the trees, only to collapse back against the tree in defeat.

Anything could have happened. He might have been delayed, his orders might have changed, he could have met resistance on the road. That thought made my heart race, surely because he'd promised to show me something, and if he was plotting against the Cherusci, I needed to know. I did not need him getting himself killed before I uncovered his treachery.

The scent of horses reached me first, followed by low masculine chatter. Like before, I tucked myself out of sight. Between the mist and shadows, they'd have to know where to look to find me, and even then might not see me.

Arminius did. The moment his eyes found mine flashed all the way to the tips of my toes to the ends of my hair. His gaze slid away, and he continued easy conversation with the other soldiers in his party. I recognized a few, but the optio riding alongside Arminius was new. I had seen men like him before in passing, the ones with skin so dark they looked to have been painted specially by the sun. Before the Romans ever crossed the Rhine with their diverse soldiers, traders from across the world had ventured to our land. We weren't nearly as insular as

Rome thought we were. Haustblot in particular brought traders and merchants from the far edges of the world.

This man was small, wiry, with a wide white smile splitting his face. Arminius called him Berut.

After some time trotting behind their small party, I realized we were heading to Sugambri territory. The men talked of nothing important, but the gentle rumble of Arminius's voice, his barks of laughter, made oddly pleasant music. I gagged silently at the thought. Plenty of men had deep, bark roughened voices and strange accents. Berut certainly did, so I chose to listen to him.

The presence of an optio from the main body of Varus' army added more intrigue to the day's plot. I hoped Arminius didn't plan on killing him just to lure me into his trap. Contrary to most outward appearances, I didn't hate most legionaries on sight. Victims of Rome understood quite well the inevitability of surrender, and auxiliary recruiters never stopped crowing about the myriad benefits of joining their army. Berut appeared to be a nice enough fellow with an easy smile and bright laugh. There was nothing of the low predator in him, not like Patrin and that vile patrol.

Arminius never hinted at my presence. The group fell quiet the closer they got to the heart of Sugambri lands. Instead of staying on the main road—though calling it such was an affront to the Roman concept of a road—they paused at a trail too narrow for horses.

"What is this one's name again?" Berut asked as they dismounted. "Duter? Tuetonius?"

"Deudorix, Chief of the Sugambri, and you will address him as such if you value your limbs."

"Rome doesn't call them that."

Arminius snorted. "Of course not, but if you call them Sicambri, this will be over before it starts."

Behind them, the man Arminius called Ermin chuckled. He had some leadership with the ala, but without the benefit of proper Roman uniforms, I couldn't say what. I guessed him to be in his thirties, not much older than Arminius or me, with ashy brown hair he kept in a side knot beneath his helmet.

I waited until the whole of them disappeared down the trail before following. We traveled at least two miles before they stopped in a small clearing. Much like any other, soft green grass filled a gap between the towering, ancient trees. Birdsong added to the scene, light and happy. It would have been downright cheery had six soldiers and four Germani tribesmen not filled the clearing.

An older man, thick in the chest with a long graying beard to match his silvery braids, stood front and center. His golden torque and jewels marked him as the chief. Three younger men flanked him, no doubt sons or close relatives. When Arminius approached, the man spat at his feet.

"What do you people want now?" he asked in the Sugambri tongue. Their language was close enough to follow, having been our regional neighbors since time began.

"Deudorix, I presume?" Arminius gave no indication he even saw the glob of mucus congealing in the packed dirt. Deudorix grunted a reply, so Arminius continued. "We're here to talk."

The older man's lip curled beneath his bushy mustache. He turned his nose up as his hand fell to the hilt of his battle scarred sword.

"It's true, then? The eldest son of my great rival is now a Roman toy? Prancing about like a little girl in a fancy dress, playing at being one of them?"

Berut took a step forward, prepared to unsheathe his own weapon before Arminius reached out a staying hand. He shook his head once, and Berut obediently, if reluctantly, resumed his place.

"Where did you people find this one?" Deudorix all but shouted, inspecting Berut closely, with none of the unvarnished hostility he'd shown Arminius. "Left him cooking too long over the fire, did you?"

Berut shifted under the scrutiny and asked Arminius in Latin, "What is he saying?"

"He thinks we left you cooking too long over a fire."

"I've traded with men like you," Deudorix said in Latin, addressing Berut directly. "But none so…"

My hand fell to my sword, and my muscles tensed, preparing to pounce. Whose side I would defend remained elusive, but I knew a brewing fight when I saw one.

"So handsome?" Berut's face split into one of his blinding smiles. "You are right, I'm one of a kind."

Deudorix narrowed his eyes, and I caught Arminius reaching for his sword until Deudorix let out a loud laugh and clapped Berut on the shoulder. "Let's get on with it, then. Tell me, Ermin, son of Segimer, now… what do the Romans call you?"

"Arminius. I'm a captain of the ala and Varus' personal aide."

"So," Deudorix tipped his head in Arminius' direction, "tell me what business Varus' personal aide has for me? Raising taxes again?"

"No," Arminius said. "I've come to ask what you want for the future of the Sugambri."

I held my breath. This was it. This was what Arminius wanted me to witness.

Deudorix was aging, but his sharp warrior's eyes missed nothing. He asked the same question I'd been asking myself for five days. "If you've come to ask me to incriminate myself, I'm afraid you should have started with my sons. They're still hotheads."

The three men with him grumbled and shifted on their feet but dared not rebut their father.

"My friend, Optio Berut, comes from Carthage. Do you know it?"

"I've heard tales. You people love to crow about failed uprisings. Anything to cow us into fear, isn't that right?"

"Of course that's what they do," Arminius said. I didn't miss the way he referred to the Romans as *they*, not *us*. "They're terrified of what will happen when the people they've worked so hard to oppress organize against them. Berut, tell him about Carthage."

"Our hero, Hannibal, led many successful battles against the Roman invasion. For years he kept them out, but he became too bold. He determined we should conquer Italia and Rome herself. When he was defeated, they razed our great city to the ground. We were murdered or enslaved by the thousands. The Carthage where I grew up is Roman. They erased all traces of my people from the earth and remade us in their image. We speak Latin, worship their gods, eat their foods. Our ways have been lost for almost two centuries."

Deudorix sighed and folded his hands in that way all disappointed fathers postured. "You tell me nothing the Romans haven't already. Hostilities against this empire are futile and our people are doomed to become like this one." He waved his hand in a lazy circle toward Berut.

"Don't you wonder how things might have turned out for them if Hannibal hadn't taken his war to the steps of Rome?" Arminius seized on the flicker of interest in Deudorix's eyes. "What if, instead of attempting to conquer them, he had secured a dug in defensive force, a standing, unified army, powerful enough to keep Rome out for good?"

My heart stopped. Every conversation we'd had snapped into place. The way he'd spoken about the Romans, how he made a point of studying them. The pain that colored his features whenever I called him one of them.

No. It wasn't possible this was anything but a trap. My hand gripped my sword, ready to launch myself between the two men. Deudorix didn't deserve to die for this farce.

Deudorix shook his head. "It can't be done."

"Why?" As Arminius seized on the question, my heart galloped to keep pace with the very idea. It was too outlandish, too audacious. Unthinkable. Especially that Arminius suggested it. A Roman.

Deudorix snorted. "You know damn well why. No one will ever convince the tribes to unite for a single rebellion, let alone a prolonged war. It's not our way."

"Our people will not have a way if we don't do something!" Arminius ran a hand over the scruff of his jaw. "We will cease to exist if we don't fight back, and yes, that means making some changes."

"You mean trading one emperor for another?"

"What would you prefer?" Arminius asked. "Rome swallowing you whole, knowing everything you've ever worked for, everything you've ever believed, no longer exists? Or pledging fealty to a temporary king chosen by the chiefs to protect our people. That's no different than how we chose a war chief. No taxes. No conscripts. Our children won't be taken at random as slaves or bodies to fight their wars. We keep our traditions."

The sons traded looks between themselves, shaking their heads, but wise enough to remain silent. Deudorix hummed in thought.

"Still impossible. If you manage to get a few tribes to unite under this cause—and I assure you, you won't—even this one's great Hannibal was no match for the Roman army. What honor is there in condemning my tribe to servitude because you want glory in battle?"

A sheep bleated somewhere in the distance. We were closer to at least a homestead, if not the Sugambri village itself, than I thought. All around, Sugambri life rolled on as it had for generations, each day not unlike the last. None but those here knew their chief and chieftains were either about to die or embark on the most monumentous journey in the history of my land.

"Our armies can't win in open warfare against these people. What makes you so special?" Deudorix swatted a hand at a fly.

Arminius stood impossibly taller. "I know how they think, their tactics, their weaknesses."

"Name one."

"Without their formations, they fall apart. I know more than their tactics. They raised me as one of them. I can keep us ahead."

Deudorix had the right of it: Germani warriors mostly didn't stand a chance in a fight against a Roman legion, let alone more. Our people excelled in one-to-one combat, where warriors faced each other as individuals. Raw strength against raw strength.

Deudorix tapped his nearest son's chest with the back of his hand, gesturing to one of their horses. The younger man hesitated but didn't need to be told twice. "What makes you think they will not simply rain down upon us with all their legions?"

"They never have before." Arminius did his best to be every inch the casual, confident leader, but in just a few meetings I caught his tells.

His lazy grin didn't meet his eyes. That overdeveloped muscle in his jaw jumped. "No one has ever attempted what I'm suggesting. Not like this. Rome's armies are too spread out; they couldn't consolidate their forces here if they wanted to. They've already pulled seven legions off the Rhine to put down the Pannonian uprising. I won't tell you I have all the answers right now, because I don't. If we organize, if we prepare our warriors, I can lead us to victory."

The eldest son stepped forward, face pulled tight. "Rebellion? Father, he's mad. He will get us all killed."

"Perhaps." Deudorix took a flask when his youngest returned. After taking a slow gulp, he passed it to Arminius. "However, you forget we all must die. Sugambri do not die on our knees."

Just like that, Arminius' grin lit his eyes. He took the flask and accepted a drink.

By all the gods above and below, he had done it. With a few choice words, he'd secured the loyalty of the Sugambri, and with them their nearly three thousand warriors. A smaller tribe, they were nevertheless less renowned in battle. No wonder I'd never met this Deudorix. He harbored rebellious desires. Segestes would diligently avoid such a man.

A rebellion. A proper rebellion. There was still time for Arminius to draw his weapon and order an attack on Deudorix and the Sugambri. Plenty of time for a massacre. Instead, they shared a drink.

Arminius returned the flask to Deudorix. "Then I can count on your support when the time comes?"

"The Sugambri will fight." Deudorix raised his flask in a toast. "What would you have done if I'd told you to fuck off?"

Germani were a plainspoken people, and Deudorix wouldn't appreciate anything short of the plainspoken truth.

"If you'd said no, you all would have lost your heads out here."

Exactly as I suspected. Yet it hadn't happen. They met like old friends.

A slow smile spread across Deudorix's lips. Berut guffawed and the rest of the men followed.

Hope stirred in my chest. I quelled it as quickly as it sparked to life. If Arminius was true, if this wasn't an elaborate trick, then he had neither the influence nor the knowledge to lead such an undertaking.

It was, however, a good idea. An excellent idea, in fact, for a trusted, influential Cherusci queen.

------------------➤

The most arduous task I'd ever undertaken was concentrating on my chores the next day, second only to keeping this new secret from Jotapa. It wasn't for lack of trust, but more that I didn't know what to do with this new information. When I was sure I was going to burst, I went to the one person who always gave me a fair perspective.

Ingomar kept a small roundhouse on the farthest outskirts of our village. Brother to Segimer, uncle to Arminius, he stayed far away in what most Cherusci believed his shame; shame for not dying with his brother, for not protecting his wife and daughter, for letting his nephews be taken, for doing nothing when Segimer's wife disappeared into the wald, never to be seen again.

Insects came alive in the wet heat of late afternoon. I swatted and waved away mosquitoes and flies, though it was a useless battle. The dust at my feet puffed into pitiful bursts before quickly sinking back to the ground. I tired of the yet-to-arrive summer. Fall was my season, when the forest turned to a sea of reds and golds, when Haustblot bled slowly into the Vetrnaetr, winter in its truest and most reliable form. Our Haustblot celebrations served as a communal opportunity to celebrate our dead, of whom there were so many. Most importantly, Haustblot called for no sacrifices, since we considered the dead we celebrated an offering already made. We enjoyed a month-long festival of trading and peace amongst all the tribes.

Ingomar appeared in his doorway with a friendly smile, familial and pleased. The old man didn't suffer the benefits of regular visitors these days. He kept his peppery gray hair cropped short, close to his head, and he hadn't allowed his beard to grow since his brother died. Having at last seen Ermin as an adult, I recognized Ingomar as an older, beaten down Arminius.

I slipped into his arms for a hug and let him usher me through the low wooden doorframe. Inside was the same as always—a small fire pit in the center, an ancient bench along the far wall, thick rugs covering dirt floors, and, despite not having kept horses in the past fourteen years, the soft scent of leather bridles and a hint of the animals themselves.

"What brings my lovely niece to an old man on such a fine day?" Ingomar asked as he poured a cup of ale for me.

After Arminius was taken, I had implored Ingomar to stop calling me his niece, but he never listened. He smiled and nodded like a doting father, then called me "niece" the next time I saw him. It grieved me, in my childish way, to be reminded of the family I'd hoped to join forever ripped from my grasp. As I grew, I eventually understood that Ingomar needed a family more than I did. I appreciated it for what it was: affection, something we lacked more and more each passing year.

"I wanted to see how you're doing." I pushed a stray hank of hair behind my ear. "It's been too long."

Ingomar's eyes danced with mirth over his cup. "No, I haven't seen him. Our parting was..." He trailed off into a hum and took another sip. "But I hear tell you have."

The ale caught in my throat. I coughed it back down, all while my beloved uncle chortled at my expense.

"Just because I don't get many visitors doesn't mean I don't get any," he said. "Rumors as delightful as this have a way of reaching even my door."

Presented with the opportunity to at last vent all my thoughts and questions, I hesitated. What did he know? What did he believe? One wrong move, and I might inadvertently condemn someone I loved.

"Perhaps it would benefit you both if you approached him next time he's in the village."

Wise blue eyes—so like Arminius'—crinkled at the corners and studied me. I expected an immediate rejection, maybe even shouting over the audacity to suggest he acknowledge his seemingly wayward nephew. Instead, Ingomar watched me placidly, not the least surprised.

I drained the rest of the sweet ale only he brewed. Ingomar favored cherries in his brew, which had once been quite popular here. Now things associated with his family left a bitter taste in Cherusci mouths. I found it delicious.

"Ah." Ingomar rose and fetched a basket of old blankets. "Would you mind taking this to the barn loft? These old hands don't climb a ladder as well as they used to."

Given the strength still apparent in the older man's muscles, I doubted this, but didn't question him. If he wanted me out of the house for a few moments, then so be it.

"Of course." I took the basket from his weathered hands.

From the shadows of his roundhouse, to the scorching sun, to the darkness of the barn, my eyes refused to adjust, and I found myself navigating the barn by memory rather than sight. I ascended the ladder, blinking hard to force my eyes to cooperate, and dropped the basket in a spare corner.

As I gripped the top of the ladder to descend, my vision finally adjusted, and I discovered why Ingomar sent me out here. Arminius sat on an overturned bucket, propped lazily against a sidewall snickering to himself. I almost didn't recognize him without his usual armor. Dressed in a simple tunic, cloak, and boots, he might have passed for any other Cherusci. A bit. My worn-out clothes, covered in the dirt from the road, stains that may or may not have come from cleaning a deer, my unruly hair sticking to and fro, all popped into the forefront of my mind. I did my best to stamp the silly worries away, and instead focused on the most pressing matters.

I skipped the last two rungs and landed on the floor in a small puff of dust and old hay. "If you think you can trick me into getting myself and other Cherusci executed for sedition, you're mistaken."

Without taking my eyes from him, I pulled a scythe off the tool wall at my back and fell into a fighting stance. "Do you intend to betray your uncle, as well?"

He heaved a great, beleaguered sigh.

"Should have known you wouldn't make this easy," he muttered.

When he pushed to his feet, I hardened my stance. In the woods with the Sugambri he said he intended to kill any who didn't join with him. I tensed myself, ready to see his mask drop, ready to confront the cold monster I knew in my bones must lurk beneath his affable facade.

He started to take a step toward me, mouth open to spit more lies and venom, but he took me in and winced, freezing in place.

"You believe it," he said. "You really believe I'd hurt you. And Ingomar."

"That is what Romans do, and you are a Roman."

For a moment, he looked so aghast I wondered if he'd had an apoplexy and would keel over dead. Instead, he exploded.

"I am Cherusci!" His meaty fist snatched a leather cord from his neck, and he held out an icon of Donar's hammer.

Sweat accumulated on my palms. Tools clanked against my shoulders as I unconsciously retreated. His mask fell, and instead of cold calculation, he confronted me with a kind of rage I knew intimately: the rage of the beaten.

He ripped his cloak off and yanked at the collar of his tunic until he revealed dark blue ink etched into the skin over his heart. One more tug, and I made out the design of a wolf's head. Not just any wolf's head, but ours. The same sigil was painted on our shields and worked into our jewels.

"They beat me and threw me into the stockade for weeks when I did this. They only let me out when Flavus convinced our commander it was in honor of our mother."

"Flavus...?"

"My brother. That's the name they gave him. He doesn't remember being called anything else. They took my brother, Elda. They killed my father in front of me, my aunt, my niece. They took everything from me, but not this." He thumped his fist over the tattoo. "You don't trust me? Fine, as long as you stay out of my way and keep your mouth shut about what you saw. I am not going to lose everything because of one sentimental mistake."

My fingers tingled from the strength of my grip on the scythe handle. Of all possible reactions, I hadn't considered this one. It was too real, too unpracticed, too raw. It didn't fit any of the scenarios I'd considered when I painted him as a traitor.

In order to leave, he had to pass close to me, eyeing the scythe the entire time. I ignored the impulse to lower it. I believed his anger at Rome. I believed some part of him was still Cherusci. I did not believe *him*, however. He wore their armor and their sly smiles too well. He was a knight of Rome and Varus trusted him. His brother, his closest living kin, was all Roman, by the sound of it. When forced to choose, I couldn't say which side he might take.

Before he left, before shutting the door completely, I asked, "What did you want from me? We both know sentiment had nothing to do with it."

Arminius huffed a dry laugh. "Do we know that?"

I glared at him. "We also both know that you can't do a damn thing you promised the Sugambri. Not without a trusted Germani in your corner. Is that why you've flirted with me? You think you can get into my trousers and use my name to bolster your cause?"

He blinked several times before turning back to me fully. "I'm not sure where to begin addressing all of that, so let me say this: While I have always appreciated your imagination, I don't need your help. I don't want it. I told you what I want, and that is for you to keep your nose out of it."

This close I smelled him under the overwhelming barn odors. His scent didn't overwhelm like so many legionaries. His was subtle, and I struggled to pinpoint what made it unique.

"It's a good idea," I said, "if you have the right connections. Which you don't. You want my trust? Admit the real reason you wanted me to follow you yesterday."

One more step and he was so close our chests brushed with each breath. Without my awareness, he'd pushed my scythe-wielding arm to the side and stepped into my guard.

"You're so certain the only thing I want from you is clout, it doesn't matter what I tell you right now. Perhaps you're right and I need the beloved princess of the Cherusci to back my claims. Maybe I want you to get your Chatti prince on my side. Though," he tapped a finger against his chin, "any idiot can see that flirting with you won't get me there. Maybe I like the way you kill Romans. Maybe I just want you to trust me enough to let me have a taste of what I was promised."

He reached for my cheek and for a heartbeat, I almost let him. The way he stared at my lips with a longing I'd never experienced rocked me off balance. Before his fingertips made contact, however, I brought the edge of the scythe up to his neck.

"I don't know what you're up to, but it stops now. All of it." I pushed a little harder against the skin above his apple. "*All* of it. You're going to get good people killed. And I... I am to be queen of the Chatti."

To his credit, he didn't retreat from my blade. He even smiled as a drop of blood rounded on his skin. "Queen of the Chatti? Thusnelda, I would make you queen of Germania."

Chapter 6

She was Brunhilde, Freya, even Erde, the great Earth-mother ... once confronted with the realization of her genuine desires, she embraced at once the policy of Arminius and the man himself. (F. Matania)

"Thusnelda, are you listening to me?" Konrada prodded me in the ribs with one of her tiny fingers. "Are you paying attention?"

I was not, in fact, paying attention.

Arminius, his cohort of Germani auxiliary troops, and Optio Berut had returned to the village in full regalia, playing a ball-and-stick game with children. I'd never seen such a thing from proper legion troops, nor had anyone else. Half the village gathered around the main square. Some watched with caution, others with delight. Berut took special joy in the play, allowing the children to change the game at their whim so long as they won. Arminius knew the game, but slowed his gait and minded his strength with them.

I would make you queen of Germania. My lungs tightened, and I forced myself to keep breathing.

"That optio is a fine man to watch." Jotapa shielded her eyes from the sun and to get a better look at Berut.

I focused long enough to catch Jotapa licking her lips like a starving woman at a feast—a feast featuring the small Carthaginian as the main course. I would have teased her, but Konrada saw it, too.

"How dare you, you filthy little scalc! These men have imprisoned my brother and enslaved him to their legion."

She raised her hand to strike Jotapa, but I caught her wrist in a punishing grip so tight her bones ground together and she cried out.

"Enough!" I hissed. "Jotapa is a scalc by my father's will, not mine. Until she frees herself, you will think before striking a member of the chief's house, scalc or otherwise."

Konrada cradled her wrist against her chest when I released her, eyes cast downward. "I am sorry, Princess."

Curious eyes watched us, including Roman eyes. They of all people did not need to see discord in my tribe, and, more importantly, Konrada's outburst spoke to a hurt she was too young to contain all on her own. My anger fizzled as quickly as it sparked. "I know you're upset. I understand it, but it is not me to whom you owe an apology."

"It's nothing." Jotapa shook her dark head. The hairs closest to her scalp and neck stuck to the sweat on her skin. "They took her brother. I didn't think—"

"No." Konrada shook her head, "I apologize. I was wrong."

Jotapa looped their arms together and pulled Konrada's head to her shoulder. "Your brother will be fine. You'll see. Look at these soldiers, they are Germani, too, and they're right here. I'm sure he'll be with them soon."

The lie fell easily from her lips and I didn't correct her. Sometimes people needed a softer touch than I usually offered. Maybe, after learning what I had from Arminius, it wasn't such a lie. Maybe it didn't have to be a lie.

Arminius' voice rang out with laughter, echoed by children's cheers.

"One more, best two out of three," he shouted to his small opponents.

"Why? So they can stomp us again?" Berut put his hands on his hips, shoulders shaking with laughter.

A headache blossomed behind my eye as I wondered how much of this was a show, a farce, *panem et circenses*, like he said. How much was real, the man who etched his tribal sigil into his chest knowing it might get him killed?

But for his red tunic and shorn hair, he looked like one of us. The parents and minders watching the children smiled at his antics, at how he made their children smile. It suddenly appeared not quite so impossible, his belief that he could earn Germani trust. That put a kink in my new plans, plans that didn't include him.

Eager to be rid of this bothersome new idea, I ushered my friends away with a quick backward glance to Arminius. Donar himself stared back at me, intense and powerful as any god. His promise hung in the air between us, even at a distance: *I would make you queen of Germania*.

It took willpower, but I tore myself away and followed the others back to the longhouse, then led them to my bedroom. We might find some privacy there.

I needed Jotapa to know what I knew. After what happened to Konrada's brother, she, too, had a right to know something was coming. Given her nature, she'd nose around until she found out, anyway. We were too alike in that way. We were also too alike in that she was liable to launch a one-woman assault on the next Roman she saw.

Konrada held herself at the closed door, wide eyed and unsure. I hadn't invited her to my private quarters before. I sat myself on the bed, and Jotapa took her usual seat on my stool.

I studied their two faces. I knew these women as sisters and trusted them even more. My own brothers could not be so trustworthy.

"For your safety, I cannot share everything I know." The words tasted like sawdust on my tongue. "But Konrada, please trust me when I say all is not lost."

She nodded once and swallowed.

"I ask only that you trust me and keep your head down. When the time is right, I swear I will tell you everything. You are on your way to becoming a fine warrior. For now, please leave us to talk."

Konrada sucked in a shallow breath through her nose and her cheeks went pink. To her credit, she didn't argue. Once the door shut behind her, I turned my full attention to Jotapa.

"Tomorrow I'm riding to the Chatti to visit Reimar. Will you join me?"

Expecting something far more dramatic than a day's ride to visit my betrothed, Jotapa frowned. "Of course."

"And I assume I can trust that anything you witness or hear will stay between us?"

Jotapa rose and placed a hand on my shoulder. "Whatever it is, you can trust me."

"Thank you. Do you mind if I have some time to myself for the afternoon?"

"Anything you need," she said. "I'll prepare provisions for our journey."

The door had scarcely shut behind her when Arminius cleared his throat at my window. That I knew him by a single forced cough was too much.

Without turning around, I said, "Levin saw us when we fought by the backdoor. You know you can't be here."

"Do you trust her?"

I turned. The bastard had pushed my thick woven tapestry aside and finagled those outsized shoulders of his—armor and all—through the window. He practically stood inside my bedroom.

"It's you I don't trust." I crossed the floor to pull the tapestry back over the window, but he made no effort to move. "Get out."

"Maybe it would be safer all around if you invited me in." He pursed his lips, feigning his way through a facade of deep thought.

"Fine." I reached my trunk in two steps and unsheathed my sword. "I will make you leave."

Segestes and Wout were most likely training with the newest warriors. Levin and Lennart were supposed to be helping in the fields this week, but Lennart's recent attitude meant he could be anywhere, and Levin would go with him out of loyalty. Any of the scalcs could be lurking by my door. Arminius had to get the fuck out.

"Look, I understand why you don't trust me, but I feel like we've established that you don't need to be armed every time we're alone together. If you were my wife—"

There it was again, the suggestion he'd made at our less than fortuitous reunion. It was easy to dismiss as a ribald joke, but after the other day... My skin prickled at the idea. Over the course of many made and broken betrothals over the years, I'd felt nothing but revulsion. Not the case when the words slipped so easily off Arminius' tongue.

I saw it clearly, the two of us riding as one at the head of an army.

"Stop talking that way," I interrupted.

"Why?"

Light reflected off the growing whiskers on his chin, as fine a chin as I'd ever seen.

"It's nonsense." I reluctantly lowered my weapon. "It's a game you're playing that I don't understand, and I refuse to play along. You want me out of your way? I will go, but you need to stay out of mine."

He shifted to rest his weight on both forearms. Those were fine, too. "Why are you going to see the Chatti tomorrow?"

A frustrated scream bubbled up in my throat. "Did I not just tell you to stay away from me? It is none of your business."

"They would make excellent allies." He hummed and drummed his fingers on my windowsill. "Chatti warriors numbered well over 8,000 at the last survey."

Tyr damn him, he knew exactly why I intended to see Reimar.

"Wildberry," he lowered his voice, "if you want a part in this, you have to join me. Otherwise, you need to stay out of it. There is no middle ground here. It's too dangerous and I won't risk... I won't have us at odds."

There was no scenario in which I'd join him. The simple fact remained that he didn't have the connections to unite more than a few of the smaller, weaker tribes, like the Sugambri, for his venture. And when it began to collapse beneath his feet, would he go down with his allies or would he turn Roman again?

"I am princess of the Cherusci, and I have business with the Chatti that has nothing to do with you. I certainly don't need you following me around simply to provoke me."

He grinned. "Maybe I should accompany you tomorrow, and we can talk to the Chatti together, see how things go when we're working toward the same goal."

"Stop." I put enough bite into the order to silence him. My heart thumped uproariously in my chest and a dim buzzing filled my ears. "Stop playing these games with me. It must be so easy for you to flit about the tribes making wild promises you can't possibly keep, but the consequences are real for us. Stop it. Stop your flirting and whatever it is you've been plotting because you can't do it. It's you who needs to stay out of it."

For once, he sobered. Some of the color drained from his face, and he took his time in responding, choosing his words carefully.

"I am sorry I've made you feel this way." He straightened as much as possible in the window. "That was never my intention. I won't trouble you with the... other matter again."

Well, that was too easy.

"But Thusnelda—"

There it is.

"I assure you I am not playing any game with you. I think you and I would make unstoppable allies, and I think you would make one hell of a wife."

——————▶

We rode hard to Chatti territory. From dawn to early sunset, we rested only once for an afternoon meal of corn cakes, dried fish, and gooseberries, whatever Jotapa had grabbed from the kitchens. Neither the horses nor the dogs complained, though the animals wore frothy coats of sweat by the time we arrived.

A bedraggled boy materialized from the stables adjacent to the chief's longhouse while Sunna and Donar made a dive for the nearest water trough, lapping sloppily to their hearts' content. The groan of relief from Jotapa dismounting her horse echoed my own. As fit as we both were for riding, I didn't ride enough to condition my legs for the length and duration of today's adventure. What did the Romans call good health? *Vis and vigor*? I shook my head at the strange phrase.

The water in my flask was low and lukewarm. Somewhere inside that longhouse was ale that promised to slake my thirst. A scalc ushered us inside, though it was an unnecessary gesture of hospitality. Most Germani considered the hall of a longhouse communal space and always open to travelers.

Reimar's, or rather his father, Raginmar's, longhouse wasn't so different from our own. Shields lined the walls, each painted with the Chatti lynx. The smell of burning coals, roasted meats, and fresh bread filled the hall, and a handful of scalcs scurried about, preparing for the evening meal.

The woman I was soon to call Mother stood from the central fire, looking far more regal in her old work dress and apron than she had any right. I'd only met Wiltrud once, when my family and I had traveled here to finalize my betrothal to Reimar, but I'd know her anywhere. Tall and graceful, topped by a head of loose ginger curls, she wore command as naturally as her own skin. Her very presence inspired deference.

I dipped my head at her arrival, but she clucked her tongue.

"You are my good-daughter," she said, lifting my chin with a work-calloused finger, "I won't have family bowing to me."

A deep sense of calm warmed my tired limbs, much the same as when I visited Ingomar. Yet another reason my union with Reimar filled me with a tentative hope, despite our future promising no love.

She urged Jotapa and me to take seats at the nearest table and sent a scalc for ale and fresh water. "I know you didn't come all this way to spend time with me. Reimar and my husband are still in the fields, but I can fetch them if you wish."

"No, we'll wait." Somehow, sharing a table with her again made me equal parts happy and nervous. I was to take on her role as queen. Arminius' outlandish voice stole into my mind. *I would make you queen of Germania*. Our people would no sooner bow to a single king under one banner than bow to the Empire. It violated our way of life. He spoke nonsense.

Ruling the Chatti wasn't nonsense. I longed to emulate Wiltrud as much as I feared I'd never live up to her reputation. Wiltrud was known across Germania for her compassion, which belied a rock-hard spine, not to mention her younger days as a warrior. Rumors spoke of her regularly leading their tribe into battle in Raginmar's stead, though these rumors were dismissed as soon as spoken. Germani women were free to achieve many things in life, but surpassing one's husband in combat wasn't one of them.

Wiltrud was the only woman with whom I allowed myself to be openly awestruck. Should that emotion reveal itself in the presence of a man, he'd dismiss me as simpering and weak. Wiltrud would never mistake my emotions for weakness.

"I have something I'd like to discuss with him, but it can wait until dinner," I said.

A scalc returned to the table with ale and a small plate of dried fruits, nothing so heavy as to sate our appetites for the meal ahead. When Jotapa accepted her drink, I remembered my rudeness.

"I'm sorry," I gestured to Jotapa, "this is—"

"I remember." Wiltrud smiled and inclined her head. "She joined you the last time we had the pleasure of your company. Jotapa, yes?"

Jotapa's eyes widened at the acknowledgement. "Yes, ma'am."

Again, Wiltrud waved a hand to dismiss any show of deference. "As Thusnelda's personal scalc, I presume you will join our family soon enough, as well. Are you close to paying your freedom?"

A faint color bloomed in Jotapa's cheeks, and she shot a glance at me, seeking assurance to answer. It was customary in most tribes for scalcs to buy their freedom or only serve a designated number of years, but not every master enjoyed being reminded of this, particularly as Roman influence grew. Some saw the Roman practices as an opportunity to leach more from their property. I trusted Wiltrud, however, and nodded for Jotapa to answer.

"Very close, ma'am." A lifelong scalc did not easily silence courtesies. "A year, perhaps two, until I finish payment."

The lines in the corners of Wiltrud's dark eyes crinkled and danced. "And if your debt was to be paid much sooner, can I presume you will seek your family? Return to your homeland?"

"No." Jotapa shook her head. "I was born to slaves. Before Segestes bought me, I had spent my life in service to a traveling merchant and his family with my mother. She died when I was young, so I'm not even sure where my people's home is, except somewhere in Scythia."

Segestes had purchased her as a gift when I became a woman, his attempt at a consolation for refusing to foster me to another family after Mama died. We were close enough in age that it hadn't taken us long to form a relationship more sisterly than the limits of social station defined. We'd discussed this many times, especially when we were both so young. We swore we would never leave each other and, in the way of a child, I promised that together we would ride around the world until we found her native people. Knowing nothing more than that she descended from a horse tribe in steppe lands far to the east, we once believed finding her relations would be easy. Everything seems easy to the young.

"Then of course you will stay on with us as a freedwoman," Wiltrud said. "You can seek others like yourself. You might even solve your mystery."

The color in Jotapa's cheek deepened. "Thank you, ma'am."

A weight I hadn't known I carried lifted. We hadn't discussed this possibility. "Is that what you want, Jotapa?"

"We promised, didn't we?" she said.

I felt rather than saw Wiltrud's silent assessment of our exchange. Warm approval washed over me in gently lapping waves. Apparently, I had succeeded in a test I didn't know she'd laid before me.

The main doors burst open, and our quiet sanctuary became a hall full of men. The stench of sweat and manure overshadowed that of the pleasant meal to come. The only hint that it surprised Reimar to see me was a slight furrowing of his bushy red brows. Raginmar clapped him across the shoulders and guffawed.

"Looks like someone couldn't wait to get to know you better." Raginmar laughed all the way to Wiltrud, taking her face in his enormous hands and kissing her soundly on the mouth. I watched with unabashed curiosity. They were affectionate the last time I was here, and it continued to fascinate me. Reimar was a reserved man, but his parents lived with joyful abandon, even if Wiltrud held herself with more dignity than her long-haired husband.

Raginmar's hair ran in straight locks of gray, with a matching silver beard braided to his chest. Reimar took after his mother in looks and temperament, though he and his father shared their mountainous size.

Wiltrud rose from the table, sweeping her dress and apron straight as if she wore the finest gown. "Dinner will be served soon. I insist the men clean themselves before they ruin the meal I worked so hard on."

It sounded like a rebuke, but she wore a wry smile. Raginmar kissed her on the cheek before shuffling off down the hall. His limp had grown more pronounced even in the past months since I first came here. Reimar followed and stopped before me.

"Is everything all right?" he asked.

"Everything's fine. I simply thought of a matter I'd like to discuss with you. After the meal."

His eyes narrowed at the corners as he studied my road-weary appearance. No use hiding that we hadn't rushed. With a grunt, he ambled the same way Raginmar went, and I clamped my mouth shut. After dinner, then.

Chapter 7

To give ground, provided you return to the attack, is considered prudence rather than cowardice. (Tacitus)

Reimar paced in the village grain cellar—the only place we were sure no others might walk in on us. Jotapa sat on the narrow steps leading up to the door, periodically peeking through the wooden slats to ensure no eavesdroppers lurked. A single candle illuminated the chilly space.

He paced and paced and paced until my eyes crossed. Now and then he grunted, shook his head, and then continued pacing. My skin prickled beneath my tunic the longer we remained below ground.

Finally, he stopped and focused his attention on me. "How am I supposed to trust the word of Arminius? Is he Roman? Is he Cherusci? He has no loyalty, he has no—"

"You're not." Somewhere above us, a child shrieked, followed closely by a scolding mother. "If we do this, we move forward without him."

Reimar chewed over this for at least a minute, maybe longer, before resuming his pacing. "Did he say how he plans to defeat entire legions? And when Rome comes back to suppress the rebellion? We might unite the tribes for a battle, but they'll never stay. They have eleven legions posted across the countryside and Gaul. We will never match their numbers."

I expected his questions and still they frustrated me.

"I don't think he has a plan." Reimar was stuck on the wrong parts of my admittedly haphazard pitch. "Let's say we get the numbers, even for just one battle. One well orchestrated ambush. Think about it. No more taxes. No crucifixions. No more of our people taken and sold across the Empire."

My heart pounded. If I couldn't convince Reimar, who hated Rome as much as I did, then my idea to win over the other tribes myself was meaningless. I would have to sit back and watch Arminius drag our people into a doomed rebellion, condemning us all.

He sat heavily on an empty shelf, watching me until the small hairs on my arm stood up beneath my sleeves. "My father will throw his support behind whomever he believes is winning. Until I am chief..."

He shrugged his big shoulders.

"What about Wiltrud?"

It was a bold question, even for me. Wiltrud's martial leadership remained locked behind rumors and doubt for good reason: No man called himself chief while letting his wife rule. Instead of looking shocked or angry, he considered the question as casually as if I'd asked him what he thought about the coming winter.

"You are of like spirits, but it will be Raginmar's decision."

"What would convince him?"

Apparently, discussing sedition made it easier for the two of us to converse. What would convince Raginmar? If I couldn't answer that question, then I had no answers for the others who'd be just as doubtful and mercurial with their loyalty.

As it did more often than I cared to admit, Arminius' voice entered my mind: *panem et circenses*, he said. He'd told me, and the men of the auxiliary he trusted, to watch the Romans, learn from them, absorb their ways. We needed to make a study of it because it ran so contrary to our blunt, open natures. Our people hid nothing, especially not in confrontation. It was our downfall in open battle against the discipline of a legion.

"We have to show them," I said. "We gather them all into one place and put everything in the open."

He looked at me with the dawning realization of a man who had expected one thing, only to find another in its place. The spell I cast over him broke and his quiet amusement—or was it pleasure?—took its place.

"Our wedding celebration, then," he said and returned to his feet. "At Haustblot, we can all speak freely. Healthy portions of ale will soften them up. Until then, you and I will need to beat Arminius to the other chieftains."

I deflated. Of course I would forget that detail. "Segestes won't like me traveling so much, even if I tell him it's to see you."

Reimar scoffed. "He'll do what I tell him to do."

Now there was the easy arrogance I appreciated in a potential husband. He had a point, after all. Segestes desired this match more than any of us.

"Good. That makes my life much easier."

He cast a look at Jotapa—probably the first since entering the hall hours ago—and turned his attention back to me.

"You know he wants you for himself, yes?"

I would make you queen of Germania.

Yes, I did know that, though I still didn't understand it. My mind continued to insist Arminius saw me as a game piece he needed in order to win.

"Yes, but—"

Reimar waved a hand. "I know you don't want him. You came all this way to make sure he doesn't stab me in the back, and I appreciate that. But you need to be careful, as well. Don't forget that he will say and do anything to get what he wants."

With that rather unnecessary warning, he stepped aside and let us leave the cellar.

Despite Wiltrud's insistence that we take a room, Jotapa and I slept in the hall that night, as was customary for guests. Though comfortable and warm, sleep eluded me until the embers ran low. Thoughts ran round and round through my mind, never settling in just one place. I wanted to focus on which tribe I should contact next, but I kept circling back to Reimar's warning. He hadn't say anything I hadn't already thought.

Arminius said one of the most outlandish things I'd ever heard in his bid for whatever it was he wanted from me. Queen of Germania, indeed. Another hollow promise from a man used to saying anything to get his way.

When I at last drifted off, I dreamed I rode at the head of a massive army, and the battle chief riding beside me had fair hair.

➤

"Are you going to talk to me?" Jotapa rode slightly behind me. This morning we kept a much slower pace, neither of us concerned with arriving late. The dogs appreciated the change, periodically darting into the brush after a small animal or bird.

It was true; I'd hardly spoken a word to her since we'd left the grain cellar. Rather than sort through the increasingly tangled web in my mind, I concentrated on keeping my horse from chomping at every stray bit of greenery in her path.

"I think we should pay a visit to the Bructeri next, or maybe the Suebi, or—"

Jotapa's bright laughter cut me off. "You have plenty of strong men to discuss alliances with who absolutely live to listen to you speak like this. No, I mean to discuss your rather large problem."

I turned in my saddle to fix her with what I hoped was a withering glare. Or maybe my utter bewilderment. "Organizing a rebellion is a significant undertaking."

"Are you really going to pretend Arminius hasn't been slobbering after you like a stud after a mare in heat?"

The question hung in the air between us. I scrambled for an answer to shut her up, but all that came out was sputtering and choking on my tongue. Jotapa nudged her mount to come abreast with mine, shaking her head and grinning.

"I know you don't understand it," she said, not even bothering to hide her amusement at my expense, "because most men are too scared of you to act the way he does, but I promise that no matter what other plots he's involved in, his desire for you is genuine."

My mouth dropped open. "That's not... I don't..."

Jotapa sighed and took a deep breath of the crisp morning air. The cloudless sky promised heat to come, but the confines of the trees blessedly shielded us from the worst of it.

"We're so close in age," she said, "sometimes I forget how you've held yourself apart from the indulgences other girls enjoyed so freely. He may not want anything but your body, but his interest is genuine."

The comment made me bristle. I thought back to the low ache of jealousy I felt watching the young scalcs giggle with each other over their latest romantic interludes. How I wished to shed my identity for a day or two to join the fun. "Of course I hold myself apart. I am princess of the Cherusci and my reputation—"

"You invented a burden where none existed." She tossed a leg over her horse's neck and sat to the side, relaxed and never breaking control of the horse. Though she may have never even seen her homeland, horsemanship came as naturally to her as breathing. It ran in her blood. "The Romans have tried their damnedest to instill their prudishness, but Germani never held to that nonsense. You've brushed aside all suitors, every betrothal, every handsome boy who knuckled up the courage to flirt. I think I understand now."

"And what do you understand?"

Jotapa cocked her head. "You've been waiting for him."

"Reimar?" I recoiled at the notion. "I didn't even know him."

"Not him." Her laughter tinkled through the forest like bells. "For Arminius."

I gawked at her before practically shouting a single laugh. "Why in the gods' assholes would I have spent my entire life waiting for him?"

She pushed up to her feet on the animal's back, arms out for balance and struggling against her body's quaking laughter. "You'll figure it out."

"What I'll figure out is whether to carry your body back to the village or leave it here in the woods for the crows when you break your neck. Get down!"

As children we'd played like this on the horses all the time. Small, agile children. Jotapa raised a challenging brow at me, leaned down to grip the pommel on the simple leather pad we used instead of a Roman saddle, then brought both legs down on the horse's other side before quickly twisting and letting her torso hang on the opposite side. Sunna and Donar circled around the mount's feet, yipping and licking Jotapa's face.

"Like this?" She grinned merrily up at me.

I had to accept her minor diversion, entertaining though it was, rather than a shred of clarity. If Jotapa didn't want to tell me something, she wouldn't. She would tell me when she was good and ready. Or until I gave her what she wanted.

She resumed her proper seat, and we rode on in amiable silence. It took me a while to screw up the courage to relent and confess what she'd likely already guessed. She wouldn't speak to me in anything except riddles until I did.

I heaved a sigh. "Arminius came into my window and promised to make me his queen after you left the other afternoon."

The last thing I heard before temporarily going deaf was her delighted squealing.

———————➤

Home featured none of the easy companionship of a day on the road with Jotapa. At least Segestes and Wout waited until dawn's light to send for me.

I paused before the door to Segestes' private quarters. That we weren't having this conversation in the main hall didn't bode well. Never to be mistaken for a coward, I raised my fist and knocked.

My father's voice answered. "Come."

I wasn't with Arminius. At least not yesterday, I told myself in a running mantra. It should thrill Segestes I'd gone to see Reimar.

One thing became clear when I entered the room: Segestes was not thrilled. Wout, Lennart, and Levin stood around him. A single empty chair sat in the center of his large room. At least Levin didn't look at me like an insect to be squashed.

I sat in the chair without needing to be told, then awaited the onslaught. It started a little quieter than I expected.

"I told you," Segestes let his head fall into his hands, "I told you to stay away from him."

Offense stiffened my shoulders. "I did. I visited Reimar yesterday. I thought you'd be pleased that I've finally shown an interest."

Segestes erupted, all spit and bulging veins and purpled skin. "You went there on that traitorous fuck's bidding! Don't lie to me, girl. You didn't really think you were the first person Arminius approached with his lunacy, did you? He couldn't get to me, so he went to you."

Fear spiked in my veins. I don't know why it hadn't occurred to me that of course Arminius went to Segestes first. Segestes was chief of the most powerful tribe east of the Rhine. If I truly intended to mount a rebellion parallel to Arminius' plans, of course it would look like we were working together. Since my father was so committed to staying the course with Rome, it wasn't as though I could explain the truth.

"I want what's best for all of us," he went on. "I want what's best for my children. You know that includes you, yes?"

His dark eyes bore into mine, pleading. I never had to doubt the sincerity of his belief Rome was our savior. My father didn't lie, not really. Our opinions simply differed about what constituted "best" regarding our people and myself. Sadness and pity stabbed me in the heart as sure as any blade. He believed every word. It would be so easy to hate the man had I known he lied to himself and all of us for personal gain, but he didn't. He liked the Roman promise of wealth, sure enough, but it wasn't what drove him. In Rome's love he imagined a world where Mama lived.

Some part of him still loved me as he loved his sons. Something in my face must have broken because one moment I was studying each aged line in his flesh, each gray hair at his receding temple, each ounce of genuine honesty in those brown eyes I thought warm as a child, the next he knelt at my side and pulled my head into his chest in a hug. It had been long years since we last embraced.

"I'm so sorry, daughter," he said into my hair. "You always wanted it to be him, but you must know his talk will spell doom for us all."

My shoulders curled against the accuracy of his words. Jotapa and Segestes found a subject on which they agreed without ever exchanging words. Of course part of me yearned for my childhood hopes, but they were both so very wrong. They had to be wrong. Arminius was not our people's future, he certainly wasn't mine, and I damn well knew it.

My eyes burned and grew wet. I didn't cry because Segestes was right; I cried because he was wrong. I cried because of how much he loved me, us, the Cherusci, and I cried because our differences made us enemies. I cried because I didn't want to be enemies with this man, so fervent to protect me.

"Father, I—"

"I'll watch her." Levin stepped forward. The sneer in his tone colored everything except his eyes. I stared up at him, my little brother. Before Segestes or Wout reacted and studied him for themselves, his chin jerked down once just for me. Levin marked himself my ally and with that I could breathe deeply.

"I will ensure he no longer harasses her," Levin said. Confident. Superior. Absolute in his belief that all should bow to him. A proper chief's son. Wout didn't even spare him a look.

While Segestes rubbed between my shoulders, a thousand words passed silently between Levin and me over Segestes' shoulder. Like the time he'd found me in the woods with a sprained ankle and knew instinctively I wanted secrecy. We'd all be punished if the truth came out about my plans. Things would be better for the entire tribe as long as Levin remained silent and played along. That I trusted him with just a look? I didn't have a name for the relief. I couldn't thank him, not with Wout and Lennart looking on.

"Thank you, father," I whispered, realizing how long I'd allowed this embrace continue. "I want you to know how happy I am to be Reimar's bride. I went only in my excitement to see him. I hope to make a fine Chatti queen and give him sons."

Segestes' eyes shone with tears of his own when he finally released me. I'd said precisely what he wanted to hear, after a lifetime of contrarian behavior. One would think he'd be suspicious, but he only sagged in relief.

"Good, good." He cupped the back of my head and ran a thumb down my cheek. "You are always my daughter, yes?"

"Yes, father."

It was the darkest lie I'd ever told.

———————▶

Konrada begged me for more training, anything and everything to distract her from her brother's absence and her mother's continued convalescence. Her distraction proved too strong to engage in any sort of combat or hunting training, so we spent three days on leather—tanning hides, boiling pieces, and shaping them to our will, going over the best waxes to seal it. I showed her how to use different tools to carve designs into our pieces.

Each task I assigned her was painfully intricate, anything to force her concentration. Today, we painted the ceremonial gauntlets we'd carved and treated yesterday. I'd made sure her designs formed tight whorls interlaced in a dizzying pattern. Painting such a meticulous pattern would keep her busy until nightfall.

My thin horsehair brush stuttered on the wolf's head I'd carved. These gauntlets would be mine, but not until they were perfect. They would not be if I couldn't keep my brush steady and my mind off the rebellion. It ran wild with possibilities and plans. An ambush itself was no problem, it was getting the Romans and multiple disparate tribes all in the same place at the same time that proved difficult. No matter how I turned the problem over in my head, I always came back to the same place: I needed someone inside the legions. Someone with power.

Someone like Arminius. No. He was a terrible choice. In the end, he'd no doubt side with his brother, the avowed Roman. Perhaps Ermin, or Berut. Yes, Berut had a rebel's spirit and already knew about Arminius' nascent plot.

A quick glance at Konrada's work showed no errors. She chose bright colors and her gauntlets steadily transformed into little rainbows a person wore on their wrists and forearms.

She didn't look up or stall her painting when she said, "I will kill them all."

"I believe you." I set my brush aside. "You won't do it alone."

Her breath came out in a shaky exhale, and she set her work down. "I think if I keep it up, my eyes are never going to un-cross."

"Very well." I moved my own work next to hers. My own fingers ached from the intricacy of the work, and it wasn't as though I lacked things for us to do. "You can accompany me to the kitchens. I need to ensure our new mothers are getting the right portions. After that I want to check in with the weavers. Our fabric was popular at Haustblot last year, so they should be making more, but..."

I trailed off at the expression on Konrada's face. She didn't want to do any of this with me, that much was clear, but these were things that had to get done. Overseeing a tribe required a significant amount of work, very little of which was as exciting as hunting or mounting a defense against raiders. People became busy, they forgot things, they didn't see all the troubles spread throughout the tribe I saw.

"Konrada," I said, "you wanted to train with me. This is what being a leader in the tribe is. It's not all fighting and—"

"I'm sorry," she interrupted, "I was only thinking it was strange."

"What's strange?"

She shrugged. "Well, it's not like the cooks and kitchen scalcs have never prepared the meals for new mothers. Everyone knows who's pregnant and who just gave birth. Do you have to check on them every time?"

Together we left her family's small shed and headed toward the kitchen house regardless of her questions. Sunna and Donar fell in with us, each taking turns rubbing against our legs. Of course I'd had to double check the meal rotations before. When I was twelve, a woman and her babe almost starved to death after her husband put her out for infidelity and barred the cooks from feeding her. Two, no, three winters ago, no one in the kitchen noticed when a pregnant woman stopped sending her scalc for rations. What we found in that roundhouse hardly bears repeating, but suffice to say, I always make certain things my business.

"Most of the time there's no need for my supervision," I said, "but periodically things go wrong. My supervision minimizes mistakes."

Konrada ruffled Donar's ears, which he tolerated with infinite patience. "Sure, but don't things just go wrong sometimes? You can't control everything all the time."

If she expected an answer, she didn't wait for one. She scooped up a stray stick, waved it until she had the attention of both dogs, then hurled it toward the kitchen house, chasing after it and the dogs.

Even after our violent brush with the legionaries, she still didn't appreciate the necessity of my work. My inattentiveness, my carelessness nearly got us raped and murdered. The moment I became lackadaisical, that's when things fell apart. None of us could afford that.

Chapter 8

They even believe that the sex has a certain sanctity and prescience, and they do not despise their counsels, or make light of their answers. (Tacitus)

"I can't believe you talked me into this," Levin grumbled.

We walked on the outskirts of the main Sugambri village, ostensibly there to trade with their healer who, according to the Sugambri hunters who'd passed through our longhouse last week, was in possession of a garlic poultice that cured every ache. I carried a satchel stuffed with dried herbs our healer swore cured every ague. I didn't often trade, but it seemed like a reasonable excuse for the trip.

My true target was Deudorix and convincing him to ally with me and the Cherusci, not Arminius.

"You say that like you actually wanted to spend the week repairing the bog roads."

A heavy storm had damaged too many sections of our nearest roads to ignore. The rickety wooden pathways lacked the straight brutality of wide, stone-paved Roman roads, but they allowed us to traverse our lands safely and quickly. Whenever we found damage, we worked to fix it as quickly as possible. That didn't mean any of us enjoyed spending days on end wading through bogs in sticky summer heat.

"That's not what I'm talking about, and you damn well know it."

I grimaced. Levin didn't particularly care for my big plan to organize the tribes to ambush the legions. He somehow liked it even less than

Arminius trying to accomplish the same thing, which apparently the men in my family had all known about before I did.

Unlike Arminius, I was his sister, so when I twisted his arm, he relented, but not before making me swear that if I didn't get the allies, if I didn't come up with a foolproof plan, that I'd let it go.

"If we're being honest, I can't believe I talked you into this, either." I chuckled.

"It's not funny."

"No." I reached for his hand and he let me take it. "It's not funny. I'm grateful you're here."

In truth, I was grateful for much more than his presence and, if not support, willingness to be my alibi with our father. While Wout and Lennart had grown into angry men, Levin remained my brother in all ways. His innate good humor never left him. He didn't blame me for every misfortune that ever befell our family.

He squeezed my hand, and we released our grip as noise from the village grew louder. We were almost in sight of the village proper when the all-too-familiar jangling of Roman armor joined the native chorus. Levin and I froze, a hesitation that cost us the ability to dive into the trees, out of sight.

No common patrol rounded the bend in the road before us, but at least a full century complete with standard bearers and a small supply train marched our way. Fortunately, no prisoners marched with them.

Toward the back road a few officers, including a helmet topped with the elaborate white plumage signifying a legatus. My blood chilled. Even at a distance I recognized the hard lines and sunken planes of Vala's face, and I had no doubt he recognized me, as well.

"We're here to trade," I murmured, more for my own sake than Levin's. "We haven't done anything wrong."

We shifted to the side of the road as the soldiers passed, a sea of silver mail, red tunics, and dark, watchful eyes. More than one man tightened his grip on the pommel of his gladius. Were they so afraid of two lone Germani?

Vala and two other mounted officers stopped before us. His implacable stare bore down on me, and I sensed most deferred to him, like dogs averting their eyes and showing their bellies to a superior. He waited while I simply stared back, then his lips twitched in what probably passed for him as a smile.

"Princess Thusnelda, I'm surprised to see you so far from Cherusci territory. How fortuitous that we've crossed paths."

His unspoken question lay between us, and I debated the merits of answering. "Fortuitous" was not the word I'd have chosen. No, I'd have gone with "unlucky," or maybe "cursed." The gods frowned on the day's endeavor.

"Legatus." There. That was sufficient. If possible, Levin stiffened even further.

Vala's lips twitched again. "What brings you to Sugambri territory? And with only one brother? I thought after your incident your father wouldn't let you out of his sight, at least not without a small army."

My hackles rose at each successive word. *My* incident? Segestes wouldn't *let* me? Before I opened my mouth and got us into trouble, Levin intervened.

"Some Sugambri hunters stayed with us recently and told us their healer has a remedy we ought to try. We've come to trade for it."

One of the other officers laughed as though Levin told a wry joke. Vala cleared his throat, and the man's laughter abruptly cut off.

"If the Cherusci have need of medicine, you should send a delegation to the fort. We have some of the finest doctors in the world among our ranks. Our medicine has advanced quite a bit past your quaint rituals."

The officers struggled to smother their laughter.

"We'll keep that in mind," Levin gritted out.

Vala leaned closer in his saddle. "It does strike me as odd."

When he said nothing further, I relented. "What does?"

"That you would see to this errand. Not only were you the victim of a violent attack not so very long ago, but you are princess of the tribe. Sending the princess and a lordling suggests important business is afoot."

Those fathomless black eyes tracked over every pore in my face. I kept my mouth shut.

"Is important business afoot, Thusnelda?"

Levin started to answer for me, but I stopped him with a squeeze of his forearm.

"It is as my brother said, Legatus. I like the fresh air, and after all of the governor's assurances, I didn't think I was in much danger from stray legionaries anymore."

"Very well." He sat back up in his saddle. "Whatever your true business with the Sugambri is, you've come at a good time. We've just completed our inventory, and I'm sure in their joy at being rid of us, there will be much celebrating tonight."

I spoke before I thought better of it. "Isn't that sort of thing Arminius' job?"

Vala waved the other officers on. "It is, but you know, I am an old soldier who can't help but wonder if the local recruit is helping his local friends avoid paying taxes. You don't think he'd do such a thing, do you?"

Growing up with brothers, I knew most boys went through a stage during which they felt compelled to torture bugs. I remembered Wout and Lennart—naturally—huddled over beetles, grinning and gleaming as they dismantled the insects piece by piece. That same look filled Vala's eyes.

"No, I don't think he'd do such a thing." Later, I'd feel shame over the softness of my voice.

When Vala smiled, it was a ghoulish thing. "And you'd be correct. His numbers and mine matched almost perfectly. It seems Varus has chosen his aide well, and you have no serious business with the Sugambri."

I swallowed hard and reminded myself that I didn't have wings, so that odd wrenching sensation between my shoulder blades couldn't be from Vala ripping them off.

"I'm sure I'll see you again soon." He wheeled his horse around and cantered away without waiting for my reply.

As soon as he was out of sight, my breath left me in a great gust of air. Levin unhelpfully patted me on the back, causing me to cough a few times before getting my lungs back under control.

"There, that wasn't so bad," Levin said.

"Not so bad?" I wheezed. "That man is a demon and he knows. He knows we're up to something."

"I have to be honest. I stopped listening after he called me a lordling."

"Is that really all you got out of that conversation?"

"Well excuse me if I stopped listening to the rude man. A lordling? Is that what they think I am?"

I cuffed my idiot brother on the back of the head and together we resumed our journey.

Vala suspected Arminius, and he was right to. Vala suspected me, and he was right to. There was one significant problem with recruiting allies: People talked.

How many allies could either of us recruit before someone talked to Varus?

—————————>

Contrary to Vala's assessment, Deudorix and the Sugambri had no plans to celebrate. Based on the muted welcome we received in his hall, I suspected he was hard pressed to offer us so much as a meal and a blanket for the night.

First he sent us to his healer to conduct that business. The garlic salve smelled wretched, but it was worth a try, and the grandmother who came up with it happily imparted her precise instructions to Levin. I made note of each step and ingredient, knowing Levin was as likely to forget all the steps as he was to forget a few of them.

Then Deudorix left us waiting in his hall. One hour turned to two, then three as the sun sank lower in the sky. Not even his wife appeared, nor any of his daughters, if he had any still residing in the village. He was an older man, so it stood to reason if he had daughters, they were long married off to other tribes. He had sons lurking about, I knew that much. Even his scalcs avoided us, except to offer water while we waited.

"You'll have to forgive me." His voice boomed from across the longhouse, in the back where I saw a door tucked away. "I've spent the evening soothing wounded prides and raw nerves. I'm hungry and tired, so please tell me what really brought you two all the way to my home. Don't waste my time with that healer business. I think we all know better than that."

Apparently the only person who believed my reasons for visiting the Sugambri was Segestes.

He sat heavily upon a thick, well cushioned chair at the head of his table, and we slid onto benches opposite him. I glanced around the curiously empty hall. No dinner. No ale. No sons or chieftains. No other guests. It was dinner time, past that for most tribes and families, judging by the low sun. In the summer months, the sun didn't set until well into the night. Orange and purple light outside meant it was late, indeed.

Too late to play games, and the odd privacy meant I could speak freely.

"I know you made a deal with Arminius," I said. "I'm...we're here to see if you won't deal directly with us, the Cherusci. I've already negotiated with the Chatti, and they stand with us. If it's a rebellion you want, we're the ones to provide it."

I'd practiced that short speech all day, all through the night and day prior. Now that it was out of my mouth, it seemed insufficient. I wanted to appear direct, a contrast to Arminius' silver tongue. Instead the words felt deficient.

Deudorix looked much the same as I last saw him, though today's tunic offered brighter colors and more beaded necklaces hung down his neck, playing a hide-and-seek game in the braids of his beard. As I last saw him, his impassive expression betrayed nothing.

He whistled once, and a male scalc I hadn't yet seen appeared.

"Ale for the table. And bring out that boar I know Cook is hoarding."

At least he was willing to listen. We waited in silence until the scalc returned with cups and a pitcher of ale, all while sweat dotted my forehead and palms. Not until a platter of roasted boar appeared on the table did he speak again.

"Apologies for your reception." He tore off a hunk of cold meat and indicated for us to join him. "My wife is ill, and we had to send most of the village scalcs to deal with this inventory business. It would appear Arminius doesn't quite have the full trust of his superiors he claimed."

That morsel of bait fell between us. I hardly tasted the seasoned boar as I chewed, nor the ale I washed it all down with. This was exactly the sort of politicking and dissembling at which I was terrible. Just awful. Give me a sword and tell me who my enemy is. Tell me what needs to get done and I will do it. But this? Verbal games, truths packed into lies designed to test each other? It went against my nature.

Was he gauging my loyalty to Arminius? No, my presence here attested to the fact that I had none. Perhaps it wasn't a test at all, and I was reading too much into his words. My footing was uncertain here.

"It's not surprising," I said. "No matter what titles they bestow on us, they will always view us as barbarians first."

"Perhaps, perhaps not. The Gauls are happy enough, aren't they?"

"We're not Gauls."

His face lit with a smile. "No, we are not Gauls. So, you're here to make me choose between you, an untested woman whose father and chief I know for a fact remains loyal to Rome, and Arminius, the Cherusci turned Roman who may be plotting to fuck us all in the end?"

Yes, that about summed it up.

"She's been tested plenty," Levin said, sitting forward and driving his forefinger into the table as he made his point. "She's been fighting since she was a girl, and our tribe would fall apart without her. Segestes may be our chief, but Thusnelda is the one they all turn to. They'll go with her."

My chest swelled with affection. Levin had never said anything like this before, and I warmed all over with the knowledge that he appreciated all I did. There was at least one family member who *liked* me. Segestes loved me, I knew that, but in a strangled way. His love was tempered by the fact that he didn't understand me. He wished

I was something else, a biddable and compliant daughter. Wout and Lennart… I shuddered at the thought.

"Does he speak true?" Deudorix asked.

I lifted my chin. "He does. I can't promise you all the Cherusci will follow me, but most will. Much the same as your tribe, I'd imagine."

"We are free people." He raised his cup, and Levin and I did the same thing. After we took our drinks, he said, "I don't know about this business, though. You and Arminius raising competing armies for the same purpose. Don't mistake me, you seem capable and had you come to me first, I would have joined with you. But you can't raise two confederations at the same time. Why not join with him?"

My teeth ground. "As you said, he can't fulfill his promises. He doesn't have the trust of his leaders, and frankly, he doesn't have the trust of our people."

Deudorix shrugged a big shoulder. "I'm not so sure about that last part. He's got a fire to him other warriors like. And we need someone the Romans like, which Varus seems to, even if these other officers don't. I just don't know. I'll tell you this: Nothing you just said can't be resolved by you and I joining with him. He doesn't have to be the war chief, only the man on the inside. What do you say?"

I didn't know what to say. Prior to coming here, I thought there were two likely outcomes: Deudorix embraced me and we supplanted Arminius' ill-formed plot, or Deudorix chased me out of his territory himself.

When I failed to respond, he stood from the table. "Think on it. You're welcome to stay the night here."

We bid him goodnight, and when we rode out the next day, I still didn't have an answer for him.

——————➤

Konrada's brother, Ualter, returned to the village with the other arrestees, along with a small coterie of Germani auxiliaries hungry for a good meal and a break from their training. The more seasoned auxiliaries hailed from a few tribes to the south of us, and they kept weather eyes on the new recruits.

They only had two days before they had to return to the main body of the ala, so I corralled Konrada with me to help prepare a feast in celebration of their return. She followed at my heels, chattering and eager no matter what task I put before her, including cleaning fish. When Segestes grumbled about the extra resources our impromptu feast called for, I assured him I would personally see to it that the best fishers hauled in extra for drying. Dried fish was often the only meat we consumed throughout the winter.

I was helping the cooks haul bread from the ovens when Ualter himself found me.

"Princess." He bobbed his head and looked anywhere but directly at me.

"Ualter."

His cheeks turned a ruddy pink, making him appear far younger than his almost twenty summers.

"Can I talk to you? Um, outside?"

This should be interesting. I couldn't remember a single time he and I had ever spoken privately. I dusted my hands off on my tunic—it was soiled, anyway—and led the way out of the sweltering kitchen house, then down a path between buildings until we emerged alongside a spelt field. The green shoots stood a few feet high and swayed lazily in the breeze. No one could sneak up on us out here, or lurk around a corner and listen.

He swept a hand out to the tops of the plants and chewed the inside of his cheek.

"Well?" I folded my arms across my chest.

"I know, um, it's just..."

"Wodan's sake, spit it out." Frankly, I expected more of a backbone from the man who so brazenly tried to steal from a Roman supply store.

"I thought you should know that Arminius is planning something, against the legions."

He surprised me, but not for the reason he likely expected to surprise me. Either Arminius was feeling out potential traitors in the ala or word had spread quickly. Too quickly.

"Yes, I've heard this."

His face fell with the disappointment unique to children when you aren't nearly as excited about what they have to say as they were expecting.

"Oh. All right. I just thought, you'd, I don't know, want to talk to him or something. Maybe you could get our tribe committed to the cause."

My eyebrows shot up. May the gods spare me from another man suggesting I work with Arminius.

"He already approached me." Ualter didn't need to know more than that, especially if he ran right back to Arminius.

That crestfallen look on his face unfortunately brightened at this news. "Excellent. I knew you'd be with us. Will you be going with him next week, then? He's going to try to get the Mattiaci on his side while we're there doing our inventory."

Despite my effort to remain cool and detached, a smile stretched my lips.

Not only did I now know where Arminius was off to next, but I also had an unwitting informant among Arminius' own troops.

Chapter 9

The barbarians were adapting themselves to Roman ways,
were becoming accustomed to hold markets, and were meeting
in peaceful assemblages. (Cassius Dio)

Cooking up a fresh excuse to visit yet another tribe took the collective efforts of Levin, Jotapa, and me. Since the Mattiaci were known for their smiths, we decided I was desperately in need of a wedding gift for Reimar, something more than the traditional weapons. Something only a Mattiaci artisan could create.

The corners of Segestes' eyes had crinkled in suspicion at my sudden interest in my betrothed, but his desire for me to be that kind of daughter overrode his better sense.

We arrived almost two days after Arminius. Fortunately, all appearances suggested he hadn't yet cornered Foldruff, their chief.

Unlike the chaos that ensued in our village when the Romans conducted their annual inventory of our crops, animals, and textiles, the Mattiaci ran like a smooth river, unencumbered by boulders and felled trees. It was a sight to behold, watching the villagers and Romans working together, laughing and smiling.

Most Cherusci simply endured these encounters. I watched an elder Mattiaci woman with a delighted grin on her face carting a jug of ale to sweaty legionaries who raised their cups in toast to her.

The Mattiaci were a lost cause.

As soon as we arrived, I sent Jotapa to talk to a few of the smiths and kept Levin with me. Whether I liked it or not, some chiefs preferred dealing with a man. The best option we had was to pay our proper respects to Foldruff and his family and leave at first light. Hopefully we'd avoid Arminius as much as possible.

Just as I considered the best ways to avoid him, the man himself stepped into our path, a thunderous scowl set into the lines of his face.

"What are you doing here?"

I tipped my chin. "It's none of your concern."

"I beg to differ." His hand shot out to my biceps when I moved to step around him. Sparks ignited where his calloused palm held my bare arm, a shock of awareness I didn't want to acknowledge. At the same time, I heard Levin unsheathe his sword behind us. Arminius' grip relaxed, but he didn't get out of our way.

"Oh no," he said with a dark chuckle. "You don't get to do this. You turned me down, remember? The agreement was, if you turn me down, you stay out of my way. You don't get to—"

"I have no memory of actually agreeing—"

"—run around, creating more problems-"

Levin cleared his throat. Loudly.

We stopped talking at each other long enough to see Foldruff lumbering our way, along with a collection of large warriors. Without needing to be told, Levin tucked his blade back into its sheath. The last thing we wanted to do was present ourselves as a threat.

Foldruff eyed Levin and me. "You must be the Cherusci I heard about. You really came all this way for some wedding trinkets?"

A noise choked out of Arminius. He smothered it with a cough.

"Yes," I said, pasting on my most vapid smile. "I've always admired Mattiaci jewelry and thought I could get Reimar a little something extra."

Satisfied I was no more interesting than a puffy cloud, he har-rumphed then turned his attention to Arminius.

"You had something to show me?" he asked.

Arminius' eyes flicked to me, and I was pleased to see the muscle in his jaw twitch. It was an obvious tell.

"Yes, my optio found a few things near your burial ground. If you wouldn't mind..." He held out his arm, indicating Foldruff should lead the way into their wald. Away from prying eyes, I knew. The sun was beginning its downward journey, turning the wald into a forest of shadows where anyone or anything might hide.

More than a dozen men accompanied Foldruff, seasoned fighters by the look of them. I didn't know how many Arminius had waiting in those woods, but it had to be fewer than this Mattiaci war band.

Foldruff harrumphed again. "I thought you might say something like that. Very well, let's get this over with."

"Actually, my brother and I came that way," I said without thinking. "I'd love to see whatever it is they're so worried about. Just in case there are deficiencies in our burial grounds, as well."

I swear I heard a vein burst in Arminius' forehead. Folduff merely shrugged and marched away, surrounded by warriors and clearly aware of what was coming.

"That's not—" Arminius began.

"Let them come," Foldruff called over his shoulder. "Unless you have a problem with Cherusci witnesses?"

He left Arminius with no choice but to step aside and allow us to follow.

➤

"Want to tell me what the fuck we're doing out here?" Foldruff crossed his arms and glared at Arminius.

Five. Arminius had five men, including Berut and Ermin, waiting among the small cairns where the Mattiaci interred the ashes and bones of their fallen. Foldruff had brought nearly twenty.

When this confrontation inevitably splintered into violence, I had no idea whose side Levin and I would defend. The Mattiaci weren't ever going to be our allies, but Arminius was a madman bent on leading us into disaster. At least that's what I kept telling myself. It was far better than entrusting my and my people's future to such an unreliable figure.

My skin tingled in anticipation of the fight to come. Arminius had to know after two days with the Mattiaci that they were a lost cause. Nothing would sway them from Roman loyalty. Two days with them, and he was still committed to this course, and only brought five men?

Arminius had the audacity to grin instead of answering Foldruff.

The man was a menace against whom I was ill prepared.

Foldruff grumbled something in the Mattiaci dialect, too low for me to parse, and his men grumbled back. Each among them had his hand on a weapon. Tension cramped around my lungs.

Arminius had chosen their meeting place well—a stone cliff at their backs at the base of a narrow draw, and the cairns provided an excuse to draw the Mattiaci from the relative safety of their village.

"What couldn't be discussed in my home?" Folduff rested one hand on his thick leather belt and the other atop the pommel of his sword, a gladius. The Roman weapon. Goosebumps rippled down my arms.

Arminius removed his helmet and passed it back to an auxiliary. "How do you envision the future of our people?"

Folduff thumbed the pommel of his gladius. "Future? Only more of the prosperity and security of Rome, Equestrian. My people quite enjoy good food, money, an end to raids and tribal wars." He paused and pulled his lips into a smile neither warm nor friendly. "Not sure why you couldn't ask me this over a meal this evening. We're all Romans now, just like you."

How many of his people disappeared into the Roman slave machine? How many faced crucifixion? How long would it be before the tribe vanished entirely, supplanted by Romans whose predecessors once called themselves Mattiaci? In this, at least, Arminius and I agreed.

A spear would be nice. This needed to end immediately and permanently. The Mattiaci stood to ruin everything.

Often worse than the fight itself is waiting for the fight, though this case might prove otherwise. The question of which side I'd defend answered itself. Either I fought with Arminius, or I ran like a coward. I'd never run from a fight in my life.

"I'm no Roman," Arminius said. A menace and a fool, still convinced he'd win this with words. Or was he? His cheeks twitched with a suppressed smile. His chest rose and fell beneath his armor faster than normal. He wanted a fight. For reasons that eluded me, he wanted this fight.

A spear, a bow, and a full quiver would make me feel much, much better. Without needing to tell him, Levin inched closer to Arminius' group and I followed. For good or ill, the best chance we had for escaping this situation was with them.

The Mattiaci men tensed when Arminius stepped closer to Folduff. "Do you care so little about your nation's freedom? Your own identity?"

Folduff threw his head back and guffawed. "Boy, the future is Rome. You are a suicidal fool to imagine otherwise. What are you going to do?" Folduff tracked Levin's and my shift toward Arminius' men and his lip curled in disgust. "Your eight against all these men, seasoned warriors who've been butchering jumped up shits like you since before you were born?"

Arminius turned to share a grin with Berut. Menaces and madmen, all of them.

"I'll tell you what," Arminius said. "I'll let one live, so he can tell the others what happens when you cross me."

Like everyone else in the clearing, I tightened my grip on my weapon. Without shifting my gaze, I observed the closest target, a big lout, scarred in the face and arms. It wouldn't be a pretty fight, so I'd make it a quick one.

He watched me openly, smirking and licking his lips. On second thought, perhaps I'd make it a slow fight.

"That's what I thought." Folduff huffed. His nose twitched, drawing his lips up a fraction to bare his teeth. With a roar, he lunged for Arminius. I paused long enough to witness Arminius spin out of the way and slit the next closest man clean across his belly, taking both men by surprise.

The clearing erupted. I ducked a wild swipe from the lout. Earlier rain had left the earth slick, so I slid to my knees and cut him across his inner thigh as momentum carried me to the next man.

I pushed back up to my feet just in time to parry his attack. My bones rattled with the impact of blade against blade. The coppery tang of blood hit my nostrils, and I sucked the scent in deep, letting it fuel the fire in my blood.

I spent my days managing a household and village, solving everyone's problems. Since I was nine I'd learned to some degree of basic competency nearly every skill required to keep the village alive, from cooking and sewing to gelding horses and field dressing prey after a hunt. But fighting was what I did best. Fighting made my blood sing. Fighting narrowed the world down to one simple problem: I live or I die. Nothing more than the fight to survive.

We exchanged ringing blows, and a meaty hand fisted into my hair and tossed me backward. I rolled in the mud and looked up to see the lout and another man advancing on me.

Shit.

I clenched my free hand in the mud and hurled a glob of muck into the lout's face, dancing out of reach of the other man. The lout's leg wound bled profusely, but in the heat of a fight, he hadn't noticed yet.

The lessons I'd been driving into Konrada repeated themselves in my mind. *Be smart. Choose your targets. You are small and they are big. You are strong and they are stronger. It will never be a fair fight.*

I feinted back to the lout, narrowly avoiding the other man's sword. The lout swiped furiously at his face. While he did that, I dove in for the kill, ramming my sword into his belly.

With a mighty heave, I twisted the blade side vertically, then yanked the weapon up as far as it would go before it stopped against his sternum, before withdrawing.

He didn't scream for long before collapsing.

Sweat dripped into my eyes. My arms and legs burned from exertion. The other man ran at me with a mighty howl. There was no time to be tired.

Another man crashed into him, and they tumbled in a tangle of limbs and cursing. I rushed forward and cleaved my attacker between his shoulder and his neck while he struggled to untangle himself from his compatriot.

The compatriot regained his footing and kneed me in the chest and gut while I struggled to remove my sword. The blow knocked the breath from my lungs and drove me to my hands and knees.

He didn't stop there. His fist glanced across my cheek. The force of it sent my vision dancing. One moment, I had my hands and knees supporting me. The next, my face was in the mud.

Then I was flipped onto my back, all while blackness encroached and the sound of the battle faded behind a high-pitched humming noise in my ears.

How utterly foolish, to die before our grand rebellion.

His sword flashed in the shifting light and shadows. I reached for the dagger in my boot, the same one I'd carried since I was nine, the same one Arminius had first put in my hands and told me it was my last resort, the same one I'd never stopped carrying, even now. I had half a heartbeat to wonder why I clung to it before the sword came down.

It never made contact with my dagger. I blinked against the sweat and mud, and Arminius was there, holding the man's sword near the base in one hand and backhanding him with the other. More mud blurred my vision. No, not mud, the sweet oblivion of unconsciousness.

"Answer me! Are you all right?" Arminius shouted, and I winced, yanked back into the world of the living by his voice and arms. He cradled me against his chest, holding me in a way I hadn't been held since before Mama died. Between the rush of the fight and my near-miss with a premature end, being held by Arminius did something strange to my heart. It was too much.

"I'm fine." I wiggled to find my own feet, but he only held me tighter. The quiet around us indicated that the fight was over, yet he wouldn't let me go.

When he finally set me down, he didn't release me. Instead, his busy hands went to work patting me from the top of my head to my boots, even turning me around for a complete visual inspection. Everywhere his left hand touched left a smear of blood. He brushed a thumb against my cheek, and I hissed at the sting. He dropped his hand abruptly, but only long enough to pull me back into his arms.

"I saw you on the ground and I thought..."

"I had the situation completely under control." I briefly squirmed in protest, then stilled. One big hand coasted up and down my back. The sensation was so unfamiliar, so shockingly pleasant, I had no choice but to let myself feel it.

He laughed, and this time, the sound was genuine.

"I got four. How many did you get?"

I narrowed my eyes and glanced around the clearing. My head cleared enough to remember Levin had accompanied me. Amid the mess of bodies, Levin was fine, merrily collecting plunder in true Germani fashion. As far as I could tell, all of Arminius' men were fine. He chose his compatriots well, I reluctantly admitted to myself.

He chose allies well and risked losing his hand to save me. The realization coalesced with enough force to knock me back a step. I snatched for his left hand, but he held it out of reach and stepped back into my space, catching me by the waist with his good hand, lest I stumble again.

"Just a scratch," he said. "It's nothing."

"It's not nothing. You could have lost your hand. You say you want to lead a rebellion, and then you throw it all away to save one woman."

He let out a slow breath and shook his head. "You aren't just one woman to me, and you damn well know it."

"Why?" I stared up at him, searching for the truth. It didn't make sense. We barely knew each other. I was working against him. He had to know that.

His forehead furrowed. "It's always been you, don't you know that? Fuck, you just fought by my side when we both know you didn't want to. That's who you are, and that's why I want you at my side for what's to come." He held his good hand out to me. "Ride with me. We'll talk this out, and I'll get you back in the morning."

It wasn't sensible. It wasn't right. And I didn't want to be anywhere else than with him.

I took his hand.

⟶

Though Levin didn't voice his questions, I watched the play of suspicion and concern when I left on Arminius' horse. The fight was over, and explaining myself to Levin joined the mountain of other problems, concerns, and potential catastrophes I faced.

Arminius and his men didn't leave any survivors in those woods. Berut assumed command of the inventory team and intended to corroborate Arminius' story that Foldruff and the others attacked unprovoked. An assassination attempt on two Roman and ala officers not only justified the killings, it also eviscerated the Mattiaci's precious relationship with Rome.

I clung to Arminius' back on the ride out, letting each catastrophe turn over in my head, not the least of which was a newfound discomfort in the back of my mind over killing so many fellow Germani in an effort to liberate the very same people. That discomfort fought its own battle against my newfound comfort with Arminius, though I reasoned his saving my life at great personal risk to himself went a long way toward that end.

We stopped before the sun set fully and night made riding too dangerous. When we dismounted, we fell into a rhythm setting up camp as though we'd done it a hundred times before. After doffing his armor, he erected a small Roman tent while I dug out a fire pit and got a small blaze going. He produced a waterskin, which I promptly used to wipe the dried mud from my exposed skin, and a sack of field rations before settling next to me. When he offered the skin across his body instead of using his injured hand, I batted the skin away and tugged his wrist before he could snatch it out of reach again.

I sucked in a breath at the depth of the still oozing wound. "This isn't a scratch. This needs stitches."

Without waiting for him to argue or agree, I stood and dug through his saddle bags until I found a small medical kit. Thankfully, he didn't put up a fight when I settled back next to him and took his injured hand. His whole body tensed, but he held himself in place as I poured water on the wound to flush out any detritus.

"Use that next." He indicated a small clay bottle that, when I unstoppered it, contained a foul smelling liquid. At my grimace, he said, "It cleans better than water alone. You only need a little. Use one of the—"

I pulled a clean rag from his kit and poured out just enough of the liquid to saturate one corner. This time, he hissed through his teeth when I made contact with the deep cut. Once clean, I was relieved to see it hadn't gone all the way to bone. It still needed stitches.

Next came the hook-shaped bone needle and thread. I paused before pressing the needle through his skin and looked up to find his attention focused solely on me, not the painful thing I was about to do to his hand.

"Ready?" My question came out in a whisper, which made no sense. There was no need to whisper.

"I trust you."

I almost dropped the needle. As simple as that, he trusted me? Then again, he'd shown me his trust already, when he let me see his plot in action. When he didn't kill me for refusing to join him.

He risked his hand, and thus his rebellion, for me, and he trusted me. My hands shook until his good hand covered mine.

"It's all right, Thusnelda."

I couldn't look at him. With one last squeeze of my hands, he released me and I began stitching. I made each stitch as quickly as possible, with a care toward keeping them even and tight to minimize his scarring. Throughout it all, he kept still and quiet. When I was done, he produced a knife to shear off the excess thread before I rubbed a cool salve over the wound and wrapped his palm in a clean bandage.

"Thank you," he spoke quietly.

"It's nothing." I repacked his medical kit and returned it to his saddle bags. There weren't adequate words to express how his saving me made me feel. My stomach churned and my lungs constricted against the swell of emotion. For the second time, Arminius had saved my life. But when everything went to the underworld—and it would, I knew—would he again disappear, this time forever lost to Rome?

When he cleared his throat, I realized I was standing over his saddle-bags, staring at nothing.

"We should talk," he said.

I returned to my seat, happy for an excuse to watch the fire instead of face him. "We should."

Arminius cleared his throat. "I know you've gone to the Chatti. I know you want this rebellion as much as I do. Why won't you work with me?"

Hot shame poured over my flesh like candle wax. I'd never once in my life felt shame for taking matters into my own hands and resolving difficulties myself. For the first time I wondered if this well-honed habit was a shortcoming, rather than the blessing I'd always assumed it was.

"I." My throat clenched. "I don't know you. The people don't know you. If you can't fulfill your promises, then we'll all suffer for it."

As soon as the words spat from my lips, I wished to take them back. Not because I suddenly disbelieved them, rather because for the first time since his return, I didn't want to hurt him. He not only trusted me, he cared about me. In the heat of battle, he chose me over his cause, over even himself.

I didn't trust him to lead this rebellion, but I trusted him with myself. There were few about whom I felt the same.

"Then join me. Be my ally. Fuck, be my partner. I have the intelligence on Rome, you have the local clout. Together we will get the tribes. We'll be unstoppable."

Saying yes to him held all the ease and terror of stepping off a cliff. It was a free fall into the unknown, and I did not deal in the unknown.

"Look at me." He smoothed a hand over my cheek and turned my head until I was forced to obey. In fairness, I didn't fight him. "I know you don't trust me. I accept that. I'm asking you to give me a chance. Work with me. Let me show you what we can do together. We can sever Rome's hold here. We can make it so they never come back. No more Germani have to die to feed that beast."

Hadn't I thought of Rome in the same terms? Arminius was uniquely skilled in saying all the right things, and it was this very skill that made me the most nervous.

"If, *if*," I emphasized when his entire being brightened, "I agree, then I have terms. I require complete honesty from you at all times."

He nodded eagerly. "I will never lie to you."

"And we will make choices together or not at all. You will not take action without first consulting me, and I'll afford you the same courtesy."

His lips pursed. "That's fine for some things, but you and I can't be together all the time. There will be issues that arise that need an immediate decision."

"Then we have to agree on basic values going forward. For instance, I don't like that you killed all those Mattiaci today, and I suspect you knew all along what would happen once you confronted Foldruff. That's no way to win allies, and what is the point of fighting for the Germani if we're busy killing everyone who doesn't agree with us?"

"I don't think I'll have to do that again." He frowned. "I don't like it, either, but I've helped Rome quell rebellions. I've seen firsthand what inter-tribal conflict does to a rebellion. Any who refuse to join us need to fear us enough to keep their mouths shut. Unfortunately for the Mattiaci, their leaders like running their mouths to Varus."

This topic bore more discussion, but not tonight.

"Very well. About honesty, before I agree to anything, I need you to tell me why you've been so bent on my partnership. I know you didn't suggest we should marry because you fell in love with me when I was a child."

His head cocked to the side and he half-smiled.

"You're almost right. In the spirit of total honesty, I think having you as my wife would solidify my reputation among the Germani. But

Thusnelda, I like you. My first impression of who you are now was that you stood against a small patrol and killed three of them before they subdued you. That's my kind of woman. I like your sharp tongue and the fact that in a sparring match, I'm pretty sure you could beat me at least half the time. I like ruffling your feathers when you get too serious. I like that I can trust you to be serious when the situation calls for it. I like that you still wander the woods when you need space. I can't imagine a better queen at my side."

If I hadn't been watching his eyes, I wouldn't have believed him. Arminius believed every word he spoke. He truly felt this way.

My face warmed and not from the fire. No man had ever spoken to me like this.

"Easy." He caught my hand before I bolted. "No need to run, I won't push anything. I like you so much, I'm not even going to insist we share that tiny tent tonight, even though the idea delights me. I don't know where you're going to sleep, but it won't be with me in there, that's for sure."

A laugh burst from me and he grinned.

"By all the gods, would you look at that?" He traced a finger over the curve of my cheek. "When she isn't thinking about kicking my ass, I can make her laugh. Good for me."

I slapped his hand away but kept laughing. A weight lifted from my shoulders. I didn't know if trusting him, even this little bit, was the right decision. I only knew that I felt better than I had in weeks.

"Don't push your luck," I said. "I can start kicking your ass right now for that tent."

He groaned and licked his lips. "Don't tease me."

When I shoved at his shoulder, he didn't move at all. "Well? Do you agree to my terms or not?"

"That depends."

"On?"

"If I kiss you, will you stab me?" He held up his hands in defense before I replied. "Just a kiss. I have an extra bedroll, and I swear on my uncle's life I will sleep out here by the fire all night and push for nothing more."

A kiss, another cliff to step off into the unknown. Reimar never asked me for a kiss. The Marsi warrior I'd once given myself to had kissed like a sloppy wet fish. Something told me Arminius would be better than that. He was no fumbling boy.

Just a kiss weighed against the rest of my life with a man who promised to never love me. That wasn't so much to ask, to take for myself.

"Very well," I said. "I will not stab or otherwise harm you if you kiss me."

His laugh was warm and intimate, something just for us. "Exactly what I've always wanted to hear."

Our laughter died as he leaned in, still smiling ear to ear like a little boy who'd found a prize. My heart thundered the way it did before a battle. I was really going to let him kiss me.

His nose brushed mine, then his lips ghosted over mine, the faintest touch. His good hand snaked behind my neck and our lips fully met. My breath stalled. The mere meeting of our mouths set my skin aflame. When he deepened the kiss, tugged my bottom lip between his teeth until I gasped, I became an inferno. My hands curled into his tunic, and he groaned into my mouth. I gasped again and his tongue found mine. After a little coaxing, I returned the gesture with strokes of my own.

After almost fifteen years of waiting, I was at last kissing Ermin.

I froze. Ermin. Arminius. A boy swearing he'd come back for me only to disappear. A man promising me the world, a thing he couldn't possibly give.

Jerking free from his embrace, I stumbled to my feet.

"I... we... Don't do that again."

Blindly, I ensconced myself in his tent, leaving him gaping in my wake.

A long while later, he said, "Goodnight, Thusnelda." No sounds came from him after that.

Sleep eluded me for hours. I'd stepped off a cliff and was still falling.

Chapter 10

*A race without either natural or acquired cunning, they
disclose their hidden thoughts in the freedom of the festivity.
(Tacitus)*

The fall harvest provided a unique opportunity to meet with our allies during Haustblot. Once a year, we gathered for a month to trade our respective hauls: anything grown, raised, crafted over the spring and summer. Nights were for celebrations. Each tribe established their own encampments in the open fields we'd used for generations, taking a month to live as one people free from the conflicts that often separated us.

Reimar was to be here. Every time I thought of him now, my mind turned right to Arminius' kiss. True to his word, he'd left me unmolested the rest of the night and talked of nothing but the rebellion the rest of the way back to my village. The only hint that our relationship had changed was the way his hands lingered on my waist when I dismounted.

His voice had been husky when he promised to see me soon, at Haustblot.

Well, Haustblot was here, and I caught myself looking forward to seeing Arminius, despite the way his kiss had been too much, too overwhelming, and I'd given too much of myself. A voice whispered in the back of my mind that there was still so much more to give, a greater distance yet to fall.

I didn't look forward to meetings with Reimar, few as they were. He didn't make me feel simultaneously peaceful and burning. I didn't crave his touch. I couldn't imagine lying with him. It was Arminius' damned fault these thoughts plagued me at all.

Dispassion carved a gulf between Reimar and I. Our conversations centered on duties and expectations, nothing more. He politely rebuffed my attempts to learn him better and made no attempt of his own to learn me. He made it plain that he didn't want *me*, per se, just a wife.

Though I might never trust Arminius, though his passion might be a facade to gain my cooperation, I would never be just his wife, the woman responsible for his house and children. If our fragile agreement held, he and I were going to lead a revolution together.

I could be so much more than a wife. So much more than one tribe's doting queen.

Images of a life far bigger than I'd ever considered for myself followed my every action as we spent the day constructing our camps outside the trading space.

Since this site had been used for generations, it had long ago been beaten into a flat expanse of grasslands. The unencumbered wind meant tents had to be staked in deep. A wide river bordered the eastern edge of the land, but otherwise a featureless expanse stretched into the horizon.

Jotapa said this was how her mother had described their homeland. I imagined the roving bands of horsemen, wild and free on land like this. The grass was their sea, their mounts were their fleet, and the entire world was open to them. Older warriors spoke of the horse people with reverence. The horse tribes were rumored to be magnificent in combat. That Jotapa and her mother had been taken at all was unusual.

She told me, with secret smiles and wistful eyes, of whole bands composed solely of women. They wandered the plains, raiding and warring like the men, and were feared for their viciousness. She said they never took husbands, only lovers, and gave their boy children back to their lovers, who happily raised sturdy sons.

What a glorious life, never worrying about marriage arrangements and placating fickle male pride. Once Jotapa purchased her freedom, she and I might go together, find one of those bands, and live out our lives in ultimate freedom. I could walk away from Segestes and Reimar without ever looking back. The very thought made me miss Levin. And Arminius... this time, I'd be the one to disappear.

Nothing could make me walk away from my people. The Romans leached our lifeblood away year by year and pushed to consume us whole.

There was no word about whether or not the Mattiaci would take part this year. They had to be hungry for vengeance, and the festivals provided ample opportunity to call Arminius and I out in public. It was their word against ours.

I shook off the thoughts. If I wasn't careful, my fears and worries tended to drown me.

With Sunna and Donar at my heels, I sought Wiltrud. Arminius had his way of sussing out allies, but I had ideas a man might never consider. Ideas a man used to being in command might dismiss without ever seeing the results. If Wiltrud agreed, I'd honor my terms with Arminius and tell him my plans.

I found her outside her family's tent, directing her scalcs. When she saw me, her smile was so warm, guilt stabbed me in the chest. What I had done with Arminius, what I still wanted to do, betrayed her son and the motherly affection she showed me. That Reimar didn't mind what happened before our wedding was irrelevant.

She opened her arms and hugged me close. Reimar might never hug me. This aspect of marrying Reimar came with the mother I'd lost so many years ago.

"You're looking lovely." She smoothed a hand over my hair. "Are you here for my son?"

I shook my head. "No, I was looking for you actually."

She looped an arm through mine and guided me inside their tent. "What can I do for you?"

I bid the dogs sit outside before entering. A low fire burned in the center of the space, surrounded by soft furs and bedding. More furs and hides hung against the tent walls to ward off the fall chill. She set a stone kettle over the fire to heat water.

"I'd like to meet with the other queens and princesses, any woman of influence, especially from the tribes we haven't approached yet; the Bructeri, the Chauci, the Suebi. I'd like to contact the Marsi, the Usipetti, the Angrivarii, Tencteri, everyone."

She fetched two cups and a flagon of cider before settling herself before the fire. I followed only once she was seated comfortably. If she noticed my rambling, she didn't comment on it.

"The Suebi will be tricky," she said. "There aren't many left after the first Caesar. But the others I can corral. What do you have in mind?"

I thought of the scene in the forest with the Mattiaci. Arminius' method had merit—those who resisted met the sword, leaving no witnesses to counter his word, only the suspicions of the tribe. There had to be a better way, however, then massacring any who rejected his offer. There had to be a way to ease them into the idea, to plant the seeds of friendship. Something less murderous.

"I want to feel out their minds on the Roman invasion, perhaps encourage them to our way of thinking."

She poured us each a portion of cider topped with hot water. "Smart. The wives bend the husbands' ears. But you still need more. Our people respect strength."

"What do you have in mind?" I unconsciously echoed her earlier question, sipping at the cider and wishing she hadn't watered it down.

"A contest. Let them see you and Reimar's strength for themselves."

A contest. A series of fights without weapons. It wasn't out of the question and often happened during Haustblot. We all enjoyed the show, and the winner enjoyed the glory of besting the strongest tribesmen from across the land.

Another pang of guilt hit me squarely in the chest. I meant to tell Reimar as soon as I saw him. After the case I made for not trusting Arminius, my change of heart surely appeared flighty. To make that change, wait to tell him, and tell his mother first? That was an insult of the highest order. Lying to her was out of the question, however.

I cleared my throat. "I meant to bring this up to Reimar earlier, but I haven't seen him. I've reconsidered my position on leaving Arminius out of this rebellion."

She hummed and checked the water. Satisfied with its rolling boil, she moved the pot from the fire and dropped in a sachet of herbs.

"I'm not surprised," she said when she settled back into her cushioned seat. "Honestly, I was shocked you wanted to cut him out in the first place. He has access to Varus and control over the auxiliaries."

When she put it like that, it sounded silly. There wasn't an easy way to explain my instinct to run from him. He represented a danger I couldn't define, more so now that I knew how easily his kiss charged right over all my better judgment.

He hadn't arrived yet, but he would. Varus had sent cohorts to monitor this event for the past two years, a little reminder of their power and presence when we gathered en masse. Arminius wouldn't miss a chance to convene with this many chieftains at once, nor would he shirk an opportunity to put his strength on display.

"I'll let you tell Reimar. Regardless, I think you've made the right call, and I believe the three of you will raise an army unlike anything they've seen." She raised her cup in a toast. "To the end of Rome."

"To the end of Rome." I finished my cup.

She took another sip and refilled my cup without the hot water this time.

"I've been reading runes for you," she said.

When she didn't elaborate, I swirled the cider in my cup and said, "Oh?"

"I always get the same answer. I admit I wish I didn't, so I keep trying again."

We weren't getting anywhere at this rate. I put little faith in runes and bones, the flights of crows, or the guts of sheep, but clearly Wiltrud did, and she saw something she didn't like.

She set her drink down and folded her hands in her lap. "You have a choice to make, Thusnelda. Down one road is obscurity, a quiet life and after your children's children pass, you will fade from memory. No one will tell your story."

"And the other?"

Her lips pressed downward before she spoke. "Your life will be hard and unforgiving and short, but no one will ever forget your name."

Everything inside me stilled.

"Does Reimar wish to withdraw his alliance?" I asked.

She chuckled and shook her head. "No, of course not. This isn't some backward way of telling you something like that. You have our unwavering support, no matter what you choose."

"What are these two paths?"

"I'm not sure. I want grandchildren, and my son has been terribly remiss in that duty. Since his first wife, Irmhild, died, he hasn't been the same. I suspect the path you want to choose, which is why these runes make me sad."

This is why I didn't care for fortune telling. The reader always posed more questions than answers. It had something to do with marrying Reimar, though I didn't know what and it left me unsettled. A short, hard life and renown, or a long, happy life and obscurity. The latter offered more appeal, and I couldn't envision ever choosing renown over happiness.

I left her tent before Reimar arrived, relieved to not see him yet, unsure how he was going to take it when I revealed our new alliance with Arminius. The sun shined freely here, where acres and acres of forest didn't surround us, warming my skin despite the crisp air.

Wiltrud believed a question hung in the air over my marriage to her son, and I feared that question aligned with my own fear: Arminius.

The gods conspired to make my day worse when Wout and Lennart cornered me on my way back to our tents. They fell into step alongside me, and Wout threw a beefy arm over my shoulders to steer me away from the tents. To an observer, I appeared the recipient of brotherly affection.

The force of Wout's grip and our direction away from prying eyes and ears into the nearest tree line suggested otherwise.

"Send them away." Lennart kicked out a leg at Sunna and Donar nipping at his heels.

That was the last thing I wanted to do, but I also didn't want them hurt. With a quick command and flattened hand gesture, they dropped to their bellies. I heard them whining in our wake.

Once inside the protective shade, he released me with a shove, and I stumbled to avoid the spiny leaves of a holly bush.

I whirled on him. "What is the matter with you?"

The words barely left my mouth before he lunged and snatched me by my hair. Lennart banded my arms behind my back. I struggled, but between the two of them, I was stuck. Unless I resorted to extreme violence. For all their faults, they were still my brothers.

"Now you listen, you little whore." Wout growled in my face, spraying drops of spittle against my skin. "You're going to keep your mouth shut and your legs closed until father marries you off at the end of the month."

I winced against further spit and his aspersions. Calling me a whore was a new low, even for him. From behind the screaming along my scalp, the painful twist of my shoulders, and a furious Wout, I heard it. Segestes wanted my wedding to happen within a matter of weeks. It was truly going to happen. My fight left me, and I sagged against Lennart.

"That's right." Wout's smile was more a baring of the teeth than an expression of happiness. "You're going to submit to this. While you're at it, you're going to stop running around like Arminius' little errand girl. You're going to explain to Reimar what we'll do to him if he stays this course, if he thinks he can betray Rome and ruin everything Father has worked for."

Lennart shook me, further wrenching my arms. "Do you understand?"

My breath hissed in and out of my nostrils against the blossoming pain. "That's what this is about? I should have known you'd—"

Wout backhanded me across the cheek. Since I didn't see dark spots or immediately lose consciousness, I knew he'd held back.

"You're done ruining things for our family," he whispered. "This is your only warning. If we see you with Arminius, you're going to spend the rest of the festival chained to a tent pole. If we hear any more about this rebellion, we'll kill your dogs and we'll kill your scalc."

I flexed my jaw. I'd be bruised by nightfall. "And our father is amenable to all this?"

Lennart leaned his face close to mine. "He's the one who told us to ensure you behave for the next month."

My eyes focused on the square repeating pattern of Wout's tunic. "Why do you hate me so much?"

Instead of answering, they abruptly released me.

"You do what we said, and there won't be any problems." Wout straightened his tunic, and they stalked away.

I sank into a crouch and laced my fingers together behind my aching scalp. Married by the end of the festival. Jotapa in danger if I proceeded with my plans. A threat to my damn dogs. All this because at some point two of my brothers decided I was to blame for everything that ever went wrong in our lives, from Mama's death to a tear in their trousers.

I was so damned tired of it.

———————➤

All good festivals started with music and libations, and Haustblot was no different. Our hospitality practices took a strange turn at this event, where everyone traveled, yet everyone played host to someone else. It made for a friendly gathering, regardless of tensions between tribes.

At the end of the first week, musicians assembled with their drums, horns, pipes, and even the odd stringed instruments favored by the southern tribes. With the musicians came the dancers and flagons of various drinks shared with abandon. Young warriors split into small groups to show off their sword dancing, an elaborate practice of juggling and tossing swords back and forth. A good sword dance displayed skill and bravery. A poor sword dance ended with dismemberment.

When the legionaries arrived with Varus, few looked at them askance. With the drinking, however, came more forgiving attitudes, particularly since one cohort was entirely composed of auxiliaries more than happy to take part in their favorite event of the year.

Arminius acknowledged me with a nod and nothing more. Though I understood his reticence, and most certainly did not want to run to him and purge the events of the last few days until he offered possible solutions, his impersonal brush off chafed. The bruise on my cheek was now a sickly green, almost more noticeable as it faded, and he hadn't so much as blinked.

What happened to the man who almost lost a hand defending me?

I brooded over taking my the incident with my brothers to Reimar. When I told him about my shifting allegiances, he took it in stride and accepted my easy lie about a sparring accident. I could tell him. I should tell him. As my intended, he ought to know about the brewing catastrophe that was my family.

However, I suspected two possible outcomes to telling him. The first was his intervention. He'd pull me into the Chatti fold immediately, maybe even force a marriage before the end of the month, and I wasn't ready yet. The idea of being married within days left me cold with terror.

Not yet, my mind rebelled.

The other outcome was his indifference. It was my problem, after all, and wouldn't be a problem as long as I avoided Arminius and let Reimar handle the rebellion. Not only did I reject outright the idea of anyone taking charge of this rebellion in my stead, but the idea of his indifference infuriated me.

Did I not deserve more than my husband's indifference? Instead of venting my anger over an imagined scenario, I avoided him altogether. Conveniently this meant I avoided Arminius, as well. I chose not to think about the fact that my self-imposed isolation played right into Wout and Lennart's hands.

Segestes kept himself out of our tents most days and late into the nights. When he did see me, he eyed me warily, harrumphed, and went about his business. Fine by me.

I couldn't hide myself away for the opening ceremonies, which is how I found myself trailing after a merry Jotapa on her way to hunt down Berut and Ermin. She'd declared an end to my sour mood and those men the cure, despite my numerous protestations. Where Berut and Ermin were, Arminius was sure to follow.

Ceremonial Roman armor—the sculpted bronze breastplates and silver pieces polished to a high shine—glinted in the firelight. I pulled to a stop, wrenching my hand free of hers.

"You go on," I shouted over the general din of a party. "I'll get us drinks."

"They have—"

I turned away before she argued that we could get drinks anywhere, from anyone. She'd gotten me away from the Cherusci tents. I made my appearance, might socialize a little, all as I worked my way back to those tents. A foolproof plan to avoid Arminius; namely being seen with Arminius.

I almost made it before a strong hand found the small of my back and gently urged me into the shadows between two cooking tents. It was almost louder here than near the musicians.

"Did you think you were going to avoid me all month?" Arminius said, just loud enough for me to hear him.

I shied away from his touch and looked around him. "Did anyone see you follow me?"

"Is that what this is about?" He brushed a thumb over my bruised cheek. "Who the fuck did this to you?"

The threat in his voice made me shudder. Somehow, he had the exact reaction I wanted. I wanted someone who not only gave one good damn about my welfare but could actually do something about it. Aside from subterfuge, Jotapa was nearly powerless. Levin walked a fine line between being a good brother to me and placating the rest of our family. Konrada was hardly more than a child. Reimar's casual acceptance of my lie told me he didn't truly care.

The one person I'd decided was unequivocally my enemy upon laying eyes on him was the only one who soothed the ragged edges worn into my nerves this week, while also shredding them further.

"Who saw you?" I repeated, ducking out of his reach. "If they saw you..."

I couldn't think about what my happen to my friend, or my dogs, for that matter. I would sacrifice them, if necessary, but I certainly didn't want to. Not if it could be avoided.

Arminius' eyes narrowed. "Who are you worried about? Did they do this to your face?"

"It's not your concern."

Fighting with him came so naturally, I wasn't sure how to not turn our every interaction into a confrontation.

He growled. The man actually growled in the shadows. "I don't know, damn it. I don't know if someone saw us, because I wasn't aware you were so concerned about being seen in public with me. Now tell me who the fuck hit you before I start beating it out of your brothers."

I must have flinched. He sucked in a breath. Through his teeth, he asked, "Which one? Wout? I'll kill him."

He turned to do just that, and I grabbed his wrist to stop him.

"No, I mean, yes," I admitted. "It was Wout and Lennart. But if you take retribution, they won't just punish me for it. They'll kill Jotapa."

"They won't do a damned thing if I slap them in chains and sell them to the lowest bidder."

"No." I yanked at his wrist when he tried to march away again. "They're doing what Segestes told them to do. You can't arrest all of them and...and they're my brothers. I know you don't understand it, but they're my brothers. I can't let you sell them."

Finally, he stilled. "I understand better than you might think."

Flavus, I remembered. His Roman brother. Of course he understood some part of my reluctance to hand my brothers over into slavery, no matter how they treated me.

"I will," he continued slowly, choosing each word with care, "leave them alone as long as they leave you alone. But hear me now: If they lay one more hand on you in anger, they're dead men."

Shadows turned the angles of his face into sharp edges, made to slice and kill.

"Thank you."

"They don't want you associating with me?"

I huffed. "As I told you months ago, Segestes knows what you're up to, and now they all know I've involved myself. They want me to keep my mouth shut, stay out of this mess, and marry Reimar at the end of Haustblot."

Arminius recoiled. "You're going to marry him now? Right now?"

"Not right this moment, no."

He grabbed me by the shoulders. "I'm being serious! You're to be married this month?"

"Yes."

His cursing punctuated the next several minutes. For those several minutes, I vacillated between shock at the vehemence of his reaction and smug satisfaction. Here was someone who appreciated my hesitation, even if his reasons had nothing in common with mine.

As if to prove the point, he whirled back and gathered me into his arms. My good cheek pressed into the cool, unforgiving metal of his ridiculous molded breastplate. A metal nipple tickled my skin.

"Don't. Don't marry him."

"I have no choice."

"Yes, you do. Marry me. I'll protect you. We'll raise an army. We'll conquer the world. I'll make you queen of Germania."

My breath froze, and I jerked back to look him in the eye despite the darkness. He'd said it before and in my rush to disbelieve him, I blocked it from my memories.

"You don't mean that."

"Yes, I do." His face sank closer to mine, so close his breath whispered against my lips.

These words were somehow more preposterous than his promise to free us all from Rome. Germania didn't have a king or queen. We didn't even have a single identity to rule. No one would support our rebellion if they thought he intended to make himself their king and me their queen.

"No. We need the Chatti, and we will lose them if I betray Reimar."

The excuse sounded weak to my own ears, but in the moment, tucked safely into his arms, with his lips and the promise of his mind-altering kisses so close, it was my last line of defense. As with the first time he'd said those things, I skipped right past the audacity of making me the queen of this whole region.

"Is that what you're telling yourself?" His lips danced too close to mine.

I pushed free of his embrace, and he let me go.

"You can't say things like that. No one will follow us if they think you mean to make us their sovereigns."

His laugh was low, warm, and only a touch bitter. "Whatever you need to tell yourself, princess. But I know you don't want to marry him. And I know you don't hate the idea of marrying me. If that's all I have to work with, so be it. Don't worry, your brothers won't be a problem for long."

Arminius left me standing between two kitchen tents, gaping for an answer that never came.

Chapter 11

*For the Germans had a custom, handed down from their
ancestors, of resisting anyone who made war upon them, and
of not suing for peace. (Caesar)*

"...and then Berut said, 'you'd be surprised just how many legionaries don't mind getting on their knees!'" Jotapa said. When I remained silent, attention focused on sorting through the collection of old sewing tools, shells, broken beads, and arrowheads some of the more enterprising children had "traded" for a sack of dried apple slices, Jotapa nudged me with her hip. "You haven't heard a word I said. Where is your head today?"

We were alone in one of the tribe's supply tents. The children's collection was mostly trash, but I didn't have the heart to turn them away.

Another thing I lacked were the words to tell her what had transpired between Arminius and I the previous night. I still couldn't believe he'd said it again.

I'll make you queen of Germania.

No, it was unthinkable. Germania had no sovereigns, and that was not going to change with us. And I certainly wasn't going to betray Reimar and the Chatti to do it.

Jotapa looked over her shoulder and lowered her voice. "Will you please tell me what's going on? First you show up with a blackened face, then you warn me away from your brothers while you make a hermit of yourself. You've avoided Arminius like he has a pox, even though you must have things to work out with him. Now you've been acting like a ghost all day. Tell me. I can't help if you won't tell me."

Sometimes I hated it when she was right.

"All right." I pushed the basket of junk away and sat heavily on a barrel. "The short version is that my brothers threatened to kill you if I keep going with this rebellion and after Arminius got me to agree to let him help, he kissed me and he has repeatedly asked to marry me."

Her jaw fell open and her eyebrows shot almost all the way to her hairline. "You've kept all this from me for more than a week? He kissed you after that fight with the Mattiaci and you haven't said a word this whole time!"

Her voice rose to a squeal, and I hushed her in a panic.

"Anyone can hear you," I hissed.

She composed herself, took a deep breath in and released it. "Tell me every single detail."

By the time I finished, the sun was lower in the sky and I'd had to hush her no less than five times.

"I hate to say this," she said without an ounce of regret, "but Arminius may be right. Wiltrud is too committed to freedom to abandon you if you break your betrothal."

"That cannot possibly be the point you derived from everything I just told you."

Jotapa shrugged. "You don't want to marry Reimar. Marrying Arminius would at least be interesting and from the sound of it you're far more amenable to his proposal than Reimar's bloodless 'I'll never love you' shit."

To emphasize her point, she dropped her voice an octave and exaggerated each word in the poorest imitation of a man I'd ever heard. Still, it made me laugh.

"And, this 'I'll make you queen of Germania' shit is at least romantic. Lunacy, but romantic. If you're his wife, you can curb that sort of thing."

Now it was my turn to gape at her like a dead fish. "I don't know how you managed to draw any of these conclusions. I have no more desire to marry Arminius than I do Reimar. And you shouldn't take the queen comment lightly."

"Please." She rolled her eyes. "You have never, not once in the time I've known you, spoken about a man like this. And the way you tried so hard to cut him out of the rebellion? It all makes sense now."

"I cannot fathom what makes sense about it."

She laughed. "You poor thing. As usual, you're thinking too hard about it. I know it's hard for you, but my advice is to trust him, as much as you can. He saved your life, Thusnelda, with no thought to his own. That means something and you know it, or you would never have let him talk you into working with him."

Oh yes, I hated it when she was right. My skin crawled with the need to run. Had he truly bought my trust so easily? He caught the top of the sword, where the blade is dullest.

"I see that look on your face." She took my hands in hers. "No need to panic. I'm not saying you need to hand him the reins and start taking orders. I only mean that it might be good if you think a little less where he's concerned. It might even be fantastic if you let yourself enjoy him."

"I don't know what you're talking about." I knew exactly what she was talking about, and I needed to change the subject. "Speaking of Arminius, will you please deliver a message to him? I can't be seen with him, and he needs to know Wiltrud and I will be meeting with the chiefs' wives and other other important women."

The words spilled out of my mouth in a rush, and thankfully, Jotapa kept her thoughts to herself. For once.

"Very well."

Long after she left, I remained in the supply tent, blindly sifting through a basket of junk and arguing with myself over Jotapa's advice. She couldn't be right. If she was right, that meant I had more at stake than I realized.

True to her word, Wiltrud gathered the most prominent women from the attending tribes under a hastily erected canopy. We sat on furs and stuffed pillows drinking ale. Some women stitched tapestries and clothing, but most were content to laze about and enjoy a few rare hours of idleness and luxury.

I stayed quiet, listening as they spoke of their harvests, their children, plans for the coming season. My nerves strung tight. Arminius knew this was happening and knew the risk I ran by being here. I could only hope that meant he was keeping my brothers distracted. It was my first real test of trust where he was concerned, and I kept wringing my hands in the fabric of my trousers to dry the sweat on my palms.

"Our winter stores are looking scant," Wiltrud said. "The Romans take more every year."

While it was true that Varus increased his taxes at every opportunity, I'd seen the Chatti's winter stores and they were far from scant.

Chatter dwindled beneath the canopy. The women's eyes darted to each other and their cups and needlework. Anywhere but at us. A Chauci woman, Rihilt, spoke first.

"We may not survive this winter. They gutted our stores. We've brought all the bronze works we have here to trade for more grain. If they tax us before we leave..."

The space erupted. Stories and complaints poured like wine from a broken amphora.

"They took my sons, all of them."

"They left us only sick livestock. We can't breed them, and I'm not sure they're safe to eat."

"A patrol raped my daughter. She hasn't spoken since."

"The road to our village is lined with crucifixes."

The three women of the Mattiaci remained silent, staring at me without flinching.

"It doesn't have to be this way." I raised my voice to be heard. "We outnumber them."

"No, we don't," one woman scoffed.

"Yes, we do." I rose to my feet. "If we unite—"

Another woman spat. "I'll be dead and buried before aligning with the Marsi."

"They'll come back even worse than they were before. Look at the Marcomanni and the Gauls!"

"Enough!" I clapped my hands. The open canopy allowed us to see in all directions. The soldiers were far away, uninterested in a gathering of women. I gathered my strength to say the most dangerous thing I'd ever said. "If we unite, temporarily, we have everything we need to push them out."

"How temporary?"

"A few seasons," I said. It would get me nowhere to relay to them what Arminius told me: The alliance must hold for years before the Romans decided we were no longer worth the trouble. "Only a few seasons. They're spread thin—"

"Did your Roman lover tell you this?" The tallest of the Mattiaci women stood. We were of an age, though she was fiery haired and thicker with muscle. A tapestry of tattoos down her bare arms told the stories of her victories in battle.

"He's Cherusci, and he's not my lover. He knows things about them, things we can use to our advantage." I snapped out a defense of him I'd never once considered. Something about hearing her, this Mattiaci warrior, level any kind of criticism at Arminius raised my hackles.

"She says this," she pointed at me, "but what she doesn't say is that she and Arminius are no better than the Romans. You fall in line with him or you die, isn't that right, Thusnelda?"

Eyes narrowed in suspicion, whispers rippled through the gathering.

"My husband and brother were killed after Arminius came and ordered them into the woods," she went on. "They killed more than twenty men, even men from the Chauci and Vangioni. My husband wanted nothing to do with that whoreson and—"

"Whatever happened to your husband, he was a coward." I rose to my feet. "Any who choose subjugation over freedom because they fear the cost are cowards. The Romans will not stop until we are all slaves or dead. Next winter will be worse if we don't do something. Arminius can stop it. The Chatti and I can stop it. We have to unite now while we still have the chance."

She lunged for me with a shrill cry, but the other women, including the two Mattiaci with her, grabbed and restrained her.

Wiltrud jumped to my defense. "If you must fight among yourselves, save it for the contests. Settle your differences there and be done with it. Thusnelda is right. We must act decisively as one people if any of us has any hope. There will be no Chatti, no Cherusci, no Mattiaci, only Romans if we let them have their way."

She swept back into her seat, her descent graceful. "We will sit down and discuss everyone's concerns."

Under Wiltrud's guiding hand, we listened to each woman over the next several hours. By the time we finished, I discovered who we could count on, who still needed to be convinced, and who Arminius and I could discount.

Sunna and Donar greeted me with joyous abandon when I finally emerged. All things considered, it had gone better than I expected. Attacking the issue head on was best, especially if it meant we didn't have more confrontations like we'd had with the Mattiaci.

The fiery-haired woman appeared in my path with her compatriots.

"My name is Arin. My husband was Fusco. You would do well to remember those names."

"I won't forget."

They parted to let me pass. My hounds dropped their ears and the fur on the backs of their necks rose as we walked by.

The combat contests couldn't come soon enough.

→

Haustblot could not, of course, be a festival entirely devoted to peaceful trading and celebrating. The Germani were too quarrelsome for that. Fortunately, we had a time-honored tradition for settling all but the most egregious of quarrels: the contests, during which an aggrieved party challenged their enemy and they fought to submission to determine who was right. The winner named their recompense, and the loser paid.

Sometimes, however, the contests were an opportunity for competing leaders to set themselves apart. Which is why I found myself sneaking to Arminius' tent to order him into the contests. Reimar was going to settle a matter about a choice fishing hole and to fight potential challengers for the Chatti throne. I intended to fight Arin to put that matter to rest. Arminius had to fight.

He met me behind the Chatti horse corral with crossed arms and a scowl.

"I thought I told you I'd take care of your brothers," he said. "But then you send Jotapa to tell me things we should have discussed, and now you have us meeting like two criminals."

"We are two criminals."

A shaggy horse swayed its way between us and stopped to sniff at Arminius' chest in loud puffs, ruining the stern effect Arminius clearly wanted to impress upon me. He unfolded his arms to nudge the animal's head out of the way, then snorted a laugh when it lifted its upper lip and jutted its head and neck as far as they could stretch.

"Fine, we're two criminals. What did you need to talk to me about?"

"The contests." I gave the horse's rear end a gentle push, and it drifted in the direction of a clump of grass still clinging to life. "You need to fight. Reimar has three fights, something about how he settled a property dispute, but you—"

My mouth clamped shut when I saw his expression fall flat.

"Yes, Thusnelda. I know I need to fight in the contests."

I'd done something wrong and couldn't for the life of me think of what. "You've been gone a long time. I don't know what you remember about us and what you don't."

"When—" He reached as if to grab me by my shoulders and shake me, but instead ran both hands over his scalp in rough pulls. "I will say this once more and that's it. I'll never repeat it again. I am Cherusci. I remember everything. I damn well know what our people like to see before they choose a war chief. And this may have escaped you, but

I've risen quite high through the ranks. I do know a few things about winning allies and proving myself. To everyone but you, apparently."

Another horse meandered to us, sniffing at his hands as if he hid treats.

"Augh!" He threw up his arms and the old, fat animal trotted away. That was probably as fast as it could move.

I laughed. I couldn't help it. Other horses had been gathering as we spoke. They had almost no interest in me, but something about Arminius called to them.

"This is funny to you? Of course this is funny to you. I'm just the Roman who doesn't know anything about the Cherusci and can't be trusted with washing his own ass let alone knowing that he should be at an event guaranteed to secure allies."

He kept on grumbling as he walked away and my laughter died. I jogged after him and put myself in his path.

"I did not tell you about wiping your own ass." Almost instantly I regretted the words.

He cocked his head. "Maybe, maybe not. You either think I can't be trusted because I'm too stupid to know what to do, or you think I can't be trusted because I was taken hostage when I was a boy and for some reason have yet to make you believe I am not a Roman."

I scoffed. "It is not that simple. Someone has to ensure we're all in accordance. Someone has to ensure we're all doing all we can to make this a success."

"And it has to be you, doesn't it?" He hummed under his breath and the corners of his eyes softened.

His words were too close to Jotapa's. Reimar didn't give me nearly as much trouble when I approached him about his participation in the contests, and he had grown up here.

"I understand you're used to people taking your orders, but I am not one of your soldiers," I said. "We're supposed to be equals. Since you and Reimar can hardly stand to look at each other, let alone sit down and discuss a plan, it only makes sense that I act as the go-between. If we're all acting without informing the others, we don't have a plan. We have chaos and the makings of a disaster."

At some point during my rant, we'd drifted closer together. His familiar scent snuck up on me beneath the cutting stench of horse manure. Suddenly, I wanted to know how his hand was healing. I wanted to know if my memories exaggerated the power of his kiss. I wanted to know if he kissed me, would I feel better about trusting him?

Down that road lay catastrophe.

The way his jaw flexed told me he wanted to argue, but he surprised me. Whatever argument boiled on his tongue, he swallowed it.

With a solemn nod, he said, "Very well. I will let you herd me as you see fit. You'll be pleased to know, four men have accepted my challenge. There's one more I need to secure, but, and I know this will be hard for you, I want it to be a surprise."

First Jotapa, and now him. Not that I didn't want to know whom he'd be fighting. Not that I didn't think it was important to know to ensure his opponents were strong enough to impress, but not so strong that he truly risked losing. Not that I didn't think it was important to challenge people from tribes more likely to support us. No. I didn't need to know any of that.

I could trust him. Yes, as long as I kept repeating it to myself, I could trust him.

———————➤

"These games make us look like barbarians," Segestes said with a sneer.

I stretched my aching neck and bent first to the right, then to the left to give my throbbing ribs the same treatment. Arin and her friends kept themselves unavailable to meet my challenge. That left me challenging on the spot when my turn came. Fortunately, two women and a young man stepped up, each hoping for their chance to improve their reputations. I denied them that chance with three resounding victories to the cheers of the crowd. My current pains were a small price to pay to be seen by all and sundry as a fierce warrior.

"To them, we are barbarians," I said. "Do they not have the same practice?"

"It's different when they do it. It's a sport for them, not this disorganized rabble in the mud."

Pointing out that a similar, though smaller, disorganized rabble had been how he'd claimed the Cherusci chieftainship so many years ago was pointless.

The crowd cheered on the current match between two men fighting over breeding rights to an aurochs. Perhaps it was barbaric to settle squabbles with our fists, but matters settled in a contest were settled, not to be revisited. The endless arguing that defined the Roman way seemed to always leave both parties unsatisfied. When Varus or his agents presided over our quarrels, more often than not someone ended up with a knife in the back.

Almost directly across the fighting pit from where I stood, Arminius, Ermin, and Berut pushed through the crowd to get the best view. His gaze flashed to mine, just long enough to let me know he saw me, then back to the fight. Segestes shifted next to me, leaning in close.

"Do you think I am stupid?" He asked in a voice for my ears alone. "Do you think I don't know where you've been disappearing to? Who you've been with despite my word?"

He wouldn't do anything here, not with so many witnesses, not while Arminius stood so near. Letting myself stop pushing back against against trusting him offered a wholly unfamiliar emotion to take the place of conflict: comfort. Security, even. If Segestes so much as raised a hand to me, I could fight him, of course, but I also knew with certainty that Arminius would be at my side in an instant. It was a warm kind of feeling to know such a thing.

Women from across the tribes came to me with their struggles and assurances they'd secure their husbands' loyalties. In one move, I became more than a single tribe's princess. I had powerful allies in Reimar,

Wiltrud, and Arminius. I had Levin and Jotapa. Yet I remained under my father's thumb.

"Keep it up, and it won't be Levin who watches you anymore," Segestes said. "So help me, I'll keep you in chains until your wedding."

He meant every word.

Just a little while longer, I reminded myself.

"Thusnelda." Konrada cleared her throat and shuffled into my periphery. "I don't mean to interrupt, but the weaver women are about to go to war with some shepherds and I thought..."

I would take care of it, because I always took care of such matters, even when my own father threatened me. I put Segestes' threat out of my head, as I so often did, and dug back into work. Weddings and rebellions and icy eyed Cherusci in Roman armor would have to wait.

------→

Wout's fist landed like a hammer against Arminius' jaw, and for the dozenth time, I regretted watching. Arminius had beaten one man after another, each triumph a little slower than the last. Against Wout, a man his equal on the battlefield, his energy flagged.

It turned out Arminius' decision to "surprise" me with his final opponent had less to do with a surprise and more to do with keeping me from interfering. There were plenty of good reasons to fight Wout. As his sister, I knew that better than most. But Arminius fought with a sneer on his lips that spoke of motivations much darker than proving himself stronger than those loyal to Rome.

Half the tribespeople were present, watching, waiting to see the victor before making their choice. Many watched Arminius with loyal eyes already. This demonstration of his skill was crucial. Our people never trusted a war chief whom they hadn't witnessed on the battlefield. Since we couldn't engineer a battle, least of all one in which he fought on our side, this was the next best thing and thank Tyr, it was working.

Wout was smaller than Arminius, but faster and just as strong. He moved like lightning, like Donar had blessed him for just this purpose.

Segestes watched at my side, cheering him on and casting sidelong glances at my silence.

Dressed in only their trousers and mud, Arminius' body sported unnatural lumps and bumps from his earlier bouts. I imagined that once clean, he'd be a walking bruise, a wall of blacks, purples, and sickly greens. One man hadn't been shy with his nails or teeth. Those wounds could fester if not treated appropriately.

Despite the fall chill, moisture gathered on my tunic from my unrelenting sweat. Blows, grabs, throws, kicks, the sickening crunch of bone against bone, the gasps and shouts, and I could do nothing.

Wout caught Arminius under the chin and, for a heart-stopping moment, I feared Arminius wouldn't get back up. He lay on his back, eyes closed, as Wout strolled closer, putting on a show for the crowd.

My breath froze. I flinched in anticipation of the finishing blow but didn't turn away. Wout stood directly over him and placed his foot on Arminius' face, driving it into the mud. He raised his arms to a mixed response of cheers and boos. Then, with more speed than I thought possible, Arminius grabbed that foot and launched his legs up to tangle with Wout's, bringing my brother down.

With his legs locked, Wout struggled fruitlessly. Arminius held on with all his strength and twisted his body, wrenching Wout's leg into an impossible angle.

People shouted for Wout to surrender. Arminius' lips moved, speaking too low for any but Wout to hear him. Wout kept struggling.

My heart sank for Wout, who would no sooner surrender than Arminius. He frustrated and disappointed me more often than not, but he was still my brother.

With a stomach churning series of cracks, his lower leg snapped. Arminius released him and rolled away to the cheers of the crowd.

I gasped for air, somewhere between relief and horror. Wout might never recover from that wound, but Arminius' victory was decisive. The three of us had successfully showed the tribes we were uncommonly strong warriors. We'd have no shortage of allies now.

Segestes' palm slammed into my shoulder. "Is this what you wanted? Are you happy now?"

My hand fisted, ready to settle this now, but Segestes sniffed and stepped back. Arminius found his way between us, his broad, mud-covered back seething with deep, heavy breaths.

"You and your son should learn to accept when you've been beaten."

A scream worked its way up my throat, where I locked it away. I wanted to beat my fists against his stupid back.

"Stop it." I shoved my way between them and squared off with Segestes. "You are a fool if you think I wanted my brother crippled."

He raised his hand to slap me, but his eyes flashed over my shoulder. He lowered his hand and stomped into the pit to help Wout.

"Perfect," Arminius said. "Now I've undermined Segestes, too."

"Perfect?" I whirled on him. "You made me look weak. I don't need you to handle him. I didn't need you to break Wout's leg."

His brows drew in. "I'm not permitted to defend my—"

"I am not yours," I hissed, dropping my voice in the presence of our increasingly curious audience. "We're supposed to be partners, and you make me look like...like one of your whores."

He recoiled. "I don't have whores."

"Oh, for fuck's sake."

"Am I interrupting?" Reimar's flat voice startled me. "You did well out there. The talk among the Marsi is they will follow you into the underworld."

That was good news I was in no mind to appreciate.

"I was just leaving," I said. "Reimar, our families should share a meal soon."

"You won't stay and tend my wounds?" Arminius winked at me. The bastard.

"I'm afraid there's no medicine for the illness in your mind."

Chapter 12

Besides issuing orders to them as if they were actually slaves of the Romans, he exacted money as he would from subject nations. (Cassius Dio)

Reimar paced in front of Segestes, who watched my betrothed through narrowed eyes.

"Varus asks too much," Reimar said. "He's out there picking every tribe clean."

I sat on my bedding with Jotapa nearby, sorting through our remaining stores for the trip back to our lands. Though I usually dreaded the long walk back, this year I might skip the entire journey.

"He is already getting another hundred men for his army. Is that not enough to sate his greed?" Reimar paused with his hands on his hips, chest rising and falling with labored breaths.

Arminius had approached us with an idea a week earlier: He recruited Reimar and around one hundred Chatti for the auxiliary. Ostensibly, this placed loyal fighters within the Roman ranks, but it offered a secondary benefit I didn't believe was a coincidence. It conveniently meant Reimar and the other recruits were to leave immediately for the garrison, with no time for a proper wedding.

"You will not speak of him that way," Segestes hissed. His eyes darted about our shelter, as if he sensed ears listening to their conversation. "Varus takes only what is owed to Rome. As for your enlistment—"

"What about it?" Reimar cocked his head and took a threatening step closer. "Is there some reason you object to our people fulfilling their duty to Rome?"

"Isn't this what you wanted, Father?" I sat up. "To make loyal citizens of us all?"

He curled his lips, his fists, and I tensed. Would he strike me with Reimar present? Would I finally, finally beat him so bloody he never raised a hand or his voice to me again? A sharp wail cut through the camp. I jerked to my feet, but Segestes pointed a finger at me.

"Stay with your brother."

Before I snapped a reply, Reimar said, "Don't worry, I'll see to it."

I bristled. First Arminius, now Reimar stepped in to fight my battles in the most unwelcome fashion.

He and my father left the tent, leaving me alone with Wout's glare and Jotapa. Unfortunately, Jotapa was no match for Wout, least of all an angry Wout. She kept silent.

"Reimar will never have you once he finds out you let Arminius fuck you."

I gave him my back to roll up my bedding, while Jotapa crouched to do the same with hers.

"No," Wout went on, "not when he won't know if he's raising another man's bastard."

A cold fissure of anger flashed in her eyes, but it wasn't directed at me. She shared my opinion of Wout and was free to express it only with me. More than once she'd offered with a smile on her face to slit his throat in his sleep for me.

Perhaps I should have let her. Anything was better than sharing a tent with my more-hateful-than-usual brother. All that pitiless rage radiated from him, burning hotter than our cook fire.

"You'll be killed." He stared into the flames. "They'll kill you all."

"You should be so lucky."

"Do your damn duty. Stop this nonsense with Arminius. Marry Reimar. Talk him out of the madness you've concocted and bend the knee to Rome."

"And make slaves of our people?" I shouldn't have engaged with him. Perhaps it was my boredom and frustration, or that he already knew the truth.

He laughed, a bitter sound. "Better slave than dead, wouldn't you agree, Jotapa?"

The truth of his question slid deep into my belly. I was a hypocrite of the worst sort, dragging Jotapa along my mission of freedom while she remained in bondage.

I never cared for the practice, but let myself overlook it because our servants were indentured. They were free to make their own households and buy their liberty. I had no power to change our tribe, let alone any of the others. That was no longer true, though. The women listened to me. Reimar heard me out, as did Arminius. I'd been quietly supervising our tribe since before my blood came.

Arminius, Reimar, and I were uniting the tribes. We were reshaping the future of our people. Who was to say we couldn't halt the slavery? That's what it was, by a different name with different treatment, depending on the tribe.

The tribesmen wouldn't like it. They might abandon us. Arminius was unlikely to ever consider it. A multi-tribal alliance alone was unheard of, let alone *this*. It was a way of life for us; scalcs were the spoils of battles and fair trading. We found the Roman way offensive, but the only difference was the scale and expectation of release.

The problem vexed me: the hypocrisy of fighting for freedom while denying that same freedom to people not at all different from us. The hint of a solution nibbled at my brain, no more tangible than mist, an idea on the tip of my tongue I couldn't yet remember.

I looked at Jotapa, but her attention was focused on mending a tunic. None but me would have noticed the faint tremble in her fingertips.

➤

While our carts and pack animals were loaded for the return journey, I cast a sidelong look at Wout, his splinted leg stretched straight out, propped up in the back of the wagon. For all our bickering and lost love, I didn't envy the agony of a broken limb.

It wasn't unusual for an injured person to die from their wounds. Thoughts of infection, of a permanent limp, must have plagued him in addition to the pain, for he was a surly beast, snapping and growling at any who dared acknowledge him.

Jotapa's porridge breakfast was too hot. The water in his drinking skin too cold. The tribe moved too slowly to his liking. I, apparently, smelled like a week old pig carcass and would hopefully die soon.

Even Segestes caught his wrath. Segestes, who, according to Wout, had taken no action against Arminius for breaking his leg. Segestes, who was too tepid to keep Arminius away from me, too weak to resist when Varus' men claimed our best horses.

If I snarled and spit at our father that way, I'd probably have a broken leg, too. Wout, however, was the favored son and heir, therefore free to speak his mind.

I ignored him and instead watched the other tribes packing their things. The leaving was always a subdued affair. After weeks of trading, celebrating, and reconnecting with old friends, parting ways to return home for a long, cold winter never inspired joy. This day, though, was different.

People squabbled over minor grievances and shot evil eyes to the legionaries mingling between the carts and horses.

The longer I watched, the more I saw legionaries seizing property and passing it back to their own baggage carts. People put up little, if any, fight. The men's shoulders slumped and the women wept. They directed their ire at each other.

Then I saw Arminius walking alongside a cheerful Varus, smiling and laughing in all those stricken faces. Arminius' expression remained impassive while he responded to whatever Varus said, periodically redirecting a legionary.

"What's going on?" I eased over to the wagon, conflict with my brother be damned.

Wout grunted. "Varus is collecting all the unpaid taxes."

That couldn't be. The Romans were relentless in their tax collection and from listening to the women express their grievances, they'd already surrendered a dangerous amount from their food stores and animals.

There were more of us than them. If everyone stood together, we could put a stop to this.

Varus noticed our carts and pawed at the extra animals now in our possession. With the snap of his fingers, two legionaries hustled forward to collect the bounty, as if they hadn't already taken a dozen horses.

Wout, who'd been so vocal about Segestes' weakness, said nothing. Only the slight stiffening of his shoulders and quick hiss of breath through his nostrils betrayed him.

I couldn't recall the first time I understood how weak my family was, only that I'd known it a long time. My mother hadn't suffered their deficiencies. Strength was a trait I could only have inherited from her.

"Arminius," I called.

He said something to Varus before heading my way, every inch of him resplendent in that cursed armor.

"What are you doing? Our tribe paid our taxes and then some. Why are your soldiers taking more, and from everyone?"

Wout grumbled, but didn't speak up.

"Varus wants to ensure we're well stocked before we break for winter quarters." He spoke from the side of his mouth, never quite making eye contact with me.

"That sounds like a problem for your army, not our people."

He turned his head away. That muscle in his jaw jumped.

"I cannot argue with him about this and you know it," he said.

"There's more than enough of us here—"

"Shut up," he cut me off. "I've let you have your meetings—"

"You *let* me?"

"—and mostly, you've done an excellent job quelling any unrest here, whether or not that was your intention. But Varus is concerned about our own stores and if I fight him here and now, if any of us fight him, we may win the day, but believe me when I tell you, we will lose the war. Need I remind you there are three legions currently posted across Germania?"

Gods, I wanted to strike him. All I could do was seethe.

"Do you know what I've learned from Rome?" He cocked his head and stared me down with a banked fury that rivaled my own. "Pick your battles, Thusnelda. Pick the time and place where it best suits you and not right now, not when you're angry. Think of the future."

All I did lately was think of the future. I wanted something now, something I could hold in my hands and know it was real and mine. What I didn't want was my co-conspirator talking to me like a child.

"Our people are going to starve," I said through clenched teeth.

He nodded. "Some might, yes."

"And you'll do nothing?"

His eyes flickered to Wout. "What makes you think I'm doing nothing? Do you truly, after everything, believe I'm not doing all I can?"

We locked horns in a silent battle over the things we couldn't say aloud so near to Wout. My brother didn't need to know everything.

I thought back to the day Arminius bid me to follow him while he secured more allies. He'd taken a serious risk by trusting me then. Whatever my frustrations were, I knew enough to trust he wanted this rebellion as badly as I did. I closed my eyes and nodded once, resignation settling like a damp blanket upon my shoulders.

"I met with the Marsi and Bructeri, and they've pledged their support. We're doing well. Take the winter to rest," he said. "I'll be back in the spring and we can resume our verbal sparring then."

"You mean my berating you and you talking me out of violence?"

He chuckled, took my hand, and held my eyes while he placed a lingering kiss on my knuckles. "Exactly."

That light brush of his lips soothed some of my ragged edges, damn him. How dare he talk down to me than flirt.

"Take care of yourself, Arminius," I said with a cruel smile. "If you don't come back, I'll be forced to start burning things down."

"Don't worry about me. A march is a march. Keep an eye on your food stores. People are likely to start raiding if they get hungry enough."

He spoke lightly, a joke, to mask the genuine concern wrought on his features. It was so easy to hate him when he came at me with snide arrogance. Mistrusting an arrogant Roman came naturally. The daring Cherusci warrior made me want things I dared not.

I tried to smile, but it was a sad thing. "We'll be fine. Go, before I change my mind and lead the women in a revolt."

He laughed outright. "I'll see you soon, Wildberry. Before we leave."

He returned to Varus before I my mouth could make a witty rejoinder. My throat turned thick and too achy for words.

The sun had no promise of breaking through the gray, overcast skies. Sheep bleated in the distance and angry voices carried across the field.

"You're not even trying to hide it," Wout said.

I observed my resentful, sullen, beleaguered people watching the Romans behind hooded eyes. There was rage here. Even the Mattiaci and other Roman supporters felt it. Even Wout felt it, try as he might to hide it. All that furious energy boiling just beneath the surface, ready to break free.

"What's the point?" I asked. "You can't stop this."

Chapter 13

I downed my ale while Varus droned on at the head of the table. The man certainly knew how to speak. Arminius caught my eye, lips twitching.

Back in our home, life continued as usual with one significant change: Every man in my family save Levin refused to look at me.

The main body of the legions was ready to march out in a few days. My stomach churned at the thought of Arminius leaving for the winter, though I couldn't determine the source of my discomfort. They were unlikely to encounter any resistance along the route back to Vetera, their winter base. He would return in the spring. Everything calmed during our winters, when harsh temperatures dampened unrest and the Romans left behind were too few to collect more slaves and taxes. It's not as though I needed him for any reason.

And yet his coming absence troubled me. The only reason it could unsettle me was that I'd miss him. His presence had worked its way seamlessly into my life, like he'd never been gone at all. More than that, I looked forward to seeing him. Damn it, I liked him, with his amiable smiles, his teasing, the way he heard me. When he chose to.

The entire concept of missing him left me unsettled. We were partners, friends of a sort, and nothing more. We couldn't be anything more, and missing him wouldn't lead to anything good.

I sat at the table with my teeth on edge listening to the Romans congratulate themselves on all their accomplishments against our savage race. Fortunately, I possessed a convenient excuse to leave.

"My apologies." I stood and pressed a hand to my belly, as though in pain. It was a weak excuse, but men seldom questioned a woman hinting at stomach cramps.

Segestes' only acknowledgement was a quick nod in my direction before returning his rapt attention to whatever grand story Varus told.

Once inside my room with the door pulled tight, my pulse settled. I untied the laces of my belt and set it atop my trunk before loosening the braids Jotapa had crafted. These little things had the power to lighten my entire being.

I sank onto the end of my bed with a sigh and flexed my tired feet. Hours of preparation to welcome Varus and his officers took their toll. Simply being in their presence took its toll.

A throat cleared outside my window. I dragged myself up to push the covering aside, knowing it was Arminius, before revealing his grinning face.

"You sneaking away?" He frowned. "Or is your stomach really bothering you?"

I hummed and shrugged. "How did you get away?"

"Told them I had to piss."

"Exactly what I wanted to hear." I rolled my eyes.

He shooed me away from the window. "Unless you want me to crawl in on top of you, make some room."

Before I could stop him, he squeezed his bulk through the window and slid inside with a thunk as his big feet hit the floor. I whirled at the door, certain someone must have heard him.

"Get out of here," I whispered.

He straightened, filling the small space of my room even without his armor.

"There are two dozen people in the hall; no one can hear anything." His eyes took a turn around my room and he ran the tips of his blunt fingers along the rushes in the ceiling.

"They'll notice when you don't come back." I said. "Segestes will know you're here."

"And what will he do about that?" Arminius sank into my straw mattress, and I ignored the way my stomach dropped at the sight of him on my bed.

"Probably have Lennart and Wout hold me down while he beats me senseless before chaining me to a post in the hall until Reimar claims me." The three of them had threatened as much, and I believed them.

His eyes narrowed and he grew, expanding into himself until he looked even bigger. "Elda, if he so much as puts a hand on you again, I'll have him crucified. I swear to our gods and Rome's-"

"You will not." I crossed my arms and leveled my most fearsome glare at him. "For the last time, you will not make me look weak."

He cocked his head and reached for my hand, tugging me forward until I stood between his knees. "Are you upset with me?"

"No." A lie. I was always upset with him. His every word, every look, every touch drove my senses into a lather. I didn't want him to hurt yet more of my family to defend me, and I really didn't want the strange way my belly flipped at the thought of him being so wild for me that he'd truly do anything to protect and keep me.

He raised an eyebrow, waiting. I couldn't tell him any of this or how every day my marriage to Reimar drew closer, the fire burning me apart from the inside grew hotter. The days went too fast, tumbling over each other, racing to their terminus when everything would change. Putting off the marriage only delayed the inevitable.

All my life, marriage had been my future. That had been plenty of time to decide what I wanted; a powerful man, someone to be my equal, a man who wouldn't beat me or hold me back. I wanted a chief, a warrior, and a tribe of my own to lead. Affection never entered my expectations. A partnership didn't need it and what was marriage, but a partnership?

Arminius made me want things I had no right to want; silly, ir-relevant things, like the way he rubbed my inner wrists with his thumbs and looked at me with eyes that saw everything. Humor wouldn't feed a village. A quick smile wouldn't protect us from our enemies. He made me want to believe his feelings were true.

Our war could end before it started, all because I wanted him.

He brought my hands to his lips and pressed a kiss to the back of each one. "Whatever it is, you can tell me."

If he suspected what I felt, the clawing need to break my betrothal and finally surrender to him, he'd never relent. Like the best hunters, he'd sight in on that opening and wouldn't stop until I surrendered.

I jerked away from him and paced the floor. "You know, this room is my only sanctuary. I've been on my feet all day organizing this wretched dinner, after a week spent working from dawn until midnight getting our villagers ready for winter. I'm exhausted. I wanted a few moments to myself, one night to just rest, and here you are, on my bed, demanding more of my attention."

At some point during my raving, Arminius stood from the bed and silently crept up behind me to capture my shoulders in his hands. I tensed under his sudden nearness, then locked up entirely when those strong, large hands kneaded into the tight muscles of my upper back.

"Easy," he murmured against my ear. Gooseflesh rippled down my arms. "You need to relax. Let me help."

"I'm not going to fuck you."

His breath puffed against my neck in a soft chuckle. "No, that's what would help me relax. I said I can help *you* relax."

His kneading took on a rhythmic quality that almost made me surrender.

"What is this? What are you doing?"

With a little push, he kept on kneading while guiding me on dragging feet back toward my narrow bed.

"You," his thumb dug into a knotted muscle and I hissed in pain and relief, "need help, whether you want to admit it or not. If this is the only thing you'll let me do, then please let me do it. We're leaving in the morning, so if you want to spend all winter convincing yourself I had ulterior motives tonight and nothing I did actually helped you, then you go ahead and do that."

The man knew how to make an argument, especially when his fingers worked a special kind of magic on my shoulders.

To my disappointment, he released me and sat on the edge of the bed with his legs spread. "Sit here. I won't even make you lay down. You'll have an easy escape any time you want it."

A smile tugged at my lips. Arminius could be charming, when I let him. Feeling like each movement ripped away small bits of my flesh, I sank into the space between his thighs and let him brush my hair out of the way and resume rubbing my angry back into submission. With each press and knead and dig, my resistance to him waned until I slumped into his embrace.

A strange thing happened in his arms, subject to his touch. I relaxed. The fog encircling my brain, which came on so gradually I never realized it was there, dissipated. He promised to help me relax, and I did. For the first time in recent memory, I felt downright good.

A little too good. The physical pleasure of my muscles releasing their tension gave way to something languid and warm. Everywhere we touched, even through our clothes, sparked tingles through my flesh. It went beyond the simple pleasure of human touch. I wanted more. I wanted to burrow into his heat and strength against the cold air coming through the window we'd left open. I wanted to let myself fall completely, right off the cliff into the abyss, knowing he was there to catch me.

The feeling was as heady as his skin against mine, the flex of his thighs around mine, and the sharp intake of his breath when I leaned further into him, exposing my neck.

He dragged his nose along the column of my throat and took a deep inhale. His hands tightened almost to the point of pain. Baduhenna help me, I chased that pain as surely as I chased the indulgence his touch inspired. They melded into a sensation altogether new to me, and heightened to an extreme that had my chest rising and falling almost as fast as Arminius'.

"Say the word, and I'll stop." One hand disappeared from my shoulder, then the laces at the back of my dress loosened and the neckline gaped open.

I didn't want to say anything. There was something liberating about letting him have his way without a word of protest or a demand for explanation. Especially when his lips pressed into the juncture of my neck and shoulder and sucked. Especially when his teeth scraped over the skin there, chased by his tongue. My body delighted in learning that as long as I allowed it, Arminius could, in fact, make me feel good.

He made a disgruntled rumbling noise when he discovered that even loosened, the neckline of my dress didn't open enough to push down over my shoulders. Not to be deterred, he slid a hand beneath the fabric, over my chest, and not a moment too soon. My breasts grew heavy and aching, so sensitive I mewled in shock when his palm dragged over my nipple. His other arm banded tighter around me, tugging me so close I felt the press of his erection against my backside.

If my eyes hadn't fallen closed, they would have crossed when he closed his thumb and forefinger around my distended nipple and squeezed, a slow pressure he steadily increased until my hips rocked uselessly against him. A grasping emptiness opened at my core and pulsed in time with my rapid heart beat. That kind of thrumming need usually came under my own fingers on my sex, though in fairness I'd never done *this*. It wasn't fair that Arminius should know secrets to my pleasure I didn't. For instance, I didn't know if I could achieve completion just from his hands on my breasts, but he might.

I didn't protest when he started pulling the skirt of my dress up, the first man to take such a liberty since the night that now felt so long ago that I had given myself to a Marsi warrior and prayed it would change my future. There was no sense in praying for such a thing now, not when I was wise enough to know better.

"They'll wonder where you went." I shifted restlessly against him, my body seeking more contact, more pressure, *more*.

"Varus will congratulate me when I tell him about the delightful creature I found outside." His hand finally moved to my other breast, plucking and playing me like a skilled bard.

"Oh? Was she very beautiful?"

"She is unparalleled."

Once he hiked my skirt up my thighs to his satisfaction, he wasted no time swiping two blunt fingers through my sex. I bucked at the shock of his calluses, his unyielding touch, and the immediate wet gush that followed.

"Do you still want me to leave?" I felt his lips smile against my neck, where there was surely a bruise forming.

As I suspected, he knew how to touch me there, too, as if we'd done this a thousand times. He unerringly found the bud at the apex of my sex and touched me exactly how I often touched myself. If possible, I melted deeper into his arms and let him carry me away. No matter how often I did this to myself, it didn't compare to the relief of letting someone else do it. And not just anyone, but the man I'd dreamt of for so many years, acting as my lover if only for this one night.

"One day," he rubbed in hard, fast circles, "I'm going to fuck you." He dragged his teeth up my neck. "And you're going to see." He pinched my nipple until I cried out. "It's you and me, Thusnelda. It's always been us."

I broke apart beneath his words and his hands, pulsing and rocking, so far out of my head I saw the stars in the night sky. Never, not once had I brought myself to such a peak. His words swam in my head, reduced to a murky bog by his expert onslaught. If he wanted me confused and amenable to anything he asked, he certainly knew how to achieve it.

Belatedly I realized his hand covered my mouth. When I scowled up at his smiling face, he only grinned wider.

He *tsked* under his breath. "Screaming that way with your father and brothers practically on the other side of the door? You're insatiable."

His hands were still all over me, beneath my clothes. When I began to struggle, he tightened his hold on me, and I hissed at the sudden pressure against my overly sensitive sex.

"Easy, easy," he said. "You're safe, Wildberry. I just wanted you to feel good."

As if to reassure me, he removed his hands and straightened my dress, then lightly brushed his palms up and down my arms, chasing away the flash of tension that returned. My heart still thundered, and the enormity of what I'd let him do sank in. Few Germani tribes troubled themselves over chastity the way the Romans did, but it also wasn't looked kindly upon for a betrothed woman to fool with a man who was not her intended.

More seriously, fooling with Arminius—or letting him fool with me —gave him false hope. He thought he could convince me to abandon Reimar with promises of a queendom and physical pleasure.

There was no us, not the way he wanted.

"I can't." I whispered the half-formed thought.

"Shh." He kissed my temple. "It's all right. Will you do something for me, this winter?"

I shrugged. "Perhaps."

His kiss turned into a laugh. "Very well. Please try to stay out of trouble, and please don't think too hard about what we just did."

"You know I can't promise either of those things, don't you?"

He tilted my chin and kissed me, slow and deep, almost enough to reignite the fire that had only just moments ago pushed me beyond reason.

"Yes, I know."

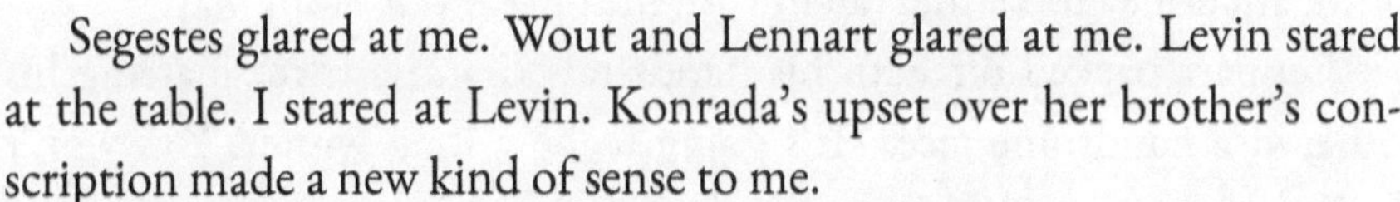

Segestes glared at me. Wout and Lennart glared at me. Levin stared at the table. I stared at Levin. Konrada's upset over her brother's conscription made a new kind of sense to me.

While I'd been in my room losing my head to Arminius, Varus had been making insinuations about our family. Insinuations about our loyalty. Insinuations so serious Levin had volunteered for the auxiliary.

He was to leave with the legions the following morning. My lone ally at home, the only brother I had left in both name and action, gone all winter. Gone forever, maybe. Yes, I understood Konrada's pain and fear in a way I hadn't before. I owed her an apology.

My stomach turned, and I worried I'd vomit in the center of our hall.

"I told you to stay away from him." Segestes refused to look at me, instead keeping his attention on the hunting knife he always kept on his belt, digging the point into the scratched surface of our head table. "I told you to stay out of this sedition."

There was no point in denying or arguing the charges laid against me. I hadn't stayed away from Arminius, and I had made myself extremely involved in the rebellion.

Wout still couldn't stand without a crutch and spent most of his days in an opium-induced stupor, thanks to Varus' medicus. It had worn off. Not only was he in pain, but his flesh craved the Roman drug now. There was a reason our healers avoided using those opium tinctures. Wout's red eyes pulsed with the need to hurt me, and the need to sate his new hunger.

Since Wout was disabled and out of his head, Lennart took my discipline upon himself. He took two steps toward me before I brandished my own knife, the one I always carried, ever since that horrible day when Mama died.

"So help me, I will gut you." I ground out each word. "I will finish what Arminius started on Wout. And you," I turned to Segestes, "I will unman you. If any of you so much as raise your voices to me again, I will end you. I am done. I have kept this family afloat for almost fifteen years and I am done. You either fall in with me or stay out of my way."

Lennart backed off with his hands raised and a sneer marring his otherwise handsome face. "It's going to be a long winter. You won't have the upper hand while you're sleeping."

I raised my eyebrows. "Segestes, did you hear that? One of your precious sons thinks he's going to dishonor your name by coming for his opponent while she sleeps."

Whatever Segestes was going to say, Levin cut him off. He jumped between Lennart and me.

"Stop. I volunteered. I'll be back in the spring, and that's the end of it. Don't make me return to find you all killed each other in my absence."

I didn't lower my knife, but I also didn't push any further.

"Levin," I said, "I'll say my farewells in the morning."

Levin nodded and stayed between me and the rest of our family until I backed into my room. Once inside, I propped my spear against the door and checked the wooden bar securing the winter shutter on my window. No one was going to sneak up on me in my sleep.

An endless, snaking line of red tunics and polished armor marched past our village a few hours after dawn. I joined most of our people at the tree line to observe the procession. A new kind of fear chilled my blood, and it was only three legions. What if they returned with more?

On and on it went. How could we possibly think to best them?

Levin was down there, as was Ualter, and so many others. I missed him already. I missed him the way I imagined I'd miss a limb if I lost one, and he hadn't been gone a full day yet. With a deep breath, I reminded myself that he'd be back when the snow melted, just like all the auxiliaries.

Rhythmic footsteps and clanging armor drowned out the natural sounds of the forest. Sunna and Donar flanked me, their ears attuned to the soldiers. If only I had a Roman tunic and armor of my own, I could spend the winter training them to attack legionaries. Perhaps when Arminius returned, he might supply what I needed.

My eyes scanned the march, searching for him. He'd be easy to spot, no doubt riding alongside Varus and the senior officers. I waited to find him, throat tight and palms sweating.

"Oh, look!" Jotapa squeezed my arm and pointed to a familiar face marching at the head of one square formation of soldiers. "It's Berut."

The man cut a fine figure, and like Arminius, always sported an easy, honest smile. I nudged her with my elbow.

"And how much time have you spent with Berut?"

"No more than you've spent with Arminius." She spoke through her big grin, waving an arm. Somehow, Berut seemed to know exactly where to look to wave back and, Gods above, blew her a kiss. "His heart is still set on Ermin and like you, we spend all our time plotting."

Berut preferring the company of other men hadn't deterred Jotapa in the slightest, who declared he was still beautiful to look at and a delightful storyteller.

"There's nothing going on between me and Arminius," I said.

She snickered. "Please, Princess. You can lie to many people, including yourself, but not to me."

Or Arminius, apparently. There were no gods powerful enough to help me if those two ever joined forces against me.

"It doesn't matter and you know it," I said. The wind blew more bitterly than usual today, so I pulled my cloak tighter about my shoulders. Snow would come tonight. A heavy snow would suit my mood. *Let it come. Let it come and bury me until spring so I don't have to face this winter on my own.*

"I won't pretend to understand everything about the situation," she went on, "but perhaps you're making too much of nothing."

I spun on her. "You think I'm making too much of our path to freedom?"

To her credit, she didn't flinch or back down. No, she tilted her chin up and held my stare. "Your freedom, Princess, not mine."

Her aim was true and cut to my marrow.

"I can pay the rest of your bond," I said, regretting the words as soon as they left my mouth.

"And what of the others?"

This wasn't the first time we'd had this conversation, and I imagined it wouldn't be the last. What she wanted—no, what we both wanted—was outrageous. Unheard of. No one would join our alliance if I called for freeing all the scalcs.

"Impossible. I'm sorry, but—"

Jotapa huffed. "Do you know why everyone is quick to follow Arminius?"

I turned my attention back to the marching troops. He still hadn't appeared and it could be a while yet.

"He's charismatic and offers the people something they want."

The words didn't sit right in my gut. There was something more to Arminius I couldn't identify. He drew people to him. When he spoke, you believed him. People followed him without question.

"That may be part of it," she said. "I think it's because he doesn't know the meaning of the word 'impossible.' I don't think it's even occurred to him that he might fail."

Jotapa had the right of it. Arminius was many things, but doubtful wasn't one of them. Was that truly all it took to win these people, unencumbered confidence?

It seemed a frivolous reason to embark on a rebellion, but perhaps it was merely a convenient excuse. My people clawed for any reason to act, and Arminius, with his brazenness, his skills, and his knowledge, positioned himself as the answer to their needs.

What remarkable timing he had to arrive when Varus pressed his advantage too far and exhausted Germani yearned to fight again. Maybe this was the will of the gods. If that was so, he was right: Now was the time and he was the one to lead it.

No, not the only one. A man so convinced of his invincibility needed careful supervision. A man like that didn't exist in the realm of mere mortals. In our mortal realm, such men were mad and dangerous.

At long last, the command element rode into view. I could have picked Arminius out if he'd been shuffling along in the auxiliary, mixed among fellow Germani. Mounted atop his horse next to Varus, he was impossible to miss.

His eyes scanned the crowd, brow pulled tight and lips turned in a small frown until he found me. The change was immediate. He grinned. He didn't wave, no doubt to avoid any undue attention from Varus or the other high-ranking soldiers.

I got an eager nod and a wink and tried not to imagine that it might be the last time I ever saw him. Anything could happen between here and Vetera. Anything could happen while he was there. He could be discovered and executed. He could fall out of Varus' favor. The emperor could decide Arminius was needed elsewhere.

Our rebellion seemed held together by the thinnest of threads, and that wasn't the worst part. I would miss him terribly, damn it. No matter what he asked of me, I intended to think of our last night together through many dark, cold nights, all without turning it into something it wasn't. It didn't have to be a mistake I cringed over. I could let myself enjoy the memory, and let that memory warm me.

A woman to my left jostled my shoulder as she jumped and waved to someone marching by. Utterly shameless, that one. I supposed it couldn't be helped after so many years of occupation.

I was no better than her, not really. Some part of me longed to make a show of myself leaping and shouting at my man. Had I not been raised to be a queen, had I succumbed to Segestes' love of Rome, I could very well have been that woman. How much simpler my life might have been. Not that Arminius was mine.

Arminius and I watched each other until his head could turn no further, then I watched him ride away.

For now, I told myself, *not forever*.

Jotapa's hand found mine and she gave it a gentle squeeze, the way we did when we were younger whenever one or the other was afraid.

"Let's go," I said. We'd lingered long enough and Segestes would be restless. Levin was gone and Arminius was gone and Wout was useless and I'd shamed my entire family into submission. At least for now.

Chapter 14

*The most complimentary form of assent is to express appro-
bation with their spears. (Tacitus)*

Winter droned on, gray and dreary and cold as ever. My days passed
in a haze of repetition: wake, dress, eat, tend the animals; meet Konrada
for training; join Jotapa for the more mundane tasks around our home;
serve dinner; sleep. During the warmer months, my days weren't so very
different from this, except I spent more time in the wald. It was the wald
that offered a sense of freedom.

Not only was I hemmed in by wooden walls and a blanket of snow,
the tension in our family reached new heights in our confinement. I
slept with my knife in hand and my door barred.

Between sniping at each other over the smallest thing, oppressive
silence reigned supreme, punctuated by the inaudible whispers of our
scalcs and periodic chuffing and clucking from our animals. It didn't
matter that Levin was gone and there was one fewer person taking up
space in their room, not when our hall became a barn for the season.
Every last inch of space in every last Cherusci building housed animals
through the winter. My room featured a makeshift pen for three goats.
The smell was not ideal, no matter how often I changed their hay.

Each day, I took first our horses, then the two cows, outside for
a brief interlude of physical activity and a blessed respite from indoor
confinement. We marked ourselves lucky to have such a large space
compared to others. The family who managed our village's sheep spent
each winter inside a great barn brimming with the creatures. I made a

point of visiting them only when necessary. Between the stench and the volume, I couldn't imagine how that family hadn't simply snapped and slaughtered every one of those bleating things.

Given the course this winter had taken, I almost envied them. Give me one hundred bleating sheep and take my brothers and father in trade.

My only true respite was when Lennart and Wout patrolled together, Wout's limp be damned. The men deftly avoided other chores to accommodate the punishing patrol schedule my father set. Segestes didn't exempt himself or minimize his role in the patrols and spent as many hours slogging through the snow and slush as any other man of our tribe protecting our interests. He had these brief, shining moments of being the kind of chief I respected.

"Here." Wout dropped a pile of trousers and tunics on the table where Jotapa and I worked on the pile from last week.

With our confinement came the free time to catch up on tasks that normally fell to the wayside during the warmer months, like mending and stitching new clothes. The calluses on my fingers thickened from the pressure of our bone needles, and my joints ached from the repetitive motions and so many hours spent hunched over mindless work.

Wout hobbled away, each step followed by the thump of his crutch. A Roman doctor had set and braced the bones and our healers pronounced it a job well done, but it would be months before we knew if he'd ever be able to use his leg properly again. He blamed me for his pain and fear that he might never be strong enough to fight again.

Part of me saw truth in his reasoning. I could have refused to join Arminius and help him along the path that had led to those contests. I could have talked Arminius out of fighting, though that option was unlikely.

That didn't mean it was my fault Wout had foolishly accepted the challenge, nor did it make it my fault when Wout refused to yield. He was lucky Arminius hadn't killed him. Warriors seldom killed each other in the contests. Most often, deaths in the contests were accidents, sad tricks of fate when a fighter fell just so or a hit landed in precisely the right spot with the right force to kill. When a fighter did intentionally kill their opponent, they then had to prove before a council of chiefs that their victim intended to kill them. As that was difficult to prove, most kept their murder attempts secret.

Wout should have had the common sense to yield when it became clear he lost the fight. Instead, he got his leg broken and blamed me for it.

Jotapa shifted the pile across the scarred surface of the table with a sigh.

"Perhaps we should thank him for keeping us so busy," she said.

I sifted through some items. "I think he tore a few of these just now."

He'd always begrudged me my own room while he shared with the twins, but this winter was worse than ever. The fact that Segestes never saw fit to foster me out to another family left ours in the uncomfortable situation of a girl child without a mother. Segestes' solution had been to treat me like a woman grown, shove me into my own room, and wait for me to take Mama's place. I never understood his reasoning, and apparently, neither had Wout.

"The only thing special about you is your cunt," he'd once told me. "Had you been born with a cock, you would be nothing. Another spare son to work the fields."

He wasn't wrong. My sex was a trick of fate. Had I been born a man, many things would have been different for me. I could have chosen my bride, for one, instead of being assigned a husband based on the man who would best benefit Segestes. I wouldn't have been raised expecting I'd one day rule over a tribe of my own. I would have been just another Cherusci man, eking out a life. Opportunities for glory might have been few, yet so much more freedom would have been mine.

Had Wout been born a woman, he'd be the one married off to Reimar. The thought made me chuckle as I imagined the two of them exactly as they were in life, attempting to balance a marriage. *Reimar wouldn't care about the change.*

"What's so funny?" Jotapa didn't look up from her needlework.

"Imagine Wout in a dress fussing around an oven."

She snorted. "That is a good reason to laugh."

A plump chicken circled our feet on the hunt for crumbs and Sunna whined nearby. No creature in the world wanted to kill a chicken more than Sunna. It had taken weeks of training to get her to stop mauling them, during which Segestes threatened over and over to kill her. He never did.

A familiar grief gnawed at my soul. Grief for the relationship my father and I once shared, what we could have had. Grief for my brothers, who looked at me with such hate in their eyes. Grief for my childhood, when life had been so simple. Grief for Levin, for being apart from him for the first time in my entire life.

Life would never be the same, and there was no sense in pouting over it, so I pushed the thoughts aside and focused on forcing my tired fingers to keep a straight stitch in the trousers before me.

The main doors of the hall pushed open with a bang, and I started and jammed the needle into the pad of my forefinger. I hissed in pain and prepared to offer a tongue lashing to whomever had burst in.

Wiltrud, Reimar, and a dozen Chatti warriors entered in a flurry of snow and foreboding. Nothing good came from a winter visit.

⟶

"When we last saw them, they numbered at least a thousand," Wiltrud said.

We gathered at Segestes' table, too tense to eat the food or drink the ale the scalcs hastily served. A raiding party of Mattiaci, Tencteri, and Sugambri were cutting their way steadily north, pillaging outlying villages and disappearing into the night with much needed food, healthy animals, and slaves.

"And your man said he saw them turning eastward?" Wout sat up straight, preening under the opportunity to assert himself in some meaningful way.

"Yes." Wiltrud nodded. "My guess is they'll hit the Marsi lands before heading here. We have perhaps a day to prepare."

They'd brought with them a few hundred Chatti warriors, currently occupying barns and homes across our village to stay warm. We could marshal enough warriors to face this threat, but the Sugambri were allies. Like the Chauci, the Tencteri remained undecided, though some of their chieftains had expressed sympathy for our cause during Haustblot. We stood to lose both an ally and a potential ally in one fell swoop if we met them with force.

The Mattiaci had more in mind than pillaging resources when they started all this.

"We can more than match them," Segestes said. "We'll send them back where they came from as a message to any with an eye toward raiding our united tribes."

That was exactly the sort of response we needed to avoid.

"We should talk to them first," I said. "See if we can't share our resources and prevent unnecessary bloodshed."

The scalcs froze in place. Every eye turned to me. Lennart looked at me askance. After a beat, Wout's lip curled.

"I didn't realize you'd turned coward, sister."

Lennart laughed and clapped him on the back as though either of them accomplished something with that insult.

"We will handle this like Cherusci," Segestes bristled, "and show them what happens when you stand against tribes united under Rome."

"Aren't you concerned this will foment unrest among the tribes?" Wiltrud asked. "Thusnelda is right. This is an opportunity to show them that kneeling to Rome is the right choice."

Segestes studied her as if he could divine exactly how he was being led, knowing only that he was.

"Don't worry," Reimar said. "There will still be a fight. It doesn't need to be a slaughter, though, and I agree we can redistribute food to see these people through the winter."

"We don't have enough to feed every starving mongrel," Lennart said.

Wiltrud spread her palms out over the table and stood, looking every bit the queen she was. "We won't know what resources we have or don't have until we all sit down and discuss it. Killing a thousand starving people will only create more enemies," she said.

"If they keep going like this," Reimar cut in, "more Germani will starve. We could have an all-out rebellion by spring. If you want the Romans to be happy upon their return, we must resolve this."

Segestes' nostrils twitched at having his own reasoning used against him. He ground his teeth, unused to being challenged, least of all by the leaders of the tribe he viewed as somewhat inferior to us. Better than the Marsi or Tencteri, certainly, but not our equals.

"If we crush this little uprising now, everyone will know they cannot stand against the tribes united by Rome."

It was to me he spoke these words, his threat clear. I stifled a laugh.

"If we show them mercy and ensure most survive winter, then they will see the benefits of remaining Roman clients. After all, our tribes have been clients for a long time now and we are successful. If the goal is one nation united as Romans, we must show them the way," said Wiltrud.

Somewhere along her journey to becoming the true Chatti chief, she'd become adept at managing men in such a way as to make them think her ideas were theirs. I grew up butting heads with a pack of brothers, diplomacy be damned.

Segestes couldn't argue this, but that didn't stop Wout and Lennart from scoffing.

"What would you suggest?" Segestes dragged out each word, as if it physically pained him to speak them.

"Aye." Lennart raised his cup in a mocking toast. "Shall we go out there to face a thousand hungry, angry men and tell them we'd like to have a little chat by the fire?"

"Women, brother," I said. "I'm sure there are women among this horde, as well."

He and Wout scowled at me and I smirked, knowing that no matter what we decided this evening, Wout wouldn't be part of the solution. I didn't want to hate him, yet the feeling grew with each passing day. He wanted so badly to blame me for his predicament, but he'd wanted to punish me for existing long before Arminius broke his leg. I couldn't let any of my family stand in the way, not anymore.

Segestes sighed and rubbed a hand across his forehead.

"Fine," he said, "what do you all suggest we do?"

"We have to gather warriors, send out scouts to locate this group. We'll meet them on the field and present our case," said Reimar.

I had to admire him as the seasoned warrior he was. There was no denying his skill, or that he'd make a fine chief. He'd make a fine husband, I reminded myself. Wanting to want someone and failing was its own kind of agony. Wanting him would make everything so much simpler.

"Wout, you'll stay here with a contingent of warriors in case raiders make their way to our village," Segestes said. "I will accompany this party to meet them."

Fine. Let him see.

The horde was easy to spot in their dark furs and heavy wools against the white blanket of knee-high snow. Horses loaded with covered parcels, some pulling carts, made blocky lumps interspersed between the bodies. They were still far enough away to give us time to settle into our loose formations. We didn't fight like the Romans, with their neat lines and in-step marching. For the Germani, battle was an opportunity to achieve personal glory and acquire wealth we might not otherwise ever gain. Weapons, armor, jewels, anything a warrior carried into battle was subject to plunder should the warrior fall. Dying bravely in battle was also, according to our priestesses, a pathway to glory in the afterlife. Cowards were left on the mortal plane to linger as unhappy spirits, slowly deteriorating into madness before decaying altogether.

Instead of tight rectangles and squares, our people stretched out into a thin line mingled with horses, each warrior jockeying for a place in the front. Only cowards willingly accepted a place behind another warrior. Once Reimar, who'd been elected our war chief for the day, gave the signal to attack, it would become a melee, every warrior for themselves with little thought to strategy.

I spared a moment to worry over taking a sword or spear to the back by one of our own warriors, such was the general confusion to follow. We had painted our faces a deep blue, some in patterns or stripes, others a solid mass of color, to ease the confusion, and hoped the raiders had chosen another color or no color at all.

I shivered and my breath puffed out in little clouds. In a short while, my cloak would be too hot to wear. Sweat from anticipation for the fight to come dampened my palms. With any luck, it would be a short one, with minimal casualties.

Those of us with horses mounted once the raiders were within shouting distance. My animal stamped its foot and snorted, knowing what was to come.

One thousand or so warriors assembled before us was an impressive sight to see. Not as impressive as our larger number and certainly not as impressive as the Roman legions when they marched, but impressive nonetheless.

Many of these people faced starvation. Others merely wanted a chance to raid, thirsting for violence and the satisfaction of seizing another man's property like predators. The Mattiaci wanted their revenge.

Their leader stepped forward, a tall man with a long, scraggly beard and braids he should have taken down, cleaned, and re-braided weeks ago.

"Look," he shouted, turning to his people for effect, "they come to take what's ours by right."

Shouts of outrage met his words, insults slung our way. Nothing too creative, of course, mostly descriptions of how we sucked Varus' cock to gain favor.

"We don't want to take anything from you," Reimar replied. We'd rehearsed these words at length last night and on the way here. "We're here to—"

The man silenced him with an outraged roar. "We don't care what you want, do we?"

The raiders cheered their approval and shook their weapons over their heads.

"No," he went on, "get out of our way, and we'll let you live."

For now, he omitted. They'd let us live for now, until they swept our lands for any usable food and left us to starve.

Our warriors tossed insults of their own, overconfident in our numbers.

Wiltrud raised her voice before Segestes got his own words out. "If we work together, we can see that none of us have to starve."

The man spat at us. "They say that. We," he beat his fist against his chest, "have been loyal to Rome since they came. You are traitors and still Varus rewards you with fewer taxes!"

Now both sides bellowed at each other, heaving like two massive living bodies. My horse stamped and danced in place despite my efforts to keep her still. It was a fruitless endeavor. The energy pulsed around us, far too strong to stop.

A fight was coming, and we would not solve it with words.

Segestes shot me a glare before saying, "The only traitors I see today are you, Mattiaci. Rome compelled us to peace and you violated that because of your own failures."

He paced out past Reimar and Wiltrud, now red in the face at the insults, no matter how true they were. I needed to stop him before he made everything worse. If I didn't, no one would.

"The Chatti have insisted on making you all a fair offer, of us all sharing in the hard work our tribes have accomplished for the season. I'd rather wipe you all out. It's your choice," he shouted.

Just as I spurred my horse into action, intent on running him down, both armies surged into action. It was too late.

Chapter 15

In the case of the barbarians, the readier a man is to be daring, the more trustworthy is he regarded and, when things are in turmoil, more influential. (Tacitus)

We came at each other in a thundering rush of bodies and battle cries. My well-trained horse charged without hesitation, eager for the battle.

All my senses sharpened. I heard every breath and growl, each thump of a foot or hoof. The scent of unwashed bodies, fir trees in the distance, and the tang of blood overwhelmed my nostrils.

I crashed my horse into the enemy's line and pulled hard on the reins to stop her while I swung the flat of my spear against any with the misfortune of being too close. Each blow reverberated up my arm.

It was a struggle to hold myself back from the instinct to slaughter. Our goal was to subdue, not massacre, despite my father's insistence otherwise. Keeping nearly fifteen hundred warriors on that same path was nearly impossible.

I aimed for arms and legs, the backs of heads to render a fighter unconscious. It was slow going, a slog through men and women alike. When my horse screamed, a chilling noise no matter how often I'd heard it, I tossed a leg over her neck and slid back into the snow, dropping the spear in favor of my sword along the way.

Thought plays little part in a battle, beyond moving from one opponent to the next. There's no space for much of anything else. I didn't notice the bite of snow soaking between the seams of my heavy wool trousers and down through the tops of the fur wraps encasing my calves and the tops of my winter boots. Pain registered in the back of my mind, quickly silenced.

My heart raced, and my lungs pumped like bellows.

A sword swung at my head. I ducked, just in time for the wind of the blade to kiss along my cheek and temple.

I spun around my attacker and cracked him across the skull with the flat of my sword. I raised the weapon for the next opponent and pulled up short when he whirled to face me. Reimar's eyes glowed brightly behind his warpaint, bright with the lust of battle.

He had his own weapon raised, now frozen, over his head in a stalled strike. For the first time since I'd known him, he laughed, a full belly-shaking guffaw. I was so stunned, I almost died for a second time. Fortunately, Reimar was paying attention, and he felled the warrior who came at my back with a quick thrust of his sword.

"We have to end this," I growled and swung on another attacker.

Exhaustion would set in soon for all of us. Even the most well-conditioned warriors couldn't maintain a pitched battle for very long. Seconds felt like minutes and minutes like hours. Hours seemed as days, weeks, months stretching into eternity as we pushed ourselves beyond our breaking points in the name of victory. As friends and family died around us.

"Their leader," he thunked the pommel of his sword against a woman's head and she crumpled like a dropped sack at his feet, "we have to find him."

I parried a blow and kicked the man's feet out from under him, doubting it would take one man to stop this mess. One man alone hadn't started it, and these raiders had damn good reason for their anger.

A woman ran at me and for a moment, time froze. Her cloak was threadbare, her frame dangerously thin. About her neck was a collar in the style Rome used to mark their slaves.

I batted her weapon aside, nothing but a short length of wood crudely shaped into a club. Bruising mapped her face and her neck was inflamed, openly bleeding in sores around the collar.

My stomach twisted into a knot so painful, bile rose in my throat. She wasn't a scalc in the Germani fashion, but a slave. The Mattiaci were taking true slaves and forcing them to fight. To bleed. To lose limbs. To die. Her eyes rolled to their whites, like a panicked horse. Open blisters pocked her nose and cheeks, and the fingers desperately clutching an ax looked black. They made her fight, after letting her succumb to frostbite.

In that frozen moment, I made a decision. I made it without consulting Reimar, and certainly not Arminius who was long gone from the territory. And I didn't care one whit about what they might say. I didn't care about what it might cost us in the future, because the cost staring me in the face was too high to pay. I refused.

I snatched her by the front of her tunic and cringed when the fabric tore. She cried out, dropped the ax, and tears sprang free. The scent of urine mingled with the other foul smells of battle.

"Tell the other scalcs," I shouted to be heard over the din of battle, "any who fight for me, Thusnelda of the Cherusci, will earn their freedom."

She continued crying and wincing away from the blow I had no intention of delivering.

"Did you hear me?" I gave her a shake. "Spread the word among every scalc you know and tell them to repeat it. Any who join my rebellion will earn their freedom. Say you understand."

"Yes, yes, yes." She nodded with each affirmation.

A warrior leapt for us, swinging a long sword to cleave us both in one motion. I dropped her and ran him through, just above the gut, under sternum and angled up for maximum effect. His blood ran hot over my hands. I pushed him off my blade with a sickening squelch.

The scalc looked up from the snow, no longer crying, eyes wide with new understanding.

"When the time comes, any who fight for me and the Chatti will be free, do you understand?"

She nodded again.

"Go. Tell every scalc."

She scrambled away and disappeared into the melee. I hoped she lived long enough to be heard.

A female voice screamed my name, a voice I'd seldom heard and recognized instantly. My head fell back on a prolonged groan. Not this bitch. Like this day wasn't already long enough.

Arin charged me on horseback. Her shock of red hair blew free behind her, all flames and fury. The melee parted for her assault. Any who stood in her way, she and her horse knocked aside, no more an obstacle than a breeze in her path.

I readied my sword and planted my feet. She was right-handed and would expect a feint to the left. She was also a seasoned enough warrior to know I knew she expected a feint to the left.

The Romans flipped a coin for such a choice. I only had my instincts. At the last possible moment, when I heard nothing but her horse's hooves and saw nothing but her wild eyes, I sidestepped and swept my blade along her thigh, barely avoiding her horse. No sense wasting a perfectly good animal.

She screamed, and in her shock, fell from the saddle pad. Her blood turned the surrounding snow bright red.

I grabbed her hair and pressed the sharp edge of my sword against her throat.

"Tell them all why you're really fighting," I screamed.

The surrounding warriors didn't pause their own fights, but a few cast looks at the scene we made.

"Food—" she started.

"The truth!"

Her hands and fingernails latched onto my wrists, but on her knees, bleeding badly from the leg, and already worn from battle, she batted uselessly at me.

"She killed my husband!" she cried. "She and Arminius the traitor killed him."

More fighters slowed and shifted their attention our way.

"Why? Tell them why." I gave her a hard shake and let my blade draw a thin line of blood for good measure.

"We're not traitors like you. We stand with Rome."

There it was, the opening I needed.

"Do you all hear her? They kneel to the masters who would see you starve. I offer you freedom, the same offer I made to the Mattiaci and now they go hungry."

Bit by bit, person by person, my words echoed outward and combatants slowed, then stopped to repeat what I said. Stopping some two-and-a-half thousand warriors mid-fight was no easy feat.

Inspiration sent from the gods. It wasn't the speech Wiltrud, Reimar, and I rehearsed while Segestes nodded along in silence. I hadn't meant to roar treason to so many people, least of all my father or our known enemies, the Mattiaci. Still, I raised my voice, so loud it cracked.

"You go hungry because Rome puts you on your knees. The Cherusci have food because they are fickle masters. Stand with me, with the Chatti, and Arminius, and you will be free to make your own futures. Germani do not kneel."

Again, my words echoed to each warrior.

Then they returned, quiet at first, growing louder and louder in a single chant.

Germani do not kneel.

⟶

The Mattiaci refused to stay and discuss the redistribution of food. They trudged away clinging tightly to their loot, and I watched them disappear into the woods, wondering what might come of my message for the scalcs. The word would spread, but would any defect from their masters?

Reimar said it was a mistake to let Arin live. I disagreed. To my surprise, he and Wiltrud deferred to me. More than that, others came to me in the aftermath seeking guidance. Warriors watched me, awaiting my word to lead negotiations. Though I'd never been in such a role, I'd never been the one they all turned to, I didn't intend to start with an execution.

Though I'd grown up as the head woman of the Cherusci, I'd never been a battle chief. That was what I wanted, wasn't it? I'd made myself the critical link in our rebellion, and that meant being the leader in these moments. That meant directing the negotiations over supplies, or at least appointing negotiators in my stead, as I did with Wiltrud, who in turn gathered warriors she trusted. It was new to me, to act in such a role on this scale. But I'd been training for this my entire life.

We set up our tents and stoked fires under the relative shelter of the tree line, then gathered to work out the food situation. Segestes kept his sullen silence while Wiltrud went to work. He hadn't spoken since the battle stopped and I had openly declared the intention to revolt.

I almost pitied him. It had taken him by surprise, the way all but the Mattiaci cheered a rebellion against the very thing to which my father had dedicated his life. His every goal centered on an alliance with Rome, and with a few choice words, he finally understood exactly how unpopular his views were.

Reimar filled a leather flask with broth warmed over the nearest fire, took a drink, and passed it to me. It went a long way toward staving off the cold.

"We'll all be hungry for the next few months," he said.

"But we won't starve, and now we've secured the Tencteri to our number. We need to show everyone that it's better to work with us."

He shrugged a big shoulder. We had hard work ahead to see it done. We considered which tribes and villages were most in need and which had food to spare. For the first time in living memory, our tribes faced a lean winter while guaranteeing the survival of all but the most feeble. The Cherusci and the Chatti wouldn't have the plump winter we'd prepared for, but our bounties were a vital lifeline for the Tencteri and Sugambri's outlying villages left with almost nothing after paying their taxes.

"You drew a hard line today," he said.

"Do you think I was wrong?" It didn't feel wrong. We could only keep our rebellion a secret for so long. It seemed silly to stay silent on a rumor already running rampant.

"Segestes may prove more dangerous than he seems."

I didn't plan on underestimating my father. Arminius had propositioned him about the rebellion and let him live. I wondered if he'd done that for me and if he'd made a horrible mistake.

"Arminius approached Segestes when he first returned," I said. "The only thing that surprised him today is bearing witness to how many agree with Arminius."

I produced a small sack of dried apple slices and offered it to Reimar, who took a few. The tart fruit contrasted unpleasantly with the savory broth we shared, but food was food and drink was drink. A long march followed by a battle left my stomach growling, and my limbs tight and angry. All the talk of food didn't help.

"Maybe," Reimar said after polishing off his apple slices, "but that doesn't make him any less dangerous. He can always go to Varus."

"No, he doesn't have Varus' respect. Arminius has that, and he can make Varus believe Segestes is the real traitor."

I took a few more slices and returned the sack to my saddlebags. With an ounce more of energy, I'd have risen and fetched a portion of dried fish. My legs felt like bruised jelly. I shouldn't have sat before getting food.

Reimar eyed me sideways, grunted, stood, and lumbered away without another word. I guessed that conversation was over and flopped back against a tree trunk, knowing I couldn't risk falling asleep alone out here, yet hardly able to keep my eyes open any longer.

"Here." My eyes shot back open at Reimar's voice. He held out a portion of hot, steaming meat. "One of our horses broke a leg. You couldn't smell it cooking?"

I patted dumbly at my nose and shook my head. Exhaustion hit harder than I realized. We rarely ate our horses. They were much too valuable as working animals for that, and the Cherusci seldom reached the point of starvation when we butchered every animal in a village. Still, I moaned at the first bite. It had been so long since I last tasted horse, I forgot how delicious it was, even prepared without the benefit of herbs.

Reimar settled back next to me, and we ate in companionable silence for several minutes before he spoke again.

"I'm not a fool. I know you are not thrilled with this match. I'm not, either. Irmhild was my wife and I vowed to never take another."

I swallowed a bit of meat and washed it down with more broth. When I struggled to respond, he waved a hand to stop me.

"Things change. The Chatti benefit from our union as much as the Cherusci. But Thusnelda, I swear to you I will be a good husband, if you will be a good wife."

He spoke the truth. Reimar would make a fine husband. He supported me when I came to him about Arminius. He didn't speak over or ignore me. He ensured I had food and drink without my asking. It was a primitive thing, to provide for one's mate. As far as the Romans were concerned, we were a primitive people and his simple gesture told me everything I needed to know about the kind of husband he'd be.

My heart broke a little. I wanted to want him and I never would. Another man occupied the space in my heart that I was supposed to save for Reimar.

Chapter 16

...just as though he could restrain the violence of barbarians
by the rod of a lictor and the proclamation of a herald. (Publius
Annius Florus)

The legions returned after Ôstara, when the snow melted and our days thawed.

Arminius, Varus, Legatus Vala, Centurion Eggius, Berut, and a coterie of auxiliary soldiers rode into our village in the late afternoon two days after rebuilding their encampment. If the villagers' mostly silent greeting disappointed Varus, he didn't show it. Segestes and Wout more than compensated, as effusive as if they welcomed old friends. Varus preened under the attention, while Vala turned up his nose.

Some part of me, the little girl who wanted to marry Ermin, or the woman who'd come under his skilled fingers, itched to run into Arminius' arms and judging by the way his gaze never left mine, he felt the same. He restrained himself while I mentally berated myself. I greeted Berut first while my father made a fool of himself over Varus.

As soon as we'd seen them coming, I'd directed the scalcs to prepare a feast. Lennart and one of his friends had brought down a boar the day prior, and it would make a fine meal. My bizarre excitement over seeing Arminius again—hearty and hale, just as I remembered him—mingled with my displeasure at having to spend the rest of the day and evening entertaining his odious peers. Winter gave me enough distance to find him decent company, when he chose to be. If this buzzing feeling in my lungs at just the sight of him was any indication, I'd actually missed him.

"If you don't mind," he caught Varus' attention while Jotapa served everyone drinks outside our hall, "I'd like to visit with my uncle before dinner."

"Of course, of course." Varus waved him away and let Segestes continue prattling on about the winter, the status of the spring plantings, hopes for a more prosperous harvest come fall. I wanted to hit him. The last thing we needed was Varus thinking we had more to tax.

Before he left, Arminius nodded at me with all the meaning he could pack into one look. My heart sped up. It was going to take all my self-control to keep from running after him immediately. Baduhenna, I had missed him. Damn it all. Simply seeing him again was enough to reignite a fire I'd spent too much time trying to ignore. I didn't know when I'd first craved him, the way I felt with him, and it didn't matter. It simply was, as true as the sun rising in the east and the turns of the moon.

Once the shock of his ignominious return wore off, it took him no time at all to sand away all the rough edges of my hatred until I'd merely wanted to hate him.

It was so much easier not to fight. He and I fought and argued plenty as it was without my private struggle with things so elusive and immaterial as attraction and affection. I enjoyed arguing with him. It warmed the blood. Yes, I could allow this affection, as long as it stayed at least a little hostile.

I made myself busy being unobtrusive, exactly the way Romans liked to see women. After half an hour of feigning interest in the conversation, I commented that I'd check on the dinner preparations. No one paid me any attention, so I slipped into the house and kept going out the back door.

As tempting as it was to run all the way to Ingomar's roundhouse, I restrained myself. He didn't need to know how eager I was by a flush in my cheeks and sweat on my brow.

Smoke puffed out from the *offnüng*, what Romans called a vent, in Ingomar's roof and the savory scent of stew wafted my way. My stomach rumbled, and I was even more grateful to see Arminius for the excuse to eat before dinner. I didn't think I'd eat in the presence of Vala and his death's head stare.

I came in without knocking. Ingomar glanced up, puffing on a long pipe.

"He's in the barn," he said, "waiting for you."

"Why isn't he in here?"

His lips quirked. "I believe he wanted privacy and didn't want to make me sit in the barn. Still drafty in there, you know."

I almost rushed back out, but paused long enough to say, "It's nice to see you again."

"Go, go." He waved me back out the door.

Light filtered through an open window, illuminating the barn's interior. Arminius paced from one end to the other, only stopping when he heard me enter.

He released a huge breath, then reached me in two strides.

I loved kissing him, the way our tongues explored each other, the way he nipped at my bottom lip, the way he held my face like a precious treasure. He'd taken off his armor so his warmth, his strength, wrapped around me without impediment.

I drank in his smell—leather, Roman bathing oil, man. Baduhenna, he smelled wonderful. How had he made me crave him with just a few kisses before winter? It didn't matter, not when the end result was my craving his kisses, his touches. It wasn't something I'd stewed over in the past months, yet now that he was here, touching and kissing me, I realized how deeply he'd gotten beneath my skin.

We broke apart bit by bit, each coming back for more as we gradually slowed down.

"Did you miss me?" He smiled against my mouth.

I gave him a light push and he didn't budge, only snickered and ducked back for another quick kiss.

"I missed you," he said against my lips.

Sense slowly returned as my heart settled back down.

"I missed you," I admitted.

Arminius leaned back and quirked an eyebrow at me. "Did you just say you missed me? Are you feeling well?"

"I'm quite well, thank you for your concern." I rolled my eyes and tried to step out from the circle of his arms, but he tightened his hold and brought me impossibly closer. No. Oh no. This was not going to become a romantic reunion fit for the old stories. I changed the subject the best way I knew how. "The Tencteri and Marsi have formally pledged to our cause. We had a bit of a battle, but—"

"You were in a battle?" His voice rose, echoing off the stone walls surrounding us. "You're just now telling me you were in a battle while I was fucking off across the Rhine?"

Somewhere between his concern and outrage, I wanted to laugh.

"It was nothing." I smoothed my hands up his chest and over his shoulders, as if we often found ourselves in each other's arms. "It worked in our favor. You should have seen them once they heard me. Our people are ready to rise up. We're producing weapons, scouting for a battle site. We might have found somewhere suitable, but it will be difficult getting the legions to—"

He pressed a finger to my lips.

"As much as I adore listening to you talk tactics, I just got back from an interminably long winter and a longer march here. Can we please talk about anything else?"

I swallowed a breath. Without meaning to, he offered an excellent excuse to avoid telling him about the promise I'd made to the scalcs. A promise I hadn't mentioned to Reimar either. They wouldn't like it; they wouldn't appreciate it until the time came for the battle. Maybe they'd never appreciate it the way I did, growing up with only a scalc as a companion. Even Arminius was never truly a slave or servant in Rome.

Upon closer inspection, bruising darkened the circles of his eyes, his cheekbones stood sharper than normal, his nose bore a sunburn. Winter had drained some of the color from his skin and left him vulnerable to the sun during his march.

He took my hand and led me to where he'd spread a blanket over a mound of hay. We eased into it, with me tucked into the crook of his shoulder, and together we exhaled contented sighs. I'd never lain like this with another man, though Jotapa and I sometimes shared a bed. It felt right, though. The pressure of his body against mine, his arm curled around my torso, offered a kind of comfort I seldom experienced.

"You're thinner than when I left," he said. "I thought I made sure the Cherusci weren't overtaxed."

I nuzzled closer and wrapped an arm across his slowly rising and falling chest. It was an act of indulgence that, after a long, hungry winter, I felt I deserved. "That was your doing? Segestes took all the credit for our winter stores."

"What happened?" His body tensed next to mine and deftly avoided answering my question.

I told him about the Mattiaci and the starving tribesmen they'd encouraged into raiding and how I'd worked with the Chatti to redistribute food supplies. I related my speech as best I remembered it and the chanting that followed. I still didn't tell him about my message to the scalcs, another secret scattering its way through our secret uprising. It wasn't the right time, I told myself. He would be furious, and I wasn't ready to break this happy reunion. Frankly, the one scalc I told might have died within seconds of agreeing to pass the message. It might all come to nothing.

He pressed a kiss to my forehead. "You did well. They'll follow you anywhere now."

"It was all Wiltrud's idea," I said with a shake of my head.

"Doesn't matter. You're the one who stopped the battle. That's no small thing, Wildberry. That's what they care about, not the administration of things."

Guilt coiled in my gut. Wiltrud was the queen, not me. Yet they had looked to me, even as Wiltrud held court with the tribesmen and issued her instructions.

A lifetime making myself a leader among the Cherusci, and I continued to chafe against memories of that winter battle. I had led it, but I hadn't. I had led the negotiations, but I hadn't. Not in the way to which I was accustomed. Hela, I hadn't even initiated the battle. Segestes had done that. After working so hard to earn respect among my tribe, it seemed wrong to take credit for these events.

I would make you queen of Germania, his voice whispered in my ear, though his mouth never moved.

No. I was no queen. Not like this. Not in a way I understood. A queen had to have her hands in everything. This couldn't be right, just as being queen over multiple tribes would never be right. He was a madman. Tragically, I felt damn good in his arms, receiving his praise.

***

"Here," Arminius tapped his finger at a spot on the map spread across the table in Ingomar's house. "Have any of your scouts reported on this area?"

We had little time left before our shared absence would be noted. For all his insistence that he and I share at least a few minutes without discussing battle plans, as soon as we returned to the roundhouse, he couldn't resist producing a visual aid to share his ideas.

"That's the place I mentioned," I tapped a finger at his hastily drawn picture of the forest and swamp, "but it's too far from your marching route and through our densest forest. How will we get three legions in there?"

His lips thinned. "Four."

"What?"

"We returned with four legions."

My skin heated with anger while fear cooled my blood. Judging by Ingomar's icy expression, the older man felt the same.

"What do you mean you returned with four legions? And waited until now to say something?" My voice turned shrill. Embarrassing, but there was nothing for it.

Arminius straightened. "Because in here, their numbers won't matter."

"Nephew, that's thousands more soldiers. Your plan is good, but it isn't that good."

"They had eleven legions posted between Gaul and Germania Magna. That number is down to two thanks to another uprising in Pannonia. Before we left Vetera, there was talk that Augustus would call more from Germania. Even if all four legions stay here, and I highly doubt they will, this is still the perfect time to retake our land. They're leaving the entire territory undefended. And this spot," he shoved a finger at his drawing, "is perfect. We could wipe out fifty thousand men here if we needed to."

He practically vibrated with excitement the more he spoke. It was a gift, this ability to twist even the worst news into something positive, to make everyone around him believe it. Unfortunately for him, neither I nor Ingomar could be so easily persuaded.

"You forget," Ingomar said, "that legionaries are skilled in single combat. They are not rendered useless in the absence of a formation."

"Even if we have every tribesman on the field, we can't match four legions," I said.

My head ached. The afternoon had whipped from happiness to anxiety so quickly my neck ached as well. I dropped my head and rubbed at my temples until Arminius' strong fingers replaced mine.

"We can and we won't have to." His voice rumbled, low and soothing. "It won't be all four legions. You have to trust me. Varus won't even use his *lanciarii*. He hates them because they won't shave their beards. He keeps them in the detached cohorts when we're on the march."

The *lanciarii* soldiers stood to be our biggest threat. Unmatched in combat, they had our ability to blend into the forest combined with the precision unique to Rome, and they were utterly fearless.

I looked up at his earnest face. He believed what he said with his whole heart, and it brought me back to Jotapa's words the day he'd marched out for the winter. Arminius didn't know the meaning of the word "impossible."

A man who didn't know the meaning of the word "impossible" was a man who could lead us to ruin. He'd proceed with this uprising if the Romans had one hundred thousand men, more soldiers than stars in the sky. How many Germani would march into the gaping maw of death because he willed it?

"I trust you," I said, for there was nothing else I could say. Not yet, anyway.

"Good." He relaxed again. "You'll have to trust me to get them there, but once they're in these woods, our land will be their biggest enemy. By the time we strike, they'll be exhausted, scared, scattered over miles."

His plan was good in theory, yet still outlandish. It relied too heavily on luck, something no amount of planning and oversight could control. As it was, I now believed we had a much, much bigger problem than a suitable ambush site: a leader convinced of his invincibility.

Spring gave way to summer and with it we mobilized across our allied tribes to produce a vast armory. To the Marsi we assigned the unenviable task of molding the ambush site to perfectly suit our needs.

The Teutoburg wald was a mass of densely packed trees, sharp ravines, dotted with marshes and bogs. Our priestesses often disappeared into that wilderness for days on end to commune with the gods. It was said we mortals could dip our toes into the spiritual realm if we wandered deep enough into a truly wild place, a place seldom touched by the hand of man.

I didn't know if any of that was true, but I knew we were going to feed that wald all the blood it could drink. The Marsi spent months damming waterways to flood the widest paths, anywhere a legion might naturally choose to march. Arminius wanted them forced into the trees, where they were weakest.

More than weak, he explained, terrified.

"They don't have forests like this in Italia," he'd said. "They've already settled everywhere they've been in Gaul. They think our woods are death traps."

"And you mean to prove them right," I added.

He'd smiled at me, leonine, predatory. The smile of a man longing to sink his teeth into his prey and tear it apart. None matched his desire to rip the still beating heart of Rome from its breast.

Those who weren't busy flooding the only usable paths were constructing a rampart along a narrow ravine several miles long, squeezed treacherously between a steep hillside and a long, deep bog. A high earthen and stone-and-stick-woven wall would provide cover while allowing our fighters to spear and shoot the fleeing, trapped Romans where they made their last stand.

Assuming we got them there. All of this rested on Arminius' ability to corral four legions into territory everyone in their command knew to be suicidally dangerous. If beating four legions with our paltry numbers —no more than eighteen thousand, by my last count, assuming all of our allies actually arrived to fight with us—wasn't difficult enough, I still couldn't conceive of how we'd get them into the Teutoburg in the first place.

This forest was so forbidding, our own people avoided it. Hunters entered in groups and travelers seldom traversed it.

When I utterly failed at forcing Arminius to reveal the precise steps he intended to take to convince Varus and Vala and all those other officers to follow him into the Teutoburg, I stuck my nose into the construction of the dams and ramparts, only to be shooed away by the skilled Marsi engineers. I nosed around our blacksmiths until it became clear that they also needed no supervision to mass produce arrowheads. For want of something to do that I actually had control over, I dragged Konrada and Jotapa out for more training, nailing straw-stuffed targets to trees bordering the western edge of our village. Each carried a bow and quiver of arrows, sharpened at the end to not waste good arrowheads.

Once the last was posted, we returned to the edge of the tree line.

"I know you can both hit a target," I said. "The object of today's lesson is hitting a target from the run. I'll go first, then you follow the same path."

I pulled a clutch of arrows and placed them in my grip hand for faster retrieval. *Inhale. Exhale. Now.*

My feet pounded down the course we'd laid out, high-stepping over roots and low bushes, all while I loosed arrow after arrow into our targets. I performed the action by rote, born of a lifetime of training. I hardly needed to look where I shot. My muscles and limbs worked in concert, doing what they were made to do. While the mantle of general sat uneasily upon my shoulders—I was too used to handling things myself for that—this came naturally. I was made to be a warrior. It was the only path my life ever could have taken.

When I finished the course, I jogged back to the others, panting lightly.

Jotapa sucked her tongue over her teeth and harrumphed. We'd trained together often enough that she was confident in today's test. Konrada, however, couldn't hide the trepidation in her eyes. Her left forearm bore bruises and sores beneath a thick layer of bandages from her struggles with archery. Something as simple as a slight twist to her elbow prevented that, but she was inexperienced. My grip arm had its own layer of calluses built up from so many years spent shooting.

I yearned to tell Konrada to go back home and abandon the idea that she'd be fighting with us, but that was a lost cause. She was too much like me. She'd sneak into the battle with or without my help. Since it was far better for her to fight with some training than none, I surrendered. The only way I could even attempt to guarantee her safety was to include her.

To add pressure on Konrada, I bid Jotapa to go next. The girl had much to learn in a short amount of time if she was to fight with us, including overcoming her nerves.

"Watch her and tell me what you think she's done well and what she hasn't," I said.

She nodded grimly, brows wrinkled tight as Jotapa moved through the course. Our Scythian friend was lighter on her feet than I was; faster, but less accurate. Her arrows didn't sink as deeply through the targets and into the trees. They didn't land with the same heavy thunk. She was strong, but not as strong as me and couldn't manage the same draw on her bow.

When she returned, I looked to Konrada. "Well?"

The younger girl squirmed a bit to be put on the spot, unwilling to insult Jotapa by criticizing her performance. Much had changed for her since the day she'd called her a filthy little scalc.

"I think maybe she should have slowed down. She didn't always hit the target completely and some arrows were shallow."

Jotapa nodded along gamely and accepted the criticism.

"That may be true," I said. "But speed on the battlefield is a gift. These targets are stationary, and no one is trying to kill you here. Out there, you could be surrounded, warriors coming at you from all sides. You won't have time to slow down and measure each shot. Sometimes, firing an arrow at a person is enough to slow them down, without ever hitting them."

Her brow furrowed deeper. "I shouldn't worry about accuracy?"

"No, I didn't say that. If all you're doing is wildly loosing arrows, the enemy will notice and you risk hitting your allies."

"Then what am I supposed to do? I'm not as strong as you or as fast as her."

I pulled her bow off her shoulder and placed it in her hands. "You train. We're going to train as hard as we can, as often as we can."

There wasn't a suitable answer to her question. Jotapa's speed and inaccuracy could get her killed as easily as my accuracy and slower speed. Konrada could outlive us all by sheer luck.

She took a deep breath, pulled extra arrows into her grip hand as I had done, and burst into a run. She was faster and more agile than she gave herself credit for, and almost as accurate as Jotapa. With time, she'd be even better. Jotapa let out a startled laugh and clapped her hands in delight at Konrada's success.

Though Konrada hadn't trained since childhood—her parents were goatherds and expected their children to follow the same path—every time we trained together, she displayed an innate skill. One day, she might be better than me. I prayed she'd live long enough to get there.

I obsessed over the details again, as if I could speak the ambush into existence by repetition alone. That's how our priestesses called to our gods, was it not? By the power of their voices and rituals. This was my ritual and my shield against Arminius. As long as I kept this barrier between us, our relationship remained about one thing and one thing only: the coming war. The litany of troop numbers, supplies, weapons, the terrain, and all the ways we'd make it into our strongest weapon of all, all of it together, spoken again and again as a prayer.

I can't love him. I refuse to love him. He is a good soldier, a shrewd tactician I respect. He's a good kisser. And that is all.

"Elda." Arminius' hand covered mine. "I know all of this. You know all of this. Sit and have a drink with me. Please."

We met so often in Ingomar's crumbling barn, it was a wonder Segestes hadn't yet figured out where I spent so many of my evenings, if he cared at all anymore. Segestes no longer appeared to care about much, keeping to his own council and letting Wout and Lennart assume his role with the chieftains.

It was a wonder I'd kept Arminius at bay this long. It was a wonder I'd kept myself at bay this long. I dreamed about what we'd done last fall so many times, it was a wonder I hadn't just ordered him to repeat the experience.

He offered me a cup from Ingomar's best ale, my favorite of his heady, sweet concoctions. Romans found our ales and meads too strong. They had weak constitutions. I accepted the cup he offered but didn't sit.

"I want to ensure we're as prepared as possible," I said.

He took my hands and pulled me between his bent knees. "We are prepared. Everything is going to plan, but things will go wrong. Half of our allies have promised their support only if they see the battle going well. We can't plan for everything."

"But—"

"No," he chuckled, "no amount of grinding these plans into dust is going to change that. Please sit and let's talk about anything else. Just for a little while."

It was grossly unfair of him to look up at me with all that hope and effortless charm gleaming in his eyes. It made me want to agree to anything he asked. With nothing more than a few pleas, he had me sitting next to him, shoulder to shoulder in the lamplight.

"Fine. What do you want to talk about that's so much more important than our ambush?"

He reached out to smooth my loose hair back behind my ear, where his rough fingertips remained. I shivered at the sensation.

"Marry me. You know I'm a much better match for you than Reimar."

My cursed wedding, the only other thing we talked about anymore. I wished I had the power to speak that event out of existence.

I tried to pull away, but he didn't let me. "I know you're tired of hearing this, and I don't care. Marry me, Thusnelda. I... we will deal with the Chatti. I'm not worried about that and you shouldn't be, either."

"What we'll both do is what we must," I said. "It's what we're both good at."

"Fine." His hand sank into my hair at the back of my head and urged me closer. "But not yet, though, right?"

"No, not—"

He kissed me and kissed me and kissed me, bathed in flickering flame and surrounded by rough wood and stone walls that weren't likely to survive another winter.

This was the opposite of keeping him at bay, of keeping myself from loving him. I tore away and marched to the ladder. His frustrated sigh followed in my wake. I needed a distraction for both of us before this went any further.

"I want to show you something," I said between gasps. "Stay here."

I climbed into the barn loft and fetched the wolf pelt I'd spent the past weeks preparing for him but paused before descending with it. In the dim light, it looked inadequate. It was big enough to suit him, but in my hands, it looked too small, too old, not a garment befitting a king. According to Ingomar, it had been Arminius' mother's project around the time she took to the woods and never returned.

When Ingomar had suggested I finish preparing the pelt in lieu of another round of my obsessive need to check in with each known ally, I'd balked. This wasn't the sort of thing a woman did for a man unless they were to be married, or he was her son. I should have been doing this for Reimar. But once the old skin was in my hands, like always I saw clearly what needed to be done and couldn't stop myself from finishing it.

Swallowing my concerns, I descended the ladder and turned slowly to face him. His eyes found the white and gray fur, but he kept silent.

"Ingomar said your mother began preparing this for you, before..." Before he was taken. Before she vanished. Before everything changed. "I had to patch it in places."

I thrust it toward his chest and stepped back, worrying my hands into tight fists. If he was to lead us into battle as our war chief, he needed the mark of a chief. It was a necessity. My palms sweated waiting on his reaction. Without ever needing to discuss it amongst ourselves, we all knew Arminius was to be our war chief. Reimar didn't call warriors to him in that way, at least not in the bombastic way we needed, and most saw me as something of a shrew. A useful, helpful shrew who could be counted on, but a shrew nonetheless. One of many curses of my sex. Arminius was the one.

He unfolded and spread it in his hands, saying nothing. He draped it over his forearm and stroked the dense fur. Nothing in his expression gave away his thoughts.

"This was for me?" His fingers briefly tightened on the fur, and he closed his eyes. When he opened them again, he looked directly at me. "Thank you."

"It's nothing." I cast my eyes to the dirt floor. "It had to be done."

"It's not nothing. It's all I have left of her." He took a step closer into my space. "It's beautiful. Thank you."

My cheeks heated under his praise. He tipped my chin up with his forefinger, staring at me like he'd never seen me before.

"I'm glad you like it," I said, like an idiot.

His cheeks lifted in a sly smile. "Are you blushing?"

I batted his hand away. "No."

"Yes, you are." He tugged me into the circle of his arms. The pelt's soft fur brushed against the bare skin of my shoulders and arms. "Don't worry, I won't tell anyone you blush."

When he got me into a hug, fighting with him was useless, so I surrendered to it, breathing in his warm scent.

"I will wear it with honor."

"You'd better."

He pulled back. "I like that you only blush with me."

He got down on one knee before me. "I will wear this into battle, and I will bring you Varus' head."

Never had I heard more romantic words.

Then he swatted my ass.

Chapter 17

The sexes unite equally matched and robust. (Tacitus)

My chosen horse sensed my nerves as I strapped my bag to her back. She shied away from my brusque touch and tossed her head against her ties. Jotapa and Konrada whispered and shot glances my way, punctuated by giggles.

Their little friendship was quickly turning into an annoyance for me.

"What are you whispering about?" I tightened the girth strap on my saddle pad once more. As expected, the mare had been bloating her stomach to keep the strap loose.

"Nothing," they answered in unison, then giggled more.

Konrada jumped to sit atop a barrel, produced a small knife, and began picking at her dirty fingernails. "Are you sure we shouldn't come with you? It's a long way alone, and your family..."

She didn't have to finish that last part. Levin had provided more of a buffer than I'd realized. Without him, every moment in my home was one flint strike away from conflagration. Fortunately, Wout's limp and recovery left him weak. Lennart seldom acted on his own initiative, and Segestes had been subdued since the winter raid. None of that meant I was safe or that they weren't liable to take action against me.

It was only a matter of time before they roused themselves to the task, or I did something so egregious they couldn't ignore it. Like taking off to meet with Reimar—and Arminius—the moment the Chatti messenger told me I was needed. There was no hiding where I went and why, so I didn't bother with any lies this time. I also didn't bother to tell anyone I was leaving, except my friends.

"Don't bother arguing with her," Jotapa said. "It's no use, not when when she's set her mind to something."

"You say that like it's a character flaw." I tied an extra grain sack and water skin on the side opposite my traveling bag. "Konrada, you have your own family to see to, and Jotapa has duties here to attend."

After much discussion, I agreed to let Jotapa perform my usual rounds in the village. It wasn't as if she didn't know what needed to be done, who needed to be tended to, or that she couldn't be trusted. I trusted her implicitly. However in fifteen years, I'd so seldom passed my duties on to anyone else, it was as if I never had at all. It was always me. A year earlier, and I might have refused altogether. Much had changed in the intervening time, and my new role as a general of the uprising pulled me in so many new directions, I simply couldn't be all things at all times.

And that was, I discovered, fine. Jotapa would see to everything.

It liberated me in a way I never expected.

It liberated me until Segestes, Wout, and Lennart stormed into the barn and reminded me that not everything could work in my favor.

"No!" Segestes roared and shook his finger in my face. "I forbid this! I told you what would happen if you kept this up. I told you! You think you can carry on like this in broad daylight, for all to see? You cannot shout your treachery to the sky and expect no consequences."

Before Lennart could reach for me, I yanked my sword free from the sheath at my hip.

"What do you think you're doing?" Wout demanded.

"I'm—" I stopped as soon as I caught sight of Jotapa brandishing a pitchfork like a spear. Wout's question was for her, not me.

With my left hand, I reached out and lowered Jotapa's weapon. As a scalc, taking a weapon to a free man called for a lashing, followed by banishment. It was as close to a death sentence as we came.

"Don't," I said with a quick shake of my head.

Then I saw Konrada with a bow drawn, arrow nocked and aimed at Segestes. I hadn't even realized she'd brought the weapon with her.

Segestes blanched at the sight. He shook his head as if to clear the confusing image away. "I am your chief," he sputtered.

She shrugged one shoulder.

My heart raced. It was too much to believe they both put their lives and freedom at risk for me.

"You haven't been chief of the Cherusci for a long time," Jotapa said. I almost hissed for her silence but stopped myself. She was right, more so now than ever before. He lived in a shell, sending his crippled son out to do his bidding, little as it was. "She is the chief, and everyone knows it."

Though I appreciated Jotapa's words, if she kept this up, I'd be forced to keep her with me until the uprising. For her own safety.

"She's nothing." Lennart spat and took a half-step toward me, until Konrada swiveled her arrow his direction. May the gods above help me, she *tsked* at him.

"I'll make you a promise, Father." My sword remained ready in my strong hand. "You stay out of my way, and I won't kill your sons and then you."

Wout and Lennart made noises of protest, but Segestes silenced them. His chin tipped up, a gesture I knew I often mirrored.

With stunning clarity, I realized Jotapa was right. Segestes had his councils with his chieftains, the collection of men he favored, but I had everyone else. Even the chieftains often deferred to me without question. Some part of me had known since I first insisted the Cherusci would rebel with Arminius. For the same reason they turned to me during the winter raid and women from myriad tribes turned to me with their griefs, the Cherusci would rebel if I told them it was the thing to do. My chest swelled with a rush of pride, and I found myself standing straighter.

"The Cherusci don't answer to you. Not the way they answer to me. The rebellion will happen, whether you like it or not, and our tribe will lead it. If you come at me like this again, I won't hold back. If that's what you want, if you want us to fight to the death, then say the word and we'll finish this right here, right now."

The corners of his eyes crinkled and I noticed the deep grooves and wrinkles in his skin. "You would kill your whole family just to bring our whole tribe to ruin?"

"Of course she would." Lennart spat a thick glob of mucus on the ground at my feet. "She thinks she's better than us."

"Enough!" Segestes shouted and his voice broke. "Enough of this. We're not going to kill each other, for fuck's sake. Thusnelda, that's not what I want. But if you push me, I will take this matter to Vala and Varus himself. I will protect our family and our tribe with whatever tools you leave me."

Thanks to Arminius and his bravado, I didn't worry about Varus. I did worry about Vala, with his shrewd, sunken eyes. I kept my face in a hard mask.

"Go ahead. Tell them. They won't believe you, not over Arminius." I hoped my voice didn't shake and reveal how much I questioned that statement.

Segestes nodded and gestured for my brothers to back off. Wout took a lurching step forward, rounding on him.

"What are you doing? We have to stop her!"

Segestes nodded. "And we will, but not like this. I am not putting my daughter in chains, and I won't see you at each other's throats. I will handle this."

Wout and Lennart looked mutinous.

"I mean it," Segestes said. "From now on, you stay out of it. Now go."

With a few dark glares, they relented. I lowered my sword. Segestes stayed by the open barn doors, haloed by morning sun.

"I haven't been the father you wanted me to be," he began. "But I do want you to be safe and taken care of. I hoped your betrothal to Reimar would temper some of this in you, but I see now that was a mistake. If you think the Romans won't take the threat of an uprising seriously, you are a fool beyond measure. I will go to them, they will investigate, and all I can do is pray that you are not fool enough to get caught in their net."

He walked away without waiting for my reply, or to hear my sharp intake of breath against the pain in his voice. It was easy to hate him when we were so different, so often at each other's throats. It was easy to forget he was my Papa, once.

⟶

Reimar stared at Arminius. Arminius stared at Reimar. Ermin chewed loudly on a roll, exchanging pointed looks with Berut. They communicated through brow raises, and I suspected a silent wager was taking place in Raginmar's hall.

"What the fuck do you mean the chieftains are backing out?" Arminius ground out each word. We sat around Raginmar's table with his chieftains, the men who saw to the outlying Chatti settlements, and a squadron of Arminius' ala.

Reimar shrugged a big shoulder. "News of that fourth legion spread quickly. The chiefs still want war, but their chieftains..."

He trailed off and finished his alehorn, holding it up for a scalc to fill.

"The chieftains should follow their chief," Arminius clipped back.

Raginmar said, "Boy, you can't have been away for that long. If they lose confidence in their chief, they won't do a damn thing he says. The Sugambri are split, as are the Marsi and the Bructeri. The Chauci wouldn't commit to a fight if it was burning their longhouse down. The Tencteri remain loyal, though."

I groaned inwardly. The Tencteri were a small, weak tribe who added little to our efforts.

"What of their honor?" A vein pulsed in Arminius' neck. "It's one more fucking legion."

"No honor in suicide," Raginmar said. "They're not stupid. It's not one more fucking legion, as you say. They've got soldiers posted across our land. What about the legions across the Rhine?"

"They're gone." Arminius shook his head. "What you see out there is a farce. Augustus called almost everyone back to Pannonia to end the uprising there."

"And that," Wiltrud raised her voice, "is also a problem. What if they wipe out those rebels and come for us? I believe in your plan, but I know what the Germani are thinking."

Arminius pushed away from the table to pace behind his seat. "So, what, then? It's all over because the Germani are afraid of what might happen? The Pannonians have been rebelling for years, and Rome still hasn't put it down. Those legions are just as likely to never return to our borders. I assure you that after they're done with Pannonia, there will be something else. They are spread too thin."

Raginmar stroked his beard and hummed in thought.

"We're forgetting something important," he said. "The will of the gods. What we need is a good omen. That will lift their spirits and put iron in their spines."

"For fuck's sake." Arminius dragged a hand through his short hair. "The will of the gods? All I need is some superstitious drivel to secure the loyalty of twenty thousand warriors?"

"He's right," Reimar said. "Most of us still believe in the gods. Her included."

He inclined his head toward me, and I sank deep into my seat. Arminius narrowed his gaze on mine, and I sensed him willing me to contradict Reimar. I started to speak as he willed, then stopped. He was being pig-headed about this for reasons I didn't understand, and I didn't owe him blind allegiance. I was the third corner of this plot and a leader in my own right.

"It's true that I believe the gods express their will in ways we don't understand," I said. "Regardless, most Germani believe strongly in our priestesses, divination, omens, all of it. It can't hurt to have a priestess or two on our side."

His jaw tightened, but he nodded. "Fine. I have enough coin to guarantee a few good omens from the right people."

Raginmar hissed a breath between his teeth and colored with anger. "You were gone too long. Our priestesses are not like your petty priests. We cannot buy them with coin or sacrifices."

"What do you mean, *my* petty priests?" Arminius stood and took a threatening step toward Raginmar. The Chatti in attendance, including Reimar, jumped to their feet, hands to swords and daggers. Arminius halted and raised his hands in deference.

He looked about the room, chest rising and falling in deep breaths. "Need I remind everyone here that I'm doing this precisely because I am not one of them?"

The entire hall went silent, every eye on him.

"I am going to lead Varus and his legions into the Teutoburg." He spoke softly. "We are going to kill every last one of them, and when we're done, we will march on every outpost, every fort, and the settlement, and kill them to a man. By the time we're finished, Rome won't have the heart to try again. I don't need a damned omen."

At that, he looked at me, expression twisted with hurt and confusion. His expression was so at odds with his rousing speech, with the way it made my heart pound and my eyes go wide, seeing what others saw in him, I almost laughed. A man so convinced of his invincibility, so passionate about his goal, had no business being hurt by a perceived slight. A man like that couldn't be hurt by anything.

"I will call on our priestesses tomorrow. If the omens are good, we will spread the word. If they are bad, despite what my husband says, we can, in fact, buy their silence." Wiltrud squeezed Raginmar's shoulder.

He stewed on this for a moment before resuming his seat. The rest of the hall followed suit. They quickly forgot most of the tension as the warriors and soldiers resumed their drinking and eating, two favorite activities of any Germani tribesman, outranked only by battle and sex.

"If we don't get good omens, we will find a priestess willing to provide them," Arminius said almost to himself, an insistence that he could control something fundamentally uncontrollable. Even I knew that.

His plate remained full for the rest of the evening. I accepted a private room for the night, since I didn't desire a night sleeping in a hall full of men. Drunk men, no less, as the night wore on. I longed for Jotapa's presence at my side.

Now and then, I caught Arminius watching me from across the table. Each time our eyes met, my blood heated. Shame, anger, frustration, wanting; it all roiled in a confusing, pulsing mass. Shame because I sat next to Reimar and sided with him, or so Arminius assumed. My teeth clenched at the thought. Gods, but I desired him so badly I ached with it. My pulse thumped between my legs for wanting him so much.

When he excused himself from the table, I fought my own battle to keep from rushing after him. I wanted to soothe his wounded pride. I wanted to punch him for taking that one step toward Raginmar in the man's own hall. I wanted to be in his arms.

Sitting next to Reimar, sharing a meal with him, scraped me raw. Conversation flowed around the table, but I heard none of it. He performed the duties of a husband, ensuring my plate and cup were full, all without looking at or speaking to me. He spoke to others, gruff, but still speaking.

The prospect of a silent life with him yawned in my future, expansive and cold. I'd been naive to think I'd ever embrace such a life with open, satisfied arms. No, I wanted heat, warmth against our dark winters. There was enough coldness in our world without adding to it in the marriage bed.

When the dinner ended, I made my excuses and hurried to the small room Wiltrud had shown me earlier. It had once belonged to Reimar's sisters and now sat empty, waiting for guests or, during the winter, served as another place to pen animals out of the cold. Unlike my room, it had no window. It did have a hatch in the roof that, I discovered, led to the attic, which featured several *offnüngs*, the central of which was large enough to squeeze through.

I found Arminius tending to a horse that didn't need tending. The slight tensing of his shoulders told me he knew I was there. He kept on brushing the animal while it chomped at the already nicked-thin grass of the pasture.

"We'll get good omens," I said. My voice carried over the still night. It was late enough that most villagers were abed. With no light, he was a large shadow, marked out by his red tunic and off-white undergarments.

"I know," came his reply.

"The gods have blessed our endeavor."

He stopped brushing and faced me in the shadowy darkness. Not even the moon offered its light.

"I don't need the gods' blessings, because I have a damn good plan."

I stepped through the fence and walked to him, close enough to discern his features.

"Maybe, maybe not. You said yourself we can't control everything that happens. Blessings from a few priestesses will strengthen our cause in the eyes of other tribesmen."

He looked to the heavens and the blanket of endless stars.

"Do you not believe in me?" His voice came out small, softer and more hesitant than I'd ever heard him speak.

"Of course I believe in you." I took his hand and he let me have it. "I wouldn't be here if I didn't. It's only that we are going to need all the help we can get. That means Donar and Wodan and Tyr and all our gods. That also means you can't sneer at superstitious tribesmen and expect them to follow you."

He breathed a long sigh. "You're right. The fourth legion he brought, the Sixteenth, came as a surprise to me, too. Everyone at Vetera told him they'll get called out to Pannonia. He wasn't thinking right, bringing them here."

I brushed a hand along the bristles of his jaw with new understanding. "He did something you didn't expect, and now you doubt yourself."

"I cannot afford to doubt myself." He shook his head, took the palm I held to his cheek, and kissed it. "If the Sixteenth stays in country, we may have a more arduous battle, but we can win it."

When he pulled me into his arms, I let him take whatever comfort I could offer. "I believe in you. With the priestesses, the others will, as well."

His fingers traced up and down my back, an action with the power to quickly render me into a pleasant stupor.

"Please don't marry him," he breathed into my ear and another piece of my heart fractured and fell away. "I can protect you. Wiltrud is too shrewd to throw everything away over a broken betrothal. We won't lose them."

Whatever need I felt for him slammed against an immovable barrier: What he suggested violated our honor. In truth, I had no choice but to believe he truly did want to marry me, because there was no good reason to do it. I was already his ally, he didn't need to feign a romance to gain my support. Pursuing me only stood to hurt us.

"And everyone else who sees you as a man willing to betray an ally over a woman?" I leaned back to look him in the eye. "They won't follow you if they don't trust you."

An owl hooted as it soared overhead. Insects and toads sang their eerie songs. Horses snuffled around us on the hunt for more to chew. The night went on, heedless of two people repeating the same argument over and over.

His lips pulled tight. "You won't say yes to me, will you?"

"I won't."

He brushed his fingertips through my hair. "How long can I have you for?"

I almost couldn't form the words. They were too final, a date too soon. I had to voice them.

"We're to be married during Haustblot, as we were supposed to last year. Everyone will be there. We can complete our plans at the feast."

"Right. Right." He sucked his tongue over his teeth. "Very well."

He snatched my hand and led me on a quick march to the lean-to where his men had stored their saddles and gear. After grabbing a blanket, he set out again, faster this time.

"What are you doing?" I trotted to keep up, glancing over my shoulder at the rapidly diminishing longhouse. In moments, we were deep in the woods, surrounded by all the familiar trees. It was at once quieter and louder without the lingering traces of human settlement in the Chatti village.

He tossed the blanket to a relatively clear spot at the base of an alder and took my face in his hands. His thumbs skimmed over my cheekbones, and my eyelids fluttered shut of their own volition.

"If I only get to have you for a little while," his nose brushed against mine, "then I am going to keep you for as long as I can, my Amazon."

He spread the blanket over the ground. Around us the forest went silent.

Unsure, I stood back and watched him make quick work of our natural bed. His movements were rushed and jerky, a far cry from his typical smooth confidence. Not unlike his panic after saving me during our fight against the Mattiaci. His hands shook. He wanted this in a way I still didn't understand. I craved his presence in my life, and I craved his touch. This, however, was physical proof that he desired me in the same way, maybe more so. I'd never been on the receiving end of such need and fought my instinct to mistrust it. To declare him a liar and a manipulator who wanted *something* from me.

But he wasn't using me, at least not in the way I initially believed.

"Arminius..."

He stripped off his belt and boots.

"I surrender," he said with a rueful shake of his head.

"What?"

"I said I surrender. We won't marry, but I will make you mine first."

He held out his hand and let me come to him. He always did that, offered his hand and waited, never compelling me to do anything I didn't want to do.

I cared for him. I enjoyed his quick smiles and humor as I lusted for his powerful fists and the way he sat his horse like a great conqueror who hadn't decided to conquer anything yet. This conqueror had done more than choose me, he surrendered to me. Every reason I'd repeated to myself to keep him at a safe distance evaporated. I wanted him, he wanted me, and since I might never get to feel what he made me feel again, I jumped into the abyss again.

First, I removed my belt, then I loosened the ties of my tunic. Arminius' hungry eyes drank in my every move. Gooseflesh prickled along my arms, and my skin turned oversensitive. The slightest movement of air hitched my breath and my fingers shook clumsily.

There was no reason to be nervous. I'd done this before, and Arminius and I had already crossed every line up to this point. If I interpreted his intentions correctly, we were about to cross a line from which there was no coming back. I might even get his child. Since it was too much to contemplate, I pushed that thought away.

I took my time removing my boots. The next thing I knew, my tunic was off and he was kissing me. They were drugging, his kisses, better than the poppy a Roman medicus could offer or anything our grandmothers kept in their healing stores. My breasts brushed against the soft wool of his tunic and I wanted more.

We undressed each other in a rush. I snickered when he lost his balance doffing his trousers and almost fell, then we collapsed into each other, laughing, kissing, reacquainting ourselves with each other's bodies in the cool night air.

His fingers found my core aching and needy. Frigg, I had waited so long for this, I didn't even care that my betrothed was a short walk away. He kept at it, pumping and rubbing with his palm against the bud at the apex of my cunt until I rocked against his hand like a wanton creature, nothing but a slave to pleasure.

"Now, please," I said, unable to bear any more of this game, this teasing hint of the pleasure he could give me but withheld.

He didn't hesitate this time. There was no pulling back, no whispered pleas to marry him. To my surprise, he rolled onto his back and guided me to straddle his nude body. I let myself enjoy the sight and feel of this powerful man prone beneath me. The coarse hair of his thighs rubbed the soft skin of my bottom and his cock lay proud, hard, and swollen across his belly.

I took the opportunity to first brush it with my fingertips, then, when his entire body twitched, I wrapped a hand around it. I felt its weight, its heat, the smooth skin stretched over an iron core. His back arched off the ground, and he hissed as though in pain when I stroked once, twice, three times.

"I can't." He pushed the words out between clenched teeth and pulled my hand away by the wrist. He gripped my hips and kneaded at the flesh there. Those long fingers reached far enough to massage into the globes of my rear.

The gentle pressure of his touch made me throb. I breathed in the cool scent of wet moss and earth and delighted in the quivering muscles beneath my fingertips as I traced the ridges and valleys of his body. My very own terrain map laid bare in the wilds and I loved it.

He shifted his hips and we both groaned into the night as my sex rubbed against his. My core beat in time with my pulse, faster and faster, desperate to be filled by him and only him.

I lifted on my knees, and he took himself in hand, guiding me down by his grip on my hip. I lost control of my senses, no longer able to stop my thoughts from pouring free of my mouth.

"Yes, yes, yes." The words spilled out, no different from the trances our priestesses entered.

His cock stretched and filled me and I needed more. Climax overtook me when he sank to the hilt. I would have been shocked, or embarrassed, by my near instantaneous response had wave after wave of rippling joy not washed over me. I was so lost in it; he took over from beneath me, holding me in place while he fucked me through each throbbing quake.

Part of me must have known this is how it would be with him, from that first moment in Varus' tent when we met again, from the power of our kisses, from the way we touched.

When that endless climax abated, he supported me as I melted into a puddle of sensitized nerves.

He had his own litany for me. I was perfect, wet and warm and tight, so beautiful, amid curses that sounded more like prayers to the gods, and promises, so many promises.

His rhythm faltered and turned to a frenzy. I dropped to my forearms and we shared a messy kiss, blending the sweat of our brows and bodies.

I murmured words of encouragement, begging him to finish and take his pleasure in my body, in a way only I could give him.

Then he surprised me. Arminius lifted me free of him and spent himself on his belly. Contentment over what we'd just shared warred with hurt. Even in this moment, he kept a wall between us, a wall I was, irrationally, more than willing to tear down. I understood his reasons, his refusal to see another man raise his child. It was senseless; he was right in that regard, yet this one action still wounded me. I was the one who kept safety measures between us, not him.

We lay side by side in the dark, tucked into each other, each lost in our own private thoughts, and the music of the forest returned. The world released the breath it held and continued on like nothing had happened.

He took a corner of the blanket and cleaned himself off with a grimace. From my position in the crook of his arm, I listened to the galloping of his heart, showing no signs of slowing.

I wanted to yell at him and storm away. I wanted to kiss him and start all over again. He shifted up on his elbow so he loomed over me and carefully touched each scar he found on my body.

"I don't want to lose you," he said, pausing over an old scar on my belly. His featherlight touch tickled, and I squirmed under it. He smoothed my hair away from my face. "I love you. I'm never going to stop."

Tears burned behind my eyes. His words weren't a surprise. His every action betrayed him. There was a finality, though, something more profound than a mere profession of love. Any two people could say the words, even feel the truth behind them. This, the two of us wrapped together, wrapped in the night, was the indelible bonding of two souls.

"You know I don't want to marry him, don't you?"

He smiled weakly. "I know."

"I..." my throat closed around words fighting to break free.

"Don't say it. Not until you mean it." He cupped my face and kissed me, slow and deep. "Perhaps I should take the gods more seriously," he said when he pulled back. "Only they could be so cruel to show me what's possible and give me no way to attain it."

Chapter 18

No people are more addicted to divination by omens and lots. (Tacitus)

Children ran to the Roman road with their hands out, begging for rounds of bread and any treat they might win from the legionaries marching from Germania. With the agility innate to children, they dodged the stray smacks or kicks from the more cantankerous of the soldiers.

Much to my father's consternation, if his incessant glaring was any indication, I stood next to Arminius. We hadn't seen each other in the few weeks since the night we'd shared outside the Chatti longhouse. Varus kept him busy leading patrols, namely spying for malcontents and traitors under the guise of pacification and resolving disputes *the Roman way.*

The push to root out potential rebels came not long after my confrontation with Segestes. That Varus had put Arminius in charge of the investigation was a type of humor only the gods ever cooked up.

"Varus is furious," Arminius spoke quietly, though he didn't need to. Between the noise of a legion on the march and the villagers trying one last time to sell their wares, a steady din drowned out most voices.

"The uprising?"

"No," Arminius chuckled. "He's embarrassed. Everyone told him the Sixteenth was likely to be called out for Pannonia, and he didn't listen. Wanted to make a big show of our return, remind the barbarians who's in charge. Now it looks like he can't manage basic troop movements, and during last night's sacrifices for a safe march, he got bad omens."

That captured my attention. "What kind of bad omens?"

He licked his lips and his cheeks twitched with the effort to smother his grin. "Someone supplied the priests with several very sick goats. It appears the gods do not favor Romans marching through this country. My ala can't stop talking about it."

My jaw dropped. He didn't. He couldn't. He had. The man was unstoppable. I closed my mouth and pretended to watch the march. "You found a way to buy your omens."

"That I did."

Ermin approached and gave me a nod of acknowledgement. "Fortune smiles on us, eh, brother?"

He slapped Arminius between the shoulders with one of those man-pats, hard enough to move Arminius' whole body but with no discernible aggression. I was grateful women never felt the need to greet me that way.

"Indeed." Arminius returned the hit and Ermin grunted. "Try not to look so happy about it. We're supposed to be gravely concerned."

I'd stopped thinking of Arminius as the man once known as Ermin and this Ermin as "that other Ermin." He was right to keep his Roman name. It marked the man he'd become, not the boy he'd once been.

"Would be much better fortune if all the legions got called away," Ermin said.

"No," Arminius responded immediately. "Then they'd be back and things would go on like they've always been. Three is a good number. Few enough to be beaten, plenty enough to make Rome think twice about us."

I hated that he was right. I wanted Ermin to be right, to imagine them leaving and never returning because the weather didn't suit, the farming wasn't productive enough, we lacked the precious gems and minerals they worshiped, our people were too rough and primitive to make proper Romans.

That wasn't to be, not for the hulking beast of Rome. Such an animal couldn't be so easily dissuaded from its prey.

Ermin laughed ruefully. "I imagine you're right."

"What have you got for me?" Arminius gave him a pointed look.

"Those Chatti you brought us are as good on horseback as you promised." Ermin spat a fat glob of mucus into the grass. Disgusting. "I'd say the ala and auxiliary are well under your command."

It wasn't difficult to extrapolate the unspoken information. Now, in addition to our allied tribes, Arminius' captaincy of the ala secured squadrons of Germani cavalrymen and cohorts of auxiliary infantry who would turn against their Roman counterparts when the time came.

"Good, pass word—"

"Aye, Arminius," an unfamiliar voice called. Arminius clamped his lips shut and pasted on a congenial smile.

Out of the corner of his mouth, he muttered, "It's Vala. Look lively."

Ermin immediately straightened and offered Vala the same congenial, blank smile as Arminius, and I cleared thought from my head for fear that any harsh words floating around in there would be plainly visible on my face.

"Legatus." Arminius saluted. When Vala returned it, he continued, "I'm sure you've met Ermin, signifer of the Germani ala, and of course this is—"

"Thusnelda." Vala inclined his head toward me. "I couldn't possibly forget. Even if we hadn't met, your reputation among my men would assure you a place in my memory."

Many words that said so much and so little all at once. My brow furrowed in confusion, and he chuckled.

"Surely Arminius has told you."

Arminius cleared his throat, and Ermin buried a snort in a cough.

"I haven't mentioned it to her, Sir," Arminius said. "For a Germani, there is no higher praise than being feared in battle. If she knew every legionary this side of the Rhine kept at least an arm's distance from the local women because of what she did, I'm afraid her head would float away in the clouds."

His words had the desired effect on Vala, who guffawed loudly enough to draw the attention of a few standing nearby. For me, they only raised more questions.

"What are you talking about?" I asked in the Cherusci tongue.

"You, my dear," Vala surprised me by replying in our language, "established quite the reputation that day. I dare say we had no reason to lash the men who assaulted you. Since the story spread, my men have rediscovered their discipline. They don't leave the camp without reminding each other what an angry Germani woman is capable of."

"You speak our tongue," I replied.

"I wouldn't have gotten this far without a healthy respect for the locals."

"Have you conquered many lands? It must be difficult to learn so many languages."

Arminius' only reaction to the venom I spat was the slightest intake of breath. Ermin had no such self-control and openly gaped at me.

"A few," Vala replied at length. "I go where Rome sends me. When I leave, the lands have roads, bath houses, sewage, formal legal systems, the protection of Rome. We are not your enemies."

Arminius dropped a hand to my hip and gave it a gentle squeeze. He knew me so well. The hair on my arms stood on end. The urge to scream a war cry and launch myself at this self-important man who thought toilets were a fair trade for enslavement, the end of tradition, and freedom was almost overpowering.

Vala didn't miss the gesture and gave Arminius an inscrutable look.

He switched to Latin to say, "I understand these Germani are more... liberal in their views of women and marriage, but I hope you know what you're doing with this one. Her father is a chief, and Varus will not appreciate it if you damage all his hard work because you couldn't find someone else for your entertainment."

Arminius tightened his grip.

"Of course, Sir," Arminius said. "I assure you, nothing untoward has happened. We are merely old friends. I've known her since childhood. Germani are a familiar people, you know."

On cue, Ermin tossed a thick arm around my exposed shoulder and gave me a shake. I slowly swiveled my head to stare at him, debating between going along with this farce or punching him in the throat.

"Aye, Sir," Ermin grinned, "we aren't so standoffish like you lot."

I forced a placid smile and Vala, after a moment's hesitation, accepted that.

"Good, good. I don't need to remind you, then, that regardless of local norms, you are a Roman, an equestrian, and that is the standard to which you will be held. In all matters."

"Yes, Sir. My apologies. I interrupted as soon as you approached. Was there something I can do for you?"

Not reacting to Arminius' obsequiousness was a trial I barely managed. Who was this man, with his honorifics and bowed head and bland eyes? I didn't recognize him at all.

Even the men Rome deemed "free" were slaves. A man with rank, a Roman knight, prostrated himself before the next superior. Segestes was chief of our tribe and not a man, woman, or child would ever consider speaking to him in such a manner. That Segestes behaved in such a way toward Romans only weakened him in our eyes.

"I saw you all talking and wanted to say hello, and, of course, pass along additional apologies regarding my soldiers' behavior, Thusnelda. I'm afraid there wasn't much of an opportunity to do so the last two times we met. I had no idea you and Arminius were so close."

Those raptor eyes locked onto me, and I knew for certain Vala was a threat we couldn't ignore. He suspected something and was intelligent enough that his suspicions were often proved true. Vala was waiting for the right moment to swoop in and catch Arminius in his talons.

"Oh, he didn't tell you?" I reiterated Vala's words. "We were betrothed as children. I'm betrothed now to the chief of the Chatti. We all assumed Arminius was long dead."

Those familiar fingers dug into the flesh of my hip, hard enough to bruise. If he was angry with me, I was angry with him, too. How could he downplay the threat Vala posed? Had he even thought of it, or had he been so wrapped up in other details, the bigger issues, that he genuinely forgot to consider the enemies around him? He had been among the Romans so long I imagined it was easy, in some ways, to forget they were his enemies.

But no, that wasn't right. A man didn't force himself to bow and scrape as he just had because he forgot who had the power and who didn't. Why hadn't he told me he was being watched so closely by someone with such power?

"Not dead," Vala said, "reborn. Thusnelda, it was a pleasure. I have no doubt we'll see each other again."

With one last raptor look at Arminius, he tipped his head in farewell and disappeared back into the crowd.

"You should have said something about him," I hissed as soon as Vala was out of earshot.

"Why? There's nothing you can do about my relationship with the legionaries," Arminius responded. "I'm handling it. Varus trusts me implicitly. Fuck, he looks at me like a son. I could walk into his quarters tomorrow in full Cherusci dress, and he wouldn't believe I was anything other than a loyal equestrian until I ran him through on a spear. What we should be worried about is when our allies get drunk and run their mouths when they visit the settlements."

I got into his face, as best I could with our height difference. "If Varus trusts you so much, a few drunken tribesmen bragging about how many Romans they'll kill won't change anything. Which is it?"

Arminius seethed down at me but said nothing. Ermin cleared his throat until he had our attention, then shifted his eyes in dramatic fashion to remind us we weren't alone. The mask Arminius wore for the sake of his rank and position slid smoothly back into place, complete with that bland, dead-eyed smile and gracious nods toward those who stared at us.

"We should continue this somewhere more private," he mumbled between his teeth.

It unsettled me, the way he shifted between Cherusci warrior and Roman officer so easily. It must have been difficult for him, as old as he was when he was taken, to learn this skill to appease his new masters.

It was so very contrary to our way. I thought of the patch-worked scars marring his flesh, many incised by the lash. He'd had a choice between learning or dying, I assumed.

"Fine." I softened. There was something about the uniform, the shorn hair and chin, the lyrical rhythm of his Roman-infused speech, that always inspired mistrust and hostility in me. That wasn't remotely fair, since I saw his truth. I saw the Arminius he kept carefully hidden away, all that rage he attempted to hide from me.

A man didn't plan an ambush like his because he was only a little angry. Fury lurked beneath his veneer, deeper still beneath all his jokes and charm.

The air went out of him, and he slid an arm around my waist, guiding me through the throng. "Ermin, see if you can't—"

"Aye, aye." He waved us away.

"I'll make sure everyone knows what happened during the Roman sacrifices," I offered.

He made a sound in the back of his throat that was neither pleased nor displeased. "Let's talk about that somewhere more private, as well."

Instead of following the Roman road back to my village, we meandered into the forest along old hunting trails. A beehive somewhere nearby, high in the trees, buzzed with life, and it amused me that somewhere out there some enterprising tribesman was plotting to harvest the honey within. We liked our honey, but few among us possessed the wherewithal or motivation to harvest it ourselves. Only a select few mastered the skills necessary, and they often came away with their valuable prize covered in stings and scrapes, courtesy of falling from trees in the process. I'd watched it once, from a safe distance, and had laughed uproariously with my young friends when the man fell at least fifteen feet to the forest floor, prize in hand and well stung by bees defending their home.

A startled brown rabbit darted out of the brush across our path before disappearing again. I wondered at the sense of a creature we never would have noticed had it not made itself known.

For a long while, neither of us spoke. It wasn't a tense silence as neither of us was angry at the other. We were two people on the same path, lost in their own thoughts.

"Don't you have to go back with the other soldiers?" I asked, and after the extended silence, my voice sounded like an intrusion.

"Varus has given me leave to visit my sick uncle as often as I'd like, so long as I don't neglect my duties to him."

"Ingomar is sick?" The moment I asked, I felt like a fool. The man wasn't sick. This was Roman dissembling.

He nudged my shoulder with his. "I can't very well tell him what I'm really doing, or who I'm really seeing."

"Of course." I made to keep walking, but he caught my hand and brought me back around.

We held each other palm to palm, forehead to forehead, until our breathing matched.

"You and I certainly know how to argue, don't we?" he asked with a small smile.

"I've been practicing on my brothers my whole life."

That earned me a startled laugh. Then he sobered.

"I didn't tell you about Vala because I didn't want you to worry. Most of the men think I am as Roman as they are, but there are others who think every Germani in the ranks are nothing more than devious savages in nicer clothing. There's nothing I can do about him except keep playing my part."

"What if—"

"No." He pressed a finger to my lips. "No what-ifs. Believe me when I say that once we start down that road, we'll drive ourselves mad with it. Elda, I have been planning this most of my life. The only way we're going to succeed is if we believe it beyond any doubt. That is what our tribesmen will follow; that is why Varus will never see this coming."

He didn't know about Segestes' possible hand in stirring up fears of rebellion, and I hesitated to tell him, just as I kept my promise to the scalcs to myself. I didn't know for sure that Segestes said anything, and I didn't know if that scalc had survived to share my message. I needed to tell him these things, for the same reasons it infuriated me that he downplayed Vala to me.

But his palms felt right against mine and his scent calmed my nerves. Telling him either of these things stood to ruin what we had, what little selfish pleasure I took.

The Romans indulged in an entertainment they called a play. I'd seen one once, years earlier, on a visit to the Roman settlement at Mogantiacum with my family. They used written scripts and acted out a story on an elaborate stage decorated with sets and music and sounds that mimicked the action. I'd been thunderstruck by the show. Our bards told stories. Sometimes these were acted out, or danced and sung, but never so formally, with so much attention to detail.

I saw then how Arminius orchestrated a grand play, and we all had our roles and our scripts to read. The Romans were our audience, led down a path toward a conclusion they didn't yet see. As long as we spoke the right lines and Arminius played his role to perfection, our audience went along with it. They didn't see what was happening backstage, and they couldn't read the script. I needed to share my script with him, and I would. I swore to myself I would.

"Very well," I said. "What comes next?"

At this, he smiled.

———————————➤———————————

Arminius declared it was time to walk through the battle plan, after which we were to embark on what, for me, was the most contentious portion of the plan: convincing the small Chauci tribe north of the Teutoburg to join our cause. Strong-arming such a weak group wasn't a problem, it was that his plan now required me to lead a body of warriors in staging a revolt among the tribe, putting everyone who participated in the farce at least a day behind the ambush, if not more. Including myself.

After everything I'd done, he was cutting me out under the guise of tasking me with a seemingly important role, a role any chieftain could play. I bristled and scowled through our tour of the path Arminius intended to lead the Romans down.

Deudorix kicked at a tree root. "While I agree this place is a deathtrap for the sheep fuckers, no Roman in his right mind is going to march into this forest, because they also know it's a death trap, do they not?"

Green and brown pressed in on all sides. For an army that relied on its strict formations and tight order, it was a nightmare. Our hunting tracks were wide enough for us but would force a Roman column into a thin line. The rolling hills, streams, fallen trees, and boulders coalesced into a perfect worst-case scenario for their army. We couldn't have chosen a better ambush site, yet Deudorix was correct: No Roman in his right mind would lead his army in there. Varus was sound of mind and viciously intelligent. Vala openly suspected treason from Arminius.

This high in our summer, biting flies and gnats swarmed in force. Our party of Arminius' most trusted cavalrymen, Berut, Reimar and Deudorix with their entourages, myself, Jotapa, and Levin, made a mass of people all swiping at their faces and exposed arms, grumbling and cursing every time we got close to a water source, where the insects thronged.

"They do," Arminius said over his shoulder. "You're forgetting that Varus trusts me and when I ride back from scouting with the ala and report an uprising straight through this forest, he'll follow me without question."

Deudorix made a noncommittal sound. Reimar snorted, muttering something about Roman arrogance under his breath.

As we traveled, Arminius pointed out each successive ambush site and how the tribes would stretch out along the ridgelines on both sides of the path to fully encircle the Roman column, until the bog encroached and we only needed to fight on one side. He described the back-breaking labor the legionaries would have to put in constructing bridges over the deeper streams and bogs and clearing trees where the path became so narrow hardly two people could pass abreast. Marching through this forest would be an exercise in slow torture for them. Our spears and lightning attacks made Arminius' plan nearly foolproof. As unpleasant as the day was, my admiration for him grew.

By the time we reached the final ambush site, with its narrow passage and well-constructed earthen siege walls, the entire party's mood turned foul. If this chunk of forest was enough to do that to us, we who fought best in it, it would turn the legions into a useless mess.

We surveyed the ramparts while Arminius explained how our warriors would hurl spear after spear, slings of rocks, volleys of arrows, from behind relative safety. He'd instructed the Marsi to build it in the Roman style, which they'd mostly accomplished but for the uneven lines and heights. It stood taller than most men and thick enough to prevent projectiles from penetrating it. That assumed that by the time the surviving legionaries reached this point, they were no longer hauling their heavy artillery. I agreed that assumption seemed likely, having now walked the route myself.

From there, it was a straight march to Chauci territory.

Chapter 19

The Germans transact no business, public or private, without being armed. (Tacitus)

Reimar, Arminius, and I rode single file through the wilderness, our silence only broken by bird calls and the wind whispering through the trees. Clouds in the distance and the faint tang of moisture in the air promised a storm to come. We had another day of riding before we reached the Chauci stronghold, and I couldn't decide if our mutual agreement to say nothing at all was a blessing or a curse.

While Reimar's silence didn't trouble me—he was taciturn by nature—Arminius' grated almost as aggressively as his heavy handed declaration that I was to lead the diversion, thus being kept away from the bulk of the fighting. Who did he think he was to give me an order, especially an order like that? I fucked him once, and now he seemed to think that gave him a say over my wellbeing?

It was so very Roman of him.

Maybe it was the boredom of our silent ride. Maybe I was exactly as troublesome and irritating as my brothers painted me. Regardless, an overpowering urge to kick a hornet's nest swept over me.

"Reimar," I said brightly and rotated around on my saddle pad to look at him, "before we marry, I just want to clarify a few things. I know we discussed keeping our lives largely separate, but what about in battle?"

He raised one single, thick eyebrow. "What about it?"

"Do you intend to order me to stay home and tend the fire, or will we be more like your parents?"

"I don't know, do you intend to try to fight when you're pregnant?"

A strangled cough came from Arminius at the front of our little line and my smile grew.

"Of course not. I want to make sure you won't invent petty reasons to keep me at home during raids, fighting season, that sort of thing."

"I am not inventing a reason to keep you out of the battle," Arminius snapped.

Reimar's eyes flicked to Arminius then back to me. He sighed. "Don't be a child. We need someone we can trust to lead the Chauci."

My hackles rose. "I'm a child, now? For being upset that I've been relegated to a duty any loyal chieftain can do?"

Arminius wheeled his horse around. "For fuck's sake, woman, I've handed you what is arguably the most important mission of our entire operation, and you can't stop hissing at me like a pissed off cat."

Reimar pushed his horse to my other side, effectively trapping me between the two men.

"Don't speak to her like that," Reimar said. I puffed with a suffusion of warmth that he'd rushed to my defense, then deflated when he continued. "I am her intended, I will handle correcting her."

Warmth turned to a flash of heat so hot it burned my cheeks. "Correcting me?" My words came out in a screech, and my vision tunneled.

A heavy hand landed on my shoulder, squeezed, and I heard Arminius' voice. "Easy, easy."

Gradually, my vision cleared. I sucked in a hard breath. To my shame, I was dizzy. I'd never fainted in my life, yet it only took a few hours alone with these two creatures to make my head spin.

"Get your hands off her."

Arminius' hand tensed on my shoulder. "I think that's up to her."

They spoke with deceptive calm as our argument metamorphosed into something different. I'd set out to kick a hornet's nest and succeeded.

Though my ears still buzzed and black spots continued to blink in the corners of my eyes, I straightened and shrugged free of Arminius' hand. With a pull on the reins, I backed my horse out from between them while contemplating drawing a weapon. Just to ensure my point was heard.

"Stop it, both of you."

"You started it," Arminius muttered.

My eyes nearly popped out of my head. "You're the one cutting me out!"

"You're both children," Reimar said, the loudest I'd ever heard him speak. "Thusnelda, we need you with the Chauci because they might not agree to our proposal. We're sending you with enough warriors to put their village to the torch whether they participate or not."

"And I thought," Arminius said, "that between you and Reimar, you are far more likely to talk them into participating. Sending you is our attempt at preventing unnecessary bloodshed. Thought you'd like that."

Days of frustration bled from my pores. That was a damn good reason to send me instead of anyone else. The only other person I'd trust with this mission was Wiltrud, and she already had her role to play marshaling the vanguard. Her experience there would be invaluable.

Whatever relief I felt, the soft affection at the thought that Arminius knew and respected me well enough to know exactly where I needed to be, soured. Arminius frowned, swallowed hard, and urged his horse back around. He took off at a quick trot, leaving us behind.

Though I wanted to chase after him and force him to tell me why he was upset, Reimar saw too much as it was. He eased his mount alongside mine, never taking his eyes off me. My skin prickled.

"All I ask is that you do your duty. But woman, if you embarrass me, so help me I will shave you bald and march you naked from village to village, the way my forefathers handled disloyal women."

First he intended to correct me, now he threatened to enact the old punishment for adultery. Few tribes kept the practice up, especially among the tribes with large contingents of female warriors. Women with swords seldom took kindly to adulterous men punishing women for the crime the men committed without repercussions. Having Wiltrud for a mother, Reimar's threats surprised me. For the first time, I caught the whiff of anger lurking just beneath his usually stoic surface. Anger at me, his first wife, or all women, I didn't know.

"We're not married, yet," I said.

Reimar spat on the ground, reined his horse, and took off after Arminius, leaving me behind.

➤————

Frikkeo, chief of the Chauci, and his wife, Rihilt, whom I'd met during the last Haustblot, welcomed us with open, seditious arms. The Chauci, it turned out, needed little convincing to join our cause.

They invited us to share a light afternoon meal while Arminius laid out what he needed from them. Once again trapped between Arminius and Reimar, my nerves jangled. The rest of our journey had been largely silent, including the overnight camp. Every time Arminius looked at me, his palpable disappointment brought shame to my cheeks, though I didn't know why I should feel ashamed.

"Varus will not march three legions into this forest without good reason." He gnawed at a crust of bread as he spoke. "An uprising from a small tribe he thinks he can easily beat, that'll be a temptation he can't resist."

"What happens to us? There is an outpost less than half a day's ride from here with five hundred legionaries." Rihilt's words took a stony edge. This was not the invitation to the rebellion she'd expected. I knew the feeling.

Arminius gestured with the knife he used to spear an apple slice. "Thusnelda will lead a body of about fifteen hundred warriors here, along with your own warriors. No Chauci will die unnecessarily."

Rihilt stiffened, skin flushed and nostrils flared.

"You think we can't handle ourselves against five hundred Romans? Our tribes have—"

"My apologies." Arminius held his hands up in surrender. "I know you could handle a cohort on your own. The extra warriors Thusnelda will lead are purely to ensure not a single Roman lives. If any of them escape to tell the tale, it could upend my efforts with Varus. It's for my peace of mind."

No matter how often I saw it, his skilled diplomatic hand remained a marvel to me. In any given situation, Arminius shaped his words to exactly what someone needed to hear in order to take the path Arminius wanted them to take. The possibility that he'd used this skill on me didn't escape my notice. I took comfort in the fact that Arminius had nothing to gain by pursuing me.

I had no other choice.

"When we agreed to this alliance, it was under the assumption that we would be in the battle. Our warriors won't like being told they have no chance at glory," Rihilt said.

Arminius grinned. "They'll have more opportunities for glory than they can handle. As long as everyone sticks to the plan, the Chauci will have plenty of time to reach the Teutoburg."

Reimar grunted his agreement. "We'll have three, maybe four days if the Romans prove hearty. That's more than enough time for everyone to draw their share of Roman blood."

Arminius raised his cup in a salute. "It won't take much. Varus trusts me and that man wants his laurels."

"And you?" Rihilt shifted her eyes to me. "What do you think? Do you think this is a good idea?"

Surprise rendered me silent for a beat. I felt all eyes on me in the short hall, so much smaller than ours. By comparison to Arminius and Reimar, I had little experience planning and leading battles, and everyone here knew it. Then again, Rihilt knew me from Haustblot. To her, and most of the women I'd met that day, I was the leader, not the men.

"Yes. Arminius' plan is sound, and I've seen for myself how Varus hangs on his words. Between our warriors and yours, we will wipe out whomever responds when we light the fires."

Next to me, Arminius' muscles relaxed. He reached under the table and gave my thigh a squeeze. My whole being softened with that little gesture of thanks, his first acknowledgment since our fight. I couldn't show how much it affected me, not here, not with Reimar on my other side, not under the sharp gaze of the Chauci. For now, this silent communication remained a secret for the two of us.

------➤

I spotted the smoke trailing the sky before my village came into view and urged my horse into a gallop the rest of the way. What I found was both a relief and a horror.

Arminius and Reimar had split off for their respective destinations hours earlier, leaving me alone when I rode into the stuff of my nightmares.

Acrid smoke, fire in the village, red tunics and shining armor decimated my home in those dreams.

I shook my head to clear the childhood memories.

No buildings burned and although our tribespeople were somber in their anger, none wailed or wept over the corpses of their loved ones. The source of the fire was in our village center, where a contingent of legionaries hacked spearheads from their shafts. They tossed the good iron and steel into a pile and burned everything else. Another pile represented most of our swords, the smallest pile our arrowheads.

"What's going on?" I voiced the question to no one in particular as I dismounted my horse.

Villagers shuffled out of my way, strangely silent. The only sounds were the snapping fire and the clanking of metal on metal.

Segestes, Wout, and Lennart stood on the steps to our longhouse, overseeing the torching of our weapons.

"Father, what is this?"

Segestes didn't react. Wout took it upon himself to explain.

"The governor heard rumors about an uprising." His eyes slid to me, twin black voids. "He's disarming the tribes. Wants to send a message."

I froze. Disarming the tribes? It had never happened. It couldn't happen. It was happening right in front of me. We did almost nothing without weapons. We certainly wouldn't conduct a successful rebellion without them. I closed my eyes and searched for some answer to this, a solution. It was all smoke in my nostrils and fire on my dreams.

"You, girl," a Latin voice addressed me. "What have you got there?"

It was the sword at my hip, the same sword I'd carried since my first battle, a raid against the Angrivarii. This soldier couldn't know about the dagger in my boot. He'd need to come back with more men to take it from me.

My hand shook as I unsheathed the sword.

"Watch it." Three legionaries watched me with their own swords at the ready.

Vala materialized from behind the soldiers. The smoke and flames cast shadows in the deep grooves of his skeletal face.

"Yes, Thusnelda, be easy," he said. "You'll be hard pressed to convince Varus it was self defense if you start killing legionaries right now. Not like last time."

The lilt in his voice matched the gleam in his eye. It was stupid to ask, but I asked anyway. "Why are you doing this? The Cherusci are loyal."

"Are they?" He cocked his head. "I hear so many rumors, and for some reason more and more of them say we need to be wary of the Cherusci. Don't take it personally, we're disarming all the tribes. I merely thought it best to start here."

Vomit rose up my throat. *All* of the tribes. When Wout said it, I hadn't quite believed him. Coming from Vala, however, I knew with certainty that almost every bit of sharp iron and steel across Germania Magna was about to get locked away by the legions. We had bog iron and solid trade from the east. We didn't have time.

Orange flames glinted off Vala's segmented armor and his black eyes. He waited for my compliance. I imagined myself whipping my arm out and slicing him clean across the neck. It didn't seem possible that we had come so close to launching our uprising, to joining the tribes for a single cause, only to have it all come crashing down because of my father. He was behind this, I knew it.

There was no winning this day's fight, no matter how badly I wanted to end Vala.

If I thought too hard about giving up my sword, about the wealth of weapons we lost this day and what that meant for our rebellion, I would have gone mad. Instead, I tossed the sword into the pile and strode away.

I was a fool for not seeing this coming. I should have ensured we had hidden armories. I should have told Arminius and Reimar immediately after Segestes made his threats and let them deal with him and my brothers. I should have known. I should have *known*.

My thoughts ran round and round until I stopped at Ingomar's door. He let me in without comment and shoved a cup of ale in my hand. I swallowed the whole thing without tasting it before taking a seat at his low table.

"What now?" I asked.

He refilled my cup and sat across from me.

"I'm not sure. Some of us will have a few suitable weapons hidden, but..." *But not enough.* "We don't have the iron to replace everything, or enough blacksmiths and forges to do the work."

I worked over each detail. It was all I could do to keep from surrendering. I wanted to scream and tear my hair out. I wanted to cry into my pillow and hide in my room. My darkest self wanted to pick up the nearest sharp object, run back into the village center, and kill as many Romans as possible before they killed me.

Weapons. We needed weapons.

"Maybe you can organize the tribes like you did over winter," Ingomar said.

"Varus already suspects an uprising; he will not like hearing about us organizing the tribes." I stood; my hand clamped so hard around my cup that it creaked in protest. "Arminius said he had Varus in hand. I told him to be more careful. I should have—"

"You know as well as I there's no stopping him."

I slumped back into my seat and grimaced at the beginnings of a headache.

"Remember: Think of what you do have. If Varus knew anything of substance, we'd be facing much more than disarmament. So, he knows nothing. We have our allies, and we don't need iron to fight."

I snorted into my cup. "Are you suggesting we attack three legions with clubs and sharpened sticks?"

He lifted a shoulder. "That's how it was done for generations. That's how half the tribes still fight. You've grown accustomed to Cherusci wealth."

Impossible. A sharpened spear shaft wouldn't penetrate armor. Our iron spearheads had trouble penetrating mail. Clubs and sticks? Impossible.

I don't think he knows the meaning of the word. That's what Jotapa had said. Arminius wouldn't let this stop him. He was a madman and yet... I believed he'd find a way. If he could find a way, so could I.

I put my cup down.

"All right. We need to spread the word to our allies. They need to know we're still moving forward and if they want to fight under arms, they'd better come up with weapons."

Ingomar smiled at me. "There's the woman I know."

Chapter 20

To abandon your shield is the basest of crimes (Tacitus)

Baugulf, chief of the Bructeri, was advancing in years with gray-streaked, reddish hair and a short, well-trimmed gray beard. He met us at Ingomar's house with a son and a chieftain I didn't recognize, all polite and restrained. They didn't greet us with hostility, though they weren't happy to see us, either. A line of sweat dripped down my back.

"Let me guess," Arminius lounged in his seat, "you've come all this way to back out."

Baugulf's hesitation spoke to deeper problems within our alliance.

"I have several concerns," he said. "Not the least of which is our lack of weapons. My people need confidence, and this business with the scalcs isn't helping matters, either."

My eyes went wide, like a guilty child caught stealing honey candies. I'd spent so much time telling myself that the scalc I'd confronted probably died in that battle, I'd rather successfully blocked out the possibility that she not only lived but also had done as I instructed.

This was not how I wanted Arminius to find out, and the very real possibility that I'd only compounded our problems fell like a hard weight in my gut. He still hadn't quite forgiven me for whatever offense I'd committed against him when we journeyed to the Chauci.

He might never look at me again, and somehow the pain of that was worse than when he came back and I thought him lost completely to Rome.

"They keep those weapons under guard at all times. I can't very well steal them back, and if I try too hard to get them for the auxiliary, it will raise questions. Wait." Arminius stopped abruptly and spread his hands across the scarred surface of his uncle's table. Ingomar made himself busy doling out fresh servings of ale. "What about the scalcs?"

"Ask your woman," Baugulf's son said.

Arminius whipped his attention to me, and I almost retreated from the confusion writ large across his face. I mean really, after the Romans swept our lands clear of almost every functional weapon, what did it matter if I promised to free all the scalcs? No, the time for excuses and lying to myself about what I'd done was over.

I searched for how he might phrase it and came up empty. He had a lifetime of practice at politicking, while I had none. Cowardice seldom plagued me, but under Arminius' hard stare, I shied away from the direct truth.

"I merely restated the traditions of our people. Any scalc who distinguishes themselves in battle—"

"That's not what I heard you said," the son interrupted me. He had round cheeks, perfect for striking. "I heard you said any scalc who fights with us will be freed."

I braced myself for Arminius' fury. He blinked once, swallowed, and schooled his expression into firm resolve.

"Aye," Arminius said. "Any scalc who doesn't run from battle or lurk about just to collect plunder is free. I didn't think it needed to be said, as it's always been our law."

The son turned away with a disbelieving snort, and the chieftain, another man of middling age with a battle-scarred face and arms, muttered curses.

"Every fucking scalc in the region is going to be out there swinging a club. We'll have no one left to work."

Arminius huffed a humorless laugh. "I imagine it'll be much the same as every other time a scalc buys their freedom. They'll keep doing their labor and you'll pay them for it."

Baugulf held up a silencing hand. "Too many scalcs freed at once could be dangerous. They may not remain with their tribes. Besides, you know damn well it is the tribe's decision when they've earned their freedom, not yours. Or hers. My chieftains don't like this, nor are they comforted by the idea of launching a battle with such a limited armory. I think it's best for us to stay back and judge for ourselves if yours is a fight we should support."

"You'll stay away until it's clear I'm already winning," Arminius said with a grim nod.

"These are our ways." Baugulf shrugged and scrubbed a hand over his beard. "I have to consider the survival of my people. Whether that's you or Rome remains to be seen."

They left soon after, without confirming whether they'd honor our alliance. It had been the same with the other chieftains who shied away from such imbalanced combat. Baugulf, however, was the first to mention the scalcs.

Arminius put his cup down with an echoing crack. Ingomar, the traitor, mumbled an excuse and ducked outside.

"Explain. Yourself."

Likely any legionary unfortunate to earn this reaction quailed, but I was no common soldier of Rome. No matter how much guilt plagued me over keeping this from him, something about the way he ordered me around turned me into that hissing, spitting, swiping cat he'd accused me of being.

"I made a decision, dammit, and my only mistake was being too cowardly to admit it. I ended a raid that would have killed scores and..."

It was the right thing to do, I wanted to say, but didn't. We didn't have room in this undertaking for rash decisions based on my personal distaste for our scalc practices.

"And it's our tradition," I finished. "It's nothing that wouldn't have been called for, anyway."

Arminius turned away as if he couldn't bear to look at me. "You made a proclamation about how each man was to handle his property on the eve of the most dangerous and important thing any of us will ever undertake. I don't know if a single tribe is going to fight. You refuse to marry me because it might make enemies of the Chatti, one tribe, but you do this and don't bother telling me about it. I should have been handling this from the moment I returned. I should have—"

He stopped short and closed his eyes.

"I apologize for not telling you," I said. My throat constricted over everything unsaid, how I couldn't keep facing Jotapa for the hypocrisy of it all, how the proclamation had come to me as if the gods commanded it and I couldn't refuse them. Perhaps I'd said it with the assumption that silver-tongued Arminius would be there to clean up whatever mess I made. There was no telling him that, either.

He paced around the cramped home, then dropped to a low crouch and tugged at the short strands of his hair. He looked up suddenly and stood, face stricken.

"Gods, you don't want to marry me. You don't even trust me. You didn't trust that I wouldn't keep you out of the battle, you didn't trust me with this. Fuck, how could I be so arrogant that I never saw it?"

I lurched to take him in my arms and stopped, unsure if he would welcome my touch. He didn't think I wanted him, and nothing was further from the truth. I'd failed miserably in showing him. Or, the most traitorous idea, I'd committed myself to my betrothal because I didn't trust Arminius, because I thought if it wasn't a decision I came up with on my own, then it must be wrong.

"I want to marry you." The admission exploded out. "More than anything. I don't know how to explain it. I know I made the right decision. I know freeing the scalcs is the only way forward. And… and if I saw a way forward without the Chatti, I would marry you immediately. The tribes will support us. Not all their scalcs will fight, and they're already thinking of acquiring new ones. We will have our rebellion, and anyone who fights with us will share in our freedom. I know it in my bones. I've never done anything like it before, but I had to act."

He flinched like I'd struck him. "Fuck, Thusnelda, I'm trying to understand."

Telling him I believed the gods had spoken to me, through me, would be meaningless. He believed insofar as his upbringing dictated, and the extent of my belief remained murky, not enough to make him understand. All I knew was I'd made the right decision and I had to see it through.

I worked my hands together, tugging at my fingers. "I should have told you sooner what I was thinking. Please trust me. This is right."

With one of his big, warm hands, he stopped my fidgeting. "I don't disagree with you. We treat our scalcs a sight better than they treat slaves, but it's still slavery."

"And we're fighting for freedom. We can't—"

"We can't succeed unless you trust me, too." He pulled me close and sighed. "Do you have any idea what it's like to want to throttle you and kiss you at the same time?"

"I feel that way about you often," I said, and his chest vibrated with laughter against me.

"You made a bold move. I respect that. I probably would have done the same—a bit later, of course."

His hands smoothed up and down my back and hips, lulling away months of tension with his touch.

When he spoke, his breath whispered against the hair at the crown of my head. "How is it you can see a positive outcome for this, but not for marrying me?"

My heart ached for want of a suitable answer, for the desire to shout "Yes!" at the top of my lungs for all to hear. Winning our battle against Rome and becoming Arminius' wife ran a tight race in my mind, heart, and soul.

———————➤

Instead of returning to our respective homes, we camped under the stars sparkling through the canopy of trees and made love again on a rough blanket in a Germani wald, where wild things made their homes. I marveled at the beauty I only found with him, with his body fit snugly inside mine. My worries disappeared, the nagging pieces of some other version of myself who wasn't connected to him, to her own flesh, to the gods, to the nourishing earth.

He removed himself from my body again before finishing but not before I found my release. Arminius was a considerate lover, the type I'd heard whispered of by the scalcs while believing such a creature to be a rarity or an exaggeration. Perhaps he was both, and I was extraordinarily lucky. Again, his subtle physical rejection stung, though not so sharply this time. He cleaned my exposed flesh with a tenderness that warmed me all over and pulled me close, so that as the sweat dried, neither of us felt the night chill.

"There will never be another for me, Thusnelda, princess of the Cherusci," he said. "You are the only wife I will ever take, and if I cannot have you, then I will have no one."

"Don't say that." I pushed up on my elbow, heart hammering anew. "You are a good and strong man. You can have any woman you wish, and she will count herself lucky to have you."

The upward turn of his lips didn't reach his eyes. He pulled my hand from his chest and kissed its top. "There's only one woman I will ever want, and she's right here. Only you, my Wildberry."

Unable to face his resignation, I settled back onto his chest and let his steady heart beat settle my own. I would have traded my soul to stay there with him in the still night. Here we were nothing more than Arminius and Thusnelda, two people living freely.

I brushed my fingers over his chest, along the hard ridges of his collarbones, and he made a happy little rumble in the back of his throat, not entirely unlike a contented cat.

He caught my hand and kissed the pad of each finger.

"If you give me a few minutes, we can go again." He turned a cheeky grin I couldn't help answering. "Take our time, focus on all the good bits."

For that, I pinched him. "You don't find me satisfactory?"

He flipped on top of me in a blink, sinking between my open thighs and rocking his flesh against mine. Leaning in so close his hot breath kissed the shell of my ear, he whispered, "Does it feel like I find you nothing better than satisfactory?"

"Then what do you mean?" I mewled and arched against him. Though my body was still swollen and achy from our joining, moisture flooded back, taking with it any semblance of rational thought. In rational thought's wake was a litany of *more, more, more.*

"I've never used my mouth on you." He sucked and licked a path along my neck, eliciting more mewling and useless writhing. It seemed to me that his mouth was quite active on my skin.

"I keep dreaming of it," he said against my skin, moving to the other side of my neck while my body pulsed and thrummed, reduced to his instrument and delighted to be played. "I want to taste you as you come."

He dipped his head to take my nipple in his mouth. When he'd sufficiently driven me into a frenzy, he released me and said, "There's still plenty of time to try new things."

The night was moonless, and as we started again, blackness descended until he was more shadow against the stars peeking through the trees than defined man. I drank in his flesh through touch, warm, malleable skin over taut muscle, wiry hair along his legs and at his groin, soft where it dusted his chest and arms. I bathed in that leather and man scent I so loved as long as it was his.

With each kiss, each caress, each heated look, he bound my body to his, as he bound my soul. Unbeknownst to me, he'd been busy stitching us together in every way possible. Marrying Reimar was no longer a matter of honoring a betrothal and bidding farewell to a man I would love better but of tearing myself apart in bloody, shredded pieces. It was an act of cruelty, and I understood his motives. Had our roles been reversed, I would have done the same and more. I told him he should take another wife, but the thought of it set me aflame.

I wanted to kill her, that faceless, nameless she-demon who sought to take what was mine. I was betrothed to him first, and I'd won him fairly with a show of my fighting prowess and all the allies I'd helped him gain for his great war. It was a marvel he hadn't killed Reimar for the same reasons.

"Hey, where'd you go?" He dragged his roughened thumb across my soft lips. "You look ready to gut me. It's not exactly the reaction I was hoping for."

"It's nothing." He gave me a hard look. "I was wondering why you haven't killed Reimar. I'd do the same to any woman you swore to marry."

"Didn't you just tell me I ought to take another wife?" He arched a blond brow and smirked at me.

All I could do was shrug one bare shoulder. "I lied."

For that, he kissed me. "You told me not to kill him, so I won't kill him. If you've changed your mind, all you need to do is ask. Though I admit, when he isn't being a cockhead, he's not so bad and might be handy in a fight."

"That's all it takes?" I took his face in my hands to study him and saw only honesty. "I tell you not to kill him, so you don't kill him. I decree all the scalcs will be free after the battle, and you defend me to the chieftains, no matter what it costs us."

He leaned in close and brushed his nose against mine. He held up his left palm, reminding me of the scar he earned saving my life. "You may not have noticed this, but I will do anything for you. Anything. I respect you and if you think this is the right course, then it's the right course."

My eyes burned with tears, though I didn't know why. He made me happy, and happiness was not an occasion for tears in my experience.

"Please don't cry." His face fell in that universal look of male panic over female tears.

"Let me... let me see if I can resolve our situation with the Chatti."

I don't know why I said that. Another wild impulse. I had no idea what to do except move forward and marry Reimar and saying such a thing only gave Arminius false hope. My own act of cruelty committed in the name of what? Sparing both of us a moment of pain? Easing the throb of an open wound we both bore?

He flashed a white smile in the darkness. "Good. Now lie back and enjoy yourself while I enjoy myself. Immensely."

Then he moved down my body and committed himself to his task with all the gusto I'd come to expect of him.

Chapter 21

...for none there looks on vice with a smile, or calls mutual seduction the way of the world. (Tacitus)

Haustblot carried with it an energy I hadn't ever experienced. I could reach out and touch the excitement, the seething fury waiting for any excuse to unleash on the contingent of Romans present this year. With the weapons, the taxes, the slaves, the terror of starvation, the flagrant disregard for our justice, our people had reached their limit.

Varus hadn't arrived, though Arminius assured us all he would be here before the month was out. To Arminius' delight, Varus, in his distaste for performing administrative tasks, had delegated several cohorts to spread across the region and do his work for him. Not only did this mean his fighting force was reduced, but the way Romans resolved local disputes inflamed tensions rather than doused them.

No matter how long they made war against us, how many tribes they conquered, Romans didn't understand the Germani ways. They saw themselves as the ultimate authority in a land that had never known any authority. Chiefs and clan chieftains presided over disputes, but no one man decided anything for another. All parties had to agree. To make matters worse, Romans reveled in any and every opportunity to execute a person. I didn't want to hear of more Germani tribesmen unjustly killed, yet I couldn't deny that regular executions benefited our cause.

Any tribesman unsure of supporting rebellion had their mind made up for them when one of their own hung from a cross. Scalcs and freedmen alike spent whatever leisure time they had huddled together working the bare, raw pieces of wood into clubs and spears, all carefully hidden away. Each tribesman and scalc did their part to rebuild our armory.

We waited until the dead of night to sneak off with groups of scalcs and tribesmen, always in different directions under the guise of making merry, which Ermin's ala soldiers aided us by holding small parties of their own around our secret meetings.

To my delight, Levin returned with the ala. Seeing him hearty and hale was an unexpected balm. Also unexpected was his excitement for the opportunity to keep Segestes and our brothers too busy to spy on our nightly training sessions. I wouldn't make the same mistake twice. Levin took Ualter under his wing and together the pair of them spent their days inventing reasons to keep my family on "guard duty" around the festival site. If it wasn't "guard duty," it was late night inventories and emergencies with recruiting for the alae. Since each "order" came from Varus, Segestes couldn't bring himself to argue. When that wasn't enough, Levin kept a constant watch on them.

Though my sleep suffered, I spent each night at Arminius' training sessions. I'd grown accustomed to Arminius' speeches by rote.

"Now," he said, demonstrating with a shield made of branches and leaves and a stick sword, "you cannot forget that the shield may seem cowardly, but they're trained to stab you here." He patted his ribcage, right where a killing blow would land. "And push on. You cannot assume their armor and shields mean they're ineffective killers."

Next, he explained how long the legionaries trained in swordsmanship and the necessity of expecting their abilities in that regard, as well. After all his talk about how useless they became without their precious, impenetrable formations, his words came as a shock to most. None of it surprised me beyond the subtle way he introduced the idea to tribesmen. Each group we guided into these woods then spread the word among their own.

He'd held that information back, waiting until our most likely allies had fully invested themselves in the rebellion before revealing the combat promised to be far more difficult than the average Germani expected. It was an awe-inspiring deception.

The scalcs were especially eager for battle. They knew the taste of bondage better than free Germani; the hard reality of selling their labor to a master in trade for the necessities of life. Of the tribesmen most keen to participate, many were once scalcs themselves.

Jotapa joined me nightly, as did Konrada as often as she could sneak away from her family. Wielding a club or spear didn't come naturally to either of them, but I tracked their steady progress with pride. For Jotapa, mastering new weapons was more a last resort should her arrows—sharpened sticks— fail. Few compared to her marksmanship, and when she took up the sling and stone, her innate skill translated there, too. Konrada grumbled about that weapon, having no natural talent for it and missing her targets by wide margins more often than not.

She cursed foully as she loosed a missile that sailed into the blackness beyond our torches.

"How am I supposed to do this in the dark?" She snarled her question mostly to the night and to anyone near enough to listen. Of everyone I'd seen over the past two weeks, she was the youngest and struggled to find her place among seasoned warriors and scalcs alike.

I crossed my arms over my chest at her frustration, at her naïveté.

"The ambush will take place in an especially dense forest," I said. "Light will be limited, if there's any at all. We might have storms. It goes without mentioning that battle itself is a sea of chaos. Even with their uniforms, it will be difficult to tell friend from foe."

While she mused over that, I turned my attention to where Arminius showed the evening's group the various weaknesses on Roman armor. His gaze found mine and for a moment, his lips quirked and his speech slowed. Heat flared between us, enough to chase away the cool night breeze. A simple look across a clearing had the power to make my pulse throb and thought flee in favor of animalistic need. After this meeting, like all the others, we'd linger in the woods to properly enjoy each other, to feed that inferno. Our connection was too powerful, something I'd never have the capacity to rein in and break.

He cleared his throat and continued his lecture. Our clubs were heavy enough to fracture a Roman shield or smash a helmet, and thus the skull beneath it, to bits. Our spears were heavier than theirs, despite having varying types, which was both good and bad. They could fling their javelins a greater distance, while ours inflicted more damage. Or they would, if we still had a wealth of iron spearheads. Their double-edged swords were short yet lethal. Ours were longer and heavier, capable of cleaving a limb in one blow, though few warriors carried them, and fewer still wielded them with anything resembling finesse. More warriors than I expected had managed to save their swords, including Ingomar, who loaned me his. I kept it tucked safely away.

"Ualter doesn't want me to fight."

I jerked, startled as Konrada broke through my reverie.

"He and I have that in common," I said. We sent children as young as twelve into combat. I was younger than Konrada when I first fought. Now that I was grown and seasoned, responsible for training youths like her, the practice left a foul taste in my mouth.

She was so young.

"I have to. I'm not going to be like Mama."

For the second time in a matter of seconds, she surprised me. "You think you need to be a warrior to be strong?"

"Don't you?" Her big brown eyes blinked owlishly up at me. "She's still abed, you know? She'd rather lay down and die than deal with Ualter's absence. And my Papa is so weak, he's letting her."

Since I knew just about everything that went on in our village, of course I knew her mother remained bedridden and useless, even after Ualter's visit. I was the one who'd arranged to have a recently freed scalc move in with them. I paid the woman enough for a year of service to ensure their household always had clean clothing, swept floors, and regular meals. Konrada never asked for the help, and she didn't need to.

"Not everyone can handle a large shock," I said, knowing it wasn't true. Konrada's parents were weak, always had been. Ualter and Konrada were aberrations.

Konrada snorted. "You don't have to lie to me. I've known what they are for a long time. That's why I have to be a warrior."

I grimaced, knowing I was possibly the worst mentor she could have. We were too similar. Of course I'd wanted to follow in my Mama's footsteps, but I couldn't deny my disdain for my father's weaknesses. He was a middling warrior at best and far too quick to kneel to our oppressors. I had to wonder how much my feelings toward Segestes, my innate belief that he couldn't be trusted to look after our family or our tribe, drove me to be the warrior I was.

There were other ways to be strong, though.

"Ingunn lost a foot and she's our best midwife. Romilda has buried every child she ever birthed, and every day she wakes with the sun, and she and her husband go about their duties. Half of the thread in our village was spun by her."

Konrada chewed my words over with a little furrow in her brow I wanted to smooth away. She was too young to have these worries.

"No," she shook her head. "That's just surviving. That's not strength."

I slung an arm around her shoulders and pulled her to my side. "Sometimes, more often than you might realize, surviving is the hardest thing a person can do."

Jotapa presented my wedding gown with flourish and an impish smile.

"I know you don't want this marriage," she conceded, "but I've worked very hard on the dress in secret for months, so can you please at least appreciate it?"

That wasn't a hard request. She had meticulously woven brightly colored stripes into a visual feast unlike anything I'd seen before. Around the hem, she'd embroidered a repeating pattern of wolf heads to match our tribal sigil. Absent was any hint of my Chatti husband-to-be. That wasn't uncommon, though in this case it seemed intentional.

"It's beautiful," I said, fingering the buttery soft fabric. It must have taken months to spin the fleece into thread so fine, to dye it these brilliant colors, then weave it all together in the straight, even stripes. "I don't know what to say."

She took my hand. "Your face says enough. You will be a stunning bride in this."

I'd certainly draw the eye in all those colors, a rainbow walking among mortals. My mind conjured an image of swearing the vows with Reimar and my fingers tightened on the dress, ready to rip it to shreds. It took a conscious effort to loosen my grip.

"You're still going through with it, aren't you?" she asked.

Someone shouted outside the tent, then laughed uproariously and continued on his way. I pulled at the neckline of my tunic, suddenly too warm to remain inside, yet certain if I walked out, every person who laid eyes on me would line up to tell me I was being a fool.

"I'm not wrong," I spat. "You grew up with us. You know how seriously we take matters of honor. What tribesman would stand with us after we dishonor Reimar? No one will trust us."

"I think..." she trailed off, folding the dress back into a neat square and stowing it in my trunk. She straightened and tipped her chin up, a mirror of my posture whenever I prepared to launch a verbal battle. "I think you underestimate how much more your allies hate Rome than they value Chatti honor."

At that, I snarled and strode into the bright afternoon sunlight.

A pack of children swerved around my sudden appearance, laughing at the boy who stumbled at my feet. Sunna and Donar trotted up to me with wagging tails and expectant faces I knew too well: They wanted a wander. Since that suited me, I took off between the tents and vendors with my dogs at my side.

The air was dusty and dry here. In a matter of weeks, the fall storms would roll in, preceding months of snow and biting cold. No matter what happened in the coming weeks, that wouldn't change. People still needed food and warmth to survive. We still had to prepare for the return of Roman soldiers in the spring, and a rebellion, successful or otherwise, meant a vicious Roman return.

I had almost made it past the last of the tents when Wiltrud's familiar voice called out.

"Thusnelda! There you are." Amid vendors aggressively hawking wares available for trade—which now included coin, to pay off the Empire—and tribespeople milling about, bartering, arguing, drinking all throughout the day and night, Wiltrud was a serene pool in her crisp white gown with its intricate blue embroidery.

I swallowed the flash of annoyance for the interruption of my grand design to lose myself in the plains.

"Queen." I dipped my head in a respectful bow, knowing she'd wave off such formality.

"Please." She slid an arm around my shoulders and guided me back on the path away from the festival grounds. "You should already be calling me *mother*."

Brown grasses started low and small, then grew taller the further we walked.

"Will you?" she asked.

"Will I what?" The sun beat down on us, warming an otherwise cool day. The dogs disappeared in the fields so that only the movement of dead grasses and peaks of tails revealed their positions. The sky was a cloudless, clear blue, offering no hint of the storms to come.

"Will you call me mother?" Her arm fell away and she clutched her hands together in a nervous gesture I never imagined her making.

"Of course I will," I answered quickly. How could she think otherwise? Since my mother's death, I'd yearned for a maternal bond more than I cared to admit. Wiltrud's appearance in my life meant more to me than whatever marriage Reimar and I might have.

She let her fingers skim over the grasses and came up with a handful of seeds, pinching a few between her thumb and forefinger before letting them fall back to the earth.

"Raginmar was not my choice of husband," she said. "I was in love with a blacksmith from a small village that was as much Tencteri as it was Chatti. As you know, I married Raginmar, and he gave me a fine son and two daughters."

At my questioning look, she smiled sadly.

"My girls have long been married off to noblemen, a Tencteri and a Marsi. They have their own households and children I've met only a few times. I had hoped, I do hope, that I will have grandchildren at home to spoil."

Sunna barked and initiated a chase with Donar. He always let her win these, rolling to his back and presenting his vulnerable belly and throat for her playful bites. He was bigger and stronger, yet he only felt the need to assert his dominance when she got carried away and bit too hard.

I didn't know if I was Sunna or Donar in this scenario, but I knew there was an element of farce to this talk. Was I to roll over and let her win, or was I the fool, unaware that she'd already won? Wiltrud danced her way around what she truly meant to say and, as usual, I found myself lost in the game. Arminius would know precisely what she meant and what she wanted from me. I'd thought these verbal sports unique to Romans, but that clearly wasn't true. I simply didn't know how to play along.

"It took me a long time to appreciate what I had with Raginmar. Even though he made me a queen, I still longed for my smith and the quiet life we might have shared." She stopped our leisurely stroll and faced me. "I know how you spend your nights here."

Panic froze every muscle in my body. How did she know? Who else knew? How soon until Reimar found out, because if he already knew, then I'd already be shaved bald and on the march.

"I... it's not..." My mind refused to form words.

She took my hand in hers. "I'm not angry, and don't worry, Reimar has no idea. I've been where you are, and I don't expect you to love my son simply because you're betrothed."

"No, no." I shook my head, ready with the same denials I'd repeated to myself ad nauseam, to borrow a phrase from our conquerors. "I am happy with my match—"

"I know. I also know that being happy and being in love are two different things. I know that like me, you are possessed of both duty and honor, and you have avoided both me and my son since Haustblot began. What will you choose?"

Facing her was impossible, so I watched my dogs as they dove and tumbled through the grass. Donar caught sight of a grouse and together they raced after the frightened creature. I didn't smile at their clumsy attempts to catch it.

"I will choose what is right," I said. "I will not dishonor you or your son."

She followed my gaze and allowed herself a low, warm chuckle at their antics.

"You remember when I threw bones for you?" I nodded. "I haven't stopped and the answer remains the same. I wish I could tell you from experience and soothsaying that I knew the right choice. I don't have that sort of advice for you. What I can tell you is that what lies ahead is beyond our mortal knowing and far beyond our petty mortal honor."

I frowned, unable or unwilling to understand her vague meaning.

"What is more important than how we conduct ourselves?" I asked. "Our honor dictates our afterlife."

She hummed, then said, "What we think is honorable and what is actually honorable are often two different things. We once thought sacrificing people was honoring the gods. Men used to reclaim their honor by killing faithless wives until the wives fought back. I know the choice I made and I don't regret it. That doesn't mean you won't regret your own choices."

She gave my hand a firm squeeze, then turned and started back toward the festival grounds. I had no choice but to follow in silence while I mulled over all she'd chosen to say and everything she hadn't.

The wedding feast was coming. No matter what I chose, that event had to proceed. With our allies present, it was our last opportunity to remind them why standing aside and waiting to see how the battle turned out wasn't an option. They needed to fight.

The day before my wedding arrived with little fanfare. For the Germani, the pre-wedding feast held equal importance as the wedding itself. That was when the two families, or, in our case, the two tribes, joined as one. For smaller unions, families worked out the sharing of assets and labor. For a joining such as ours, the feast provided the opportunity to negotiate trade and protection.

That is why Arminius seized the event for his own ends. Varus wouldn't question the gathering of so many tribal leaders, and with Arminius, Ermin, Berut, and a selection of auxiliary officers present, he didn't feel the need to send other legionaries to supervise.

Arminius avoided me. Our nights together turned to arguing as the wedding drew closer, then ceased altogether. When we saw each other, he stopped whatever he was doing, puffed himself up to say something, and never did. His jaw clenched. If I was close enough, I caught the corner of his eye twitching. I wanted to smooth away all those hard, angry edges. That would only make things worse.

I let him avoid me in the days leading up to the feast, and it felt like slowly sawing off a limb gone rotten. It had to happen in order to live, but the removal burned worse than dying. The sky remained bright and cloudless—a good omen, everyone reminded me—and I saw it all through a gray haze.

Like the days before this one, Segestes watched me at all times. If it wasn't Segestes, one of my brothers lurked about, always a safe distance away, still close enough to hear my every word. I didn't worry about any of them, because I wasn't up to anything beyond the boundaries of my mind. In my head, I ran to Arminius every day with no regard for caution. In my mind, we shook off the bonds of honor and duty and rode away together, somewhere north and east, where it rained ice all year and the Romans had no interest in invading. It would be so easy to disappear together.

Abandoning our cause, our people, wasn't easy. The cause was bigger than whatever Arminius and I felt for each other, bigger than my fear that any future with Reimar was inextricably linked to the loss of Arminius.

Like every Haustblot, these last days were rife with slaughtering and slow roasting animals, preparing breads and cheeses and myriad culinary delights before settling in for the winter. Now it was all for my wedding. Our makeshift festival village swam in the various scents of cooking foods, each more savory than the last. Women laughed and called out their best wedding night advice, advice I didn't need or want. The impulse to run as far and fast as my legs could take me was powerful.

The weighted expectations of people from tribes with no investment whatsoever in my wedding constricted around me. Chatti and Cherusci hopes sat heavier upon my shoulders. The union of our two tribes marked something significant: the two most powerful tribes in the region aligning themselves for the common good.

In my dazed wander around the camp, I nearly bumped directly into my father before he caught me by the shoulders. His face pulled tight with concern, and he kept steadying hands around my biceps as he leaned closer to inspect me.

"Are you well? I called your name and waved at you, and you still almost walked through me. That's not like you." He pressed the back of his hand to my forehead and his frown deepened. "No fever. Are you drunk? Did you hit your head?"

With a grumble, I pushed away from his grasp. "I'm fine, only tired."

His concern transformed to annoyance. "You better wake up, because I will not have you falling asleep in the middle of the feast."

For a brief moment, he'd beheld me with fatherly concern. Naturally, it came right back to hostility.

"You have nothing to worry about." I tried to shoulder past him, but he blocked me.

"Don't you dare act like I'm being unreasonable here. You have given me more than enough reason to believe you will make things difficult. For once in your damned life, please promise me you'll do your duty."

"My duty." I huffed. Our understanding of duty differed in fairly significant ways. Luckily for him, I agreed that duty compelled me to marry Reimar. "I swear to you, I will do my duty."

This time when I stepped around him, he let me go.

For the first time in recent memory, Ingomar joined the festivals with his small tent and store of delicious ales. My feet found him long before I made the conscious decision to seek him out.

His weathered face brightened at my arrival. He sat behind a make-shift stall that had seen far better days with his jugs all around and an ancient copper cup for tasting.

"My niece, so good to see you." There was no censure or sarcasm in calling me his niece, even as he knew I was to marry far outside his family the following morning.

I opened my mouth to call him uncle, then shut it.

"No matter what," he said with paternal patience, "you have been a dutiful niece to me. Now, may I interest you in my newest concoction? I used your favorite wild berries, honey, and a dash of mint."

Without waiting for my response, he poured a generous portion into a cup hidden beneath his stall and offered it to me. I hesitated over the mix of sweet berries and mint, but disappointing him was out of the question. The flavors burst on my tongue, cool and sweet and perfectly balanced.

"This is wonderful," I said. "Are you having any success?"

He shrugged. "Some. The Cherusci won't deal with me, but others are less discerning."

My nose scrunched and I reached for the sword I wasn't wearing, prepared to unleash vengeance on any who didn't properly appreciate Ingomar and his brews. "Less discerning" was hardly the appropriate response to his labors.

"I'm glad you're here," I said, for lack of a satisfactory way of expressing my appreciation.

"As am I." He hefted the jug over the rickety shelf of his stall and set it before me. "A wedding gift, for you."

I froze. It was wrong to accept it, not when I should have been marrying his nephew.

"Take it," he said. "I brought something else for you. Well, it's for Arminius, but I think he'd like to get it from you."

"Why?" I shook my head. "He's your nephew and he loves you. Whatever it is, I know he'll be grateful."

"This is more…" he trailed off in a sigh. "It's not something an uncle traditionally gives his nephew."

When I didn't reply, he stood slowly and beckoned me toward his tent with a cock of his head. I waited a beat until curiosity got the better of me.

It took a few blinks in the darkness to make out the shapes at the back of his tent, and when I did, my lungs seized.

Segimer's shield and spear rested along the back canvas wall, cleaned, the shield boss polished, and all repainted.

"You gave him his mother's pelt. Soon, it will be time for him to carry his ancestral gifts into war. It should be his wife to pass these along." His hand found my shoulder. "He's told me how he feels, what he wants. If there is anyone left to perform this rite, it is you."

It was the bride's duty to present these weapons to her groom at the wedding. The constriction that had tightened for days became a noose wrapped around my whole body. I fled from Ingomar's tent on unsteady feet.

Chapter 22

She comes to her husband as a partner in toils and dangers;
to suffer and to dare equally with him, in peace and in war.
(Tacitus)

Inhale. Exhale.

In and out.

I had no arrow to loose, no spear to hurl.

My lungs refused to take in and release air. There were too many people packed inside the celebration space. The mingled scents of food turned my stomach sour, and the stench of bodies gagged me. It was too loud, too many voices, too much laughter. The clatter of cutlery rang in my ears. Sound took on a strange quality, ebbing and flowing, like repeatedly dunking my head in a rushing river. Spots danced in my vision whenever I forgot to force my lungs into their basic function.

Reimar sat next to me in our place of honor. We didn't speak beyond the most basic courtesies. My steadfast avoidance of him throughout the month didn't help.

As was custom, Reimar filled my plate before his and I filled his ale horn before mine, to symbolize how we were to provide for each other in marriage. I offered him a tight smile and took a bite of braised grouse. My stomach and throat clenched in revolt, rejecting the food as soon as it hit my tongue. I forced it down and tasted bile.

Jotapa's absence didn't escape my notice. I needed her nearby, a friendly face who wanted me to be happy. Konrada and her family took up a table toward the back, and her incessant scowling almost made me laugh. In her own way, she rebelled for me, and I appreciated her anger on my behalf. My family occupied the table to the left, while Reimar's family and a selection of Chatti noblemen took the table to the right. Reimar and I sat alone at the head of the tent, neither speaking nor touching, no better than strangers.

Reimar watched Arminius through narrowed eyes. When I accidentally leaned close enough for our shoulders to brush, he jerked away. With a start, I realized he avoided any contact with me. We hadn't touched since we sat down next to each other.

He knows. He knows and he's furious.

Fear and shame swirled hot in my chest. He'd asked for one thing and I failed.

But no, he'd asked for more than that. He'd asked for my entire life, my body, my time, my effort, my every waking moment, and in return he offered nothing. What right did he have to be so angry with me when I sought love, the one thing I shouldn't have to ask for from my husband? I understood that now, in a way I never had before. It was the height of naiveté to think I could ever accept a life without love.

When we married in the morning, it wouldn't be long before our lives diverged completely, joined by a vow, perhaps children, if we remembered each other long enough to make them. That wasn't even a partnership. That was two strangers sharing a house. Before Arminius, I might have embraced that future, believing it was my best option. Now I knew better and saw my future with Reimar as one of lifelong crushing disappointment.

I can't do this.

Representatives from almost every tribe in the region occupied the tables, the most important of which gathered at Arminius' table. They formed an island of quiet in a sea of noise and joviality. His expression was open, cocky, even; the mask he wore when he wanted something. The cowards, all of them, Chauci, Bructeri, Tencteri, Marsi, others I didn't recognize, remained aloof, sharing loaded looks, leaning away from the table. We were so close to achieving everything we had worked toward and still they turned away.

Through the din and crush of bodies, my eyes found Arminius over and over again. Each time our gazes met, his forced smile vanished. He fumed. I felt the heat of his frustration from across the temporary hall.

The few times Reimar said something to me, Arminius' muscles locked, like he was about to leap from his seat. His knuckles turned white around his ale horn. I was too far away to know for sure, but experience told me he ground his teeth. The muscle in his cheek that jumped when he was upset must have been exhausted.

My father noticed the way Reimar and I shied away from each other. He tracked every single detail of the feast. If he had his way, he'd have married us on the spot to be done with it.

Thinking of tomorrow's wedding made my head swim. Give me a cohort of angry legionaries or a wall of pissed off Mattiaci warriors. Give me a knife to the gut. *Baduhenna, do not make me go through with this.*

Little by little, Arminius stopped pretending his participation in the surrounding conversation. Berut and Ermin took over as if nothing was wrong. They answered the chiefs' questions, soothed lingering concerns. My joining with Reimar went a long way toward that end. That only increased my turmoil.

Everything was wrong. My entire body rebelled at where this night led.

Arminius shook his head once, slammed his ale horn back and drained its contents, then pushed from his table and marched outside.

He shot me one final, long look before he swallowed hard and pushed out into the night.

My heart seized in his wake. He took it with him when he left. Tears burned my eyes. The tent sweltered, and my gown, my lovely, striped gown, stuck to my skin. I reached for my ale, the same Ingomar presented to me, but my hand shook, so I tucked it back in my lap.

Every fiber of my soul screamed to run after him. He took with him the future I finally admitted was mine. A fissure opened up in my breast, and it would never knit back together. Not by Reimar, nor by any children he gave me.

A tear broke free and spilled down my cheek. If I wasn't careful, I would shame myself and dissolve into sobs. I caught a whiff of Reimar's smell—horse, cook fire, and him—something I'd never before found unpleasant, but now it revolted me. I would sob and retch, and our allies would sneer at my weakness while my world broke apart.

Reimar grabbed my arm, hard enough to bruise, leaned in close, and whispered in my ear.

"I should have cast you aside months ago." His entire body vibrated with rage. Spittle flew from his lips to the shell of my ear. "You have shamed me over and over again, now you weep in front of our allies. If you leave, if you break your word, I will see you pay. I wanted a mature woman who understood her role, not a child following whims. Follow him. Say farewell if you must and compose yourself. But woman, if you don't return, I'll tell everyone that you are a faithless whore I cast aside. I'll tell them that you begged me to take you back and I refused. Mark my words, that will be the least of the hells I visit upon you."

Curious eyes turned to us, some snickering and whispering. More than a year of assuring myself marrying him was not only right, but necessary, threatened to strangle me where I sat. My mind couldn't make sense of it, the answer I hadn't bothered to consider: Reimar might be the wrong husband. I couldn't live without love, and I couldn't live with a man who sought to punish me every time I behaved contrarily.

I'd betrayed Arminius over and over again, in ways that might cost us everything, and he had never threatened me. We talked through it.

Reimar's nostrils flared. Before he opened his mouth and ordered me to stay, I popped up so fast I nearly tipped over my seat.

"What's the matter?" Wout shouted, eyes narrowed in suspicion.

Now they all looked at me, the closest tables having fallen silent.

Don't look at Wiltrud. Don't look at Wiltrud.

"Air." My voice came out choked. "I need a bit of air."

"Better keep a sharp eye on that one," a man called from the crowd, and they all laughed.

That laughter followed me all the way outside. Reimar was right. Everyone knew. There was no choice left to make. My only choice became more clear than the springs after the snow melted.

For a few heart shattering, endless moments, I didn't know where to search for him. I successfully pushed down all thoughts about the consequences of what I'd done and focused my energy on finding Arminius. Everything else we'd handle together.

Together. I liked the sound of that. He would make it better. For once, I wanted him to take care of me. I wanted to release control and allow someone else—him, the only one—to take my reins.

First, though, I had to find him. The festival village teemed with celebrating tribespeople. Most couldn't give two shits about any wedding. The festivals always ended with a large party, and tonight's feast served as an excuse for more drunken revelry.

Those who recognized me cheered and called ribald suggestions for my wedding night. I ignored them and hurried toward the fenced pastures. His men made their camp there. I didn't want to consider the idea he may have hopped on a horse and ridden from me for good.

A wandering pack of drunks shouted curses and split apart on the path ahead of me to dodge the cantering horse and rider cutting through them, toward me.

Arminius. My heart soared with the knowledge everything would be all right. He wore his special armor, the shining metal molded into the shape of a muscular chest. It didn't do the body beneath justice. Instead of his helmet, his wolf's pelt hung about his shoulders and over his head. This was who he was: a Cherusci in Roman armor, a blend of two disparate worlds, too mixed to ever truly abjure one or the other.

His face broke into a grin at the sight of me. He pulled the horse to a stop and slid from the saddle in time to catch me as I hurled myself into his arms.

I didn't care that his armor was hard and unyielding or how many witnesses we had. He lifted me clean off my feet and spun in a circle.

"Were you coming back?" I asked into his neck. The soft fur tickled my nose and I wanted to burrow into it.

"I was ready to toss you over my shoulder and carry you out of there if I had to." He rubbed his hands up and down my back, reassuring himself of my presence, of my choice to leave for him.

I laughed against his neck. Relief ran warm and sweet through my blood. Uncertainty had cast a dark pall over my every decision. It vanished the moment he rode up in all his finery, prepared to steal me. Bride stealing was rare, but it happened. I suspected that more often than not, their stories were like mine: Women abandoned unwanted betrothals to be with a man of their choosing.

Reimar would follow through on his threats, of that I had no doubt. To save face, Segestes would declare Arminius stole me. It rankled. Arminius and I would know the truth, as would our friends, Levin, even Reimar.

It was my fault Segestes had these weapons to wield against us.

"I'm sorry," I said.

"For what?" He tightened his arms, then loosened to lean back and grip me by my bare elbows. "You came."

"I'm sorry it took me so long."

He pressed a kiss to my forehead. "You did what you thought you had to do. There's no fault in that."

"But—"

"Thusnelda!" My father's voice roared behind us, cutting clean over the other conversations and distant music.

Wout hobbled alongside him; Lennart and Levin jogged ahead.

"We should go." Arminius herded me to his horse. I cast one last look at the twins in time to see Levin snake a foot out and trip Lennart, who tumbled cursing into the dirt.

Arminius laughed as he swung back into the saddle. With a firm grip on his forearm, I followed behind him. The moment I settled into my seat, he urged the animal into a canter. I didn't know what destination he had in mind, and I didn't care. We were together.

———————◆

We rode in silence until we were a healthy distance from the festival encampment. In a small clearing lined with torches and lamps stood one of our older priestesses, Berut, Ingomar, and Jotapa. Hooves pounded behind us and Levin dismounted. He shot me a grin and joined the others before I asked him how he'd slipped away so fast.

As I slid off the horse, Jotapa met me with my wolf headdress in her arms. I'd never worn it before. Such accouterments were reserved for chiefs and their queens. My mother had made it before she died, from the pelt of an inky black female wolf she and a small group of women ha hunted. I took the silky garment and clutched it to my chest.

"How did you know I would leave?" I asked her.

She set it upon my head and arranged the pelt around my shoulders. "I know you. And Berut told me what Arminius was planning."

"And you?" I turned to Levin.

"Jotapa thought you'd want family here and I agreed." He wrapped me in a hug and whispered, "You are going to do great things with him."

Arminius took my hands and pulled me close. "Are you sure? It's not too late to take you back."

Months ago was too late. Years. Decades. I'd always been his.

"You would surrender now?"

"I would do anything to make you happy," he said.

"The Chatti will never forgive this insult. Reimar is furious. He's made threats. Segestes—"

"I don't care."

"We're really going to do this?" I searched his eyes and soaked in his unassailable confidence, his assurance that all would work out, that same assurance that had led him to plan an entire wedding without knowing if I'd actually walk away from Reimar the night before I was to marry him.

"We're going to conquer the world."

My audacious man, never afraid to set his sights far beyond where we common mortals tread.

"Are you ready?" The priestess addressed us. I looked around the clearing and our gathered loved ones and didn't find what I sought: a goat, a cow, a sheep, a chicken, an egg, anything.

"I didn't bring a sacrifice," I said. No one married without making an offering to the gods, lest they face tragedy and destruction later on.

The priestess shook her head. I couldn't see her face behind her veil, but when she spoke, I recognized the voice of Cotafrit, the eldest. Some said she'd been alive more than a century. Age had hunched her posture, and she pointed a bony, brittle-skinned finger at us.

"The gods demand more of this union than trinkets. Your sacrifices will come later," she said. "You ask much from the gods, and they will demand much in return. Are you prepared to pay the cost?"

Between Reimar's threat and Wiltrud's mysterious prophecy, I feared Cotafrit was right. A sacrifice was coming, something beyond an animal. I sought Arminius' hand. He gave mine a gentle squeeze and rubbed circles with his thumb.

"I've known my whole life what I want won't come easy," he said, his eyes searching mine. "Whatever the price, I will pay it."

My throat constricted. Could he really be certain of this? What if it cost our rebellion? Any children I might give him? What if we lost everything for the sake of calling each other husband and wife?

He brushed his thumbs across my cheeks and cupped the back of my head. "I see your mind working. Whatever you're thinking, I've thought it, too, and I would change nothing. Do you hear me? Nothing. I know our plan is going to work, just as I know I love you and need you at my side."

Everyone and everything faded around me except for him. I nodded slowly. "I love you, whatever the cost."

The priestess spoke the rites in the old tongue. She sliced our palms with my knife, my first gift from Arminius, over the raised pink scar on Arminius' palm, then bound them together with a leather strap, marking us as one body, one soul.

We each spoke the vows: Henceforth, we would live as one, caring for each other, protecting each other, sheltering each other from all that may come. The words left my mouth in a daze, as if someone else spoke them, as if I watched the scene unfolding from a few steps away.

Berut and Jotapa clapped and cheered, pulling me back into my body. Arminius leaned down for a deep, slow kiss while the priestess released our hands.

It was done and couldn't be undone. We finished the steps that started when I was born and first promised to him. Our future loomed bigger than either of us imagined as children. My heart beat faster and I smiled up at him.

"Husband."

"Wife."

Saying and hearing these words filled me with hope, though hope was an unsatisfactory word for the feelings threatening to burst out of my chest. *He is my husband, and I am his wife.*

As it was always meant to be.

Ingomar cleared his throat. He held out the shield and spear. Arminius' breath caught at the sight of his father's old weapons. I took the shield first, surprised at its heft. Segimer had crafted a fine shield.

"Your shield." I extended it to him, and he took it with reverence. Next, I passed the towering spear. "Your spear."

If I wasn't mistaken, his eyes glassed over, flitting between the weapons, me, and his uncle.

"Thank you." He spoke first to me, then to Ingomar. "You saved these. How...?"

Ingomar waved a hand and said something so like his nephew, I smiled. "Don't worry about it. They belong to you now."

Arminius stood a little taller. "I will carry these with honor."

I looped an arm through his. "We know you will."

Berut trotted to his side with a cloth-wrapped package. He held it while Arminius unwrapped it, revealing a pair of armbands and a golden torque. I reached for them, then pulled back and bit my lip. It was his duty to present these gifts to me, the jewels to replace my mother's and mark me as a wedded woman.

Jotapa appeared at my side and tugged my mother's jewels from my arms, unclasped the torque from my neck.

"I had these made over winter." Arminius held up the torque. At its center, two wolf heads faced Donar's hammer. It was the union of our houses, our souls, finely wrought in gold, cool against my skin. He slipped the matching armbands up my biceps and stepped back.

"They're beautiful."

He had commissioned them over the winter, a man always thinking ahead while the rest of us thought only of today.

Ingomar produced another jug of our wedding ale, the drink he hadn't brewed for me but made with the sure confidence it was for his nephew's marriage to me.

We passed around cups and held our own small, secret celebration deep in an unfamiliar wald. After two cups of ale, everyone made their excuses and left Arminius and me alone in the clearing. He took me by the hand and led me to a large tent I hadn't noticed before. Inside, they'd filled it with thick furs, stuffed cushions, and plentiful woven blankets. A covered trencher hid a late repast for the two of us. Our friends had been busy.

Though we'd lain together before, my nerves jangled, and my heart raced in anticipation. Our joining was no longer an illicit release of pent-up desires. He made it abundantly clear I pleased him, as he pleased me. There was no reason to be nervous, yet I chewed my lip and trembled when I felt him behind me.

Coarse fingers gently removed my wolf pelt and folded it into a meticulous square before setting it aside. His hands rasped down my bare arms and I shivered.

He scraped his chin against the smooth skin of my cheek and rumbled a contented noise.

"Wife." He said it repeatedly, finding no end to the simple pleasure of calling me his wife.

I turned in his arms and reached for his own pelt, giving it the same treatment he'd given mine, as best I could. Such precise folding didn't come naturally to me. Next, I removed his armor, piece by piece, under his unwavering gaze. He groaned and stretched his neck once free of the contraption.

"Come here." He pulled me back into his arms. "Your mind is working hard. What are you thinking?"

"This changes everything."

He leaned down until our foreheads touched and we breathed each other's air. "Not for me. Everything is as it was meant to be."

"How are you always so sure?"

"I've found I can brazen my way through almost anything." He chuckled and kissed me on the nose.

"Not me." I shook my head once. "Though you tried very hard."

"No, I had to pray you'd come to me and, if that didn't work, pray you wouldn't kill me while I was stealing you."

He possessed a unique ability to make me laugh, and I loved him for it. "I don't think I would have killed you. Beaten you, but not killed."

"You do love me."

"I do. I love you."

We met in a fiery kiss, no gentle preamble necessary. It was messy, tongues stroking, nipping at each other's lips while our hands went to work on our clothing. Once bare, he eased me back into our marital bed.

I drank him in, his scent, his warm flesh pressing me into the soft furs, the way our bodies fit together, how his light chest hair rasped against my breasts. We were made for each other, and it was long past time I embraced it.

He slid down my body, intent on doing that thing with his mouth, but I was in no mood for games designed to delay what we both wanted.

"No." I hauled him up by the back of his neck and kissed him with all the ferocity I possessed. "Now."

I wrapped my legs around his hips and attempted to guide him into me. I needed it; I needed him, his body joined with mine in the most primal way. I ached for him to fill that empty place inside me, the one only he could fill.

"You greedy thing." He laughed against my mouth. "We have all night, wife. For once, I want to take my time."

With a push and a twist of my hips, I reversed our positions and raked my short fingernails down his chest, eliciting a hiss from him. He gripped the globes of my ass so hard I'd be bruised by morning. I wanted it. I wanted his marks covering me, so everyone knew we belonged to each other. More than our wedding, I wanted his brand on me and mine on his.

His muscles flexed and rippled. It took self-control to hold himself back when we assumed this position, to relinquish a portion of control to me. He was more than strong enough to take over, even from beneath me. He let me set the pace, though sometimes it pained him to the point of breaking, and he relished it. The veins in his neck popped from the effort of holding back.

We both groaned when I rocked myself against his arousal. My body was already slick and ready for him.

"If we have all night," I leaned down to trail my tongue along the juncture of his jaw and throat, "then we have plenty of time to go slow later."

"Did I say all night?" He took himself in one hand and shifted my hips with the other. "The rest of our lives. We have the rest of our lives."

I cried out as he sank into me, both from the slight burn of his intrusion and the satisfaction of the way he touched me everywhere, impossibly full.

His talk about taking our time was all bluster. He couldn't wait any better than I. He gripped the hair at the back of my head and set a punishing pace. I reveled in the way he lost control, more animal than man when he got like this.

The trembling in my legs that preceded my completion started almost immediately.

"Look at me." He released my hair, only to lift my chin. I'd closed my eyes and dropped my head without realizing it. "You're mine, and I'm yours. Always."

"Always," I repeated, gasping against his mouth. He had me almost insensible. He might have been asking me to rip out my heart and hand it to him, and I would have agreed.

My sex fluttered and spasmed, and then I tipped over the edge with the force of a star falling to the earth. In my lust-driven madness, I bit down on his shoulder and none too gently. His thrusting turned almost violent, faltering, before he jerked inside me and his fluid joined mine. Finally, finally he finished in me. Dizzy with euphoria, I collapsed atop him, gasping for breath. The days when he withdrew and took that part of him away from me were past.

I don't know how much time passed as his heartbeat slowed and the sweat cooled on our skin. His fingers rubbed up and down my back, lulling me into a boneless sleep.

"Always," he whispered before I completely lost consciousness.

"Always," I answered.

Chapter 23

*...his hatred augmented privately because his daughter,
though betrothed to another, had been snatched by Arminius...
(Tacitus)*

Arminius sighed and rested his chin on my shoulder, though the hunch in his back couldn't have been comfortable.

"Are you absolutely certain I can't convince you to stay with my uncle?"

"Yes."

We rode back to the festival village atop a plodding horse, neither of us in any particular hurry to return.

I softened under his concern, but imposing myself on Ingomar was out of the question. Not that staying with him would do much to spare me from Segestes' wrath. No, it only meant my father had a slightly longer walk to reach me. It was better for me to return home with the added protection of being Arminius' wife. If I couldn't face my family, how was I to face Rome?

It was still hard to think of our marriage without smiling like a loon. The little girl I'd once been beamed with satisfaction to have gotten what she wanted after so many long, lonely years. Arminius was proving to be an excellent husband. He saw to my every need, heating water for a hot bath every night, which we we shared. I had to stop him from hand feeding me every meal. It was simply too time-consuming when we had better things to do.

We spent the last few days of the festival wrapped in our own cocoon, and I loathed the return home. Ermin had come that morning, declaring Arminius must return at once, under Varus' order. Neither of us liked the sound of that.

I much preferred staying in our tent, visited only by Jotapa when she brought fresh victuals. And we required much sustenance to keep up with our activities. Arminius was insatiable, almost as insatiable as me. If I wasn't pregnant yet, there was something wrong with my womb.

He skimmed my hip every time we passed each other as we packed away our little nest. We seldom stopped touching each other now that we were free to.

Jotapa and a few of Arminius' trusted auxiliaries helped strike the tent and load the bedding into a small cart. They'd only brought one extra horse, no doubt at Arminius' instruction.

He wanted us seen riding back together, by all and sundry in a simple declaration: Arminius and Thusnelda were one, their battle king and queen united.

Jotapa shot me yet another wry smile and giggle while she stowed the plates and cups we'd used that morning. She'd say nothing with so many men around, but her mischievous eyes spoke clearly enough. She bore the same look each time she delivered food and removed our used dishes. If I didn't get her alone and let her pepper me with questions soon, I feared she'd erupt.

It was a brief ride back, thankfully, as I sat across Arminius' lap in an egregious display of our relationship. The damned man preened like a puffed up bird as we entered the festival grounds and people stopped their packing to stare.

As they did last year, legionaries made their rounds, gutting people of their winter necessities. If the rumors were true, many had hidden the bulk of their food, animals, and timber. Good. Soon they wouldn't have to worry about these vultures picking them clean.

A few of the legionaries tapped each other and pointed to us like we were a one-horse parade. Word traveled quickly. That, or Arminius hadn't been shy about his intentions. Both situations were equally likely.

My husband was too cheeky for his own good. As his wife, it was now officially my job to keep him in check. I smiled to myself at the thought.

We rode straight through to Varus' expansive tent on the assumption this meeting had everything to do with our secretive wedding. Before I dismounted, I heard Segestes' raised voice.

A sentry posted outside straightened when we approached. He spun into the tent door to announce us. Arminius didn't wait for the poor man to finish.

Segestes was so red in the face, he looked purple. Veins bulged in his neck. All he needed was a little foam around his mouth, and I'd believe him rabid. Wout accompanied him, not as red, though still vibrating with anger.

What do you even care?

Then Wout's lips tipped ever so slightly up and his eyes radiated menace. He was viciously happy, and I did not know why beyond the simple desire to see me hurt. For the space of a breath, I forgot my happiness over my marriage. All that remained was the brother I'd once looked up to sneering at me and my husband, gleeful to take part in our destruction.

The same inner child who delighted in her dreams coming true with Arminius shriveled under Wout's scorn.

"This man," Segestes pointed a shaking finger at Arminius, "stole my daughter the night before she was to wed another. He has violated her and my alliance with the Chatti."

Varus sported the tight countenance of a man whose patience ran thin.

"Arminius, your new father-in-law has leveled several serious allegations against you today." He took a sip from his wine and frowned at the gilded cup. "Care to address any of them before we get started?"

Arminius tucked his arms to the small of his back in what I assumed was a posture of deference. "I can address the specious lie that I stole

Thusnelda; however, without hearing the other charges against me, I'm afraid I don't know what they are."

My heart thumped so hard I was certain the others could hear it. A pair of slaves made themselves as unobtrusive as possible while they scurried about in the tent's adjacent rooms, carefully stowing away the opulence Varus insisted on carting out everywhere he went.

Legatus Vala stood to Varus' left, his face a stony mask. Centurion Eggius stood to Varus' right.

While Varus appeared to be counting the seconds until this ended, the two soldiers kept their flint-hard eyes on Arminius. He might have won over Varus and others, but he hadn't convinced every Roman he was trustworthy.

"Go on." Varus waved his cup toward Segestes. "Tell him what you told me."

My father stiffened his shoulders and tipped his chin up. "Arminius is plotting an uprising. When the legions march out—"

"Three legions," Varus said. "How many men is that, Vala?"

"By my last count, a bit fewer than twenty thousand veteran soldiers, sir."

"Yes, twenty thousand of Rome's finest soldiers. Continue, Segestes."

A bit of Segestes' dark color paled. "Yes, Governor. He has been organizing a confederation of the tribes to assault all three legions on your winter march."

Varus looked at Arminius. Arminius looked right back and shrugged. "What can I say, sir. I have been quite busy deviously plotting how I can get more than two tribes to agree on anything, let alone fighting under a single leader. I've been running them through drills to match Roman formations. Thusnelda here has been overseeing the production of shields and swords for, what is it now, wife? Thirty thousand warriors from tribes who can only stand each other long enough for one month of controlled trading and drinking?"

I gaped at him in wide-eyed horror.

He shot Varus a grin. "All this under your nose, and I stole a woman betrothed to the prince of the second strongest tribe in the region, with no regard to Germani honor and customs, because I have so thoroughly secured their disparate loyalties that they no longer care about generations of grudges. I am an impressively cunning man, as you know."

Varus stared at him some more, then burst out laughing. He laughed so long and hard, he wiped tears from his eyes. The two Roman officers shifted uncomfortably at this display.

"Xanthes," Varus shouted between bouts of laughter, "bring Arminius a cup of wine. Don't water it."

After he collected himself, he let out a long breath, and leveled his attention on Segestes.

"I understand," he spoke slowly, enunciating each word, "that you are upset one of my men ran off and married your daughter. Normally, I would promise that I'd see Arminius flogged for his insubordination, as my men, even the local auxiliaries, are not permitted to engage in these barbaric marriage ceremonies. But I've learned enough about your daughter to know you have let her run wild and are now reaping that harvest. By Jupiter, if you come to me again with such a ridiculous accusation to assuage your pride, I will have you crucified. Do you understand me?"

Now it was Wout's turn to take on that purple hue. "You have to arrest him! He'll kill you all!"

"I have to do nothing!" Varus thundered. "I do not take orders from barbarian chiefs, and I especially do not take orders from their brats. Arminius has been a loyal servant of Rome for most of his life and a friend to me. I will address the matter of his so-called marriage with him, and that will be the last hear from any of you about it. Get the fuck out. Go back to your hovels."

Left with no other choice, my father and brother shuffled out the door. Wout paused in the frame and sent me a look heavy with threats. I was tired of men threatening me.

Varus drummed stubby fingers against his toga-clad thigh. At length, he huffed a laugh and gave his head a rueful shake. "Couldn't help yourself, could you?"

Arminius shrugged one shoulder. "What can I say? We were betrothed as children. All I did was hold Segestes to our original agreement."

"And got yourself a hellcat in the bargain." Varus' smile turned lascivious. My fists clenched.

"You know me. I love a challenge." Arminius slipped an arm around my hip and tugged me closer. He knew damn well how close I was to violence.

"I know you, my boy," Varus said. "I don't think I need to remind you that in the eyes of Rome, this is merely a *usus* marriage. Nor do I need to remind you that I brought you here to help smooth my way with the tribes, not make things more difficult."

"Apologies, sir."

Vala cleared his throat. "Segestes leveled a serious accusation against you, Arminius, which you didn't deny."

The oppressive air in the tent constricted. Against my body, Arminius' muscles went rock hard while his face kept its placid facade.

"I answered a ridiculous accusation with a ridiculous response, Legatus. As the governor said, I wounded Segestes' pride."

Vala rounded Varus' seat to face Arminius directly.

"It's not the first time I've heard this rumor. Far and wide, my men bring me whispers about you. The Mattiaci have been quite vocal regarding those men you killed."

"They say you killed them when they refused to join your treacherous confederation," Eggius said. "They say you intend to install yourself as king after you chase us back across the Rhine."

My voice had no weight here. I spoke anyway.

"Our people see him as a traitor," I said. "He leads tax collection and arbitration for Rome. Many wish to see him torn down, by any means necessary."

Vala's dark eyes locked on me, and Arminius tightened his hold.

"See," Varus chortled, "a real hellcat. Don't let her sex blind you, gentlemen. She's right. Arminius is an example to many and an enemy to some. Why, when I was rising through the ranks, some of my peers spread all manner of nonsense about me. My personal favorite was the one where I was plotting to usurp Augustus by marrying his niece."

Varus rose to clap Arminius on the shoulder, an unsubtle move forcing Vala to step back.

"When we return to Rome, I can introduce your wife to a good etiquette teacher. I can also recommend an excellent housekeeper. Something tells me that despite Thusnelda's many impressive skills, managing a household is not one of them."

They shook hands, and Arminius nodded graciously.

"My thanks, sir. I eagerly look forward to introducing her to the greatest city in the world."

I forced a smile in a pale mimic of Arminius'. Varus would return to Rome, of that I was certain. We'd return his parts in a box.

———➤———

Arminius glared at the longhouse.

"You should stay anywhere else."

"It's only for what, another month?"

The Romans always left before winter settled. A month was stretching the estimated time I had left in the home I'd known most of my life. It was a strange sort of melancholy to miss the place before I left, when I still dreaded my last days there still to come.

The coming weeks promised to be long and fraught, unless Arminius and I made a clear declaration now. I was fully prepared to face them on my own, but having him at my side eased the burden. I liked it.

"Probably less," Arminius said. "Varus is eager to return to the relative comforts of Vetera. He won't stop talking about the baths there."

Less? A shiver raced up my spine. What once seemed a lifetime away could now be counted in days.

"The ramparts are all completed?"

Nonplussed by my sudden topic change, Arminius quirked a lip and said, "Yes. I personally reviewed every mile of them."

"And the chieftains?"

He gripped my shoulders and adopted a serious, if a little patronizing, expression. "Everyone knows where they need to be. Before you say it, yes, many of them are still noncommittal about their support, but they will be there. Not one of them will miss an opportunity to scavenge for loot."

Mollified, I nodded.

"We can't keep putting this off." He tipped his head toward the longhouse. "I know it doesn't always seem like it, but I have thought of everything. I put the right people exactly where they need to be. The Chatti are still committed. All we're waiting on now is Varus' departure order."

"Right." I sucked my tongue across my teeth and took his hand. "Let's get this over with."

My home was deathly quiet inside. The central brazier burned low, hardly enough to chase out the bitter fall chill. No scalcs were present. Segestes sat on a raised chair on the dais, cleared of our usual table. To complete the eerie tableau, my brothers flanked him on both sides. Silent. Staring. Gods, how long had they sat like this waiting on us? How awkward.

The sound of Arminius pulling the door shut echoed through the hall. We walked hand in hand to the dais, and I couldn't help feeling like a wayward child coming to accept her punishment. I reminded myself that wasn't how this meeting was to go.

"You. Stole. My. Daughter." Segestes' voice cracked, as though he'd spent days yelling at the top of his lungs.

I stepped forward. "He didn't steal me. I left."

"You had no right—"

"Shut the fuck up," Arminius spoke, deadly soft. "You will not be dictating to my wife anymore."

Segestes sneered. "If you think I am going to sit back and let you destroy everything, you are mistaken. You steal my daughter. You break a treaty I have held for years. You foment a useless rebellion. It will fail. They all fail, and we will be the ones left to pay the cost. As Wodan as my witness, I will tear you apart."

My brothers said nothing, though their collective anger was palpable. For once, I took comfort in Levin's absence. I didn't want him here for this or dealing with the fallout of our family's anger.

I shoved past Arminius. Though I appreciated his help more than I ever thought possible, I didn't need him to speak for me. He could threaten all he wanted, and it counted for nothing as soon as he left this hall. This wasn't his fight; it was mine.

"What's done is done, in the eyes of witnesses and the gods. The rebellion is coming, no matter what you say. I was there when Varus laughed in your face."

Segestes said nothing, though I swore I heard his breath hitch.

"Yes, Varus laughed in your face before casting you out like a misbehaving hound," I said. "No one listens to you anymore, Father. Not the Romans, not even the Cherusci. Arminius may not be chief, but we all know he will be when this battle is won. I am his queen. I orchestrated the survival of our allies last winter. They look to me. If I were you, I'd think carefully about how you treat me between now and then."

I let the threat drop like a lead weight at Segestes' feet. Between him and my brothers, save Levin, they could beat me. They could chain me up. They could kill me. Then they'd face Arminius and the Cherusci. Any move against me now started a countdown on their lives.

"This isn't over." Segestes repeated, more to himself than to me or Arminius. He dropped his head and exhaled slowly. When he lifted his gaze back to mine, his eyes shone with the hint of tears. "Daughter, if you do this, we will all suffer for it. Please, hear me. Let this go. We can go to Varus together—"

"Shut the fuck up."

To my surprise, the softly spoken invective came from Levin. He fell in at my side, already dressed in his ala armor.

"You heard her," he said. "It's done. Give it up."

Something about hearing it from Levin, one of his sons, broke something in Segestes that my rebellion hadn't. His shoulders slumped. At length, he hauled himself out of his chair and shuffled to his room without looking back. Wout and Lennart looked uncertainly at each other before following.

My breath exhaled in a great whoosh, and Arminius rubbed a hand down my back.

"That wasn't so bad," he murmured.

I choked on a bitter laugh. True, it might have gone worse. Yet seeing my father surrender lacked the satisfaction I'd imagined it would. I hurt for him. He believed with his entire being that he was right and we were wrong. In his mind, this road led only to ruin; not just for me, or our family, but all Germani. That had to be a terrible feeling, as terrible as I felt when I saw our people in iron collars, slaving away for Rome.

"I should go," Arminius said.

I turned to him and captured his face in my hands, tracing the familiar lines and planes I'd grown to love so dearly.

"Will I see you again? Before?"

His lips thinned. "I don't know. I'll try, but..."

I shook my head. "Don't take any risks. We're too close to victory now."

He turned to press a kiss against my palm. Dimly, I sensed Levin take his leave of this private moment.

"Take care, wife. What I've asked of you is no easy feat."

As much as I bristled at my mission, at not being present for part of the battle, I understood the significance of the task he'd given me. I'd never led a battle entirely myself before. On the surface what he asked of me was paltry, nothing more than an attempt to keep me from the worst of the fighting. It was so much more than that, though. If I failed, the entire uprising might fail with me.

He trusted me with all that.

"I'll see it done," I said. "And I'll meet you in the Teutoburg."

Chapter 24

The greatest disgrace that can befall them is to have abandoned their shields. (Tacitus)

A messenger from the Germani ala squadron arrived when the sun reached its zenith in the sky, barely three weeks after Arminius had left. He sweated and puffed from the hard ride from the Roman encampment.

"Three days," he said, after draining a large cup of the water Jotapa offered. "The legions will leave at dawn in three days."

Jotapa's eyes widened, likely a match to my own. It was here. Our time had come and it was hardly any time at all to reach Chauci territory and orchestrate a small uprising before the legions passed us by.

Without needing to be told, Jotapa darted off to fulfill her duty, spreading the word around the village. Our own messengers were to ride immediately to our allies. The system worked as a relay. Where one messenger stopped, another continued.

Excitement and anxiety warred in my breast. I trusted my small contingent of Cherusci warriors, but what of the Chauci?

My traveling bags were packed, as they had been for weeks now. I threw on my sturdiest boots, strapped my belt, baldric, and sword to my hip, tossed the straps of the two bags across my shoulders, and hefted my spear and shield. The familiarity of carrying this heavy load went a long way toward soothing my nerves.

Wout met me in the hall. "You truly believe you can win this, don't you?"

For once, he bore no condemnation for me, only bewilderment. To him, I was a creature beyond understanding, not even of this world.

My lips twitched. "We're going to win, brother. Whether or not you join us is up to you."

His gaze darted away, and I almost caught sight of indecision coloring his features. Before I saw it for certain, a clamor arose outside, featuring one voice rising above the others.

In the muddled afternoon light, Segestes railed at the warriors gathering for the ride north.

"You will bring their wrath down upon us!" He crowed at the top of his lungs, swinging accusing fingers in every direction. When he settled on me, his expression flared. "She intends to steal your scalcs! She thinks to dictate how you manage your own property, and her duplicitous man plots to make himself king. They say they fight for our freedom, but everything they're doing is with the aim of subjugation."

Their attention shifted to me, some with questions, many with impatience. They wanted this battle as badly as I did. The way Konrada kept eyeing the path out of the village, she looked ready to ride off without us if we didn't hurry up.

"Scalcs aren't slaves," I said. "They earn their freedom with goods or bravery, the same as always."

Shuffling at the edge of the crowd caught my attention: At least half the scalcs in our village had assembled, each bearing a variety of weapons, from clubs to shovels and pitchforks. That would do nicely. However, their arrival sparked more unrest among those not already committed to joining me.

The sight of all those scalcs together, on their way to earn their freedom through bloodshed, made the issue a reality. I hadn't believed so many would readily join this fight.

I swung onto my horse's back and whistled for my dogs.

"If you're so worried about your scalcs," I shouted above the growing din, "then join me. There are tens of thousands of Romans who are yours for the taking."

I didn't bother waiting for a response, to hear what fresh venom Segestes spit my way. Those of us with mounts would ride hard for the Chauci. Everyone else had to keep up as best they could.

Once everyone was mounted, Jotapa to my right, Konrada to my left, I kicked my horse into a gallop.

We had more than one fight ahead, and after spurning my Chatti betrothal, I didn't know if we had any allies left. Despite my gnawing anxiety, the relief of leaving my father and brothers and all their hate behind kept me light in the saddle the entire journey.

➤

Rihilt spoke for her silent husband.

"We won't stop anyone from joining you." She measured each word like they were weighted with silver. "We are still free people here. But you have proven to be untrustworthy. If you cannot uphold a simple betrothal agreement, why should we believe any promises you make on behalf of a man who would steal another man's wife?"

My temper flared. How dare she, in a single breath, assert our freedom, then insist I hadn't the freedom to choose my husband? In all likelihood, her own marriage to Frikkeo was arranged. It wasn't as if she didn't know what it was like to be shoved into a situation not of her own choosing.

Unless she didn't. Unless, like I once did, she saw marriage as a duty that served numerous purposes, none of which required love.

I unclenched my hands.

"If it matters to you in the slightest, Arminius and I were betrothed the day I was born. My father dishonored that arrangement by breaking it while Arminius was away. However, I do not see how it's relevant to the matter at hand. We have no time to waste before—"

The Chauci's minor chieftains cut me off with their grumbling.

Faithless, they called me. *Without honor. As Roman as Arminius.*

Jotapa took a firm grip on my shoulder, and I realized my hand had fallen to the pommel of my sword. No. Arminius silenced his opposition with violence, not me. This situation was exactly why he had sent me.

Their puny little hall stank with unwashed bodies and the smaller animals occupying the pens. It made my eyes water.

"We will not trade one tyrant for another," Frikkeo said. "This business with the scalcs is—"

"It is the way of our people," I shouted above the disgruntled murmurs. "What is the matter with you? All Arminius has ever promised is that if we do this, we get to keep our way of life. All Rome offers is to take it away. How many of your people have you lost since they first arrived? The slaves, the soldiers, the murders. How many have starved after those raping bastards stole your food and called it a tax?"

They looked at their feet, each other, anywhere but our party. The fucking cowards. The bold Rihilt stared over my head, chin up in a pathetic attempt at defiance. I had to do something, something extreme. Arminius wasn't here to hold my hand, and the idea that came to mind wasn't something I'd ask of anyone else. As per usual, I would fix this problem myself.

"You're afraid?" I let disgust coat each word. "You think they can't be stopped, is that it? Fine. Fine. If you need proof that Romans bleed the same as you and I, then I will provide it."

I stormed out into the gray, chilly morning, my friends hot on my heels.

"What are you doing?" Jotapa abandoned her horse and trotted to keep pace with me, Konrada close behind.

In a series of quick, jerky movements, I stripped my horse of my extra gear. "They haven't fought back in so long, they've forgotten the legionaries are mortal. I'm going to remind them before we run out of time. If not..."

Konrada frowned at the village. "The scalcs are with us, as are our men. If you're not back by sundown, we'll burn this bitch to the ground. That should get Roman attention."

I smiled down at her. "You've certainly got the spirit."

"I should go with you." Jotapa made for her horse, but I stopped her.

"No, no. I need to show them, the way Arminius did at the contests." But bigger. Bolder. A statement they couldn't ignore. A statement designed to shame every one of them who dared call themselves a warrior.

"Thusnelda, you do not have to do this alone. We can make a contest here just the same if you take help."

I shook my head, too committed to the course to let her change my mind.

As I mounted, she said, "For once in your life, let us help you."

"No." I wheeled my horse away and urged it into a trot, then a run. No, it had to be me.

With Sunna and Donar alongside, I rode hard and fast for the Roman outpost, stopping when I reckoned it was about a mile away. I left the horse loosely tethered to a tree and took off on foot, spear tipped with a sharpened rock in one hand, bow and a clutch of salvaged arrows in the other. Our little trio ran silent as wraiths through the dense trees.

It wasn't hard to find the trails their patrols used. I followed one, then another, sweating despite the fall cold, searching for any sign that soldiers had passed one way or the other recently. Fresh footprints, a broken branch still green with life, anything. Sneaking inside the tall wooden walls of their fort was suicide. I needed to find soldiers outside the walls. One taking a piss would do perfectly, but I hadn't brought all those weapons for nothing. I'd killed how many that fateful day with Konrada, three? This time, I had the element of surprise.

A surprise that only worked if there were any soldiers in these woods. My heart sank as each path turned up nothing. Not a sound, not a single hint that these Romans left the safety of their walls more than once a month.

I slowed to a walk to catch my breath and poured water from my flask into my hands for the dogs to get a drink before I took several swallows myself. I closed my eyes and let the ambient sounds of the forest filter into my ears.

Songbirds angrily chased something away. The wind rustled through the leaves. Trees creaked and groaned in their own unknowable speech.

Something small skittered through the undergrowth, a squirrel, maybe, or a rabbit. The symphony of toads and insects calling to each other. Voices in the distance.

Voices. Men's voices and not very many of them. They talked and laughed, blissfully unaware of the danger they were in.

I dashed on silent feet in their direction. It didn't take long to catch sight of them. In the dimness of the woods, murky sunlight glinted off their armor. They chatted and ribbed each other, ignorant of my presence. They weren't paying the least bit of attention to their surroundings. It was a mockery of a patrol.

With a flick of my wrist, I bid the dogs to lie down. Surprise was essential. The shadows of the trees and bushes obscured only so much. Their shaggy brown and black fur and long snouts added to their resemblance to wolves. When they lunged after their prey, snarling and baring their long white canines, the resemblance was uncanny. These legionaries would shit themselves when Sunna and Donar burst out of the understory, aiming for their throats.

I set my spear down by my feet and nocked the first arrow, the rest gripped tight in my bow hand. My heart raced not with fear but with the excitement that only came before combat. Few people were fortunate enough to be both excellent at something and also love doing it. Whether I fought one person or a horde of warriors, I relished the exhilaration, the simplicity of it all. Either I won, or they did. Nothing else mattered. Today, I would win.

I pulled the string back, muscles flexing with the familiar action. My target was the tallest soldier, the one who stood to be my biggest problem. Our heavy arrows could puncture their armor but not always and not without proper arrowheads, so I waited until he turned his back and exposed his flank.

My arrow hit its mark. He reeled and howled in pain, and his friends scrambled to help him. One shouted in the direction I'd shot from, but I was already on the move to circle them. I loosed my next arrow, clipping another soldier high in his arm. I cursed that shot. It should have landed in his neck.

The last two men without wounds whipped their shields around to their fronts but didn't know from where they were under attack. They shuffled their feet this way and that, twisting back and forth with their wounded compatriots between them. The one I'd hit in the flank hefted his shield with a pained grimace. I had to respect the man's spine.

"Show yourselves, you gutless fucks!" he shouted.

Good, they thought I was many.

Another arrow flew right into his knee. He roared in pain and dropped onto his other knee, his shield falling into the dirt next to him.

"Sevillius," called one of the soldiers still standing. His voice quaked, betraying his nerves, and I grinned despite myself. That one would do nicely.

I sent three arrows in a fast volley toward the other one, nailing his sword arm, his shin, and, to my delight, one barreled right into his exposed throat. He staggered, then dropped like a stone.

The soldier I'd selected blanched in horror. Something dribbled down his leg.

"Go!" The soldier I'd shot in the backside pushed onto his hip. "Back to the fort. Get help."

He shook his head so vigorously, his helmet tottered. "No. I won't leave you behind."

"That's an order," the other man barked. "Get the fuck back to the fort."

He stayed where he was, turning quickly, searching the woods for his unseen assailants. His gladius trembled. I spared a moment to appreciate his bravery. This young man had probably never seen a single battle. They trained to fight as a solid unit, even in their sword play. Legionaries never fought alone. Now he stayed to defend his fallen comrades. The survivors took up their swords in a pitiful show of going down fighting. I would finish them off later.

I traded the bow for the spear. My dogs looked up at me with pure hope shining on their merry faces. They panted and shifted restlessly on their bellies, dying to join me. I indulged them.

The soldier shouted and stumbled back when the three of us burst out of the shadows. The dogs easily dodged the sword swipes of the men on the ground, growling and yipping. They thought it was a game. I rushed my target. At the last moment, I flipped my spear and smashed the butt end into his face. He had no time to react. Blood erupted from his nose and upper lip. To his credit, he quickly regained his balance and shoved me back with his massive rectangular shield and a swipe of his gladius.

When I side-stepped into a slow circle, he mirrored me, blinking back tears and sweat. One of the men on the ground bellowed in pain, and I smirked at the thought of Sunna or Donar tearing into him.

"You barbarian bitch," the soldier said. He spit a thick stream of mucus and blood to the ground. "We're going to torch your whole tribe."

I flipped my spear back around and lunged at him. It was half-hearted, more to probe his defenses than an actual attempt to hurt him. He blocked me easily with his shield and cracked his sword against my spear. Probe, block, crack. We might have been sparring for the steady pattern we fell into. It was just how I wanted him.

When I was sure he expected my next thrust, I spun and crashed the staff against his exposed knee. He dropped on an outraged howl.

I was almost disappointed by how easily I had felled four of the Empire's finest.

He released his shield and forced his way back to his feet. Perhaps it wasn't so easy after all. I dropped my spear and unsheathed my sword. If he wanted a sword fight, I would oblige him.

I let him attack first and caught his blade on the dull edge of my weapon. We attacked and parried for a few minutes. We were both tired; me from my race here, him from the shock of the attack. I didn't let it show the way he did.

"Kill the bitch," one soldier said.

Donar snapped his jaws in his face. They weren't accustomed to killing people, and I didn't know if they'd actually killed the other soldier or maimed him into silence.

At his comrade's encouragement, my opponent lunged wildly at me. I let him come. Once he was in my guard, I trapped his sword arm between my bicep and torso and brought the pommel of my sword down on his temple with a resounding crack. I had to do it three more times before his eyes rolled back and he crumpled at my feet.

I sucked in air, breathing harder than I'd realized. The sun was past its zenith in the sky and I needed to get moving, but exhaustion settled like a stone in my limbs. The dogs had torn out the throat of one man, leaving the other, with his fast sword arm, alive. They panted slightly harder than I did.

This narrow path reeked of blood, piss, and death. I tipped my head up to the sky and willed rain to fall to wash away the scent and cool my overheated skin.

"He was right," the survivor croaked. "When my brothers find our bodies, they will burn your shitty village down. Your men will be crucified and the women taken as slaves. What the fuck were you thinking?"

I kicked his sword out of his hand and sank into a crouch by his face. Pain and blood loss made him pale. He might have been handsome to another woman in another place and another time. I saw a man facing death with fire in his dark eyes.

"We're going to come back here," I said, removing my dagger from my boot. "We're going to kill every one of you murdering, raping dogs until there are no Romans left alive in my country."

His eyes narrowed. "Impossible."

"Only a Roman would think that." I gripped his hair and prepared to ram my knife into his throat, when he barked in pain. An arrow I didn't fire pinned his hand to his thigh, where he'd held a dagger close enough to gut me.

In shock, I released him and leapt back. Jotapa strode from the cover of the trees, panting hard for air and shaking her head at me.

"Do you," she gasped, "have any," another gasp, "idea how close you came to dying just now?"

I glanced down at pale, blood-spattered Roman who still had enough strength to snarl at me. "I have an idea, yes."

"Good." When she got close enough, she nocked, aimed, and shot him through the eye. "You're welcome."

My pulse skittered in an uneven rhythm. If Jotapa hadn't been there, that soldier might have gutted me.

"It's all right, you know." She toed the unconscious soldier with her boot. "It's all right to ask for help."

My mouth went dry. I'd opened myself up enough to trust Arminius, and I trusted Jotapa with most things, but apparently not in all things. It wasn't as though we hadn't fought and trained together, as though I didn't trust her at my side. My first instinct in an emergent situation was to shoulder the burden on my own, in spite of common sense.

"You'll get there." She patted me on the arm with a smirk. "What about this fellow?"

I took a deep breath. In and out.

"Thank you. I'm sorry I made you run all the way here."

"Run?" She scoffed. "I took a horse."

Together we stripped his armor, tied him, and secured him to my horse. The task was far easier with her help.

⟶➤

The entire village and all the visitors from their outlying settlements gathered in the square when we returned with our quarry. Torches lined the main path, casting their flickering orange light against the roundhouses and outbuildings. I dismounted and sliced through the binding around his feet before yanking him down. Jotapa and I pulled him down with enough force to unceremoniously dump him on his ass.

"What is this?" Frikkeo pushed through the crowd.

"This," I grabbed the legionary by his hair and drew him back to his feet, "is your great unbeatable enemy. Jotapa and I killed his entire patrol and still took this one alive. Is this who you fear so much?"

Frikkeo's eyes widened and the crowd erupted in chatter. He waved a hand for silence. "You have brought them to our door. They will be here—"

"By morning," I finished for him. "We left an obvious trail they'll pick up at first light. You can join me and strike them first, or you can sit here and wait for them to raze your tribe to the ground. Look at him. Two women alone did this. With no armor; half my arrows are just sharped sticks. By the time we face them in the Teutoburg, they will be exhausted and terrified, like this one. A child could kill one of them."

This, too, was not a job I needed to complete myself. I released his hands and shoved my sword into his grip before taking a step back and calling for Konrada. She appeared with her spear, topped with a bit of stone like mine, and an uncertain frown.

"This girl is barely a woman. She's never been in a battle. You want an omen? A demonstration? She will show you what a broken Roman looks like in a fight."

The legionary looked between Konrada and me. "What is this?"

"You fight her," I answered in Latin. "Fight her and die like a warrior."

He gritted his teeth. "I won't fight a little girl."

I came close enough to whisper in his ear. "If you don't fight her, I will tie you to a tree and feed you to my dogs while you're still alive. You saw what happened to your friend, yes?"

It was a bluff, but then again, it wasn't. I thought of how many Germani this man had slain, enslaved, assaulted, stolen from. He didn't deserve mercy, and the Chauci wouldn't follow me if I showed it.

If he had any color left in his pallor, it leached away. He tightened his grip on the sword and studied it, turning it this way and that. Heavier than a gladius but with only one bladed edge, it was unfamiliar to him and gave him no special advantage.

I joined Konrada on her side of the semicircle of villagers and gauged her readiness. We'd trained hard together these past months. I was confident enough to have brought her along for this attack in the first place, but was she? She'd never killed a person before, and the addition of a rapt audience added pressure to the situation. Her hand flexed on her spear, and though her eyes didn't stray from the Roman, they darted in rapid flicks.

"Think of the brother they tried to steal from you," I said in a low voice just for her. "Think of our tribesmen they've crucified, of the people they've taken. Think of what they wanted to do to you when we were ambushed. They are lower than dogs."

She gave a jerky nod.

"You're ready, Konrada. You do this and you're ready for the battle."

She turned her large eyes to me and something cleared and sharpened in her gaze. Without another word, she stalked toward the Roman. Jotapa filled in the space she vacated.

"What are you doing?" Jotapa whispered.

"She needs this, before the battle."

"And shaming them by sending a girl to do it is an attack on their pride," she said. "Smart."

I puffed up a little under her praise. Perhaps I was better at manipulating a group than I gave myself credit for.

Konrada and her opponent circled each other, her with measured, easy steps, him on unsteady feet. The crowd started jeering the Roman. However they felt about our rebellion, they hated our conquerors. They cheered Konrada on, and I swelled with more pride. That was my student out there.

Just like I taught her, with a great battle cry and no warning, she lunged. The soldier dodged by a hair and stumbled backward. He swiped at her, which she easily batted away with her spear.

Cries of "finish him!" and "make him bleed!" rang out from the crowd to great cheering. I couldn't argue with that. I still had to organize this rabble into a small army and lead them to take the fort before sunrise. We were running out of time.

"End it. Show them how easy it is." I raised my voice to be heard over the shouts. Konrada gave no indication that she heard me, and I silently praised her for not diverting her attention. The Roman may have been weak and frightened, but he was still armed and well trained.

She swung her spear overhead in the move I'd nailed her with many times, spinning it faster and faster as she let the length of the shaft slid infinitesimally further down her grip. The Roman watched it, uselessly gauging the moment he would make his attack. My heart beat faster. She'd never caught me off guard with this, had never successfully used it in practice.

He darted forward. Right into the blade of her spear. It caught him in the neck. Blood spurted, and in the moment before he fell, his eyes widened in shock. The crowd burst into a thunderous ovation for her. It was a clean kill in a single strike. She whipped around to me with a stunned expression, disbelieving, maybe a little green with nausea. That reaction was common after killing a person the first time.

Jotapa shepherded Konrada to her side, and I retook my place before the mass of jubilant Chauci. The legionary's body twitched a few times and his blood steamed in the chilly night air.

"Do you see?" My voice cracked, hoarse from shouting. "Your chief and your queen think you can't beat them. They expect you to bend over and get fucked in the ass by men who can be killed in one blow by a child!"

Shaming their leaders this way was dangerous. I didn't know how deep their loyalty ran, but I knew a thing or two about Germani pride. Weak leaders lost their seats, and few displayed the kind of weakness I had put on display.

I swallowed hard and willed my voice to keep working, drawing deep from my diaphragm to continue. This sort of speech-making was Arminius' territory.

"We attack the fort tonight, before they have time to organize. When every one of those dogs is dead, we march to the battle site and join my husband's army, where we will wipe them out."

Silence answered me. Germani weren't prone to silence. I looked to Jotapa and Konrada. Each one of them shrugged. Useless.

"Decide." I dropped my voice lower. "Will you let these weak bastards make slaves of you, or will you fight for freedom?"

"What of our scalcs?" a faceless voice called to murmurs of agreement.

Gods, this again. I fought the urge to roll my eyes and let my disgust show.

"There are more than twenty thousand Romans—soldiers, men, women, children—waiting for you. Whatever you lose in scalcs, this battle will get you threefold."

This soothed their worries, the same way it would soothe every Germani from here to the Alps. Finally, the fuckers cheered for me.

Chapter 25

*This young man made use of the negligence of the general
as an opportunity for treachery, sagaciously seeing that no one
could be more quickly overpowered than the man who feared
nothing, and that the most common beginning of disaster was
a sense of security. (Velleius Paterculus)*

In absolute silence, our bodies painted black, we encircled the fort. Germani warriors were nothing but shadows in the Stygian night, lit dimly by the waxing moon.

My body thrummed for the coming action. Sentries dotted the walls of the fort, more than what they usually posted at these places. They must have found the bodies of their brothers and expected an attack. All of them were up and ready. It was neither ideal nor terrible.

Impatient to start, I shifted on the balls of my feet. The rest of the warriors needed time to get into position and ready their weapons. They bore farm implements, clubs, sharpened spear shafts. Many wielded axes, allowed to keep them on account of their necessity in daily life. Some held large rocks. If we were successful here with our primitive arms, there was hope yet for the larger battle. If we failed, I'd meet Arminius in the underworld.

Every third fighter carried a clay jar of oil. Most of us had arrows wrapped in dry fabric. Once we lit the starter fires, we had seconds to launch the oil and arrows before the Romans organized a defense.

An owl hooted in the distance. To the untrained ear, the call sounded genuine. To the Germani ear, born and bred in these woods, it was our signal.

My hands trembled with excitement, both for the fight and to see these warriors following my orders with smooth precision. This was my attack plan, and mine alone. For whatever reason, everyone, including Rihilt, Frikkeo, and their more seasoned chieftains, agreed with me. No suggestions on how to better the plan. Arminius trusted me with this task, and thus far I hadn't let him down. I wouldn't.

The warriors with tinder and flint dropped to their knees and sparked small fires to life while the rest of us nocked arrows in preparation.

As shouting rose from the walls, we lit our arrows and loosed them in a fiery rain, right behind the wave of oil jars hurled up and over the walls. One struck a soldier in my line of sight. I shot him in the chest and watched as he erupted into flames before tumbling and disappearing off the wall. Grim satisfaction overtook me. The rebellion began.

The Chauci and Cherusci army unleashed our haunting, resonant battle cry. It came from deep in the chest and rattled through the throat. We launched more flaming arrows until a brilliant orange glow lit the inside of the fort. Soldiers bellowed orders, and their steps thundered as they raced to defend themselves. It was too late for them to prevent the conflagration.

Fifty feet away, a team of warriors hammered axes into a tree. It fell with an echoing crack, and they descended on it, stripping its branches and chopping away at the narrow top of the thick tree to make a battering ram.

"Thusnelda!" Konrada pointed her spear toward the top of the wall, where soldiers assembled with their own marksmen. It was time to move regardless of how ready our ram was.

I whistled and waited until it echoed around the fort, then sprinted toward the wall, loosing arrows and dodging as I went. Warriors around me cried out as they were hit, but it didn't slow our assault. Studded planks were hastily tossed on the ramparts, easing our passage right to the timber walls.

Most were instructed to lob sling stones and arrows at the soldiers guarding the walls and wait for the main gate to come down. A portion of us, myself included, were to breach the walls ourselves. Spindly ladders lurched into position around me.

Someone grunted next to me, and I turned in time to see him fall back with an arrow jutting from the top of his shoulder and out his ribs on the other side. The black paint smeared from his head down his bare chest concealed the blood pouring out of the wounds. Another warrior wrenched the arrow free and fired back up the wall. I shook off the sight, swallowed a deep breath, and leapt up the nearest ladder with my spear strapped to my back and my sword in hand.

Our ladders didn't quite reach the top of the wall. They weren't meant for climbs this high, but it worked out: The legionaries couldn't push them away. Though that also meant once I reached the top rung, I had to jump and pull myself up before a soldier ran a javelin through my chest.

To my right and left, others made the leap. We swarmed their walls in such numbers that as they fought off one warrior, three more clambered past their defenses. I glanced down the line, and it was a mistake. Jotapa kept pace with me. Damn it, I'd told her to wait for the gates to fall. Some fucking scalc she was.

I laughed at the thought, and, given the scene, I imagined I looked like a madwoman. She grinned at me, all white teeth against blackened skin. The ladder jarred and bent under the weight of the bodies following me.

I was Thusnelda, princess of the Cherusci, war queen of Arminius, and I would hesitate no more. I dipped low and pushed hard against the rungs. For a heartbeat, I floated in open air, then my arms caught around one of the spiked tips of the wall. A splinter dug deep into my palm, but I wouldn't feel it until the heat of battle faded.

With a mighty heave, I tossed a leg up and through the spikes. It was a difficult maneuver to cross them. They weren't sharp enough to hurt me seriously, but sitting on them wasn't exactly an option.

Before I steadied myself, two soldiers descended on me. I dropped and rolled beneath their dual sword swings and came up behind them. My blood pounded and sang in the chaos. I caught one with a hard slice against his thigh and ducked the next gladius that came for my head.

A body rammed into me, knocking me off the raised platform. I fell hard onto my left shoulder. At least it wasn't my head. I bit back a cry of pain and found my feet as quickly as possible, and not a moment too soon. A soldier charged at me, and it was all I could do to parry his rapid, heavy sword thrusts. When I tried to wield the weapon in my strong hand, shooting pain arced from my shoulder, up my neck and down my spine. I wasn't as strong with the other arm, and each blow from the man's sword sent me staggering backward. Our blades met with clangs and sparks. My back hit something solid—a support post for the walkway—and I had nowhere left to go.

Fighters screamed in agony and fury. More of my army streamed over the walls and, to my relief, they rushed the soldiers defending the gate. Soon we would overwhelm their pitiful numbers, pitchforks and sticks be damned. I feared I wouldn't live to see it.

An arrow skimmed across my attacker's face, taking his nose and upper lip with it. I blinked at the horrifying sight of what was once a human face, now rendered macabre. He dropped his sword, and his hands flew to his ruined visage. Bright red blood spilled over and through his fingers. I raised my sword and ended his suffering with a clean slice across his throat.

Konrada stood not ten feet away from me, loosing arrows with expert precision. Most of them, lacking arrowheads, glanced off the soldiers' armor. Smart, vicious warrior that she was, she aimed for their faces. I grinned and hurled myself back into the fight.

My injured shoulder hindered my progress, but the other warriors overtaking the fort made my work easier. For every legionary I fought, two more warriors descended to finish him. What we lacked in fine weapons, we made up with numbers.

My cheek throbbed from a hit a soldier landed before being summarily cut down, and my arm tired quickly without the help of its twin. The smell of coppery blood and burning wood and flesh assailed my nostrils.

The screams of dying men faded, and bit by bit, my warriors slowed and the frenzy of battle waned. We left few legionaries standing.

When I saw a warrior raise a gladius to end a soldier on his knees, glaring defiantly up at him, I called for him to stop.

He whirled on me, eyes flashing with bloodlust. "What?"

I raised a hand in supplication. "We need one who can still sit a horse. Someone has to bring word to Varus that the Chauci are in open rebellion."

With pained reluctance, he lowered his weapon and jerked the man to his feet.

"Your legions are on the march to Vetera," I said in Latin. "If you catch up to them, you might live."

He was tall, for a Roman, with a proud set to his shoulders and a patrician nose. He spat at me.

"I am a soldier of Rome. If you have a message for your governor, tell him yourself."

The warrior knocked the man's helmet off and slapped him across the face. The soldier was right; this was a message I could send myself. I was a war general against an implacable enemy. Lines I once would have never crossed no longer mattered.

"Find every standard you can," I said to the warrior. "Cut his throat, strap him to a horse, and make sure his body and his standards cross the marching route." I spoke in Latin for the Roman's benefit. To my satisfaction, he hissed a breath in through his nose, and my warrior nodded his understanding.

He forced the soldier back to his knees.

"I am a soldier of Rome." He stared sightlessly beyond us, beyond the walls of this fort and the forests of Germania. "I swear that I shall faithfully execute all the emperor commands. I shall never desert the service. I shall not seek to avoid death for the Roman Empire. I am a soldier of Rome. I swear that I shall faithfully—"

The warrior sliced so deeply he almost took the man's head off and then whistled for more warriors to join us, repeating my instructions before they scurried off to obey.

Smoke stung my eyes and throat. The smell made my stomach churn. Sunna and Donar trotted to me, wagging their tails, faces coated in gore. They'd taken to killing Romans better than I'd expected. I gradually noticed my warriors gathered around me, expectant in their silent attention.

Jotapa hurried to my side to inspect my shoulder. It wasn't out of the socket, as I feared, but it was badly sprained, and I had no time to let it rest. She cleared her throat and pointedly shifted her eyes to the crowd of bloodied, blackened warriors.

Rihilt separated from the main body. "It was as you said. We will fight with you, Wolf Queen."

My brow wrinkled with confusion until Sunna barked. The animals truly resembled their wild half-siblings after a hunt and hearty meal. My wolves, painted with Roman blood.

Pre-dawn twilight lightened the night sky. Sunrise fast approached.

They awaited my orders because I had led them in a successful battle and earned my place.

"Clean out their stores before they burn." My voice scratched from the smoke. "Have a good meal, get some rest. At dawn, we march to join the others at the ramparts."

They didn't turn to obey. A lone man stamped his foot and others joined him until they stomped in time, beating out an impressive sound from the packed earth.

"Wolf Queen," someone chanted and the rest joined her. They raised their various weapons overhead, and I turned in a slow circle to see them all. Konrada smiled brightly as she joined in. A slash of blood decorated her cheek.

It was more than a title. It was my place next to, not behind, Arminius as a liberator of Germania. Gooseflesh rippled down my arms at the thrill and terror of it. It wrapped around my heart like a vice, an iron shackle that defined my future: I either led them in triumph or to our deaths.

By the time we finished hauling away food, supplies, weapons, and the surviving horses, the fire in the fort had spread to the nearest trees. Part of our blessed woods burned along with the Romans.

———➤

The closer we got to the battlefield, the darker and heavier the clouds became. Brutal gusts of wind smelled of rain not yet falling. What the clouds waited for, I didn't know. I begged the skies to open or clear, to make some decision.

My shoulder ached and grew more stiff with each passing mile, no matter how I stretched it with Jotapa's help. There was no helping it except time. Time I did not have. My only option was to fight regardless and hope this weakness wouldn't be the death of me.

We came upon the first bands of Germani tribesmen on the outskirts of the battle site by dusk two days later. The warriors lazed about, more interested in drinking and debating the merits of fighting at all. Women and children bustled about the makeshift camp, far more industrious than their armed counterparts.

The legions hadn't made it this far yet. We were to circle past the great swamp and join Arminius' troops spread across the largest hill. Between the high ground and the swamp, we had successfully turned miles of this forest into a death trap.

Except the disorganized rabble here showed no intention of actually going to the battle.

"You." I pointed to the nearest man. He was younger than he looked and wore his thin hair knotted on the side of his head. He used his spear like a walking stick. "What is your tribe?"

His lip curled. Then he saw the small army at my back.

"Marsi."

The Marsi were supposed to be miles to the east with the bulk of the fighting force, battering the legions in a continuous circuit of lightning assaults.

"What are you doing here?" I dismounted, then affixed a bag of water to my mount's bridle. We had time to rest, but not long. I wanted to be in position before nightfall.

I needed to see my husband, to confirm with all my senses that he was alive and in good health. I needed his smiling face and powerful hands and scent like I needed water. Before I could get to him, though, I needed to kick these Marsi in the ass.

"Who's asking?"

"Thusnelda of the Cherusci."

The warrior sucked his teeth and tossed a shifting glance at the surrounding tribesmen. The nearest stopped what they were doing to observe our exchange.

He shrugged one shoulder. "We decided to see if there will be a battle at all. No sense going all that way and throwing ourselves in the path of three legions if the other tribes aren't there."

They wouldn't fight unless they saw others fighting and winning. Arminius and I had expected this. We'd predicted it before Varus disarmed the tribes. At least two chiefs had said as much. That didn't stop me from planting my fist in his face.

Weapons came out on all sides when he fell on his ass. I faced the working end of a hoe. Women hustled their children out of the way. The gods had their own answer to my rage. In that fraught moment, the clouds released their moisture in fat, slow droplets and thunder rumbled overhead.

Between the Cherusci, Chauci, and scalcs, we didn't quite match these Marsi numbers, but we had no camp followers or children to protect. If they wanted to fight us, while our blood still sang from the massacre at the fort, they were asking for trouble.

I didn't draw my sword. I didn't need to. Sunna and Donar growled at my feet, prepared to carry on their new favorite hobby: tearing apart men who sought to kill me.

"This isn't all of you." I knelt at the fallen man's side. "Where are the rest of your tribe?"

"They didn't come."

If only half the Marsi deigned to come this far, the odds were good others had made the same choice. The icy cold fingers of fear wrapped around my throat. No proper weapons, no army. I had to get to Arminius.

I straightened to my full height and raised my voice to be heard by all. It was no wonder Romans were so angry they made war all over the world. All this oration and arguing was exhausting. I tired of trying to convince these people to act in their own best interests.

"Fight or don't fight, I don't care," I said. "But remember: You swore to fight at Arminius' side. You will pay for breaking that oath."

"You broke your oath to the Chatti," he spat back to murmurs of agreement.

May Donar strike me down so long as I never hear that again. May Tyr and Wodan and all the others abandon me, just don't let my life be reduced to one broken betrothal.

I brushed the rain off my face to no avail, glad I'd let Jotapa re-braid my hair.

"The Chatti are fighting alongside Arminius right now. They have honored their agreement. If Reimar himself can fight alongside Arminius, then what's your excuse?"

Another bluff. Unless one of the Marsi argued the point, there was no way of knowing if the Chatti had honored our agreement. I took a threatening step toward the warrior still on his ass, then toward the next nearest warrior, a tall, thin man whose nose was too large for his face.

"Are you all cowards? Vultures waiting for the real warriors to do the hard work so you can swoop in and steal what they leave behind?"

They turned their gazes away from me.

"Who says the Chatti are there at all?"

I cast my face up toward the sky and prayed that one of the gods would take pity on me and end my suffering.

Rihilt barked a laugh, loud enough to rival the thunder.

"Did you hear that?" She cast her question over his shoulder to our army. "They haven't even been to the battle yet. They're fucking weak."

My army erupted in laughter.

"That's not—" the warrior at my feet started.

"Shut the fuck up," I said.

We had nothing to gain from staying any longer. I unhooked the water bag and nodded to my chosen trio—Levin, Jotapa, Konrada. It was time to go. The Marsi might follow us out of shame if nothing else. Securing everyone's total loyalty was an impossible dream. I had to settle for this pack of sniveling, indecisive tribesmen.

I resumed my seat atop the sturdy mare who'd taken me this far. She didn't shy from much, nor did I spend the many hours of riding fighting her impulse to gnaw at any passing greenery she wanted to taste. I couldn't remember exactly where I'd snatched her. She came from the herd we kept in our village, but I didn't know who'd trained her so well.

"Where... what..." The Marsi warrior trailed after me, unable to give his questions the right words.

"You heard her." Jotapa circled her dappled mare around him. "Be where you promised, or we'll take what you owe us."

As we rode away slowly to accommodate moving horses and a great flock of people through increasingly dense woods, I aimed a smile at Jotapa.

"You always were my favorite," I said.

"I know." Jotapa urged her horse past mine and shot me a cheeky grin as she went.

After a few hours, word traveled up our line that the Marsi trailed us at a distance.

————➤

The sounds of battle grew louder with each step, and I hurried us faster and faster until the warriors on foot had to run to keep up. Branches scraped at my face and arms, but my surefooted mare deftly maneuvered through the rough terrain. No one complained about the rain and wind. It masked the sound of our approach and concealed our painted bodies more than the natural darkness of night.

We were on the wrong side of the battle, picking our way across natural levees and out of the murky swamp. The Romans could use the same levees to escape, except they didn't know how to spot them, certainly not in the dark. Not in the downpour. They didn't know how to spot the rushes that only grew in water, not amid the other brush.

The stink of stagnant water, piss, and blood drifted all this way.

However bad I thought the battle might be, what I observed as we crossed the bog was worse. Our warriors bounced off Roman shields like children playing an adult's game. The attacks were too staggered to make a real impact against the impenetrable wall of legionaries. Too staggered to represent even half of our promised allies.

This was only one part of one legion. The track was narrow, but the Romans kept their order, beating back wave after wave of half-hearted assault.

Germani battle cries joined the chorus of clashing weapons, animal screams, and the emotionless calls of orders up and down the Roman lines.

Defeat formed a cold, hard ball in my chest. I bit hard on my tongue until I tasted blood. Then I let myself get angry.

They needed to retreat, to let the Romans advance deeper into the wald. I needed to trust someone to get across the battle line and spread the word. Someone with authority.

"Rihilt!" I called. After a few minutes, she rode to my side. "Get across the line and tell them to retreat. We need the legions to keep advancing east, not stand here and fight."

Without question, she turned her horse to the west and cantered away. She would see it done.

Once I cleared the swamp, I swung east, and my army followed. At first, the Romans didn't notice us racing down their line. They focused on the battle in front of them.

The few wounded at their backs called out the first warnings. Warriors behind me silenced them as they passed, but eventually the legionaries raised the alarm.

Mud splattered high enough to coat my boots and trousers. All along the battle line, Germani tribesmen crashed against shields and swords, spears and javelins flying in both directions. Too many of our weapons splintered like kindling or glanced uselessly off armor. I ducked as a javelin whistled past my head. A cry of shock and pain indicated someone behind me wasn't so lucky. I cringed and kept on. There was no time to worry it was someone I knew. I had to lead us as far as possible to let my warriors fan out into a battle line of their own and push these Romans deeper into the wald.

Finally, I saw it: a thick alder blocked the trail, cutting this line of soldiers off from their compatriots. A crush of wagons, panicked civilians, and braying mules stacked on the other side of the fallen tree. Here, the fighting was worse. Germani clustered around bearded, long-haired legionaries who fought like the best of our warriors. Any one of theirs faced off against two, three, even four Germani warriors and held them at bay.

These legionaries spread out, giving them room to unleash their lethal swordplay on our lightly, if at all, armored warriors. It was the *lanciarii* Arminius mentioned. Germani and Roman bodies littered the mud, and Germani and Romans alike stumbled over the corpses of their comrades. Granted, far more Germani corpses dotted the track. A wounded man swept out his sword in a pitiful attempt to stop me, but my horse swept past him.

When I pulled the reins to stop her, her previously sure feet slipped and slid in the muck, nearly launching me from her back. I yanked my spear free from its lashings and rammed it into the back of the closest soldier I could reach. It was a tricky shot, aiming for the scant inches of unprotected flesh between the cheek and neck plates of his helmet, and the chainmail protecting the rest of him.

I managed this twice more before they realized they were under attack from behind. Jotapa and Konrada fell in at my side. Down the track, my army spread out in a thin line, attacking the legionaries and shattering what remained of their order.

It became a melee, the exact sort of fight my people spent their whole lives training for and engaging in. Jotapa and Konrada kept up a volley of arrows until the legionaries got too close. I kicked my mare into a quick dash at the soldiers, running one through with my spear. The head found its target and broke off in his gut. That primitive spear lasted far longer than I'd expected it to.

My mare whinnied in terror, and my stomach dropped. The world tilted, then I slammed into the ground, my leg crushed between the mare and the armored body of a dying man beneath both of us.

I was trapped, and the legionaries nearest me knew it. So, unfortunately, did Konrada. She launched herself from her horse and charged the soldiers with a battle cry worthy of the gods, Jotapa right at her heels.

Before either of them made it to my defense, Sunna appeared, snarling like the mightiest of she-wolves. My heart jumped into my throat as she latched onto a soldier's sword arm. Where was my Donar? He'd kept pace the whole way. I hadn't given either of them a thought, trusting in their keen intelligence and strength, and now their loyalty to me was going to get them killed.

Not unlike the young girl swinging her spear in an arcing circle between me and the soldiers. I struggled and fought for freedom to no avail until the horse found her feet again. I gasped at the sudden release of pressure. She left me lying atop a dead man with a leg I feared was useless. I had both of my arms, though.

With a grunt of effort, I pushed up on my left leg before testing my weight on the right. Since I wasn't immediately wracked with mind numbing pain, I drew my sword and limped back into the fray.

Jotapa's arrows came fast and accurate around us. She kept her horse wheeling back and forth with only her legs and hips for control. In the rain and chaos of battle, hair streaming in a dark pile of braids, face hard in concentration, she looked the part of the famous Scythian warrior women. An Amazon fighting among us.

I ducked under Konrada's spear and sliced my sword up and across the belly of a soldier too busy watching the spear to notice my approach. The blade rattled and caught on his chainmail.

Damn it, I needed my stronger arm. Teeth gritted, I gripped the weapon in both hands and swung again. This time, my blade cut through to flesh. I whirled in time to parry a series of quick overhand strikes and thrusts from the next soldier. He was better armored and mostly safe behind his shield, but I was faster. I spun around him and jammed the blade in his back.

On and on we went, the three of us hacking, slicing, dodging. It might have been minutes or hours; I couldn't say. If I was wounded, nothing was bad enough to slow me down.

In a flash of lighting, I witnessed Konrada take a soldier's arm clean off with a gladius she'd picked up, as if she'd been doing this for years.

High-pitched whistles echoed down the line of Romans. They called and repeated orders to form the *testudo* formation, taking on the appearance of a giant, well armed turtle inching their way along the path to the west. Exactly where we wanted them to go.

In answer, our own horns sounded retreat.

We let them go, our people vanishing back into the woods like ghosts. I called for my dogs, but only Sunna came.

My heart sank. No Donar, no Arminius. I didn't know if Levin lived. Our people were still fighting, still organized, however few we were. That gave me hope Arminius lived and I'd simply missed him in the melee. I didn't have that same hope for my Donar. I whistled for him again and again, but he never appeared.

It was childish to mourn a dog when so many of my tribesmen lay dead and wounded, when we had so much farther to go. Yet my heart needed something to grasp, something to release the intensity of the past few days without leaving me catatonic.

Rain masked my silent tears. I sent up a prayer to Baduhenna, that she might take pity on my brave animal, that she might bless me and let that be the only thing I lost in the coming war.

Chapter 26

Never was there slaughter more cruel than took place there in the marshes and woods, never were more intolerable insults inflicted by barbarians... (Publius Annius Florus)

I led a short but steep hike up the hill from the ravine. Every muscle in my body was stiff, and mud and drying gore encrusted my skin and clothes, like everyone else in our party. Jotapa and Konrada were almost unrecognizable beneath the war paint and mess. I searched every face we passed for Arminius, or Berut, or Levin, or Ermin, even Reimar, Wiltrud, anyone I might know. Anyone who could tell me where to find my husband. I needed him, and if I didn't find him soon, I feared I might scream like a wild person.

A passing warrior said he'd be in this area. Almost ten thousand Germani tribesmen spread out behind our hastily constructed ramparts in this stretch of the forest. That was almost ten thousand people to sift through until I found the one I wanted. I was too distracted to appreciate the fact that so many had actually arrived after what happened with Reimar, though it was a fraction of the warriors we had been promised. It wasn't enough. I gathered information as I stormed through the camps—there was no word from any of the Sugambri. At least half the Chatti had refused to fight. Thousands upon thousands had their excuses, from the weapons to my marriage to the ominous flights of crows.

I would deal with them later.

Sunna stayed close, her tail down and ears flattened. She kept looking back the way we came, as if she, too, willed Donar to appear.

Warriors gathered around fires and tents, regaling each other with competing tales of their own bravery and showing off their newly plundered weapons. The forest echoed with shouting and laughter, the hiss of blades scraping against whetstones, music on pipes. As if they hadn't been getting soundly beaten when I arrived. As if I hadn't just spend hours tripping over fallen Germani.

Every person I grabbed and asked of Arminius' location gave me a vague point in the same direction, so I marched onward. Whether my army still followed me was the last thing on my mind. They could survive without me for a few hours.

"Elda!" Levin trotted out of the shadows, and I nearly tackled him in a hug. He was alive, had all his limbs, and at least enough strength to withstand my attack.

"Happy to see you, as well." He laughed, then sobered. "You're not going to like this."

The flash of relief I felt at seeing him fizzled. "What?"

"Father and the rest of the Cherusci are here."

This information did not entirely surprise me. If Segestes had any chance of retaining the respect of the tribe, he had to support this battle. That didn't mean I looked forward to seeing him or my other brothers. The good news was they significantly bolstered our numbers.

I grunted and kept limping on. My knee throbbed.

"Don't worry, your husband isn't far."

That slowed me down. "Levin..."

"I know, I know. I'm the greatest brother." His grin flashed white against his painted skin and the surrounding night. He reached behind me to chuck Konrada on the shoulder.

"You look like you saw some good action tonight. Did you kill anyone or just hide behind my sister?"

"I'll have you know—" The rest of her reply was muffled as he wrestled her head into the crook of his elbow.

The rain slowed to a steady mist and the wind settled, giving us the hint of a respite. Hopefully, it would start up again, anything to keep the Romans mired in muck and misery.

"There she is!" Berut called. He sat arm in arm with Ermin, sharing a tankard of ale. "With my favorite Scythian."

Jotapa jogged past me and threw her filthy arms around Berut's neck, tumbling across both their laps in the process. Berut and the rest of the warriors in this area still wore their auxiliary uniforms and armor.

I turned in every direction and didn't find him among the fighters.

Berut saw my distress and whistled. "Oi, General, your wife is looking for you!"

The men who heard laughed, and Arminius still didn't appear. I prepared to scream until he produced his large ass for my inspection. Everything hurt; my arm, my leg, scrapes and cuts I hadn't noticed while fighting. I was so tired; I swayed on my feet. My stomach growled and my throat ached with thirst.

After what felt like a lifetime, Arminius materialized from the night and my pains mellowed. Tall, strong, wearing chainmail over his legionary uniform, and shockingly clean, but for the beginning of a black eye. The warriors parted for my husband.

He didn't break stride until I was in his arms and we were kissing, which elicited a roaring cheer from our army. Our mouths fought to claim each other, rough, deep, clashing teeth and tongues, while our hands swept each other up and down.

He was whole. He was healthy. He was in my arms. At length, we slowed and parted, still breathing each other's air. The warriors returned to their conversations and respectfully ignored the rest of our reunion.

"You're here," he said.

"Of course I'm here."

"You're all right?"

"More or less."

He pulled back and conducted a more thorough inspection of my person, patting me here and there. When he squeezed my left bicep, I hissed in pain.

"What the fuck happened?" His face transformed into a thunder-cloud to match the ones haunting the day.

"What didn't happen?" I tugged his hands and attempted to lead him back the way he came. "Can we discuss it over food?"

Arminius relented and took me back to his tent, hardly large enough to fit both of us inside. He caught me up on the events I'd missed, and I shared the success of our attack on the fort.

After wiping my exposed skin down with a wet rag, I stuffed my face with salted meats and cheese, washing it all back with fermented goat's milk, until my belly was full to bursting.

"Varus turned three shades of purple when that horse rode out of the woods with a man's body on it."

"How did you get away?"

At this, he sported a sly smile. "I volunteered to lead a squadron ahead to scout the area. Sent a few back to report that the route was tight but passable. It was easier than herding sheep. You did perfectly." Arminius pulled me close and kissed me on the temple. "Things were, um, rougher today than I expected. The column stopped sooner than I expected. It was fortunate you arrived when you did."

He didn't need to say more. The tightness of his shoulders and the clench in his jaw said enough. It hadn't been the easy victory he believed he'd engineered. Arminius didn't have room for self doubt, and our paltry numbers and difficult first day forced him to seriously consider the possibility that we might lose. Luckily for him, he had me.

Despite my aches and exhaustion, I fell back on our thin bedding and beckoned him to me. We didn't speak as we undressed, then quietly found relief in each other. It had been weeks since I'd last felt the comfort of his touch, the exquisite pleasure only he offered, and the ease that came with knowing he stood at my back.

That security allowed me to drift off almost as soon as my body reached its completion.

Before I left the world of the conscious, Arminius cuddled me to his chest and whispered, "You saved me today."

After yesterday's rough start, the tide turned in our favor.

The order of the next day was harassment. Our ever-growing army took turns sprinting into the ravine, slaughtering as many Romans as they could, then drawing back into the shelter of the trees. Each successful assault drew more Germani out of the wald into combat. Deudorix swept in with his Sugambri like a conquering hero.

Reimar and Wiltrud kept their Chatti warriors far from us, near the end of the Roman column. That was fine by me, especially since the pair of them knew what needed to happen. We didn't have to send messengers or even wonder if the job was getting done. I also didn't have to wonder if Arminius or I were about to catch a knife in the back from Reimar.

Between the nature of our shock combat and our newly inflated numbers, we took few casualties while legionary bodies piled along the narrow track. Warriors returned from their brief skirmishes with weapons, broaches, sacks of coin, anything they could carry. The imbalance in our armament shifted with each run.

Our warriors hit harder and harder, driven into a frenzy. It no longer mattered if a warrior carried a club or a steel-tipped spear. All turned lethal. Roman officers struggled to maintain their fine order. Some cohorts had better success than others. One man's bravery bolstered another, just as cowardice bred cowardice.

Romans eyes rolled white with terror. Blasting wind picked up and rain resumed its downpour. Under the onslaught, high tree boughs broke free and crashed to the forest floor. An annoyance for us, but for the legionaries, each echoing crack might have been a signal for another assault.

It was as Arminius said; our forests unmanned them. The narrow track crippled their defenses and exhausted their march. They wasted hours constructing hasty bridges and clearing trees before abandoning the endeavor altogether. The supply wagons and horrified civilians were the first left behind, followed by their artillery—scorpios, ballistae, massive contraptions I'd never seen before.

Our army and camp followers cleaned out those wagons, and behind our ramparts, a five mile-long celebration started. The Germani love for pilfered treasure provided its own intoxicant.

Arminius spent the morning giving orders and didn't immediately join our fighters. I stayed at his side, fielding questions and issuing orders of my own.

"Spread the Chauci out through the bog," I said to Berut early that morning. "Keep the stragglers from escaping. Spare the women and children."

Arminius paused his own conversation with Ermin and a few other men I didn't recognize.

"You heard her," he said. "Spread the word. It's not my habit to conduct war against women, only armed men."

Below us, the fight raged on. Steel and clubs clashed with shields. Screeching Roman whistles, bellowing horns, and shouted commands echoed around us. Trees behind the ramparts now featured Roman heads nailed to their trunks.

It was a strange thing, to pick mercies. Taking a Roman woman and her children as scalcs was a far better fate than when they enslaved us. It was a far better fate than dying bloody in the mud, left unburied for the animals and the elements. When we found legionaries still alive, incapacitated by their wounds, choking on their own blood, we ended them quickly.

Then we robbed their corpses. We defiled them. They had done the same to us for generations. This was how we stopped it. If that meant letting our warriors violate the dead to sate their bloodlust, so be it. Numbness settled over my soul, and I turned away from the worst grotesqueries.

We were letting the Romans get another mile into the forest before launching the biggest assault of the day. That was time enough, according to Arminius, for Varus and his coterie of senior officers to cross our path.

Arminius practically drooled over the prospect of confronting Varus himself. A lifetime of simpering for Romans, a year of smiling and complimenting and soothing this one and now he excised all those indignities at once. I didn't fault him for it.

We struck camp and trailed along the hill, parallel to the ravine, following the beleaguered Romans at a leisurely pace. At first the respite was nice, a blessed relief from several long, strenuous days, but soon I itched to rejoin the fight.

We were readying ourselves for the day's assault when Arminius said, "We're about to fight at each other's sides."

I smeared black war paint across my face in diagonal stripes. The rest covered my bare arms and neck, careful to avoid my wedding jewelry.

"We've fought together before," I said, lacing my baldric.

"Not like this." Arminius donned the wolf skin I'd given him at our wedding, and I dug mine out of my pack to match. "That was a quick fight. This is a battle. It's different."

He caught me by the hips, pulled me close, and took a deep inhale, breathing me in. "I like the look of you like this."

I rather enjoyed the look of him in his Cherusci battle regalia myself. He released me to take up his shield and offered me a smaller one. The owl sigil on the boss told me it had come from a Tencteri woman.

All along the ramparts, warriors assembled with their shields and weapons.

"Well?" I asked. "Are you going to lead us to victory?"

He winked at me, turned, and banged his spear against his shield, beginning the Germani battle song. The cracking took on an even rhythm, soon joined by the deep, chest-rattling tone of our song that ascended into a high-pitched cry.

My discomfort with allowing our warriors to defile bodies, with promising to execute prisoners and truly believing I would do it, evaporated. Beyond the normal rush of battle, fighting at his side imbued me with an otherworldly confidence. In all my battles before, I thought I trusted my allies, my friends and family, but the moment Jotapa defied me and saved my life had shifted something vital.

What I felt in this moment, preparing to hurl myself into the fray surrounded by my truest family, forced me to see how little I had actually trusted them before. How little I had truly believed I could close my eyes, turn my back, and let them take care of me.

Rushing into battle without that nagging worry was exhilarating.

Arminius took the first step, hurtling down the hill. I followed, Sunna and my friends close by. The rest of our army flooded downhill and soon the world descended into madness.

Hot red blood spurted on my face. I ripped my dagger back and twisted out of the reach of a slashing gladius.

Arminius rammed his shield against the soldier so hard the man went clean off his feet before crashing to the muck. Another warrior lunged to stab the soldier in the face before racing to her next opponent.

He and I fought together as a seamless unit: one body, four arms, many weapons. It was a thing of beauty. To the Romans, we were a nightmare come to life, hacking our way through their lines as they struggled onward, ever deeper into our trap. With a few choice words and suggestions over the preceding months, Arminius had convinced Varus these woods weren't so deep, that, if necessary, they could push straight through in a day, two at most.

It was this seditious intelligence that doomed them.

Arminius barked something. It might have been a word lost to the din and rain, it might have been nothing more than an animal roar, and bolted down the line.

"Arminius!" I shouted after him uselessly. He disappeared into the sea of violence after... I saw them: Varus, his legates and select tribunes, only a hundred yards away, fighting their way forward.

I took a step in his direction and got no further. A shield rammed into my side, sending me sprawling into the slurry of mud, blood, puke, piss, and body parts that now comprised the ravine floor. I gagged against the rush of it against my cheek and nose.

Time froze and my mind refused to comprehend what just happened. He left me. He saw his target, abandoned me, distracted me, and left me to get hurt. A fist took me by the heart and crushed. I should have known.

"Up!" Levin grabbed the back of my tunic and hauled me to my feet, then shook my shoulder, looked me over, and nodded. "You're fine. Keep going."

Levin was there the whole time. I heard Jotapa's roar, and a flash of curly dark hair in my periphery revealed Konrada. More Cherusci fought around me. I wasn't alone. The grasping pressure on my heart released, and I finally sucked in air.

Clarity returned just in time to come face to face with another legionary. A stained strip of cloth covered one eye, the other was wild, feral, rolling to its white.

He struck me across the jaw with the pommel of his sword. This time when I fell, my sword left my palm. My shield was gone. I scrambled and reached for the sword, but my hands found only mud and rocks and a disembodied foot cut off at the shin. He lifted his shield to ram the bottom edge into me, but I rolled out of the way, avoiding the blow so narrowly the outer edge of the shield scraped against my back.

Sunna lunged at the man's calf, ripping at the flesh with shakes of her head.

I rolled over a javelin, grabbed it, and thrust up. He caught the strike with his shield, then discarded the implement entirely, beating at Sunna with the pommel of his gladius. She never paused. I kicked out as hard as I could. My foot landed squarely on his knee, above where Sunna's sharp teeth gouged and tore. The crack of bone was both loud and deeply satisfying. He stumbled back, howling in pain.

I scooped a stray gladius out of the mud and hurdled over his downed form when I caught sight of her. Konrada was on her knees, weaponless, bleeding from her shoulder down to her chest.

My legs couldn't move fast enough, not over the slick mud and detritus, not around the fighters. One legionary raised his sword to end her, and my heart jumped into my throat, strangling the scream I heard in my head.

A big, red-haired warrior planted a spear through that soldier's head, helmet and all. I nearly fell to my knees in relief.

Reimar and a Chatti woman formed a protective barrier around her, cutting down any who got too close. I could have kissed them both. Instead, I staggered past their surprised faces and gripped Konrada by her uninjured shoulder.

"How bad is it?" She didn't answer, so I shook her and tugged her tunic open along the tear. What I found made me sag into a crouch. It wasn't deep. She was merely stunned.

"Get her back behind the wall," I shouted to the woman, who looked to Reimar for confirmation before taking Konrada by the arm and hustling her through the fray.

"What are you doing here?" I took up a position at Reimar's back.

"Besides saving a child from death?" He casually batting away a soldier with his spear. I would feel shame for that later.

It didn't matter why he was here, only that he was, and I needed his help. With Baduhenna's blessing, I forced myself to trust him enough to get me through the battle lines. It didn't need to be more than that.

"I need to get there." I pointed toward the heaviest fighting, where Arminius, assuming he was still alive, was cutting his way to Varus.

A smaller, round shield with an ox burned into its bright green face jutted out of the ravine floor, so I grabbed it, wincing at a fresh wave of pain in my left arm. My leg stiffened in protest, as well. My tongue found a loose tooth and my mouth tasted coppery with blood.

Battle is no time for pain. The wound is either severe enough to lay you flat, where you will probably die, or you must ignore it. I ignored everything.

Reimar ran ahead of me, sweeping his spear and plunging it into the backs and sides of Romans. He cut a path, and together we ran, taking blows from all sides, pausing only long enough to defend against a brutal attack before pushing on. Sunna never left my side.

I caught sight of Wout and Levin—no, it was Lennart—taking on their own opponents. Wout's bad leg kept him off balance and slow, so Lennart took the lion's share of the fighting. I mentally cursed Wout for showing up. Fighting was dangerous enough, and Wout made the situation more fraught for Lennart.

Whatever the outcome, they chose their fate.

Romans clustered around the soldier bearing one of their eagles, and the mounted officers fought an increasingly hopeless battle against the warriors swarming to tear them down.

Arminius ripped one rider from his horse, stabbed him, and prowled on, hardly slowing down. He cut, hit, and threw his way to Legatus Vala.

His face was starkly pale, more skeletal than ever, and his sword trembled in his hand. Arminius prowled toward him, so intent on death that fighters, ours and theirs, scrambled out of his way. Even from behind, he was a sight to behold, towering with his wolf headdress, splattered with all manner of filth.

Vala shocked me all the way to the sodden soles of my boots by whipping his horse the other way and galloping back down the track to the east. Arminius stopped short, reared back, and threw his spear with all his might.

It missed horse and rider by inches.

Arminius spun to the other surviving officers and found Varus at the same time I did. I shoved a pair of combatants out of my way with my shield and bodyweight. Sunna yipped and seized onto the face of a fallen officer.

Varus didn't notice any of this. His eyes focused solely on Arminius. He dismounted and waved his sword at him.

"Traitor!" he screamed. Arminius was right: The man turned at least three shades of purple when he was angry. "The gods will—"

"Your gods, not mine." Arminius' approach was deceptively casual. The Romans were on the run, the lines loosening as the cohorts ahead broke free from our assault. Deeper and deeper west, exactly where we wanted them to go.

Before Arminius got another step closer, Varus dropped to his knees and rested the pommel of his sword in the mire.

Arminius' eyes went wide, and he shouted for him to stop.

In an ultimate act of defiance, Varus rammed his body down on his sword and died a breath later.

———————➤

Arminius dragged Varus' body all the way past our wall and into the remains of our camp. Most Germani moved down the line, many all the way to the end, to our ultimate trap.

His face was black and blue, his lip split, and blood had dried around a deep cut on his hip. He spurned my quiet efforts to get him to leave the corpse behind and let me tend him. I'd never seen him like this before, not my laughing thunder god. Not even when we'd fought the Mattiaci or when he'd put himself through our combat challenges. He'd been human then.

We were winning, but you wouldn't know it by his scowl and clenched jaw. *Tick, tick, tick.* The muscle twitched so much, I wondered if it hurt him.

Varus had stolen his victory. I hadn't known how much of Arminius' motivation rested on his desire to personally mete out justice, to be the one to deliver the death blow.

I turned away until he became himself again. A confrontation lay in our future. He'd demanded my faith more times than I could count, and when I finally gave it to him, he left me. Forgiveness might be too much to ask.

More heads adorned our trees, a macabre display for the gods. I turned away from those, too. I turned away from the Roman women and children shuffling behind their new masters, too exhausted, too scared, too broken to wail.

My hands, my arms, my legs... there wasn't a part of me not sticky with gore. I shuddered at the realization. Konrada had almost died. I didn't know the fate of my family. This had to end soon.

In all my warring against other tribes, I had never seen anything like this abject slaughter. I'd never fought a battle so fierce we tripped over the bodies of the fallen, slipped in their spilled guts, killed and killed and killed, only ceasing when it was time to let the enemy advance a little further.

The sickening thwack of a sword against flesh snapped my eyes back to him, where he hacked Varus' head from his body. My stomach jerked in revolt.

"Take this to the Marcomanni. Their chief thinks himself quite the friend of Augustus."

I didn't know to whom Arminius spoke and I didn't look to find out. I bid Sunna to stay where she was and picked my way back down the ravine.

It wasn't silent, precisely. Germani talked among themselves as they combed over the bodies, periodically thrusting their weapons into Roman survivors. They shoved all the gold and silver they could carry into sacks and left the rest for the crows.

Those dark birds, friends of our Wodan and augers of things to come, squawked and squabbled over the choicest remains. The gods blessed this endeavor, no matter how grotesque my mortal eyes found it.

I didn't know what I was looking for. Snatching treasure from dead men held no appeal. Miring myself in the depth of what we'd done, what was still to come, did nothing to lift my plummeting spirits.

A few warriors gathered around a Germani corpse, paying their respects and sending a prayer to their god of choice. When I got closer, I recognized the Marsi warrior I'd shamed into fighting.

His cloudy eyes stared up through the trees and his mouth hung open, slack and useless. A fly landed on his lips before one warrior waved it away. Two men gathered him up and began the steep hike back to the ramparts, where he could receive the proper funerary rites. He died because I forced him here.

"Thusnelda." Jotapa's soft voice startled me. She'd wiped her face clean and her eyes promised nothing but bad news. "I…"

She gestured vaguely behind her, where more warriors gathered around more Germani bodies. I closed my eyes for the count of two deep breaths, then opened them again. She wasn't as dirty as the others, owing to her preference and ability to stay mounted while she launched her arrows.

"Who is it?"

Her mouth worked, trying to form words and failing, until she said, "One of the twins. I'm sorry, I can't tell them apart the way you can."

Please don't be Levin, I thought, then shook it away. I wouldn't wish for one brother's survival over another's. Our differences didn't matter. They were all my brothers. They'd all come to fight. Once, a long time ago, we'd been so close. I made my way to the body, each step like lead.

It was Lennart. He'd worn a yellow tunic. In death, he was otherwise indistinguishable from Levin. Life set them apart, how they moved, how their eyes danced. Without life, Lennart was at last identical to Levin.

I saw the little boy who couldn't fetch eggs without stirring the hens into a frenzy, who cursed like a seasoned warrior before he was big enough to carry a sword. He'd grown into a cruel man, but once, not so very long ago, he'd been my little brother.

Segestes sat on his haunches next to him, his head in his hands, Wout holding his shoulder. Lennart looked almost peaceful, if it weren't for all the blood. My father lifted his head at my approach. His eyes were red-rimmed, though I didn't think he'd been crying.

"This is your fault."

I looked to Wout and, for the briefest of heartbeats, shame reflected at me. Then he looked away and kept his silence.

"I know." I walked away. They wouldn't want me present for his burial. They didn't want my grief. The fracture in our family was complete. There was no setting the break and hoping it healed.

Berut and Ermin encircled Jotapa. She beckoned me with a jerk of her head.

"Some legionaries are abandoning the march. They're running to the north and south," she said.

That made sense. Their own officers ha abandoned them and committed suicide rather than face us. We didn't need survivors raising the alarm at any of the remaining forts and outposts, however.

"Berut, Jotapa, gather the best archers. Run them down. I don't care if it takes all night. This ends tomorrow."

Chapter 27

They put out the eyes of some of them and cut off the hands of others; they sewed up the mouth of one of them after first cutting out his tongue, which one of the barbarians held in his hand, exclaiming "At last, you viper, you have ceased to hiss." (Publius Annius Florus)

Rumor said a single centurion took command of the surviving troops. He consolidated their number into what amounted to a legion and a half. The Romans didn't bother digging in another camp. He kept them moving at their painstakingly slow pace through the night while our raiders periodically tossed volleys of pilfered javelins and sling stones before rushing down the embankment for a few minutes of violence, nothing more, before melting back into the forest.

And on the Romans dragged themselves. I had to admire their tenacity. They gave up on constructing hasty bridges, as they'd given up on their baggage train and camp followers. Those belonged wholly to us now, along with an array of heavy artillery.

Their column shortened considerably, and one of their eagles now resided in Chatti hands. All night long I watched a stream of broken men shuffle on from my safe vantage point. Arminius eventually quit trying to get me to sleep and joined my vigil.

"Won't be long now."

"Good."

I had so many things to say to him, but it wasn't time yet. Just looking at him made my heart hurt, made me want to hit him and weep, maybe simultaneously.

Sunrise was still far off, but the inky night faded to dark gray. It hadn't rained in hours and, for the first time in three days, I was mostly dry. My war paint flaked off, and I didn't bother to reapply it. We covered ourselves in paint to become shadows. The Romans damn well knew we were there, yards away, dogging their every step.

"Thusnelda…" Arminius started and shook his head, cutting off whatever he really wanted to say. "It's time to go."

He pressed his hand against the small of my back, and I vacillated between leaning into his touch or away from it. His comfort called to me, but forgetting the carnage below wasn't an option, nor was forgetting the way he'd defiled Varus' corpse. It especially wasn't enough to forget the way he'd abandoned me.

The trouble of it was I understood his rage, no matter how he betrayed me in the process. Rome hurt all of us. He had done nothing uncommon to Germani warfare beyond the scale of it.

It was the scale that festered beneath my skin. I'd never seen so much death, though the necessity of it was clear. Rome would never leave us if we didn't wipe them from our land.

None of that made me feel better. None of it mattered anymore; there was no stopping it.

I let Arminius guide me along until we broke into a jog. He touched me like he wanted to apologize. The Marsi and Chatti remained behind to cut the surviving legionaries off from any chance of escape. The Bructeri, Chauci, Tencteri, Cherusci, and Sugambri assembled at the end of the ravine, where we'd rounded out our wall to complete the trap.

From behind the safety of our ramparts, I watched the dawning horror on the faces of the soldiers who'd marched into an impasse. Our wall completely covered the open space from the base of the hill to the marshy bog. Retreat wasn't an option, not with their numbers stacked behind them and our tribesmen harrying the rear of their formations.

A centurion, wounded and limping, barely able to keep his shield up, broke formation, drew his sword, and looked me right in the eye. It was Eggius, bold, wounded, and furious.

Others around me jeered, shouted insults and promises of his impending doom, but I remained quiet. He awed me. Despite everything we put him through he stood before us with a sword and a snarl. Not all Romans were without honor.

Here was a proper fight against a proper enemy. I let everything else fall away in favor of the simplicity of the fight. It was me or them. No more and no less. I intended to walk away from this battle victorious.

I vaulted over the wall at the same time Eggius charged forward with a roar. His army hesitated, clutched the dregs of their courage, and followed him. Arminius ran right behind me, along with the rest of our army.

Eggius disappeared in the savage pandemonium that followed. I lost myself in a murderous whirl, killing one man to move on to the next. Arminius' bloodlust hadn't cooled. At least he stayed at my side while we ended one Roman life after another. That, too, seemed to be his paltry effort at an apology. I kept an eye on my own back this time.

Surviving horses and mules went wild, driven by the scent of death and the madness hemming them in.

I took a breath to survey the battlefield and didn't like what I saw. Our warriors lingered near the wall, content to let the Romans come to them.

"Forward!" I bellowed. Attuned to me despite the battle fever driving his every move, Arminius simultaneously pushed forward and yelled for the others to do the same.

The Romans fought hard. They didn't surrender an inch, no matter how exhausted, how the events of the preceding days mentally and physically broke them. If I didn't like seeing thousands of Roman corpses littering the ravine, I imagined how it made these men feel.

These were not the men fleeing or falling on their swords. They fought with heart and soul. They made us earn our victory, and I savored every moment.

My wounded body numbed. If I didn't feel, I didn't hurt; a battle gift from Tyr. Another hit to my face completely dislodged my loosened tooth. I spat it into the gory mire at my feet and kept going.

Each time I took a hit, Arminius went a little more mad. He nearly cleaved a man's head from his neck in one blow. His savagery on my behalf went slightly further as an apology. Someone landed a good slice across his thigh, and I responded with equal ferocity, screaming as I leapt onto his back and plunged my sword between his shoulder and neck.

A flash of distinctive red hair atop a mountain of a man revealed Reimar, then Wiltrud in all her glory. She moved like the gods themselves possessed her limbs, and it was no wonder the Chatti let her rule in her husband's stead. Then they were gone, lost in the chaos.

"You!" a voice I'd almost forgotten growled. I turned to find Patrin, the legionary who'd intended to rape Konrada and me that day so long ago.

He'd made it through the past three days unscathed, though his segmented armor was dented in places and he wielded a curved Germani sword instead of a gladius. He was pale, filthy, and looked at me with enough hate to scorch my flesh from my bones.

Arminius made to intercept him before he attacked, but I threw myself in his path.

"He's mine," I barked. Arminius took another step and I didn't move. He had to blink at me several times before the battle fog cleared. He nodded and moved to take on another Roman. More shouted commands had our warriors pouring around us, compressing the Romans tighter and tighter together. He was still in there, my husband. After this ended, I was going to get him back. After thoroughly explaining all the ways he was never to betray my trust again.

This time, Patrin was ready for me. He kept his shield up and his unfamiliar blade at the ready. Its single edge was chewed up so badly the tip was missing. I shifted my shield and felt my mouth quirking. I'd picked up a gladius and though one edge was pocked, the other gleamed bright and sharp. Patrin held a steel bludgeon, and I held a functioning sword.

His lips moved in inaudible curses. In a repeat of the first time we met, we circled each other, and any thought of the battle raging around us disappeared. Despite what he'd done, no matter how scared I was, I listened to what Jotapa would tell me: He won't make that mistake again. *This time he will be there. Arminius will watch my back.* I grew larger, stronger at the thought. Patrin would not best me this time.

We met in a clash of steel and leather-wrapped wood. He had armor and I had none. My sword had a functioning blade and his didn't. We both fought for our very lives.

Tire him out. Go for his shield arm. Open his guard. I was lighter on my feet, between my lack of armor and not having been on a grueling death march for the past three days. What I needed was a spear.

A sting at my waist. The faint resistance when my blade made contact. The jarring rattle of my bones when our weapons made contact. My feet sank up to my ankles in mud and waste.

Patrin stumbled over a disembodied arm onto his back and I seized on the opportunity. His shield arm fell outward, leaving him wide open. I reared and rammed my sword straight through his shield arm and shield into the ground. With a bit more struggle, he'd sever the limb himself. He swiped at me with his sword, but I kicked it away. With one booted foot on his free arm, I pinned him.

I pulled the dagger from my belt and pressed it to his throat.

"It's over, Patrin."

If he felt pain from what I'd done to his left arm, he didn't show it. Maybe, like me, his entire body was numb. Maybe I had a limb or two hanging on by tendons and stretched skin and would realize it only later.

"I knew it, I knew it, I knew it," he said over and over. Foamy spit dribbled from his mouth. "I knew he was a fucking traitor."

With my dagger clenched in my fist, I punched his face between his cheek plates, over and over. When I finally felt pain radiating from my fist down my forearm, I stopped. Patrin was an unrecognizable mass of bruises and blood. His nose was smashed. His teeth had cut my knuckles and our blood mingled on my hand.

We both gasped for breath.

"You fucking people." Blood splattered from his lips with each word. "Rome is inevitable. They're going to send twenty legions to punish you for this. You've signed your own death warrants for nothing."

I gripped the collar of his breastplate and lifted him to hear me properly. "We will never be Roman."

And then I jammed my dagger, that precious gift Arminius gave me, into his neck and ripped it out the front in a spray of hot blood and torn flesh.

I threw my head back and screamed into the sky. It opened for me, pelting fresh rain to wash me clean.

➤

The gods had indeed blessed our endeavor. By the time the last of the Romans dropped to their knees in surrender, the clouds parted and the rain ceased. Our success pleased Donar, Wodan, Tyr, our whole pantheon. They wanted their people to live freely.

White and gray-clad priestesses milled about the battlefield, dictating which items were to be sacrifices and which tribesmen could keep. They were most excited about the two eagles we'd claimed, arguing animatedly with Arminius, Frikkeo, and Reimar over their fate. Arminius promised one eagle to the Chauci and since the Chatti captured the other, it was theirs by right, or so they argued.

Whatever became of the third eagle, it was lost.

The survivors—a little over a thousand—were corralled and bound in a clearing beyond the hill. It must have been the insult of all insults, to discover that they'd been so close to escaping the wald. Some made good their escape. We'd hunt them down soon enough.

The warriors who'd best distinguished themselves, according to their own and their peers' accounts, claimed first rights to pick new scalcs from among the prisoners. When Arminius saw one man pick a tribune from the lot, he frowned. The sight of a living tribune struck me as odd. Eggius was clearly the last man giving orders. He'd ordered the surrender, but this tribune outranked him. Perhaps, like us, they elected new leadership when the old failed them.

"Can you put a stop to that?" He leveled the question at me, quiet and a bit withdrawn, as he'd been since the fighting stopped. "The officers will bring good ransoms."

"Fine." I turned to go, but he stopped me with a hand on my arm.

"Thank you." There was something funny about his expression, lips pursed to say more, the corners of his eyes drawn low. Someone shouted for him. He let me go and returned to the other chiefs and nobles. When he spoke to them, his voice retained all his usual command and swagger, and I wondered if I'd imagined anything else.

With a sharp whistle, I stopped the warriors collecting their bounties and repeated Arminius' orders. They grumbled, but obeyed. The warrior who'd sought to claim the tribune shoved his prize back to the dirt and snatched up the next man he saw. A common foot soldier of no discernible rank or position with one arm hanging grotesquely out of socket.

Families and tribespeople who hadn't fought assembled in the field and among the trees, gleefully picking through the bounty and establishing an encampment to rival Haustblot. They slaughtered the dead horses and mules, and my mouth watered at the scent of roasting meat. It occurred to me I hadn't eaten since the previous evening, and my stomach rumbled in protest.

I wandered aimlessly until I heard Wiltrud call my name. She waved at me with a hand heavily wrapped in blood-stained linen. At my questioning look, she chuckled.

"Lost two fingers. It's about time I got a proper wound. How have you fared?"

Every inch of my body ached, but I'd only lost one part. "Just a tooth."

She nodded as though I'd said something of value. "Shedding a little blood in the name of our people pleases the gods."

"They must be quite pleased with your fingers, then."

She laughed once, a loud crack of noise that blended in with the general merriment around us.

"Perhaps they thought I was too skilled and now seek to humble me."

I hoped they never saw fit to humble me in that fashion. I enjoyed having all my appendages.

"You chose your path," she said without recrimination. "I hope I was wrong when the bones said this way lies an untimely death for you."

I didn't care if my name was remembered for an eternity. That's not what drove me to this point, nor why I'd chosen Arminius over her son. Everything I did, I did for love. I loved my tribe, my way of life, even my family for all that they didn't love me anymore. I loved Arminius, and my heart lurched at the thought of what I would say to him the next time we were alone, when the walls of war stopped pressing in on all sides.

I took my leave of Wiltrud and searched for Konrada, but she was nowhere to be found. I stumbled across a half-drunk Levin, and he pointed me toward a copse of trees skirting the bog. He didn't look me in the eye, so I added him to a growing list of troubles. Troubles I intended to address later.

Would he ever forgive me for his twin's death?

Inside the trees, the afternoon sunlight filtered in dapples and shadows. The air was wet and the kind of cool that promised a winter lurking just beyond the horizon. Konrada sat on a fallen log with her back to me, picking at its bark. Jotapa sat next to her, rubbing at her shoulders, and at their feet was not one, but two very familiar dogs.

Sunna *and* Donar.

I gasped and cried out, and both loped to me, tongues flapping, tails wagging, like nothing at all was ever amiss.

"Where have you been?" I held Donar's face and gave him a shake for good measure. *Stupid dog. Stupid, stupid, lovable, wonderful dog.* I bit back a sob and wrapped my arms around his furry body, inhaling his dog-stink like it was the finest Roman perfume. A heavy weight lifted from my chest and for the first time in days, I felt something almost like happiness. A good omen, just for me.

"He found his way to the camp followers. He's been eating his weight in leftover meat," Jotapa said.

"You idiot." I hugged him tighter. "If you ever do that again, I'll kill you myself."

Jotapa unfolded herself from the log and tipped her chin toward Konrada. Her shoulders hunched in and her hair hung in loose, tangled waves over her face. She shrank in on herself.

I released Donar and took up Jotapa's seat.

"How are you feeling?" She'd been to a healer and received a few stitches, though, thankfully, most of the cut was too shallow to need them.

After a long while, she spoke, almost too softly to hear.

"I'm sorry, my queen."

Her words shocked me so badly I reared back. I looked to Jotapa, but the press of her lips told me she'd heard this already.

I took a deep breath and settled into my second relief: a fixable problem.

"First, it's Thusnelda. Second, how many women did you see on that battlefield?"

Her nose scrunched in thought. "You and Jotapa, of course. The Chatti woman who helped me. There were others."

"Not many, though, right?" I nudged her with my shoulder until she lifted her head and let her hair fall back from her face. "We are few. They let us fight so long as we keep up."

Her skin drained of color. Before she completely collapsed under the weight of her shame and fear, I continued.

"Look at me. We are few, and we are the fiercest among the warriors because of it. I saw you facing seasoned legionaries all on your own, fighting to the end. It was your first battle and you haven't trained your whole life like the rest of us have. I am proud of you."

"But I lost." Her eyes flared and she opened her mouth to keep arguing, so I cut her off.

"I almost died out there facing just one man. Wiltrud, the Chatti queen, lost two fingers today, and she's been a warrior much longer than I have. These soldiers are skilled. Sometimes it's plain luck, who lives and who dies. The only shame is in running. You didn't run."

She chewed her lip and considered my words. "But I didn't go out and fight today."

I threw an arm around her shoulders and squeezed her to me. "It was your first battle and you almost died. Your body and mind need to heal. And they will, do you hear me? You have all the makings of a fine warrior."

Jotapa sank into a crouch before us with a small smile playing on her lips. "You didn't even see her at her best. She has that spear trick down to an art."

That lifted some of the darkness from Konrada's countenance.

"I seem to remember being trapped under a horse and witnessing that greatness keeping me alive."

Her dark eyes flickered up to mine. "I did do that, didn't I?"

"Yes," I laughed, "you—"

My next words stopped short. Cries of anguish rose from the field, quickly joined by vicious shouts and calls for something I never thought to hear in my lifetime.

"Burn them! Burn them all!"

———————➤

The three of us skirted the edge of the jubilant until we found an opening. My dogs aided our passage, nipping at over-excited tribesmen until we reached the clearing with our prisoners.

Under the direction of the priestesses, warriors hauled selected legionaries to their feet and marched them into the woods, where wretched howling mingled with laughter and cheers.

We made our way into the wald, and my horror grew with each passing step. The chosen soldiers were tied to trees, stripped of all but their tunics. Some kept their stoicism, others shivered and wept openly. Some were so far gone from their wounds, their heads slumped on useless necks.

Evil permeated the forest in tangible waves that made my stomach turn.

"What is this?" Konrada whispered.

"You," I called to the nearest priestess, bent over a bound soldier and daubing oil across his forehead, "what are you doing?"

She straightened, a ghostly figure in her flowing gray robes and hidden face. "We're blessing the sacrifices, my queen."

My stomach dropped to my feet. I sprinted, calling for Arminius, but no answer came. The tribesmen and priestesses were too busy huddled over their sacrifices to help me.

Jotapa took off in one direction and Konrada in the other. How had this happened and where was Arminius?

We don't sacrifice people. Even when our people had maintained the practice, the sacrifices were willing. These were an insult to the gods.

My feet pounded over rotting leaves and squelching mud. Arminius was nowhere and soldiers were tied to trees, waiting for death in every direction.

One face out of the blur caught my attention and I stopped. Eggius, who'd so bravely charged at the wall, who marshaled his troops in the face of certain defeat, leaned against the trunk, staring ahead even as two Germani men pissed on him. One of them slapped his cock across his face when he finished, and Eggius didn't so much as flinch.

"Stop," I said.

Three sets of eyes fell on me, two full of predatory malice.

The bigger one, with a filmy eye and bushy hair, grabbed the centurion by his hair and traced a knife along his cheek with just enough pressure to draw blood.

"This one's ours," Filmy Eye said. "We picked him fair."

I lifted my chin. "And I am telling you to stop. Walk away."

The smaller man, skinny but strong, snorted. "Who the fuck are you? Our chief said we could pick sacrifices. We're softening this one up."

"Who is your chief?" I voiced the question, then knew the answer. I recognized them. They were Cherusci, from one of our more distant villages. I'd seen them at festivals, though not many. "Segestes?"

They both laughed and the skinny one said, "Fuck Segestes. We worked it out. Arminius is our chief now."

The world tilted beneath my feet, and my vision blurred. Sounds faded to a distant echo. Not Arminius. He wouldn't have given the order to sacrifice these men.

I remembered the wet slice, tear, and scrape of Arminius removing Varus' head. His cold distance ever since. Something dark had taken root in him in the Teutoburg, and if I didn't do something now, he might never come back to me.

I drew my sword, the gladius that hadn't failed me against Patrin.

"Back. Away. All of you." I raised my voice to a shout. "I am Thusnelda of the Cherusci and this stops now."

Quiet descended, broken by Roman moaning and a great mass of shuffling footsteps behind me.

Levin and Konrada led a pack of warriors, some Chauci, some Marsi, only a few Cherusci.

Rihilt stepped out of the crowd and raised a club. "We stand with the queen. This is not our way."

The group murmured their agreement, and I was at once relieved I wasn't alone and sick with fear that my allies were so few. The Germani wanted Roman blood, and the tens of thousands we'd massacred so far hadn't slaked their thirst.

Arminius stormed through the crowd, his own coterie of warriors at his back.

"Thusnelda—"

I jerked out of his reach. "What is this?"

In answer, a shrill, chilling scream rent the air. It wasn't hard to find the source. One hundred feet or so away, a priestess retreated from a burst of flame. They were burning these men alive.

"Stop this!" I cried. "We don't do this! It's...it's..."

He spread his arms out wide. Dried blood coated his hands. "They wanted barbarians. Now they have them."

His warriors roared their agreement. My mouth fell open and that fist returned, squeezing painfully around my heart.

I leveled my sword at him. His eyes widened in surprise, then narrowed sharply.

"The gods don't want this, husband."

For a heartbeat, we stared at each other. Quick as a snake, he knocked my sword from my hand and snatched me by my shoulders. White hot lightning lanced from my injured shoulder. At my squeal of pain, his grip loosened but didn't release me. He pulled me close and spoke directly into my ear.

"They need this. Do you understand me? There's already unrest, and they won't shut the fuck up about sending Rome a message."

I struggled against him and got nowhere. "Three legions and every fort east of the Rhine isn't enough?"

"No." He shifted his grip and drew me into an embrace I didn't return. Anger held me so tightly, I shivered with it. "We won't have an army to take those forts if they abandon us now."

"This isn't right." His chest muffled my words and, damn him, his scent softened me. I needed my anger. Without my anger, weeping threatened to overtake me.

"They will walk away, and everything we've worked for will have been for nothing."

I hated him in that moment because he was right.

He's right, and I'm wrong, and I have to let him do this.

"Let me handle it." He kissed the top of my head and stepped away. "Ermin, tell the priestesses to stop the fucking fire. We don't want to burn the whole forest down. Tell them to make it quick. We have to be ready to ride out by morning."

My husband, the consummate politician. With a few choice words, he satisfied their bloodlust and lessened the atrocity to come.

A strangled groan brought my attention back to the centurion. Skinny and Filmy Eye huddled over his twitching form.

Arminius applied the same speed he used on me to grab Filmy Eye by the back of his neck and hurling him onto his ass.

"Who the fuck told you to do that?"

Eggius was missing an ear, sucking in hard breaths through his nostrils, bobbing with the effort of staying conscious.

"You said—"

"I said they were sacrifices!" Arminius roared.

While Arminius dressed down every warrior present, I knelt before the centurion.

"Eggius, right?"

"Yes."

If I'd had a waterskin, I would have offered it to him. I had nothing but my sword and my dagger.

"You fought bravely, Eggius." His eyes glazed over beyond my shoulder. "I can see you freed from this. You can live out your life as a scalc."

Awareness returned. His eyes sharpened and cleared. "I will not abandon my men."

The Roman with honor. How different everything might have been if they'd come to us in peace and brotherhood. If men like him filled their ranks and their cities. If their intentions had been to share, not conquer and erase.

I was all too aware of the frenzied army filling these woods. Mercy killing him after Arminius made his will clear wasn't an option, no matter how badly I wished to.

"They will make it quick. I'll see to it."

"For all my men?"

"Yes."

He nodded once, closed his eyes, and released a shuddering breath.

➤

It took a fair amount of arguing, but the priestesses relented and accepted my orders. Live burnings became throat slices, right on the jugular. By the time I collapsed into bed next to Arminius, death filled every corner of my mind. Cold froze me from the inside out.

He rolled and slipped his arm over my waist, pulling me close. I settled into his warm, familiar weight and willed whatever goodness that remained between us to chase away the dark.

"I should have talked to you before, when I realized what we had to do." He stroked my back and hair, and I forced myself to remember the pleasure of his touch.

"Yes, you should have." I burrowed deeper into his chest.

"It won't happen again." To my regret, he stopped his drugging touch to tip my chin up. "We can't argue like that in front of the tribes."

He left much unspoken in that simple statement. Our war against Rome wasn't over. In the morning, we were to march on the forts and two Roman settlements spread across Germania Magna. We still needed this tribal alliance, and we were at our best when we worked together.

"It won't happen again," I said. It was a bold promise to make, one I feared neither of us could keep. I pushed that thought away and leaned in to kiss him. I trusted that he'd try. That had to be enough.

We sank into each other with whispers of love and promises of a better future. Like the first warm day of spring, the ice in my soul thawed.

Morning dawned with fog, a cold bite, and the general commotion of a war band on the march multiplied tenfold. The Germani were no less euphoric than they'd been the previous day, still thirsting for Roman blood.

Jotapa brought me a horse. A purplish bruise stained her cheek, and she favored her left side.

"Will you be all right?" We had long days of riding ahead of us and more battles to follow. I didn't want her to suffer needlessly or, worse, get herself killed fighting when she was in no condition to fight.

"It's nothing I can't handle." At my scowl, she added, "And I will rest in a wagon if it gets any worse. My ribs are bruised, is all."

My only response was a grumble, and she let out a musical laugh.

"I promise I won't do anything foolish."

"Like backflips off your horse?"

"Two legs on each side the whole way. No creative dismounts."

Before I mounted, I grinned at her.

"You're a free woman now."

She answered with a grin of her own and patted the traveling sack strapped to the big Roman cavalry horse she'd claimed. "I'm free and I have more silver than I know how to spend."

"You'll think of something." She might leave me, decide none of this was for her and it was time to find her own people. The thought of her leaving usually made me melancholy, but hope suffused my spirit. This is what I had fought for, wasn't it? The freedom to make our own choices, to live our lives the way we chose. Her freedom to choose for herself was the best thing I ever wanted for her.

"You should go; your husband is looking for you." She gestured beyond the army and, indeed, Arminius sat atop his massive stallion, searching the sea of people and belligerently ignoring Berut and Ermin's attempts to get his attention.

I swung up onto my horse's back, unrolled and placed my wolf's pelt on my head, and urged the animal into a walk. Sunna and Donar raced ahead, right toward Arminius. As I walked on, warriors and tribesmen called out greetings to me.

"The wolf queen!" they shouted and cheered. From across the field, Arminius smiled so brightly he shone with it. My Donar made flesh, proud and beautiful and lethal.

"It won't last." Segestes fell in next to me on his own horse, one of the stout, shaggy geldings native to our country.

He looked older than I'd ever seen him. Every line in his face stood in stark relief against his thinning skin. His eyes were bruised and red, his hair almost completely gray.

"These people? They don't want a single king or a queen. They barely tolerate a chief." He huffed a bitter laugh. "They are drunk on victory, but mark my words, daughter: This name they call you, Wolf Queen, it will turn to poison in their mouths. They will turn on you."

On those parting words, he wheeled his horse away and disappeared among the throngs.

In a way, he was right. The Germani didn't have a king, and as soon as our war ended, so would Arminius' hold on these tribes. All we had to do was keep them together long enough to push Rome back across the Rhine indefinitely. It was as simple and as impossible as that.

I urged my horse into a trot until we joined Arminius.

"I don't think I could have done this without you," he said.

I pursed my lips and feigned deep thought. "No, probably not."

"Thank you." He leaned across the distance between us and kissed me. "Are you ready for what comes next?"

The thousands behind us took up cheers, drums, and horns. I had seen the best and worst of him. I understood the lengths we needed to go to secure victory, the lengths to which these people would follow us.

"Yes," I said.

He took my hand and together we led our army into the horizon.

Author's Note

The Wolf Queen began as a short story, mostly flashes of scenes when I first discovered the love story of Arminius and Thusnelda. I was enthralled by the untold tale hiding between the sparse details. There are approximately three lines about Thusnelda by the Roman historians who wrote about Arminius. Tacitus wrote of Segestes' complaint to Varus that Arminius had "stolen" his daughter, who was betrothed to another man. Although further details are available to anyone with an internet connection, I don't wish to spoil the next book by describing the other statements Tacitus made about their relationship. Suffice to say, what was said and unsaid suggested a tale of profound love shared by two defiant rebels. I didn't read the story of a woman stolen, but of a woman who ran willingly, who took charge of her own destiny. Imagine my surprise and disappointment to find almost nothing written about this woman and even less from her perspective. Naturally, I decided if I wanted to read Thusnelda's story, I would have to write it myself.

We know very little about the daily lives, culture, and values of these early Germanic tribespeople. They had no written language, so they left behind no records in their own voices. The written sources we do have come from Roman historians, mostly writing years, decades, even centuries after the time described in this novel. It is theorized that historians like Tacitus and Cassius Dio assembled their various texts from the works of earlier historians and record keepers, however those primary sources are lost. While there may be truth to the secondary and tertiary texts, we have no way of verifying their claims and we cannot ignore the political and social motivations they may have had for telling a particular kind of story about those wild barbarians to the north. Julius Caesar's writings on the region are notoriously flawed and contradictory (for example, in *The Gallic Wars*, he states that Germans did not practice agriculture, then later refers to their extensive agricultural practices), however Tacitus' work is considered largely reliable.

I chose to blend these Roman texts with archaeological studies about the region, such as Peter S. Wells' *The Barbarian Speaks* and *The Early Germans* by Malcolm Todd, along with texts about the early Vikings and archaeological studies of tribal cultures contemporary to the early Germans, like *Barbarian Rites* by Hans-Peter

Hasenfratz. I hope that the end result of my work is the creation of a believable world that would realistically band together to reject Rome in such an outrageous fashion.

As to the role of women in warfare, archaeology has steadily revealed numerous cultures around the world where women fought alongside men. Even Tacitus reported that Germanic women were essential on the battlefield, first to egg their men on, then to pick up weapons and fight when the battle wasn't going well. We know women regularly fought as shieldmaidens among the Vikings, who derived much of their culture from the early Germans. We also know that like the Greeks before them, Rome had a vested interest in keeping women in subdued roles. It stands to reason that Roman historians wouldn't be keen to report that female warriors were so successful in battle against Rome's finest soldiers. I chose to highlight ancient female warriors through Thusnelda and her compatriots because, quite frankly, I see it so rarely in adult historical fiction. There is more than enough evidence to assert that it is not only possible, but happened with some regularity in cultures all over the globe. You can read more about ancient women in warfare in Adrienne Mayor's *The Amazons* and Pamela D. Toler's *Women Warriors*.

Arminius' personal history is almost as murky as Thusnelda's. We do not know who he was prior to leading this rebellion, aside from the names of his father, uncle, and brother, and his standing as a nobleman among the Cherusci. We know that he had some official role in the Roman military and earned the honorary title of Equestrian, a Roman knight. We also know that he had so successfully convinced his superiors of his Romanization that they never thought to question him. We don't know how he came to achieve this position. As hostaging young boys was a common practice, it is possible he endured being taken from home and raised among Romans. However, it is more likely that he spent his life among the Cherusci and achieved his standing by service in the auxiliary. I represented his background as the former in the name of dramatic tension, as I did with a number of details in the story, from the timeline to Thusnelda having her own room (an unlikely scenario, even in a longhouse) and the number of her brothers (she reportedly had only one). Kalkriese Hill is not in the Teutoburg forest, but as the two locations are commonly associated with the battle, I merged them. Kalkriese Hill is where most archaeological evidence of the battle has been found.

Other details, however, are grounded in research. Slavery among the Germanic tribes was more akin to indentured servitude and sharecropping than the bondage slavery practiced by Rome. The tribes did not believe in capital punishment, though there is debate about when they stopped the practice of human sacrifice. Chiefs had very little power over their tribes and war chiefs were selected from among the people based on ability, not nepotism. Most important decisions were made by a council of tribesmen. The details of the battle are accurate to my sources and Eggius was a real centurion noted for his bravery and leadership. Though there are multiple accounts of this battle, I recommend *The Battle that Stopped Rome* by Peter S. Wells and, for German speakers, *Die Schlacht im Teutoburger Wald* by Reinhard Wolters.

Lastly, I'd like to address the hateful elephant in the room: since the late 19th century, Arminius has been used as a figurehead of German nationalism, Nazism, and white supremacy. This was on my mind continuously as I wrote and edited this novel, and I hope the end result is an Arminius who was too flawed, too selfish, ofttimes too lost and reckless, and certainly too open minded to ever represent anything those people would find positive. The Arminius of their imaginations never existed.

Thank you so much for reading. Writing this story has been a journey and I look forward to sharing the follow up, *Fall of the Wolf Queen*, with you soon. You can contact me and stay up-to-date with *Fall of the Wolf Queen* at my website, www.mariemccurdy.com.

Marie is a Florida native, California transplant, and has lived almost everywhere between.

She's been writing stories since she could hold a pen, but didn't get serious until she joined the Marines in 2009 as a Combat Correspondent. After five years telling Marine Corps stories, she knew it was time to start telling stories of her own.

Marie currently lives in New Orleans with her fur family; three delightful cats and one questionable chihuahua mix.

www.ingramcontent.com/pod-product-compliance
Lightning Source LLC
Chambersburg PA
CBHW030920300726
48970CB00001B/255